A CARTOON NETWORK ORIGINAL

ANTI-GRAVITY

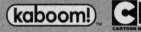

STEVEN UNIVERSE: ANTI-GRAVITY, November
2017. Published by KaBOOM!, a division of Boom
Entertainment, Inc. STEVEN UNIVERSE, CARTOON
NETWORK, the logos, and all related characters and
elements are trademarks of and © Cartoon Network.
(S17) All rights reserved. KaBOOM!™ and the KaBOOM!
logo are trademarks of Boom Entertainment, Inc.,
registered in various countries and categories. All
characters, events, and institutions depicted herein
are fictional. Any similarity between any of the names,
characters, persons, events, and/or institutions in this
publication to actual names, characters, and persons,
whether living or dead, events, and/or institutions is
unintended and purely coincidental. KaBOOM! does not
read or accept unsolicited submissions of ideas, stories,
or artwork.

For information regarding the CPSIA on this printed
material, call: (203) 595-3636 and provide reference
#RICH - 754817.

BOOM! Studios, 5670 Wilshire Boulevard, Suite 450, Los
Angeles, CA 90036-5679. Printed in USA. First Printing.

ISBN:978-1-60886-996-1, eISBN:978-1-61398-667-7

STEVEN ★ UNIVERSE ™

A CARTOON NETWORK ORIGINAL
ANTI-GRAVITY

created by
REBECCA SUGAR

written by
TALYA PERPER

illustrated by
**QUEENIE CHAN
& JENNA AYOUB**

colored by
LAURA LANGSTON
with **VLADIMIR POPOV
& ELEONORA BRUNI**

lettered by
MIKE FIORENTINO

cover by
SARA TALMADGE

designer
MICHELLE ANKLEY

associate editor
CHRIS ROSA

editor
WHITNEY LEOPARD

With Special Thanks to
Marisa Marionakis, Janet No, Curtis Lelash, Conrad Montgomery,
Jackie Buscarino, Alan Pasman and the wonderful folks at Cartoon Network.

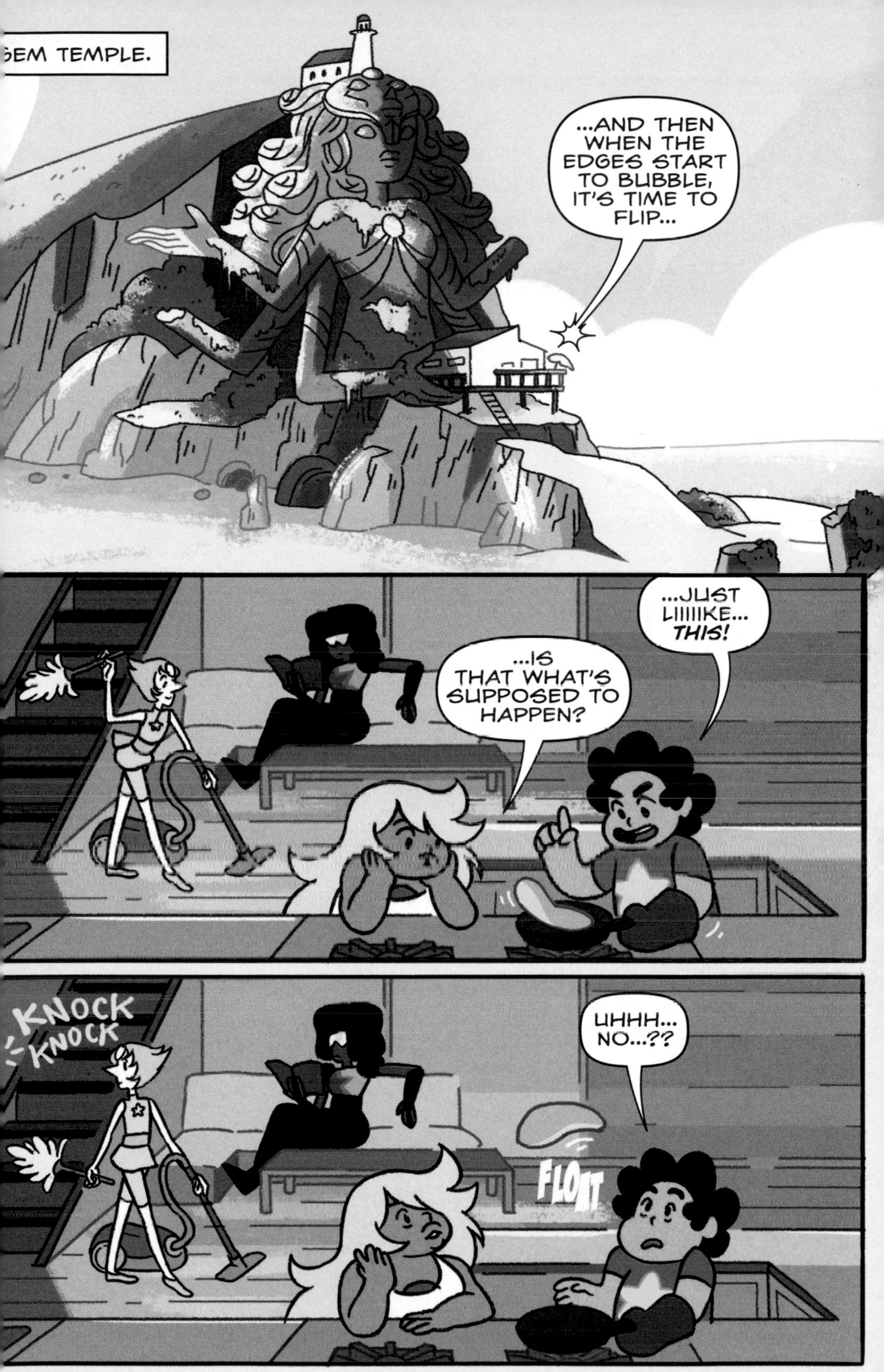

GEM TEMPLE.
...AND THEN WHEN THE EDGES START TO BUBBLE, IT'S TIME TO FLIP...
...IS THAT WHAT'S SUPPOSED TO HAPPEN?
...JUST LIIIIIKE... THIS!
KNOCK KNOCK
UHHH... NO...??
FLOAT

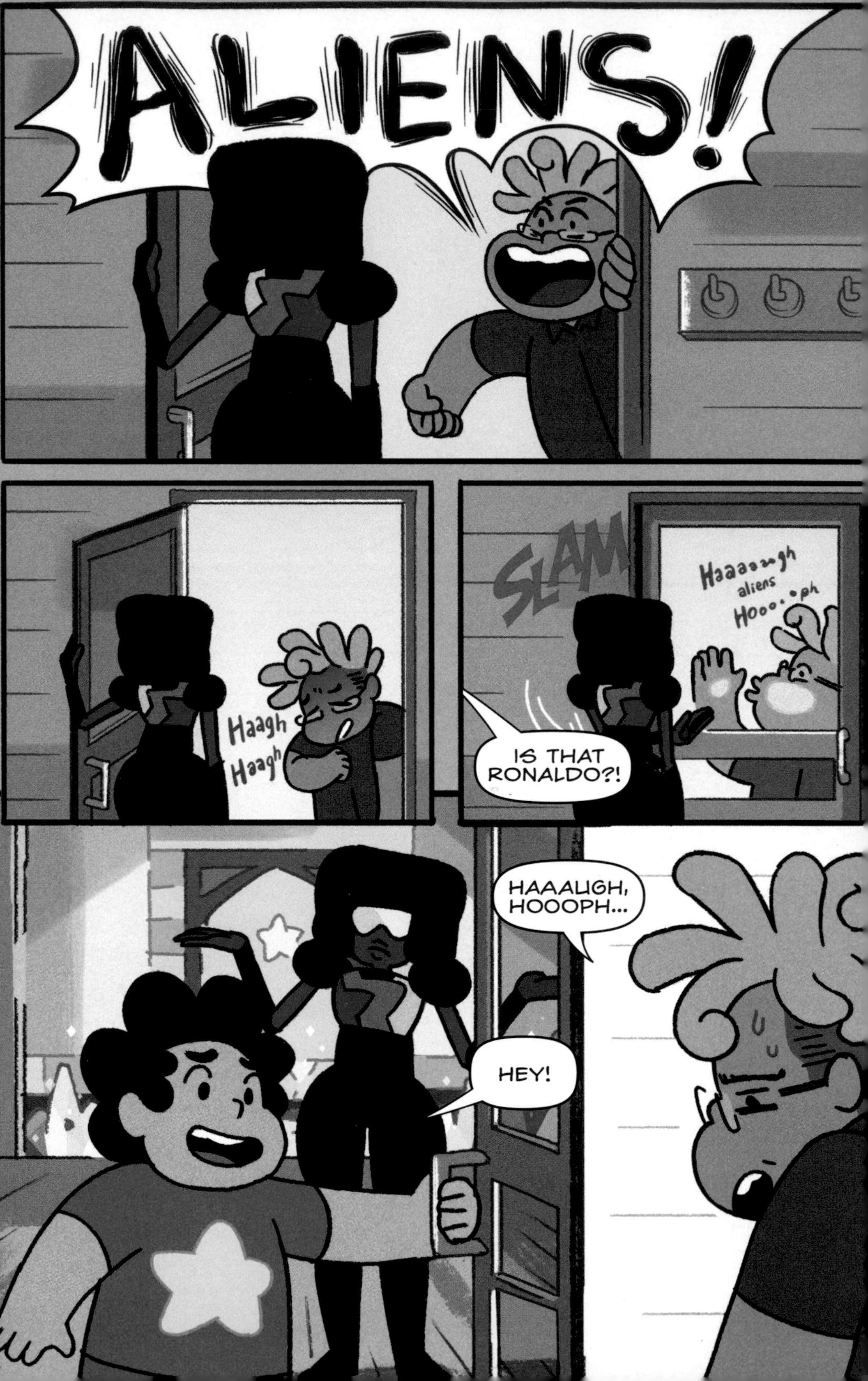
ALIENS!
Haagh
Haagh
SLAM
Haaaaaugh
aliens
Hooo..ph
IS THAT RONALDO?!
HAAAUGH, HOOOPH...
HEY!

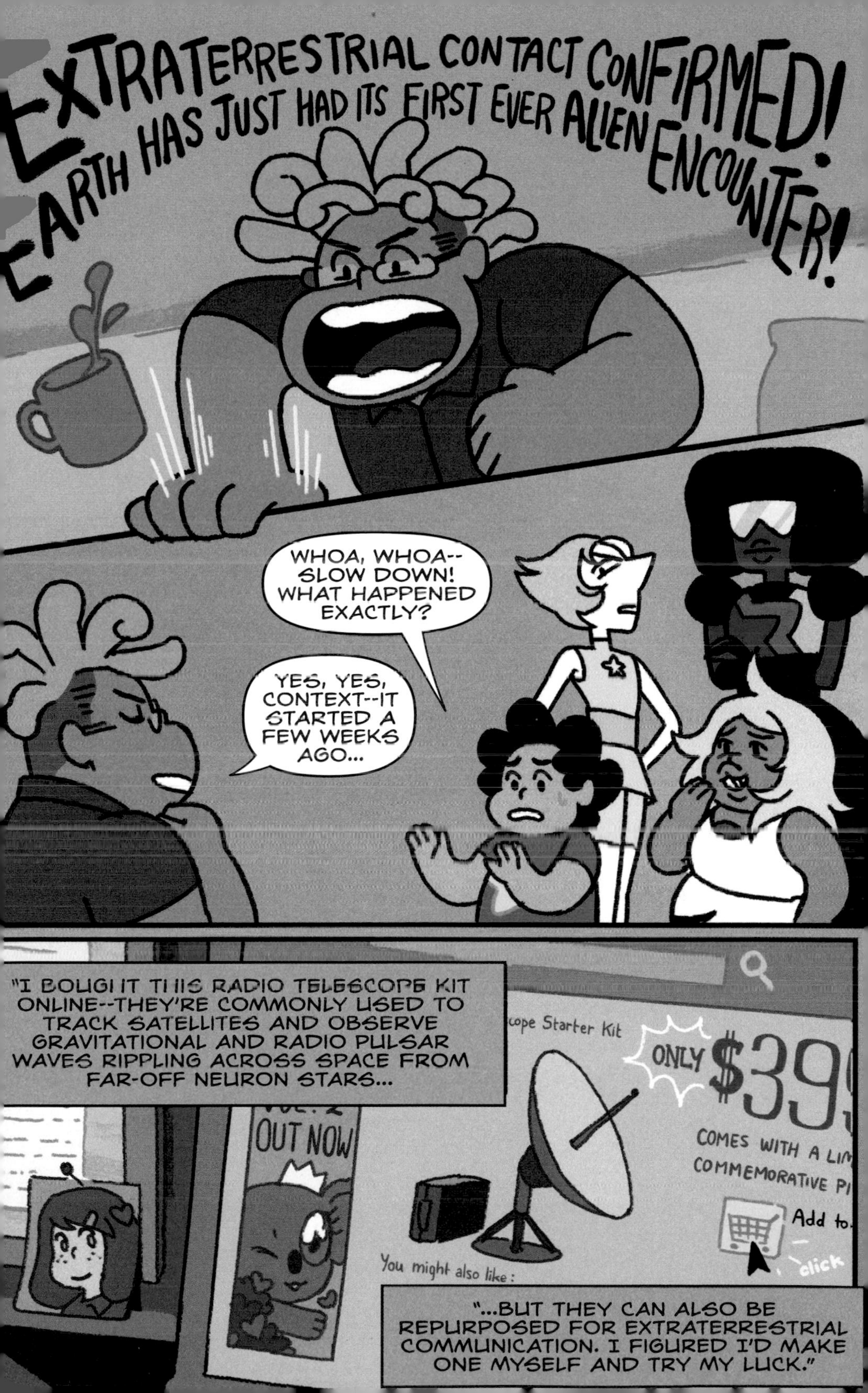
EXTRATERRESTRIAL CONTACT CONFIRMED!
EARTH HAS JUST HAD ITS FIRST EVER ALIEN ENCOUNTER!
WHOA, WHOA-- SLOW DOWN! WHAT HAPPENED EXACTLY?
YES, YES, CONTEXT--IT STARTED A FEW WEEKS AGO...
"I BOUGHT THIS RADIO TELESCOPE KIT ONLINE--THEY'RE COMMONLY USED TO TRACK SATELLITES AND OBSERVE GRAVITATIONAL AND RADIO PULSAR WAVES RIPPLING ACROSS SPACE FROM FAR-OFF NEURON STARS...
cope Starter Kit
ONLY $39
COMES WITH A LIM
COMMEMORATIVE PI
Add to
click
You might also like:
OUT NOW
"...BUT THEY CAN ALSO BE REPURPOSED FOR EXTRATERRESTRIAL COMMUNICATION. I FIGURED I'D MAKE ONE MYSELF AND TRY MY LUCK."

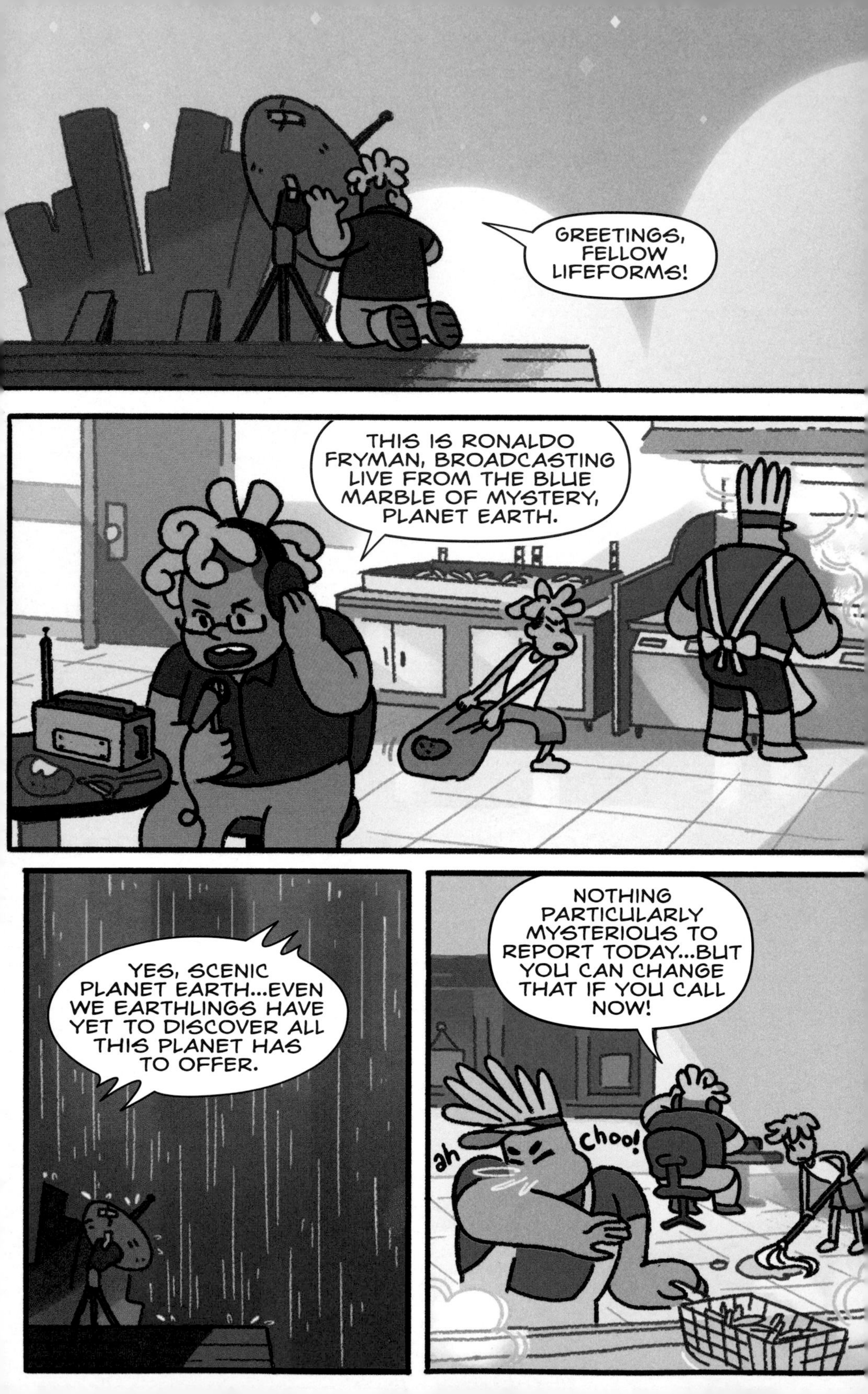
GREETINGS, FELLOW LIFEFORMS!
THIS IS RONALDO FRYMAN, BROADCASTING LIVE FROM THE BLUE MARBLE OF MYSTERY, PLANET EARTH.
YES, SCENIC PLANET EARTH...EVEN WE EARTHLINGS HAVE YET TO DISCOVER ALL THIS PLANET HAS TO OFFER.
NOTHING PARTICULARLY MYSTERIOUS TO REPORT TODAY...BUT YOU CAN CHANGE THAT IF YOU CALL NOW!
ah
choo!

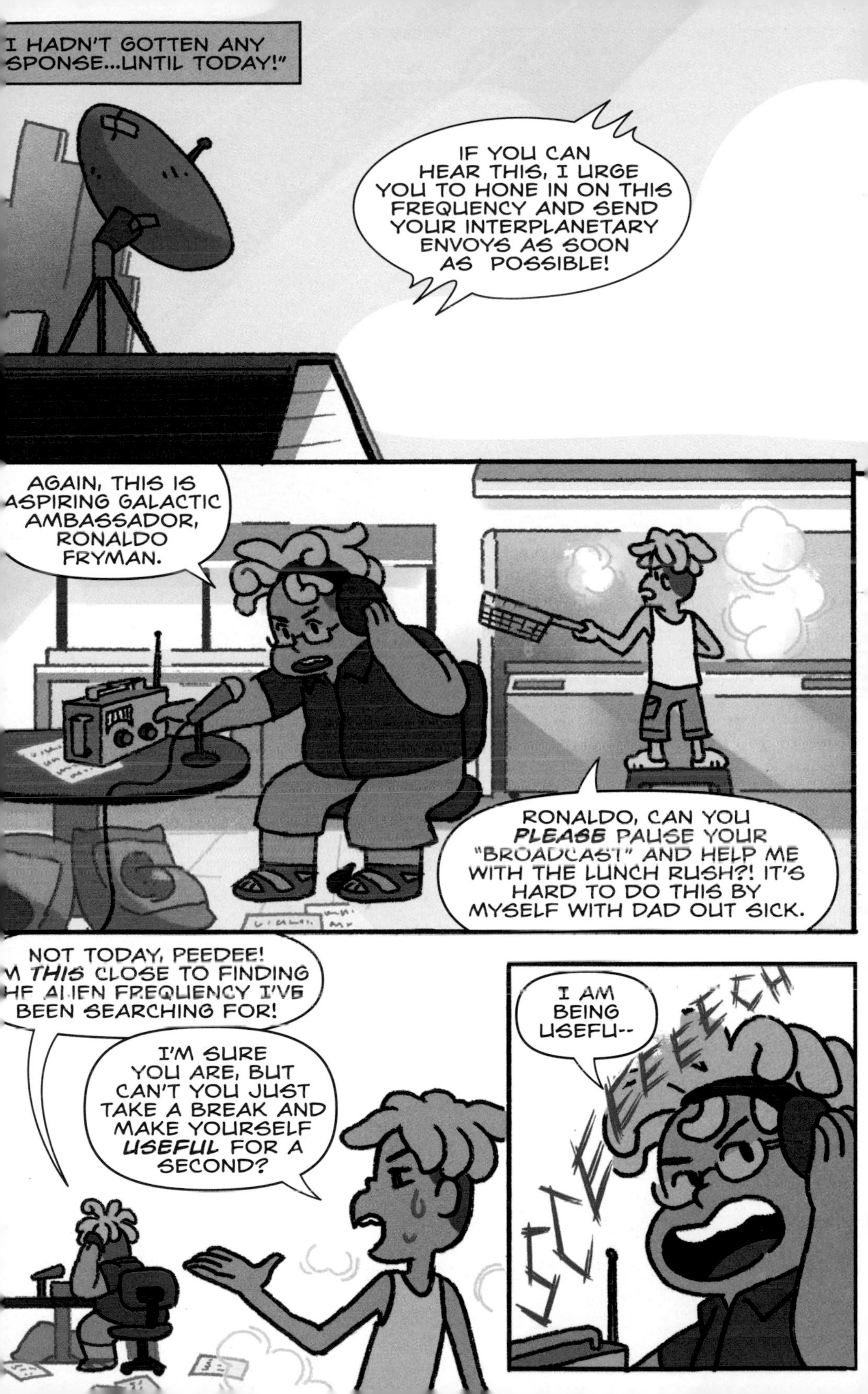
I HADN'T GOTTEN ANY
SPONSE...UNTIL TODAY!"
IF YOU CAN HEAR THIS, I URGE YOU TO HONE IN ON THIS FREQUENCY AND SEND YOUR INTERPLANETARY ENVOYS AS SOON AS POSSIBLE!
AGAIN, THIS IS ASPIRING GALACTIC AMBASSADOR, RONALDO FRYMAN.
RONALDO, CAN YOU PLEASE PAUSE YOUR "BROADCAST" AND HELP ME WITH THE LUNCH RUSH?! IT'S HARD TO DO THIS BY MYSELF WITH DAD OUT SICK.
NOT TODAY, PEEDEE! M THIS CLOSE TO FINDING HE ALIEN FREQUENCY I'VE BEEN SEARCHING FOR!
I'M SURE YOU ARE, BUT CAN'T YOU JUST TAKE A BREAK AND MAKE YOURSELF USEFUL FOR A SECOND?
I AM BEING USEFU--
SCREEEEEECH

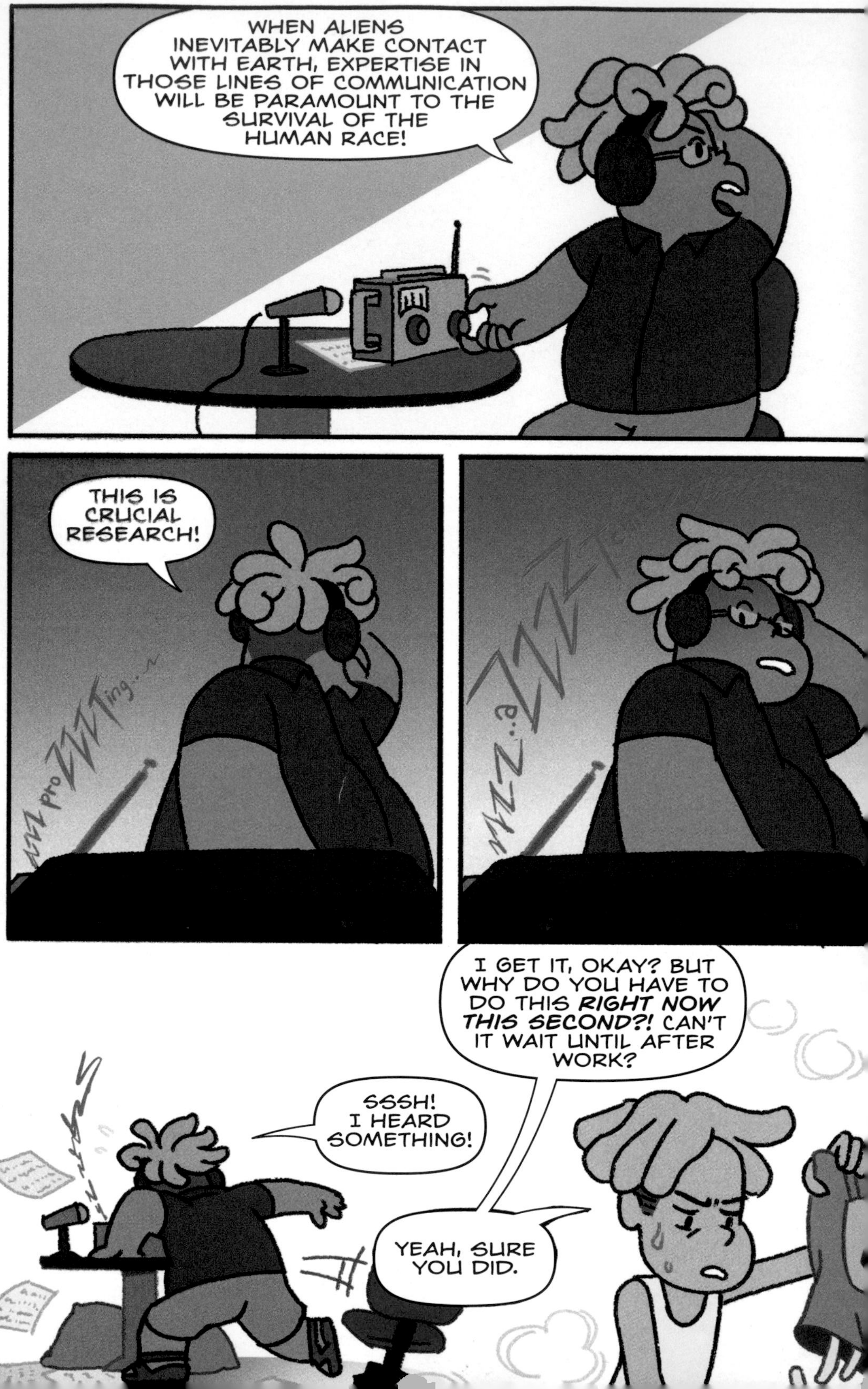
WHEN ALIENS INEVITABLY MAKE CONTACT WITH EARTH, EXPERTISE IN THOSE LINES OF COMMUNICATION WILL BE PARAMOUNT TO THE SURVIVAL OF THE HUMAN RACE!
THIS IS CRUCIAL RESEARCH!
I GET IT, OKAY? BUT WHY DO YOU HAVE TO DO THIS *RIGHT NOW THIS SECOND?!* CAN'T IT WAIT UNTIL AFTER WORK?
SSSH! I HEARD SOMETHING!
YEAH, SURE YOU DID.

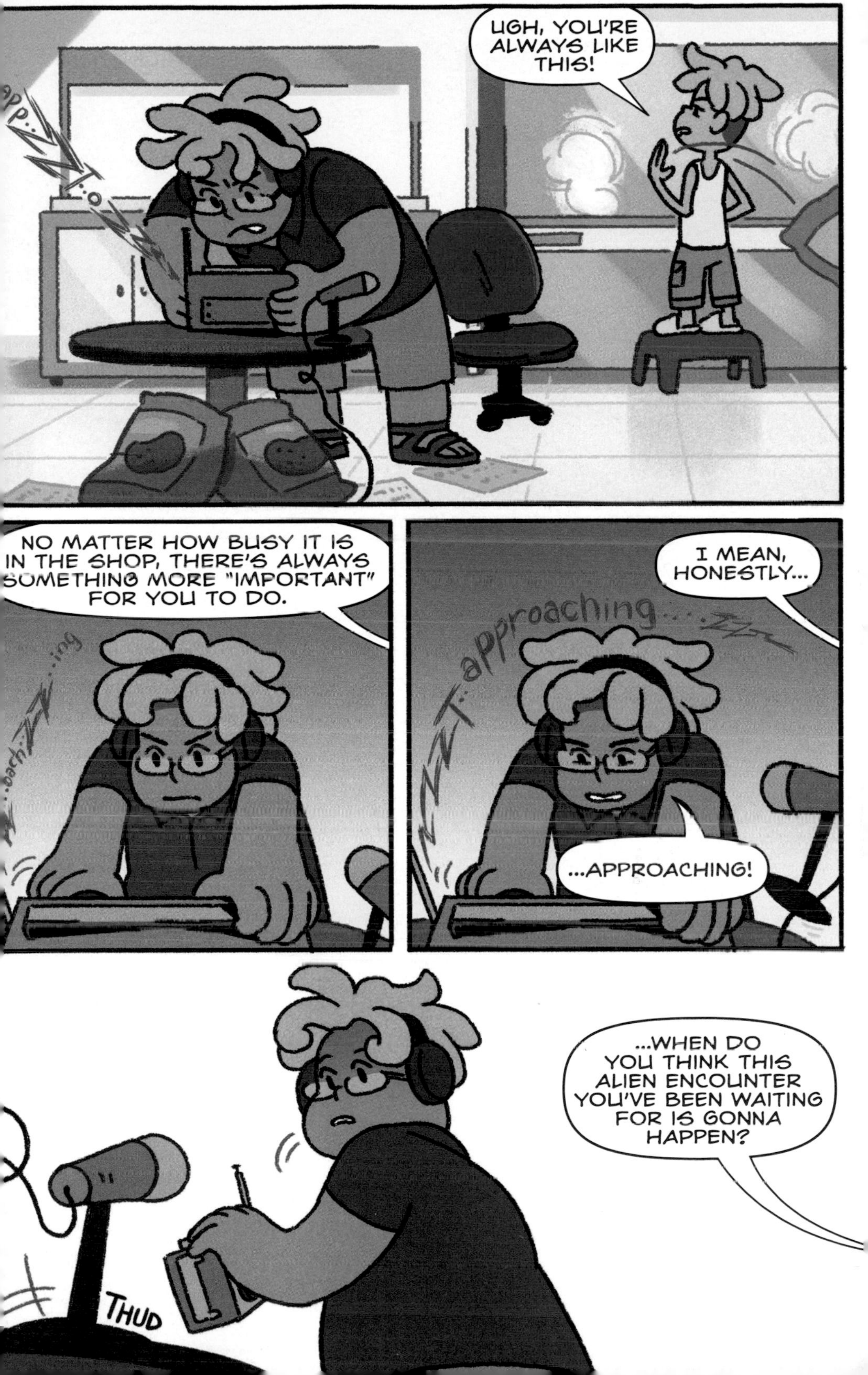
APP...ZZT...O...ZZ
UGH, YOU'RE ALWAYS LIKE THIS!
NO MATTER HOW BUSY IT IS IN THE SHOP, THERE'S ALWAYS SOMETHING MORE "IMPORTANT" FOR YOU TO DO.
...oach...ZZT...ing
I MEAN, HONESTLY...
ZZZT...approaching...ZZZ
...APPROACHING!
...WHEN DO YOU THINK THIS ALIEN ENCOUNTER YOU'VE BEEN WAITING FOR IS GONNA HAPPEN?
THUD

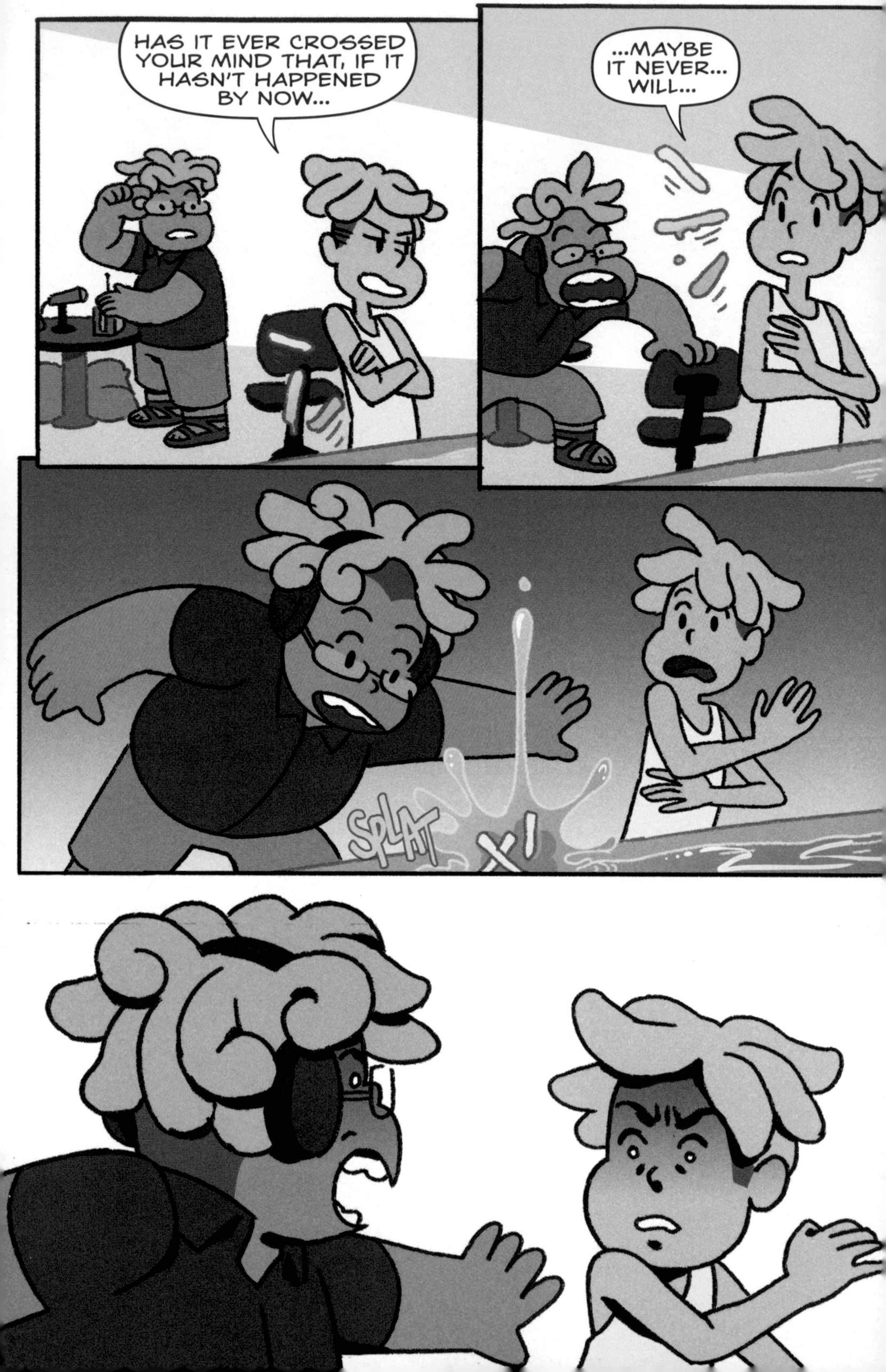
HAS IT EVER CROSSED YOUR MIND THAT, IF IT HASN'T HAPPENED BY NOW...
...MAYBE IT NEVER... WILL...
SPLAT

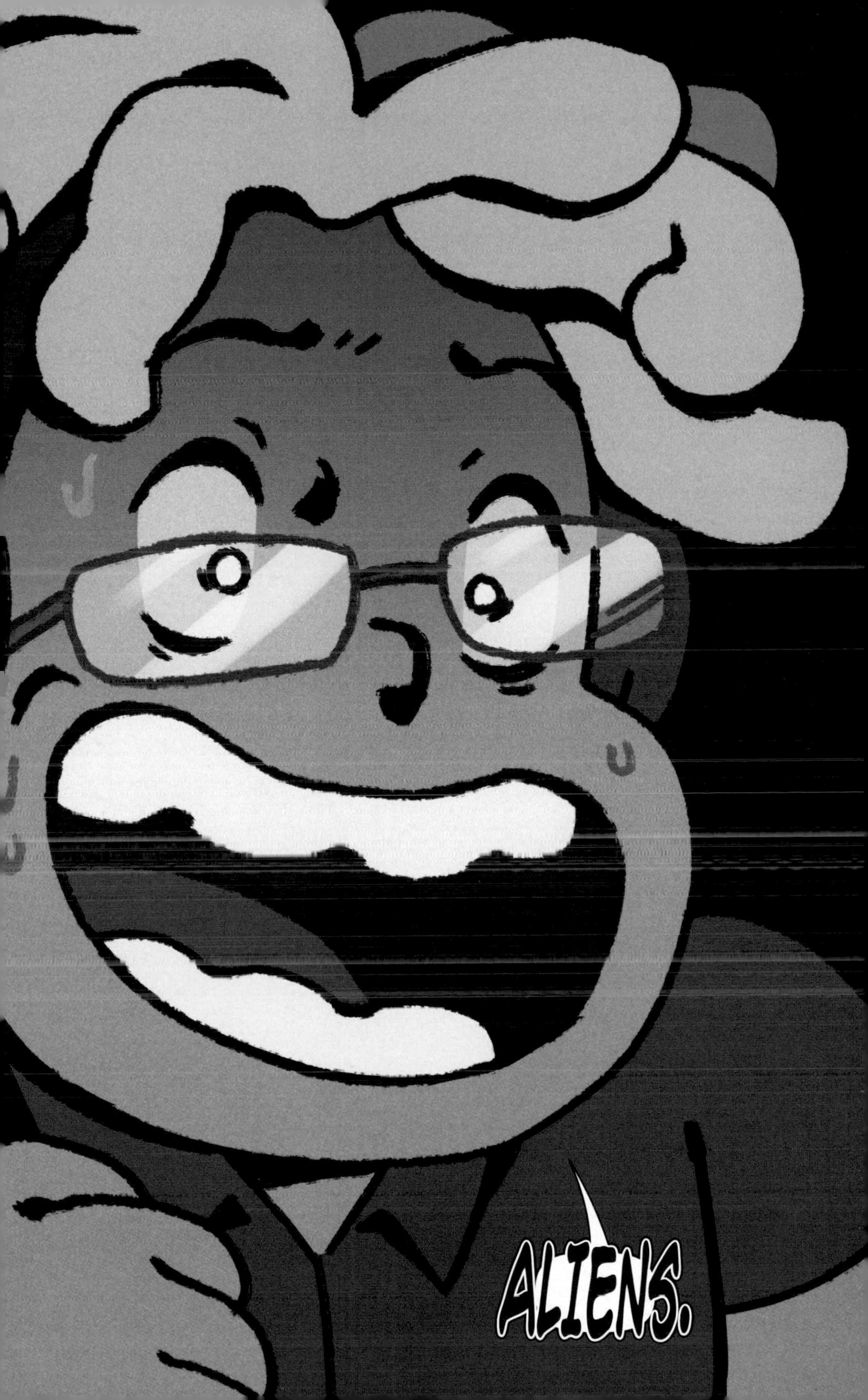
ALIENS.

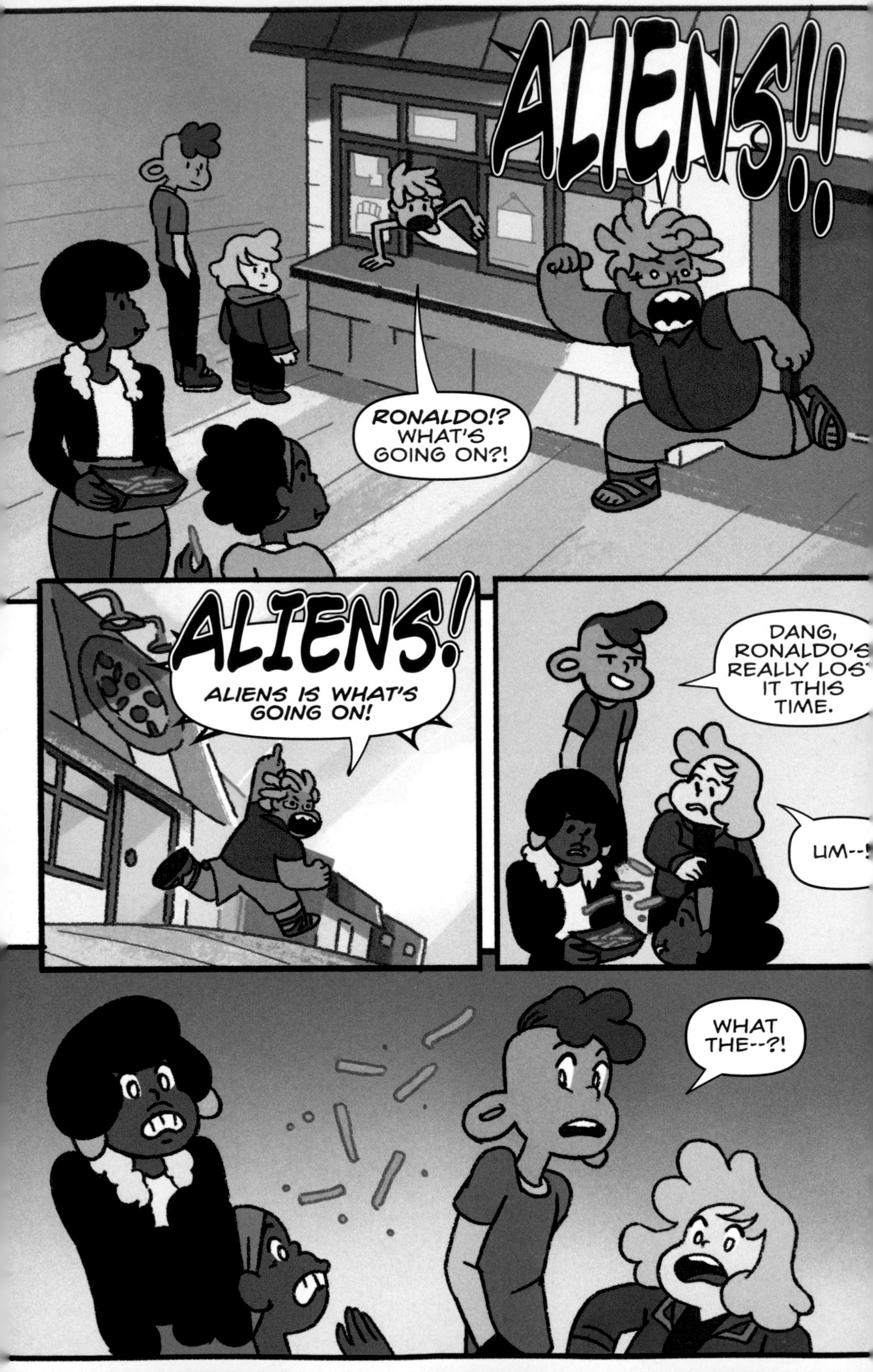
ALIENS!!
RONALDO!? WHAT'S GOING ON?!
ALIENS!
ALIENS IS WHAT'S GOING ON!
DANG, RONALDO'S REALLY LOST IT THIS TIME.
UM--!
WHAT THE--?!

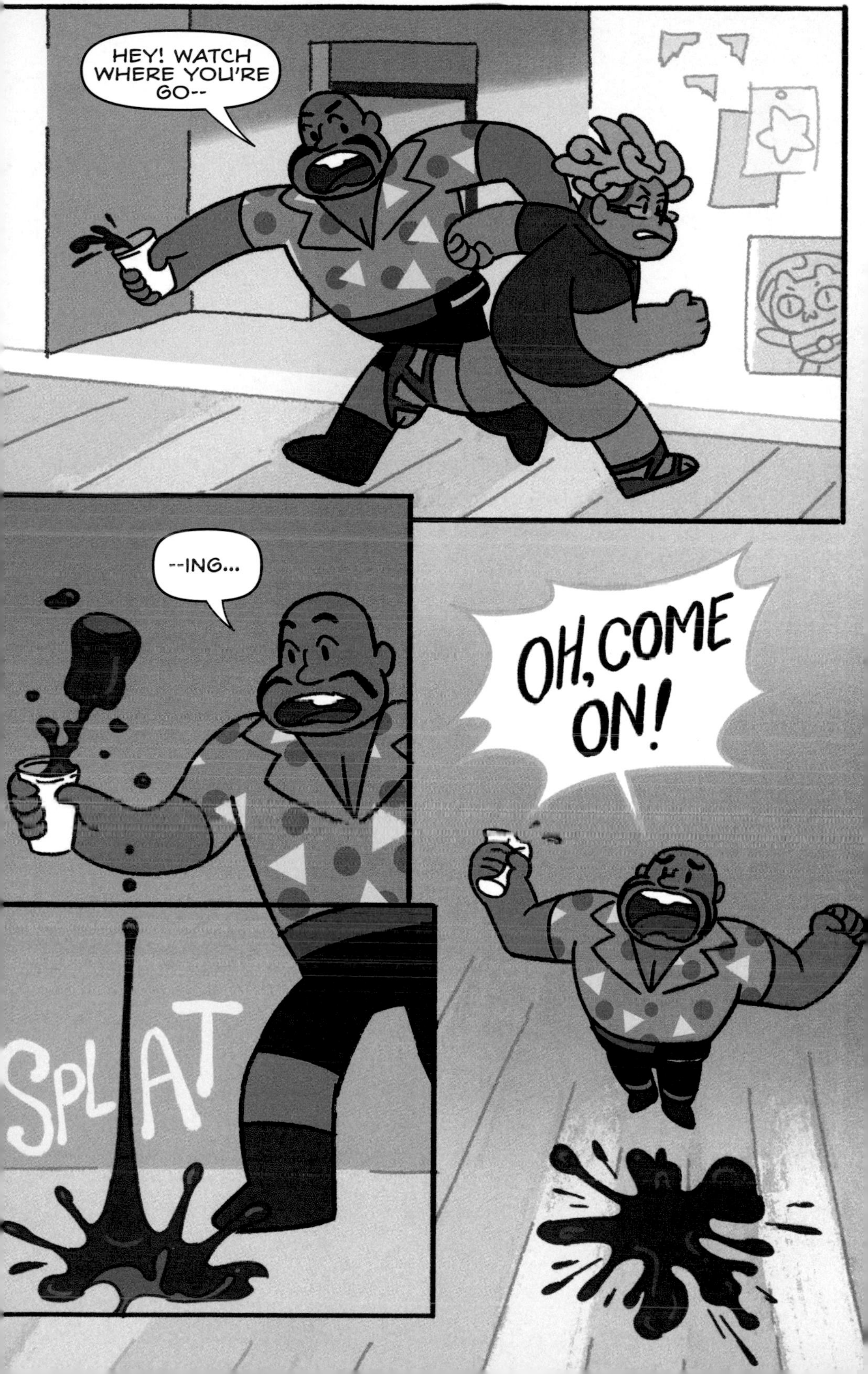

HEY! WATCH WHERE YOU'RE GO--
--ING...
SPLAT
OH, COME ON!

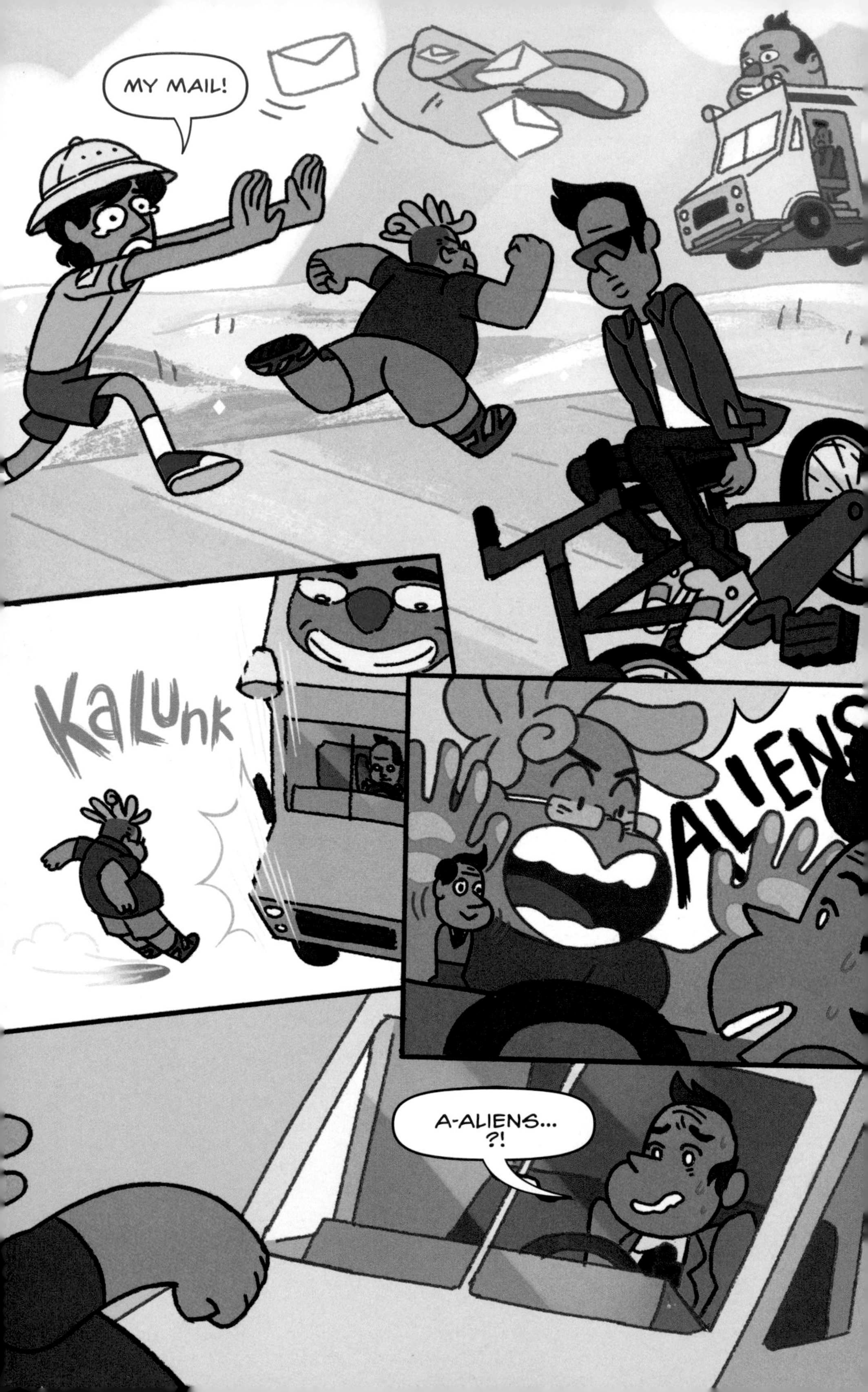
MY MAIL!
KALUNK
ALIENS
A-ALIENS...
?!

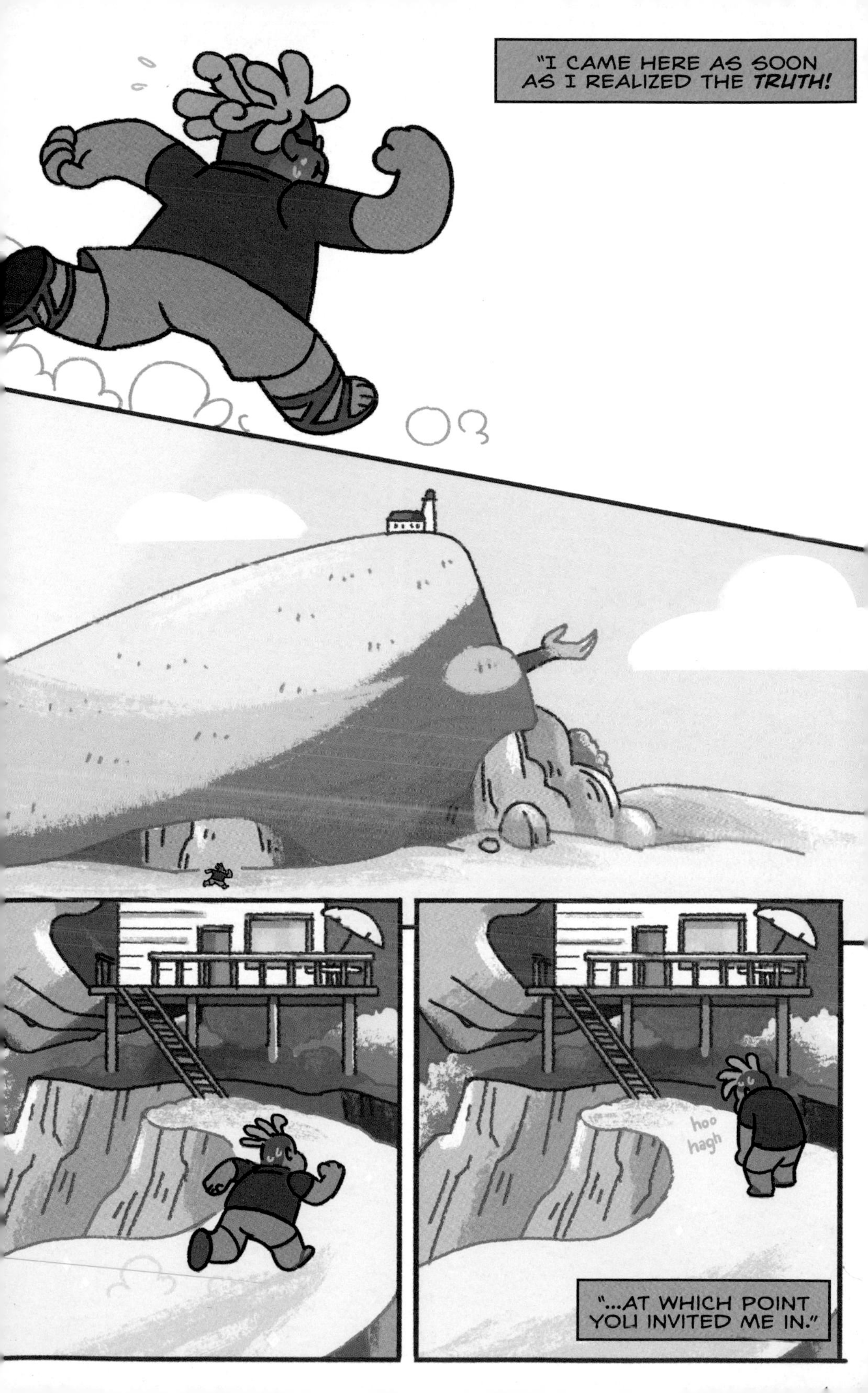
"I CAME HERE AS SOON AS I REALIZED THE *TRUTH*!
hoo hagh
"...AT WHICH POINT YOU INVITED ME IN."

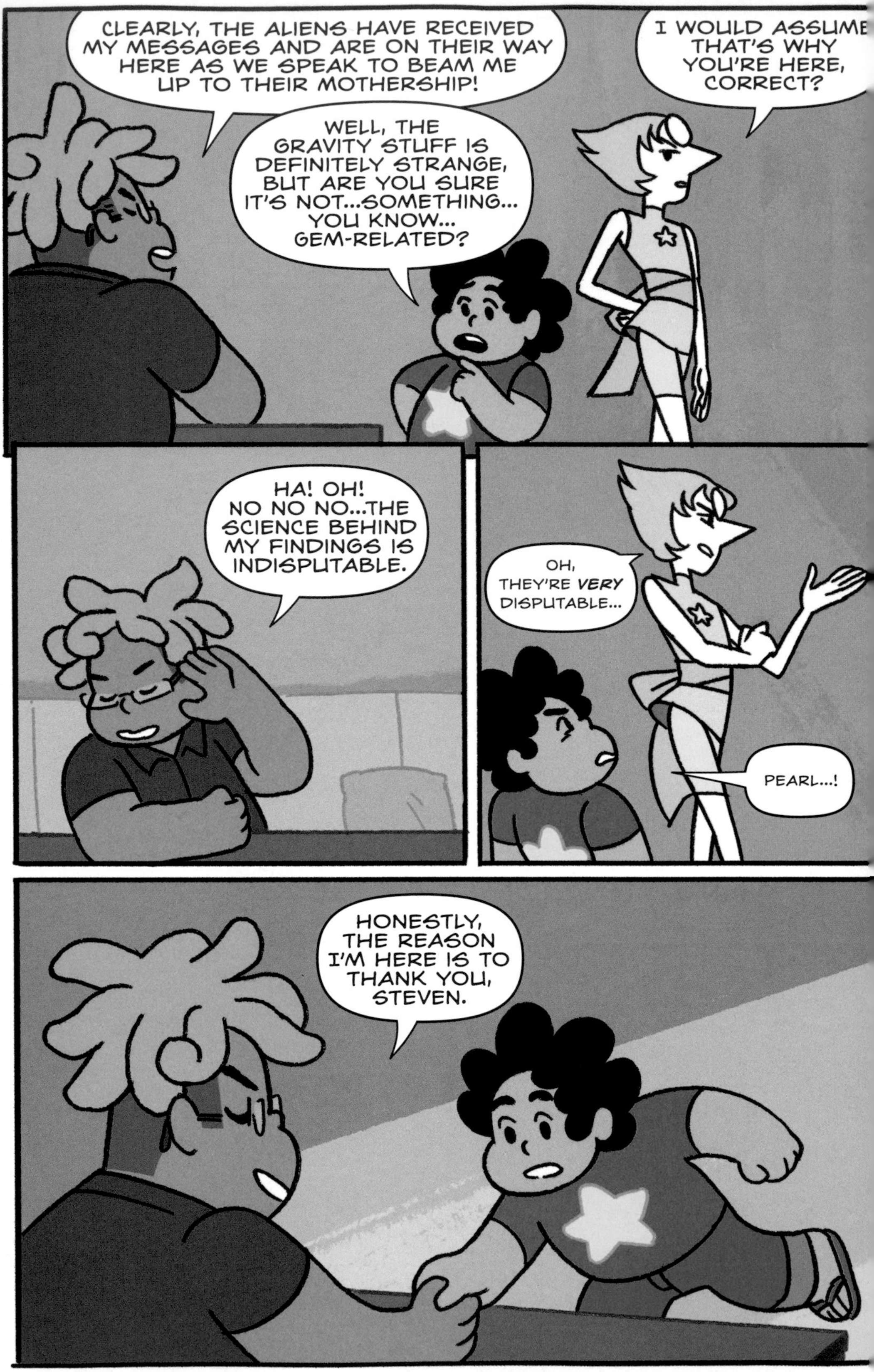

CLEARLY, THE ALIENS HAVE RECEIVED MY MESSAGES AND ARE ON THEIR WAY HERE AS WE SPEAK TO BEAM ME UP TO THEIR MOTHERSHIP!
WELL, THE GRAVITY STUFF IS DEFINITELY STRANGE, BUT ARE YOU SURE IT'S NOT...SOMETHING... YOU KNOW... GEM-RELATED?
I WOULD ASSUME THAT'S WHY YOU'RE HERE, CORRECT?
HA! OH! NO NO NO...THE SCIENCE BEHIND MY FINDINGS IS INDISPUTABLE.
OH, THEY'RE *VERY* DISPUTABLE...
PEARL...!
HONESTLY, THE REASON I'M HERE IS TO THANK YOU, STEVEN.

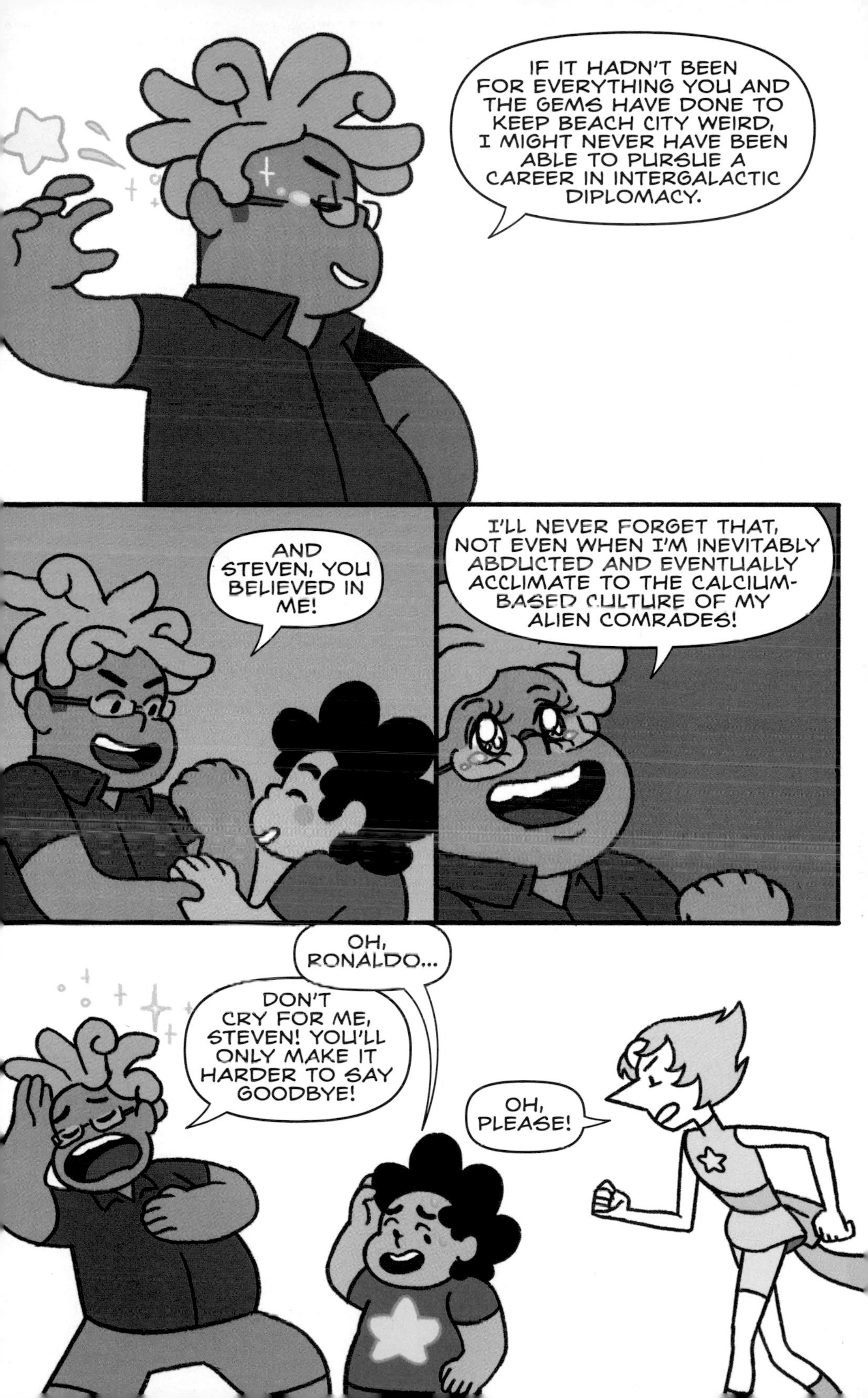
IF IT HADN'T BEEN FOR EVERYTHING YOU AND THE GEMS HAVE DONE TO KEEP BEACH CITY WEIRD, I MIGHT NEVER HAVE BEEN ABLE TO PURSUE A CAREER IN INTERGALACTIC DIPLOMACY.
AND STEVEN, YOU BELIEVED IN ME!
I'LL NEVER FORGET THAT, NOT EVEN WHEN I'M INEVITABLY ABDUCTED AND EVENTUALLY ACCLIMATE TO THE CALCIUM-BASED CULTURE OF MY ALIEN COMRADES!
OH, RONALDO...
DON'T CRY FOR ME, STEVEN! YOU'LL ONLY MAKE IT HARDER TO SAY GOODBYE!
OH, PLEASE!

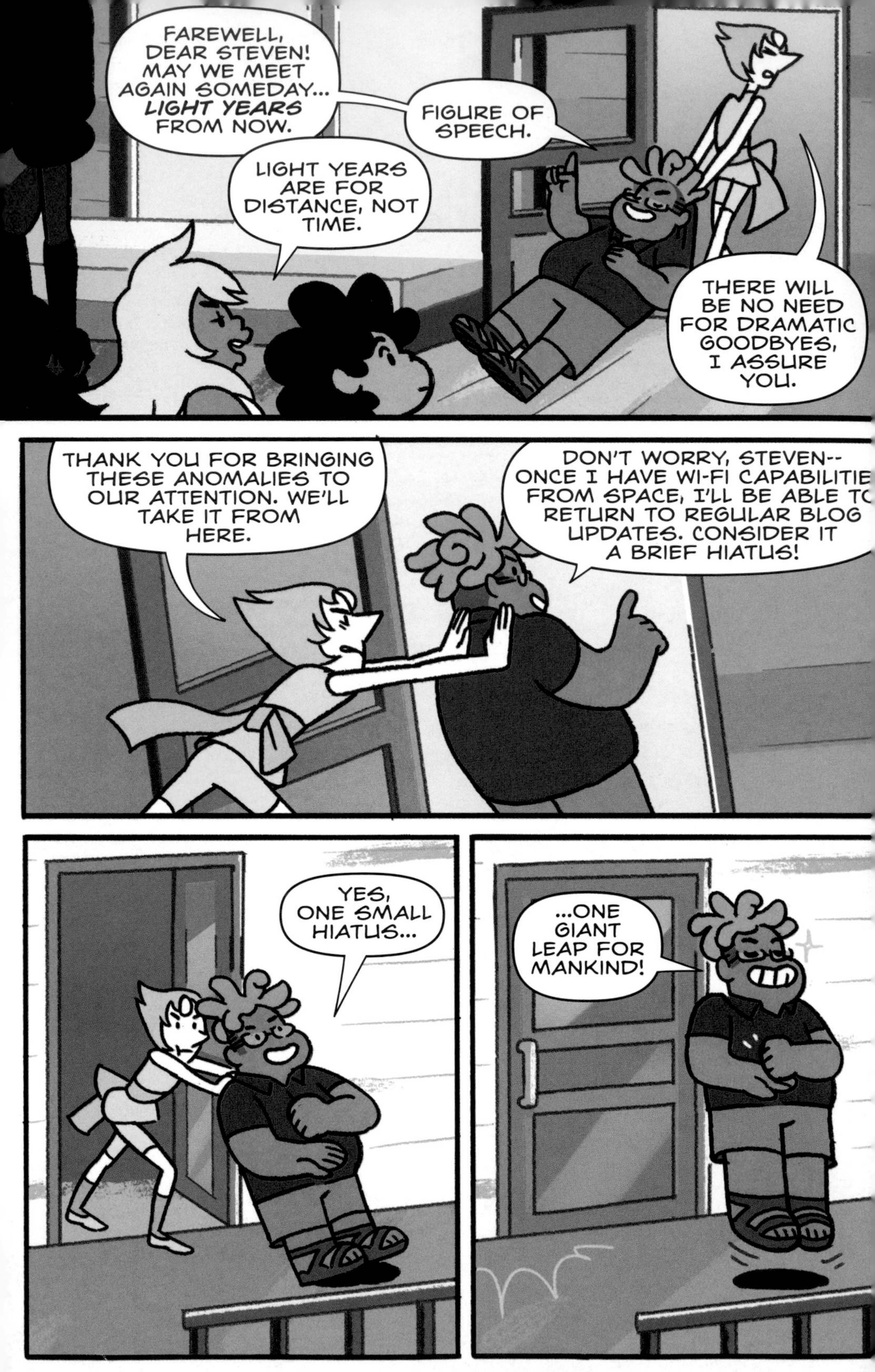
FAREWELL, DEAR STEVEN! MAY WE MEET AGAIN SOMEDAY... *LIGHT YEARS* FROM NOW.
FIGURE OF SPEECH.
LIGHT YEARS ARE FOR DISTANCE, NOT TIME.
THERE WILL BE NO NEED FOR DRAMATIC GOODBYES, I ASSURE YOU.
THANK YOU FOR BRINGING THESE ANOMALIES TO OUR ATTENTION. WE'LL TAKE IT FROM HERE.
DON'T WORRY, STEVEN-- ONCE I HAVE WI-FI CAPABILITIE FROM SPACE, I'LL BE ABLE TC RETURN TO REGULAR BLOG UPDATES. CONSIDER IT A BRIEF HIATUS!
YES, ONE SMALL HIATUS...
...ONE GIANT LEAP FOR MANKIND!

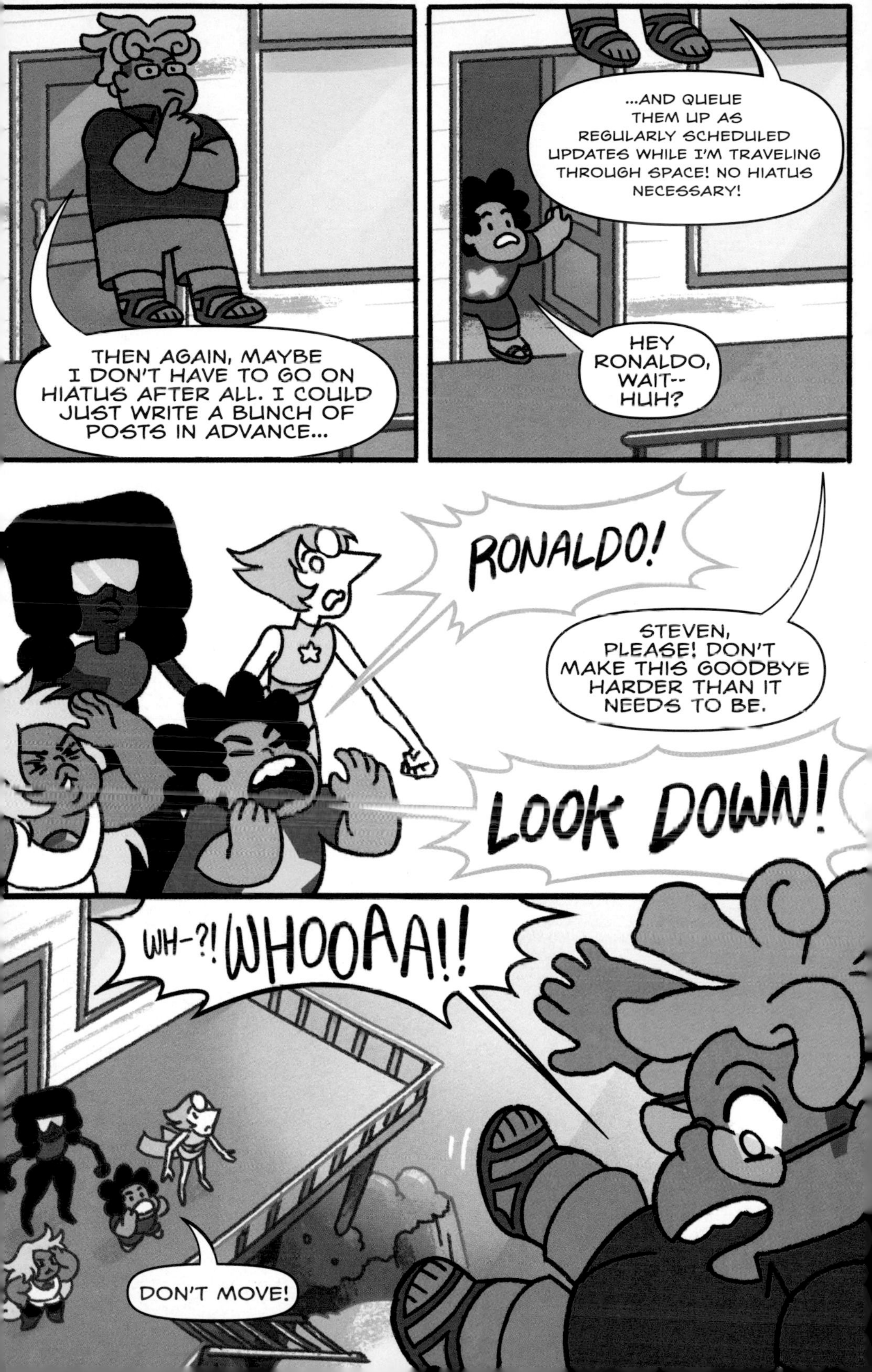
THEN AGAIN, MAYBE I DON'T HAVE TO GO ON HIATUS AFTER ALL. I COULD JUST WRITE A BUNCH OF POSTS IN ADVANCE...
...AND QUEUE THEM UP AS REGULARLY SCHEDULED UPDATES WHILE I'M TRAVELING THROUGH SPACE! NO HIATUS NECESSARY!
HEY RONALDO, WAIT-- HUH?
RONALDO!
STEVEN, PLEASE! DON'T MAKE THIS GOODBYE HARDER THAN IT NEEDS TO BE.
LOOK DOWN!
WH-?! WHOOAA!!
DON'T MOVE!

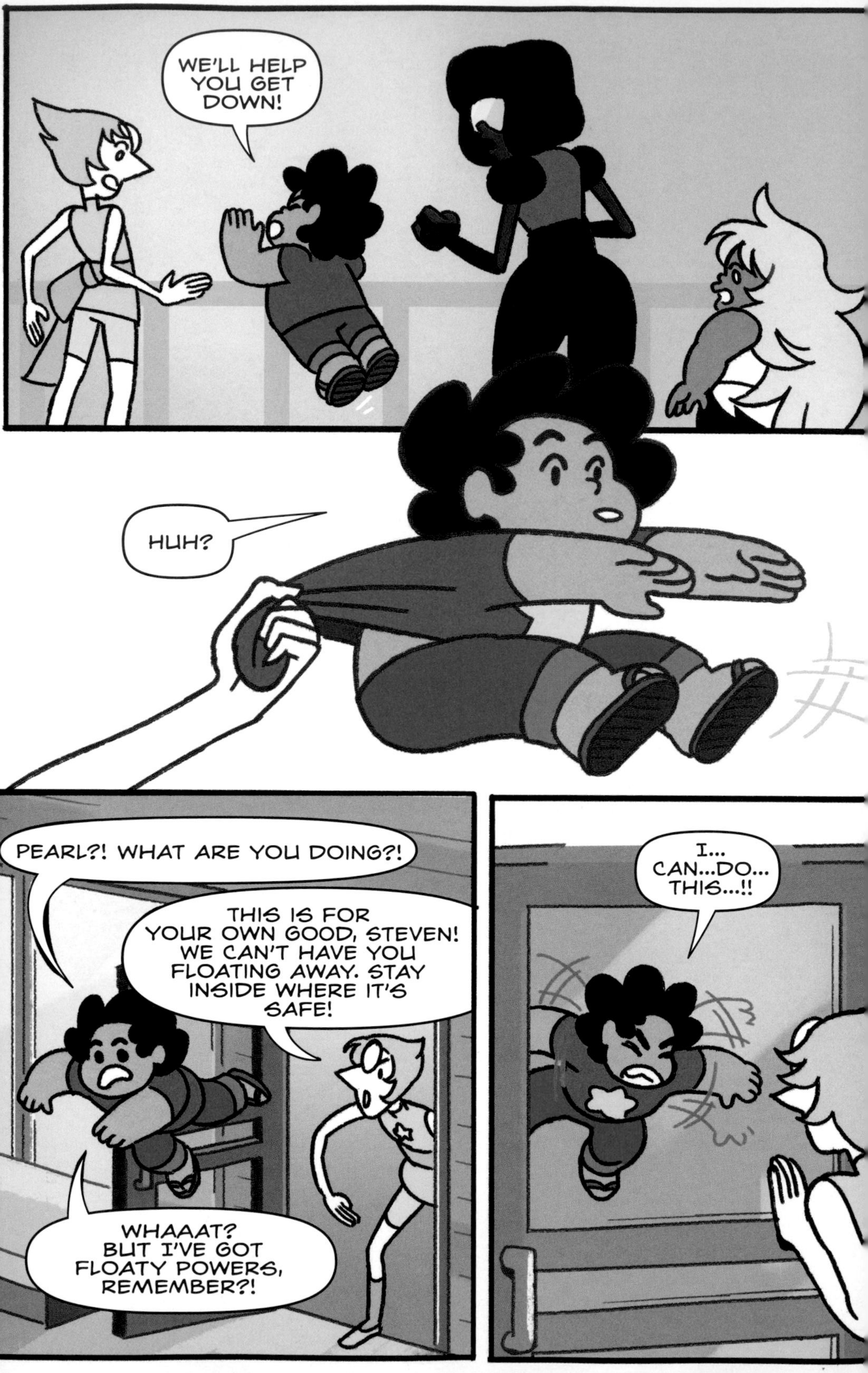
WE'LL HELP YOU GET DOWN!
HUH?
PEARL?! WHAT ARE YOU DOING?!
THIS IS FOR YOUR OWN GOOD, STEVEN! WE CAN'T HAVE YOU FLOATING AWAY. STAY INSIDE WHERE IT'S SAFE!
WHAAAT? BUT I'VE GOT FLOATY POWERS, REMEMBER?!
I... CAN...DO... THIS...!!

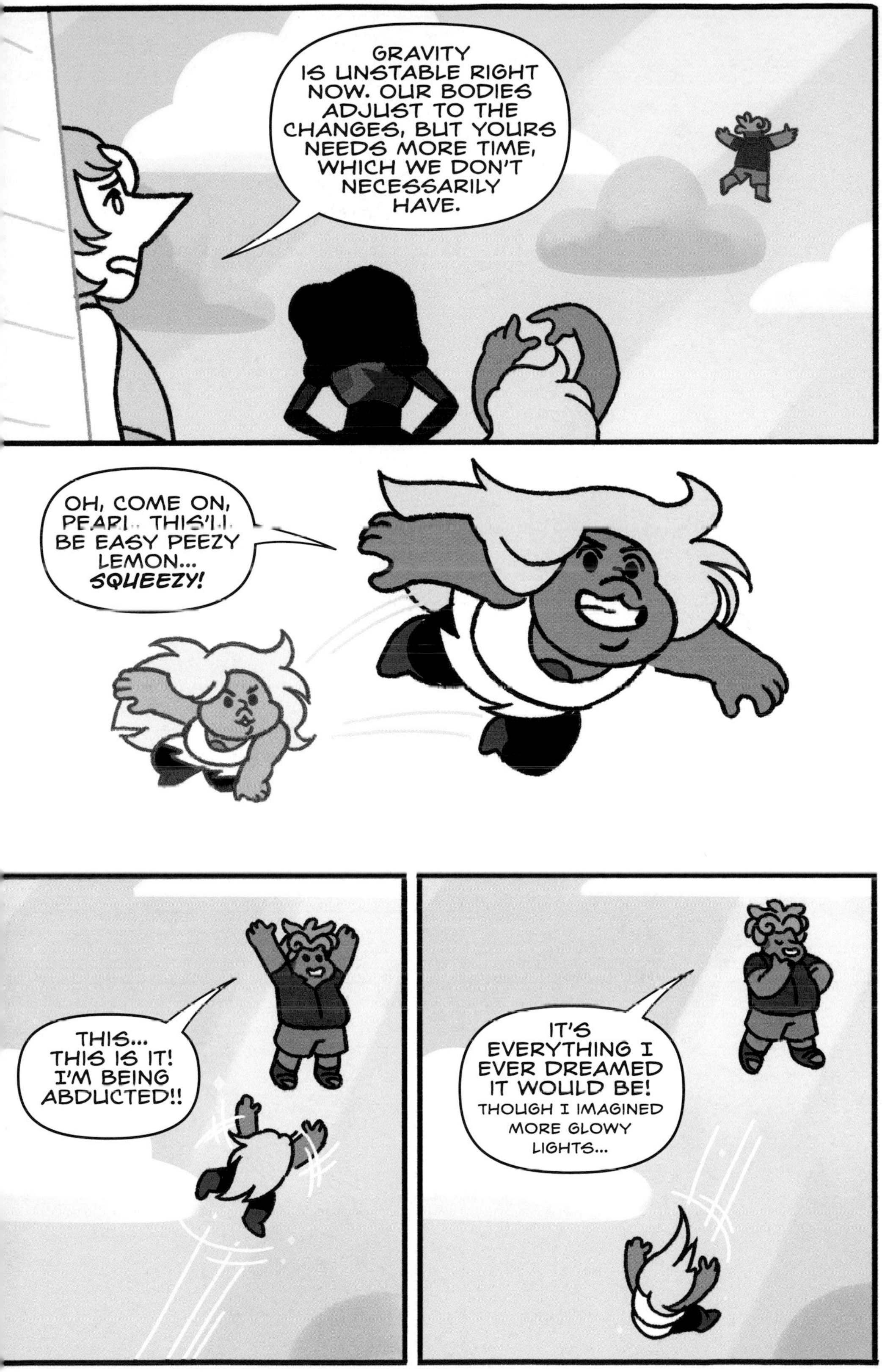
GRAVITY IS UNSTABLE RIGHT NOW. OUR BODIES ADJUST TO THE CHANGES, BUT YOURS NEEDS MORE TIME, WHICH WE DON'T NECESSARILY HAVE.
OH, COME ON, PEARL. THIS'LL BE EASY PEEZY LEMON... SQUEEZY!
THIS... THIS IS IT! I'M BEING ABDUCTED!!
IT'S EVERYTHING I EVER DREAMED IT WOULD BE! THOUGH I IMAGINED MORE GLOWY LIGHTS...

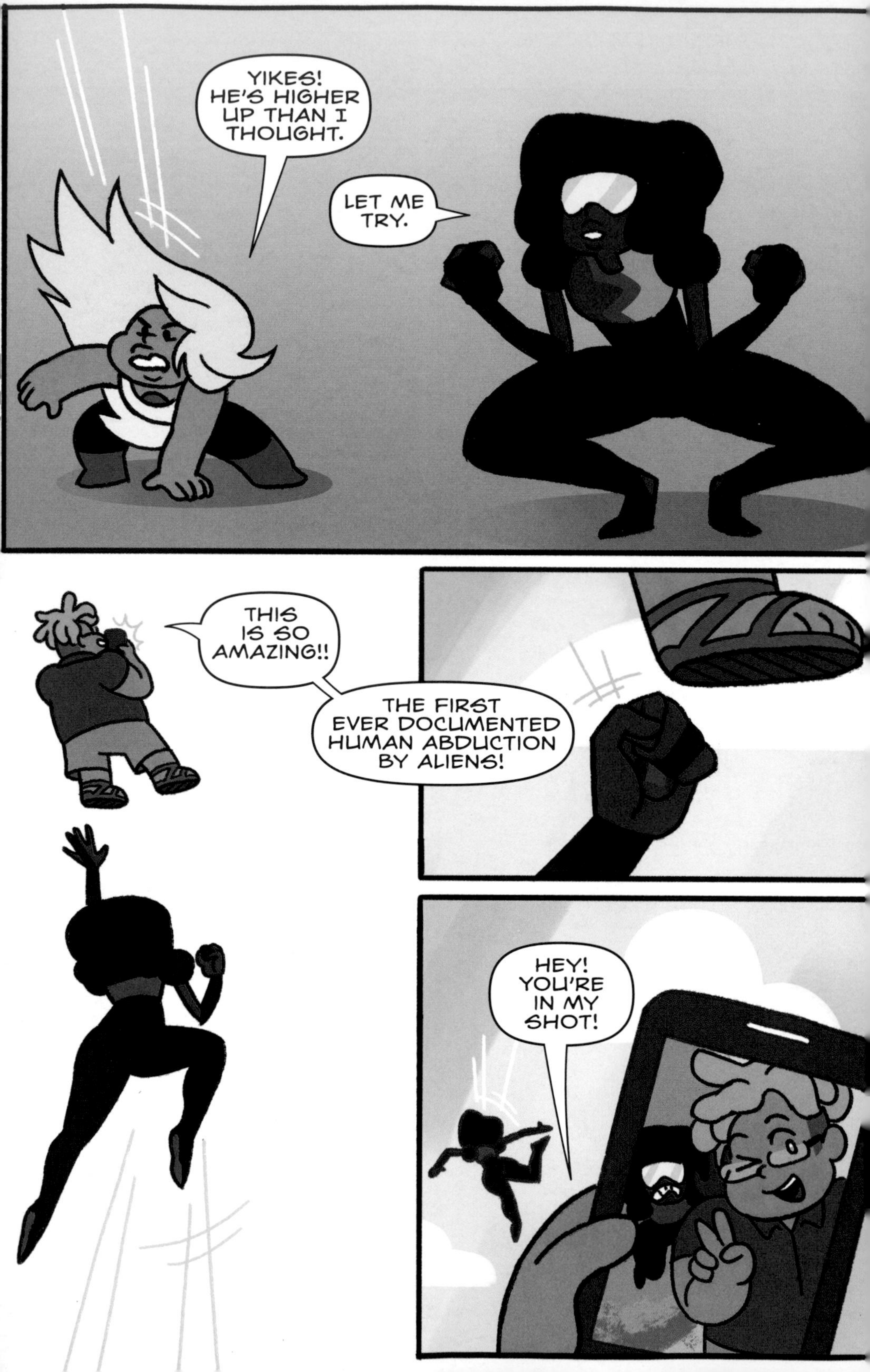
YIKES! HE'S HIGHER UP THAN I THOUGHT.
LET ME TRY.
THIS IS SO AMAZING!!
THE FIRST EVER DOCUMENTED HUMAN ABDUCTION BY ALIENS!
HEY! YOU'RE IN MY SHOT!

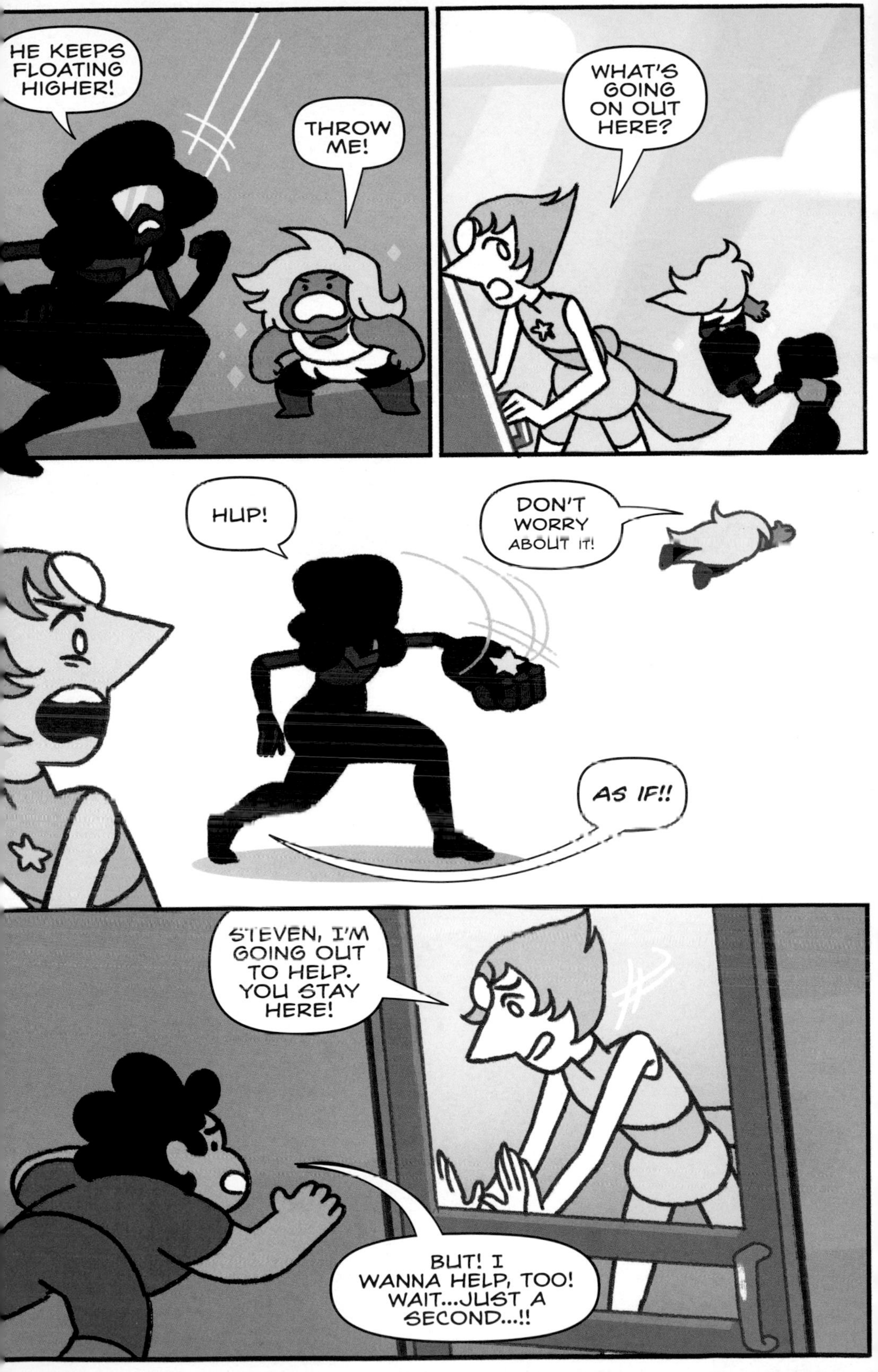
HE KEEPS FLOATING HIGHER!
THROW ME!
WHAT'S GOING ON OUT HERE?
HUP!
DON'T WORRY ABOUT IT!
AS IF!!
STEVEN, I'M GOING OUT TO HELP. YOU STAY HERE!
BUT! I WANNA HELP, TOO! WAIT...JUST A SECOND...!!

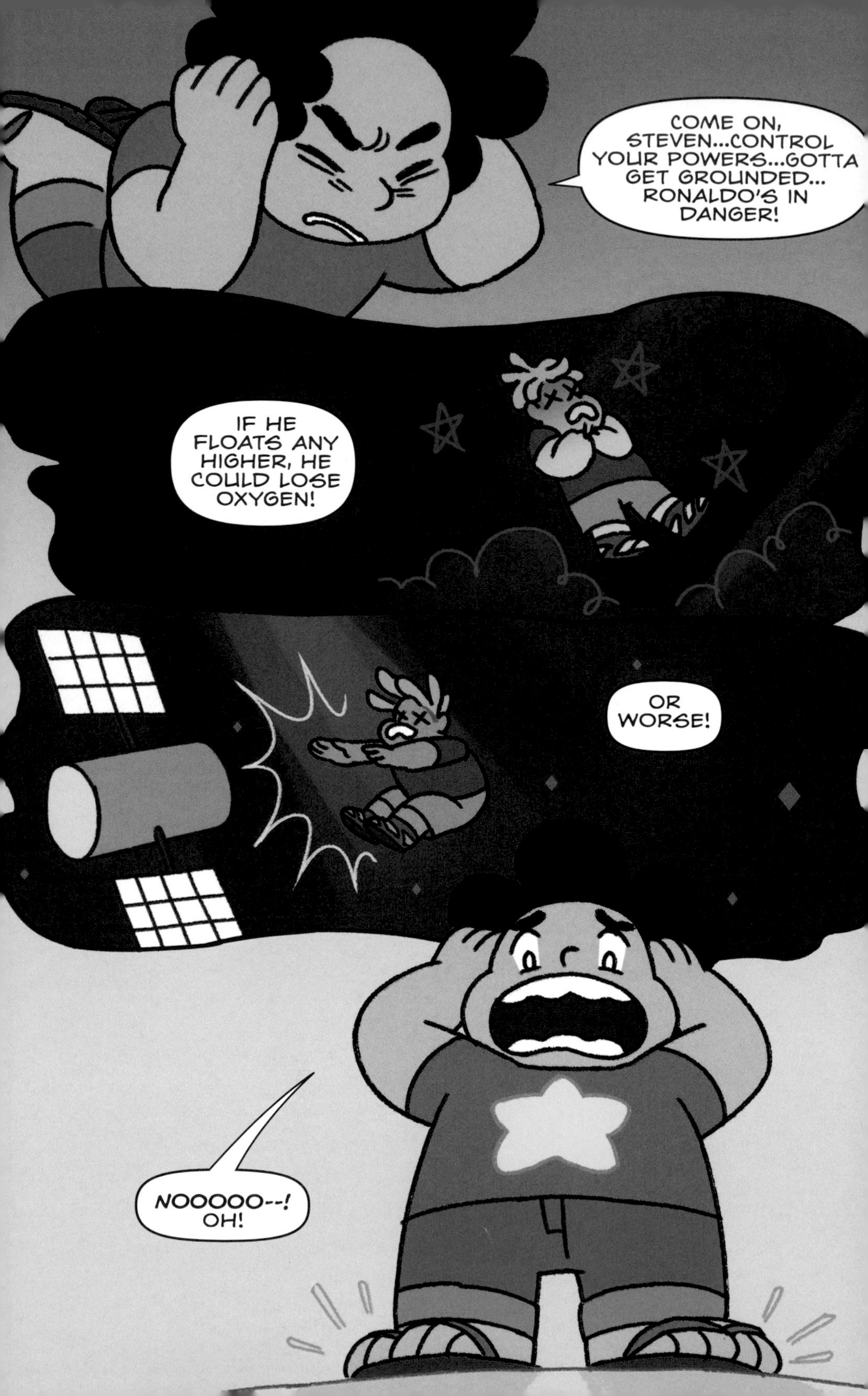
COME ON, STEVEN...CONTROL YOUR POWERS...GOTTA GET GROUNDED... RONALDO'S IN DANGER!
IF HE FLOATS ANY HIGHER, HE COULD LOSE OXYGEN!
OR WORSE!
NOOOOO--! OH!

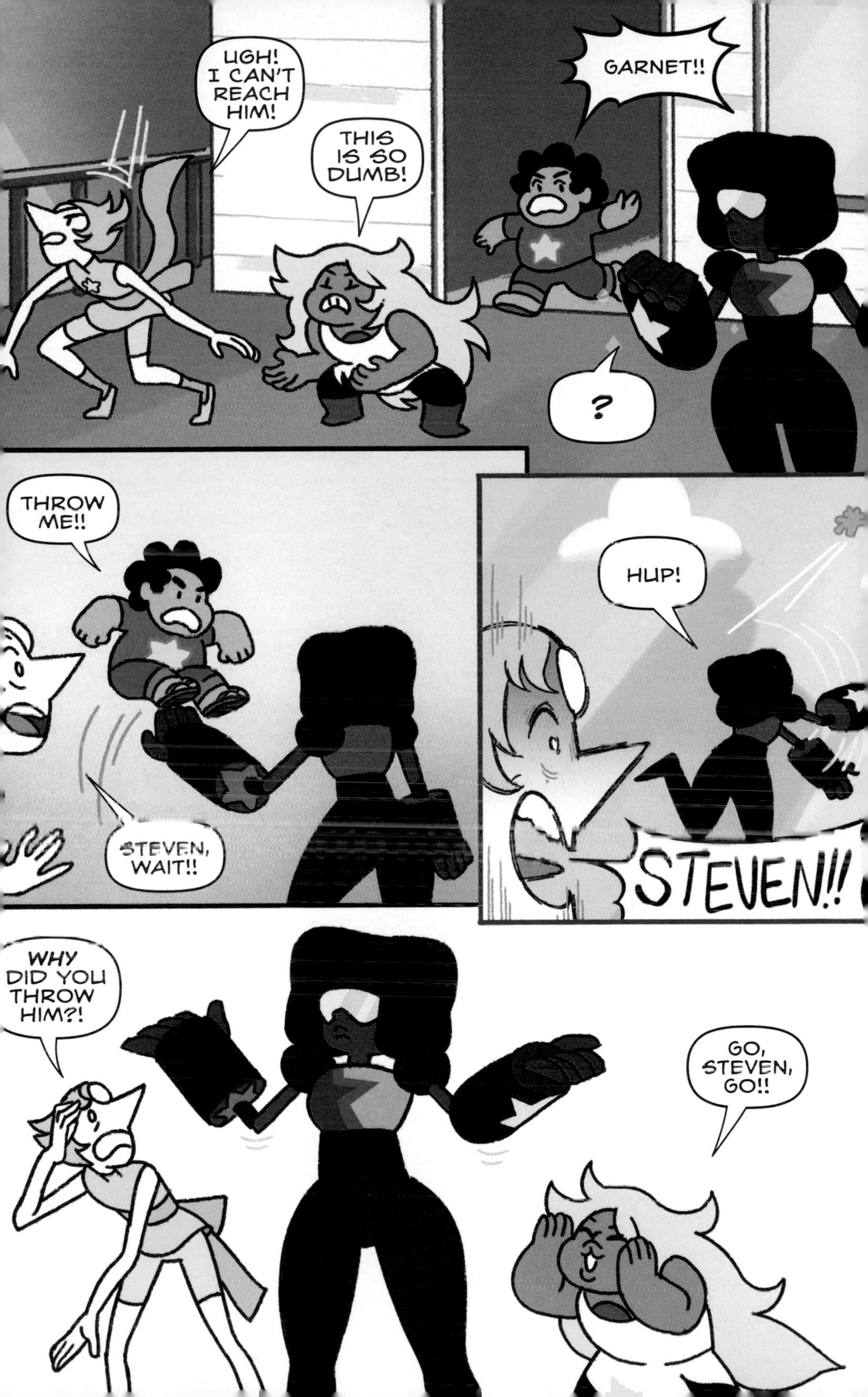
UGH! I CAN'T REACH HIM!
THIS IS SO DUMB!
GARNET!!
?
THROW ME!!
STEVEN, WAIT!!
HUP!
STEVEN!!
WHY DID YOU THROW HIM?!
GO, STEVEN, GO!!

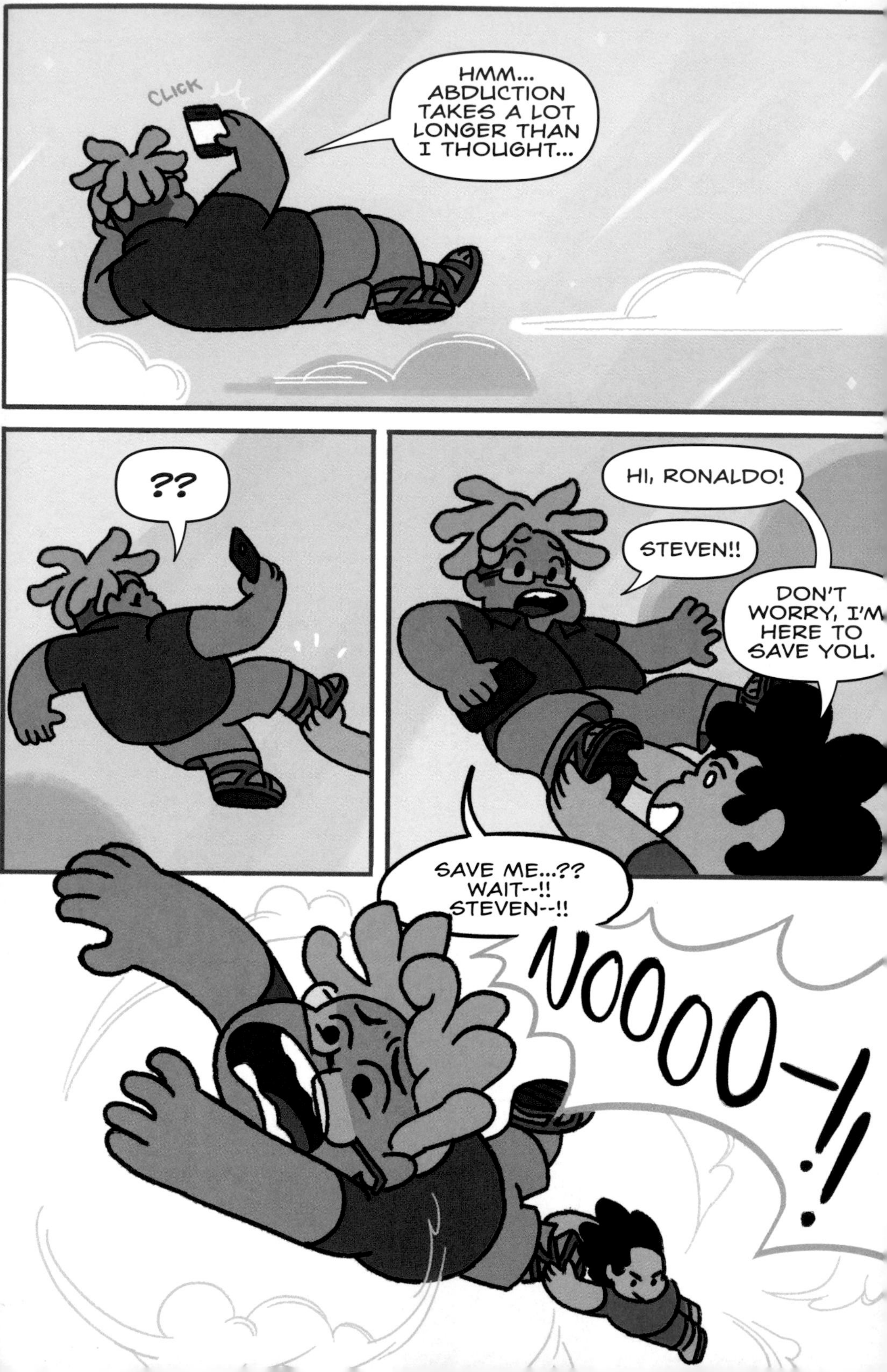
CLICK
HMM... ABDUCTION TAKES A LOT LONGER THAN I THOUGHT...
??
HI, RONALDO!
STEVEN!!
DON'T WORRY, I'M HERE TO SAVE YOU.
SAVE ME...?? WAIT--!! STEVEN--!!
NOOOO-!!

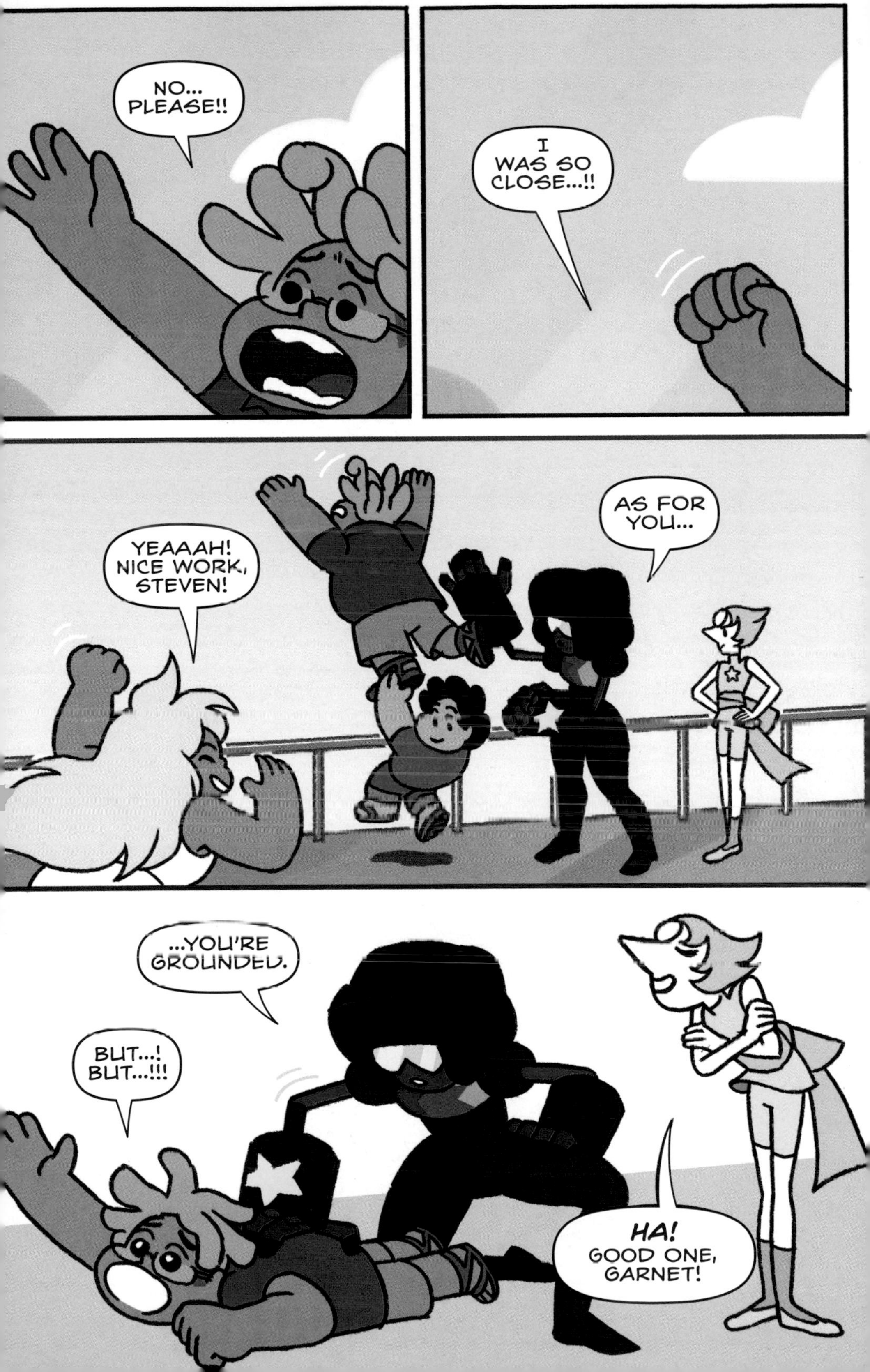
NO... PLEASE!!
I WAS SO CLOSE...!!
YEAAAH! NICE WORK, STEVEN!
AS FOR YOU...
...YOU'RE GROUNDED.
BUT...! BUT...!!!
HA! GOOD ONE, GARNET!

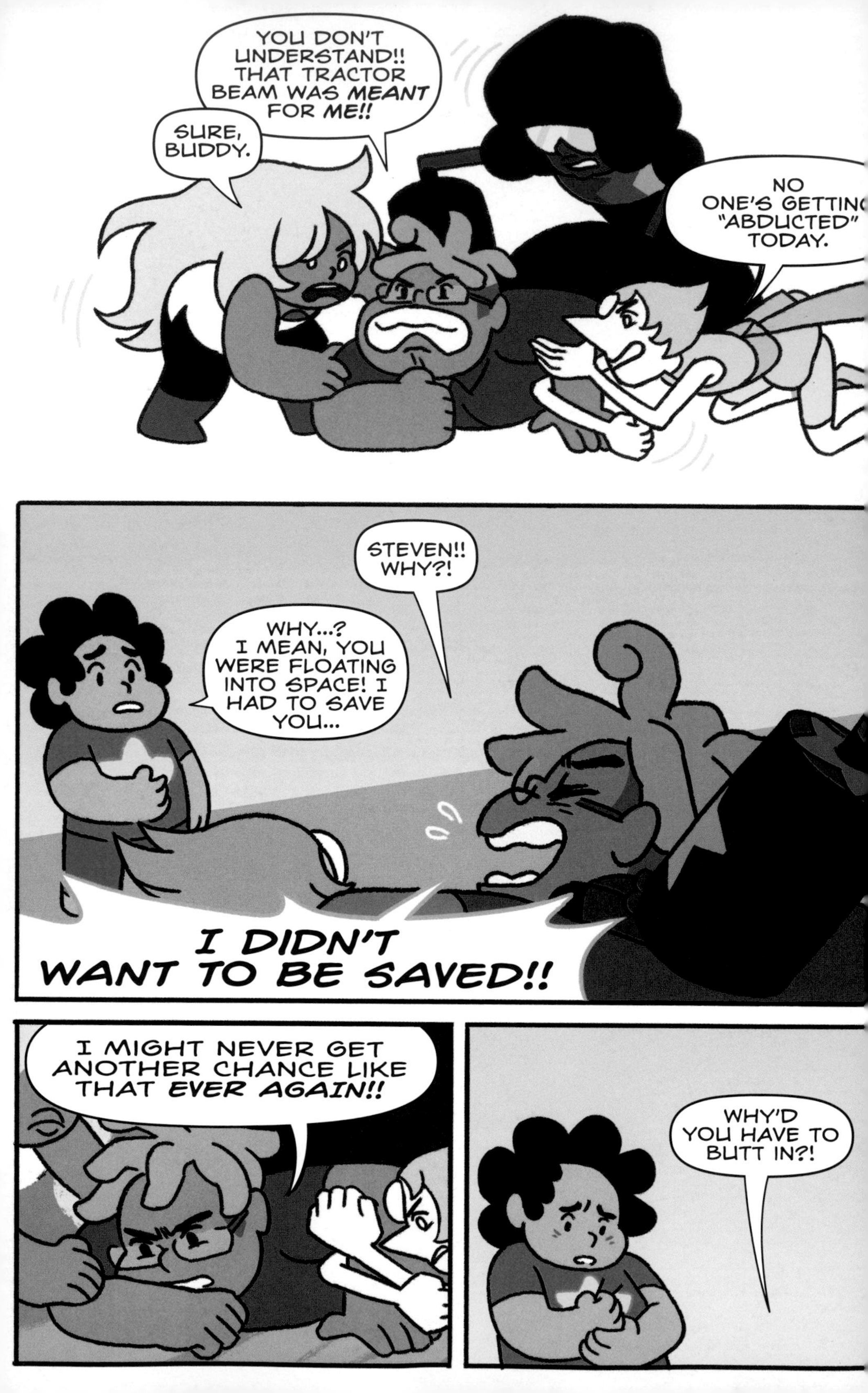
YOU DON'T UNDERSTAND!! THAT TRACTOR BEAM WAS MEANT FOR ME!!
SURE, BUDDY.
NO ONE'S GETTIN "ABDUCTED" TODAY.
STEVEN!! WHY?!
WHY...? I MEAN, YOU WERE FLOATING INTO SPACE! I HAD TO SAVE YOU...
I DIDN'T WANT TO BE SAVED!!
I MIGHT NEVER GET ANOTHER CHANCE LIKE THAT EVER AGAIN!!
WHY'D YOU HAVE TO BUTT IN?!

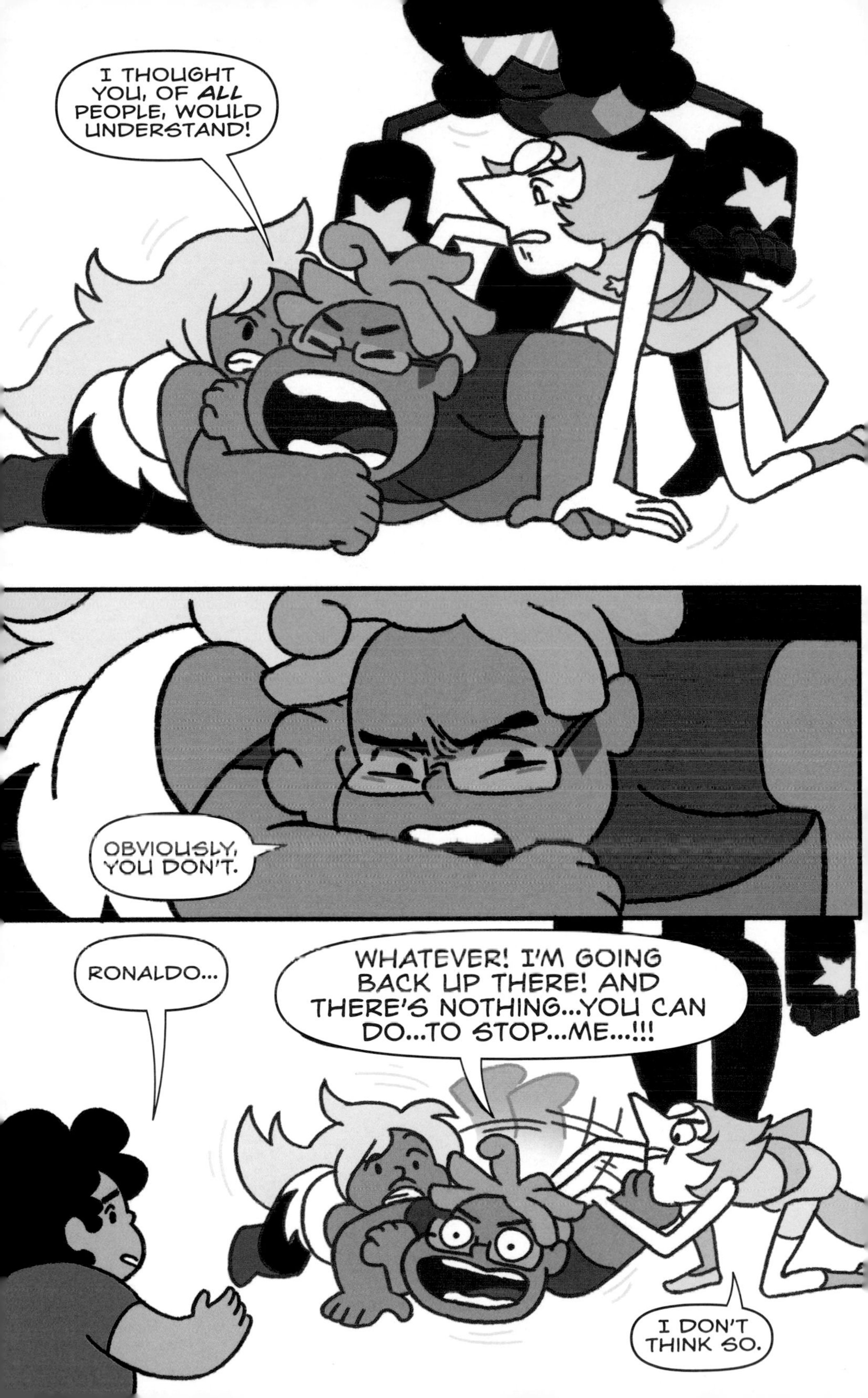
I THOUGHT YOU, OF ALL PEOPLE, WOULD UNDERSTAND!
OBVIOUSLY, YOU DON'T.
RONALDO...
WHATEVER! I'M GOING BACK UP THERE! AND THERE'S NOTHING...YOU CAN DO...TO STOP...ME...!!!
I DON'T THINK SO.

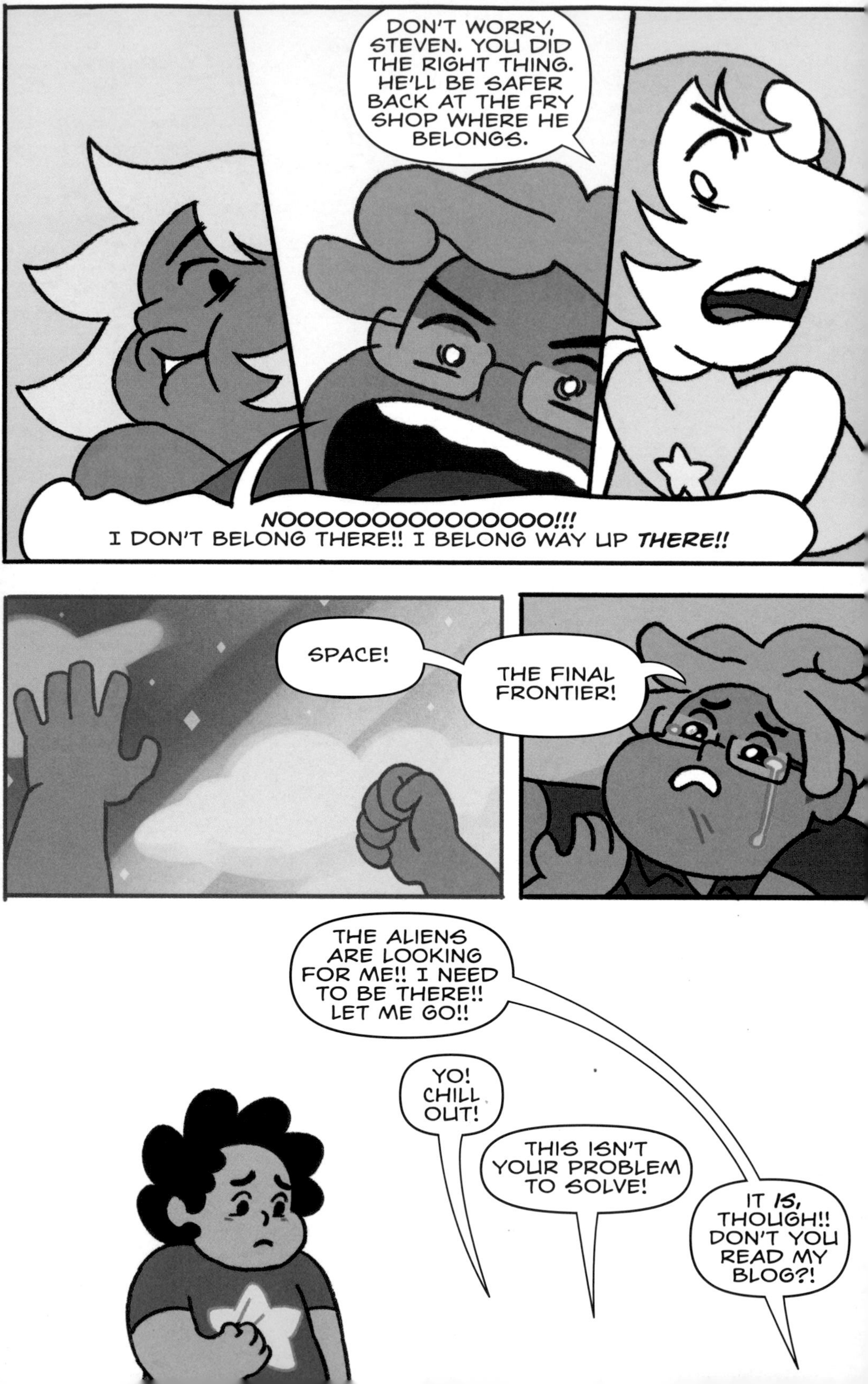
DON'T WORRY, STEVEN. YOU DID THE RIGHT THING. HE'LL BE SAFER BACK AT THE FRY SHOP WHERE HE BELONGS.
NOOOOOOOOOOOOOOO!!! I DON'T BELONG THERE!! I BELONG WAY UP *THERE!!*
SPACE!
THE FINAL FRONTIER!
THE ALIENS ARE LOOKING FOR ME!! I NEED TO BE THERE!! LET ME GO!!
YO! CHILL OUT!
THIS ISN'T YOUR PROBLEM TO SOLVE!
IT *IS,* THOUGH!! DON'T YOU READ MY BLOG?!

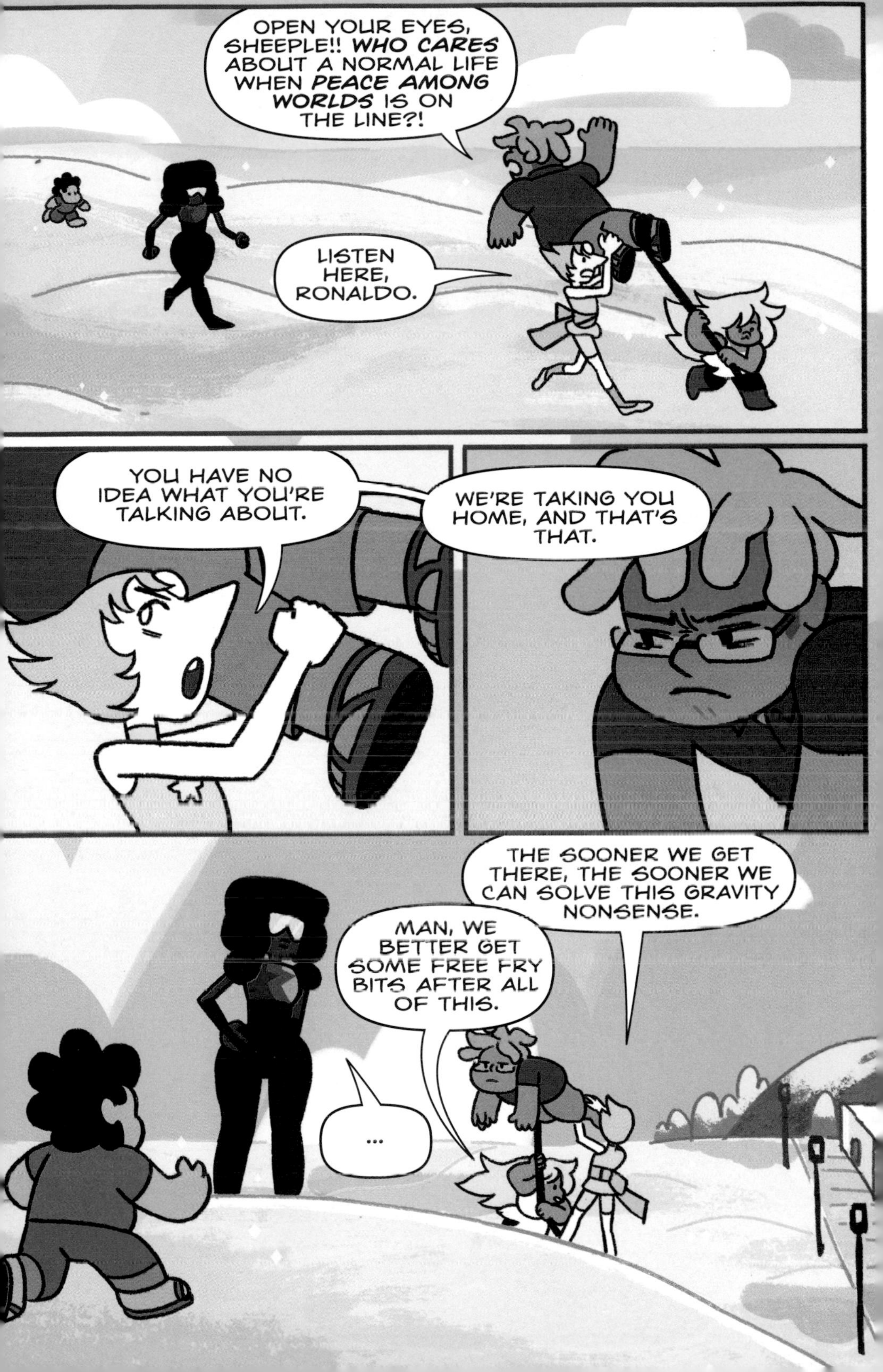
OPEN YOUR EYES, SHEEPLE!! WHO CARES ABOUT A NORMAL LIFE WHEN PEACE AMONG WORLDS IS ON THE LINE?!
LISTEN HERE, RONALDO.
YOU HAVE NO IDEA WHAT YOU'RE TALKING ABOUT.
WE'RE TAKING YOU HOME, AND THAT'S THAT.
THE SOONER WE GET THERE, THE SOONER WE CAN SOLVE THIS GRAVITY NONSENSE.
MAN, WE BETTER GET SOME FREE FRY BITS AFTER ALL OF THIS.
...

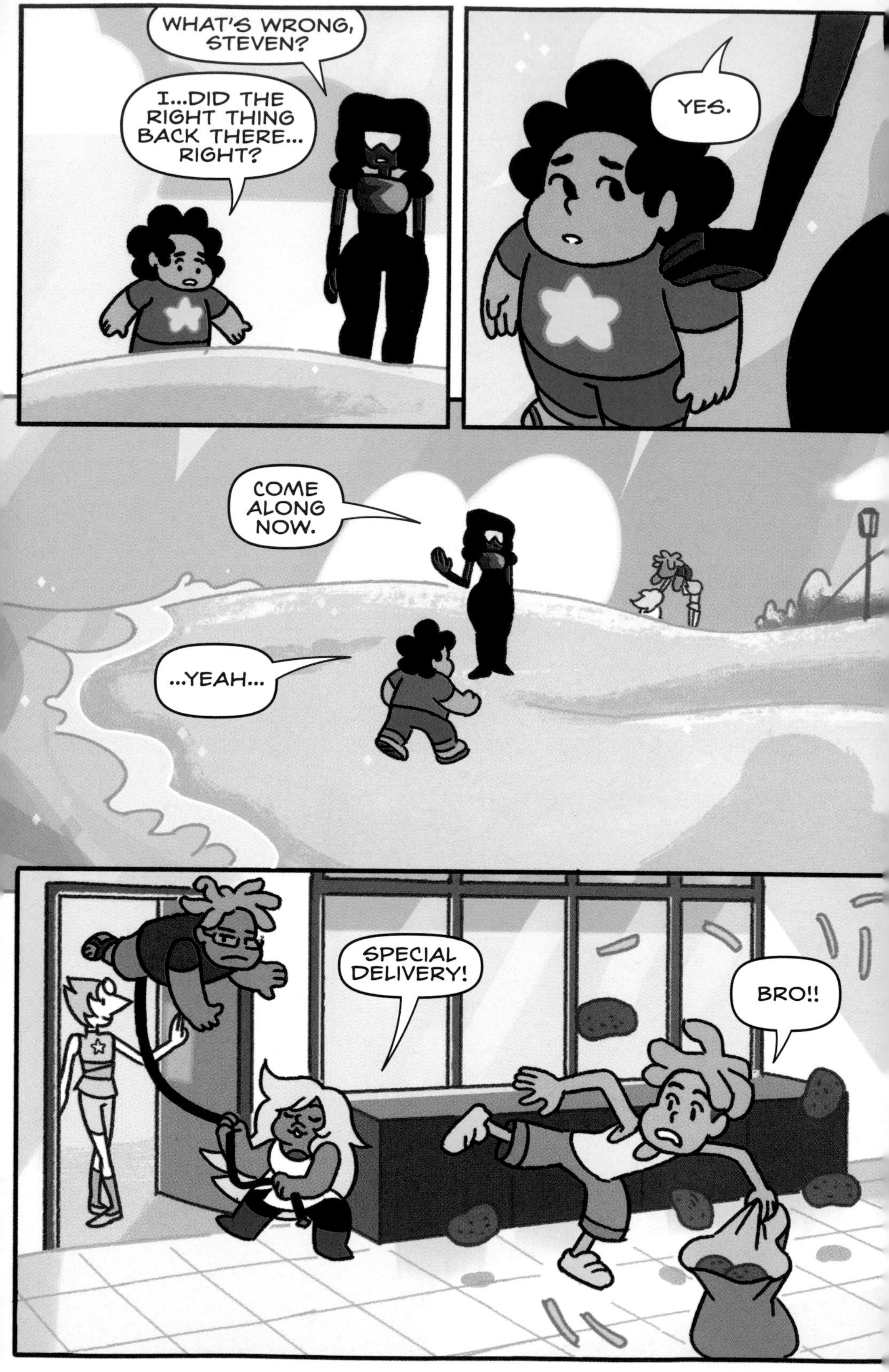
WHAT'S WRONG, STEVEN?
I...DID THE RIGHT THING BACK THERE... RIGHT?
YES.
COME ALONG NOW.
...YEAH...
SPECIAL DELIVERY!
BRO!!

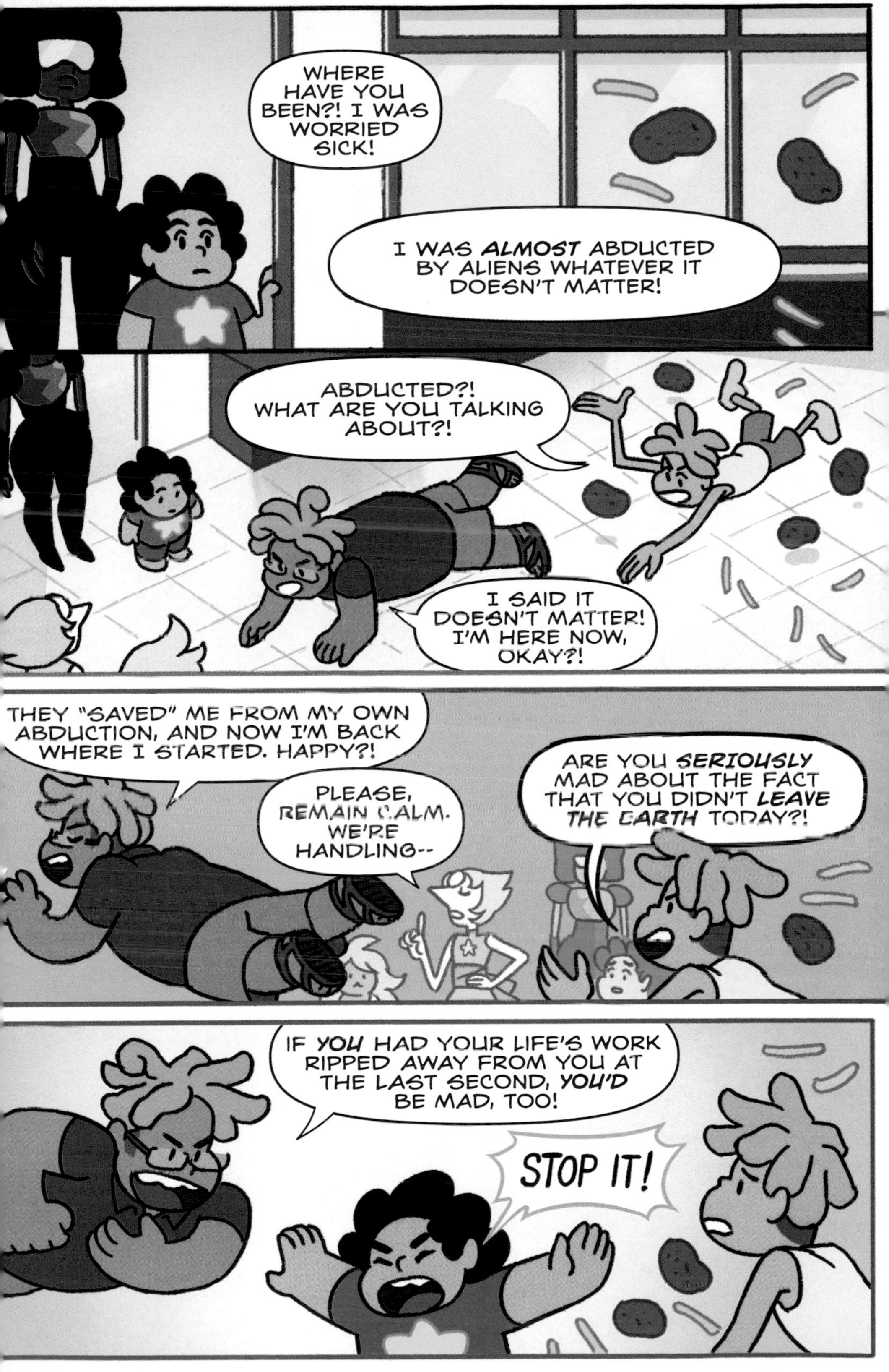
WHERE HAVE YOU BEEN?! I WAS WORRIED SICK!
I WAS ALMOST ABDUCTED BY ALIENS WHATEVER IT DOESN'T MATTER!
ABDUCTED?! WHAT ARE YOU TALKING ABOUT?!
I SAID IT DOESN'T MATTER! I'M HERE NOW, OKAY?!
THEY "SAVED" ME FROM MY OWN ABDUCTION, AND NOW I'M BACK WHERE I STARTED. HAPPY?!
PLEASE, REMAIN CALM. WE'RE HANDLING--
ARE YOU SERIOUSLY MAD ABOUT THE FACT THAT YOU DIDN'T LEAVE THE EARTH TODAY?!
IF YOU HAD YOUR LIFE'S WORK RIPPED AWAY FROM YOU AT THE LAST SECOND, YOU'D BE MAD, TOO!
STOP IT!

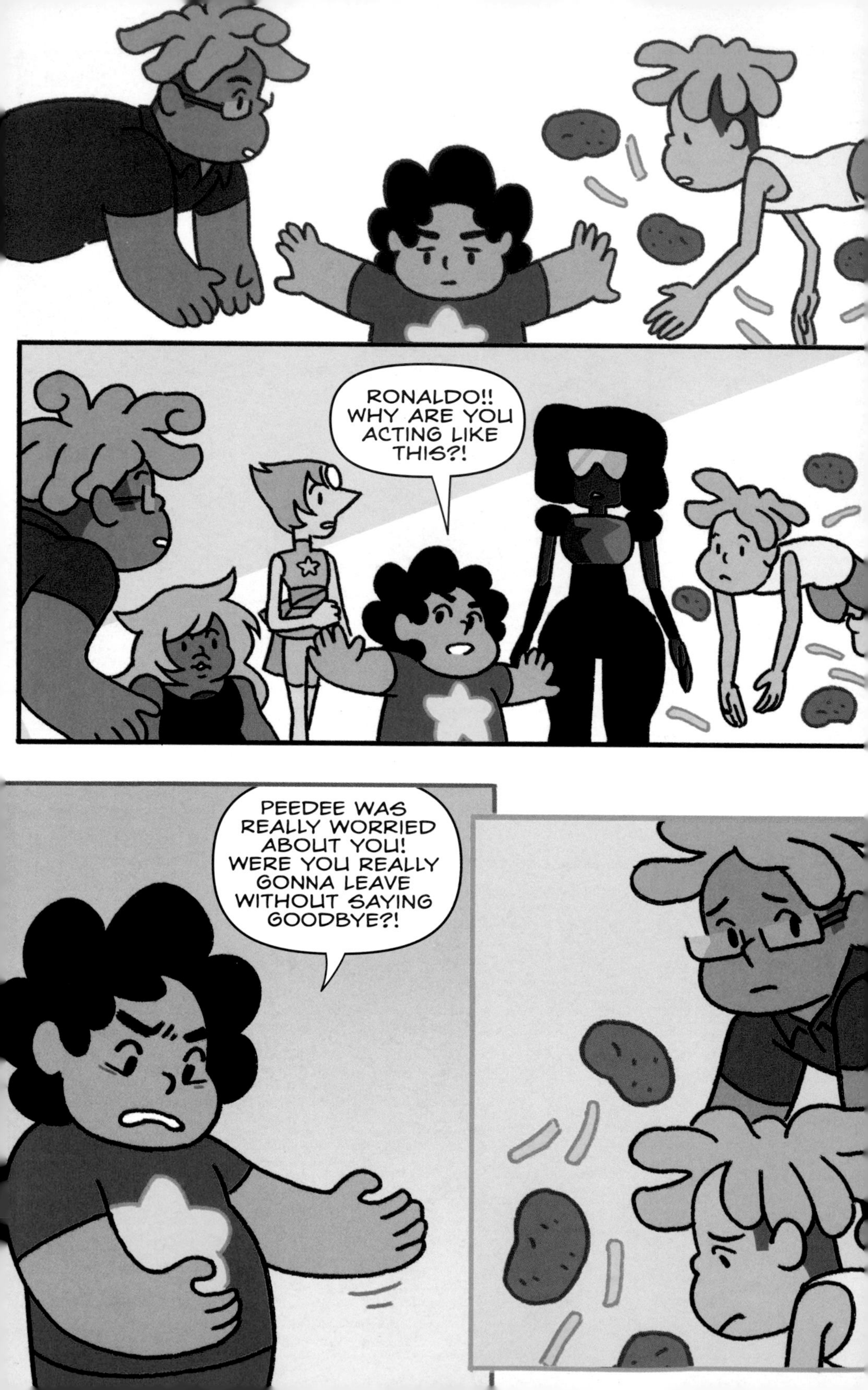
RONALDO!! WHY ARE YOU ACTING LIKE THIS?!
PEEDEE WAS REALLY WORRIED ABOUT YOU! WERE YOU REALLY GONNA LEAVE WITHOUT SAYING GOODBYE?!

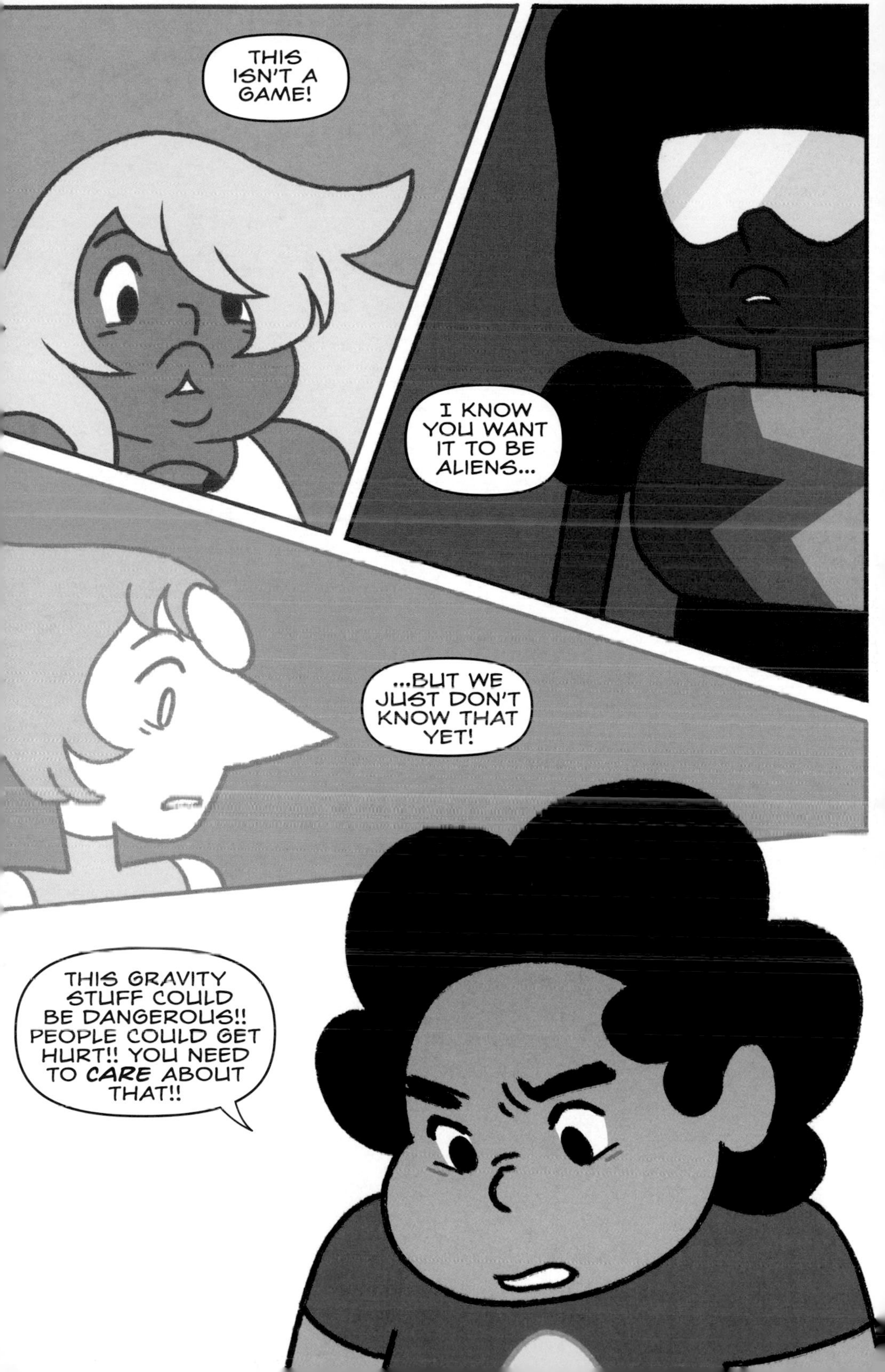
THIS ISN'T A GAME!
I KNOW YOU WANT IT TO BE ALIENS...
...BUT WE JUST DON'T KNOW THAT YET!
THIS GRAVITY STUFF COULD BE DANGEROUS!! PEOPLE COULD GET HURT!! YOU NEED TO CARE ABOUT THAT!!

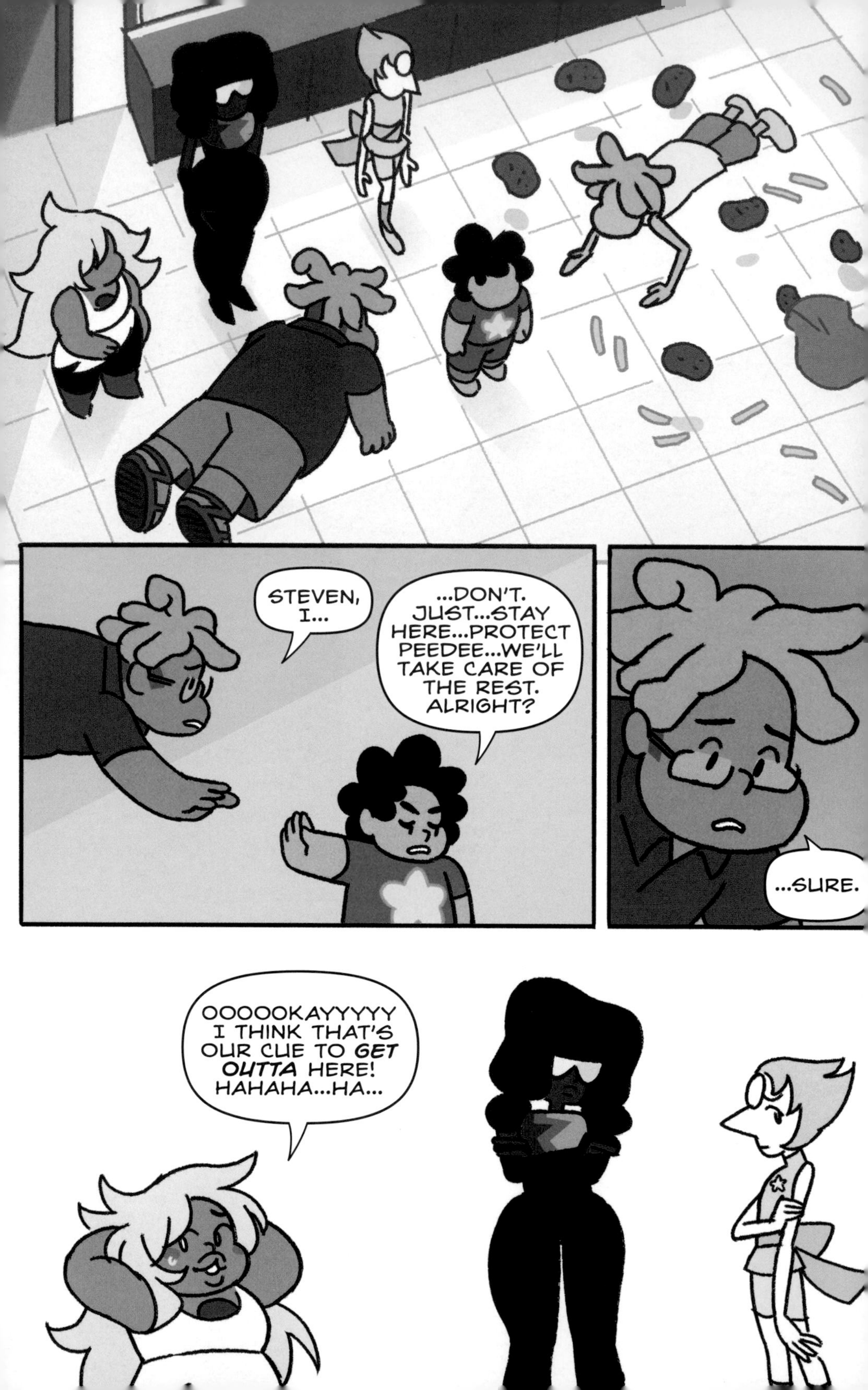
STEVEN, I...
...DON'T. JUST...STAY HERE...PROTECT PEEDEE...WE'LL TAKE CARE OF THE REST. ALRIGHT?
...SURE.
OOOOOKAYYYYY I THINK THAT'S OUR CUE TO *GET OUTTA* HERE! HAHAHA...HA...

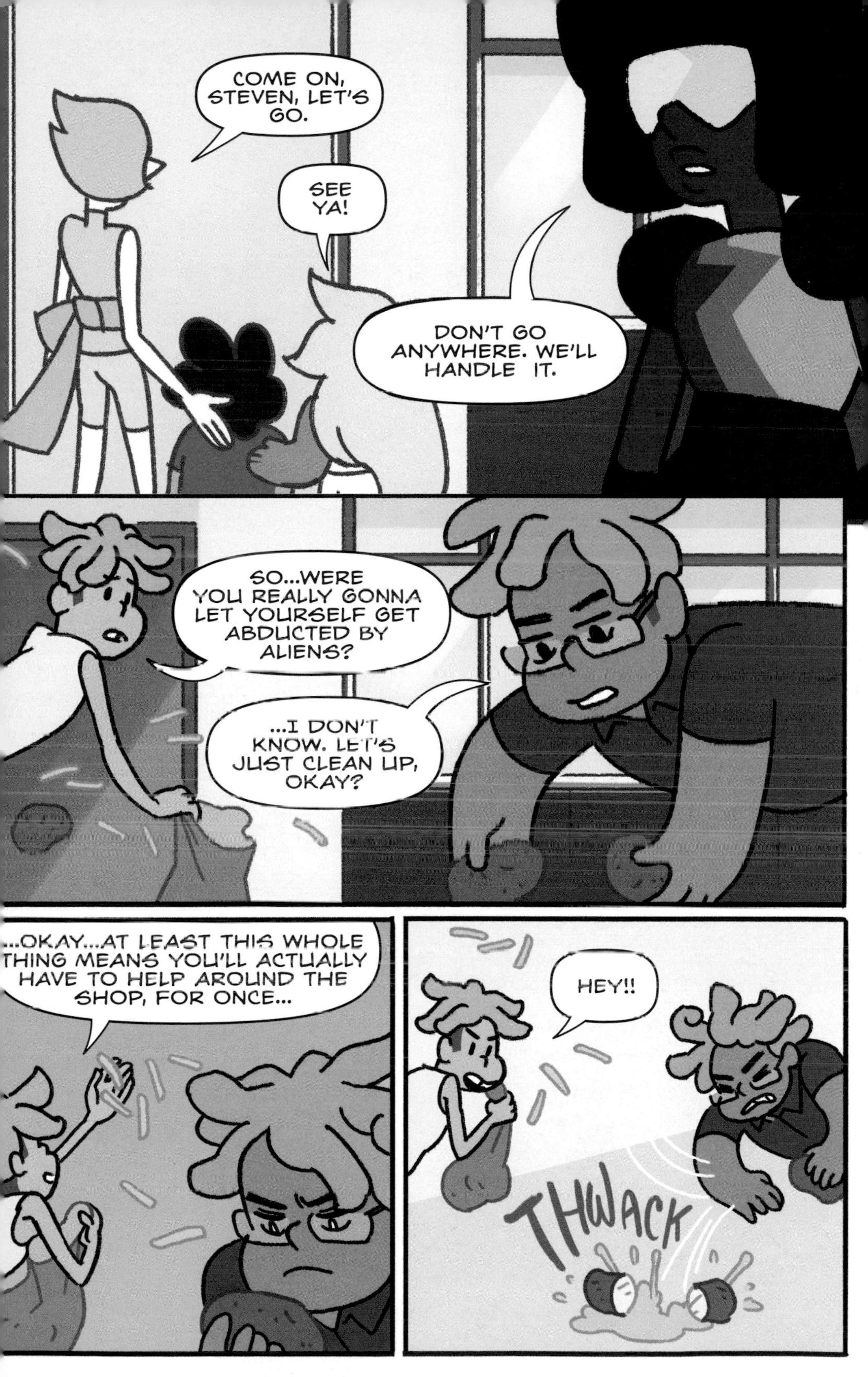
COME ON, STEVEN, LET'S GO.
SEE YA!
DON'T GO ANYWHERE. WE'LL HANDLE IT.
SO...WERE YOU REALLY GONNA LET YOURSELF GET ABDUCTED BY ALIENS?
...I DON'T KNOW. LET'S JUST CLEAN UP, OKAY?
...OKAY...AT LEAST THIS WHOLE THING MEANS YOU'LL ACTUALLY HAVE TO HELP AROUND THE SHOP, FOR ONCE...
HEY!!
THWACK

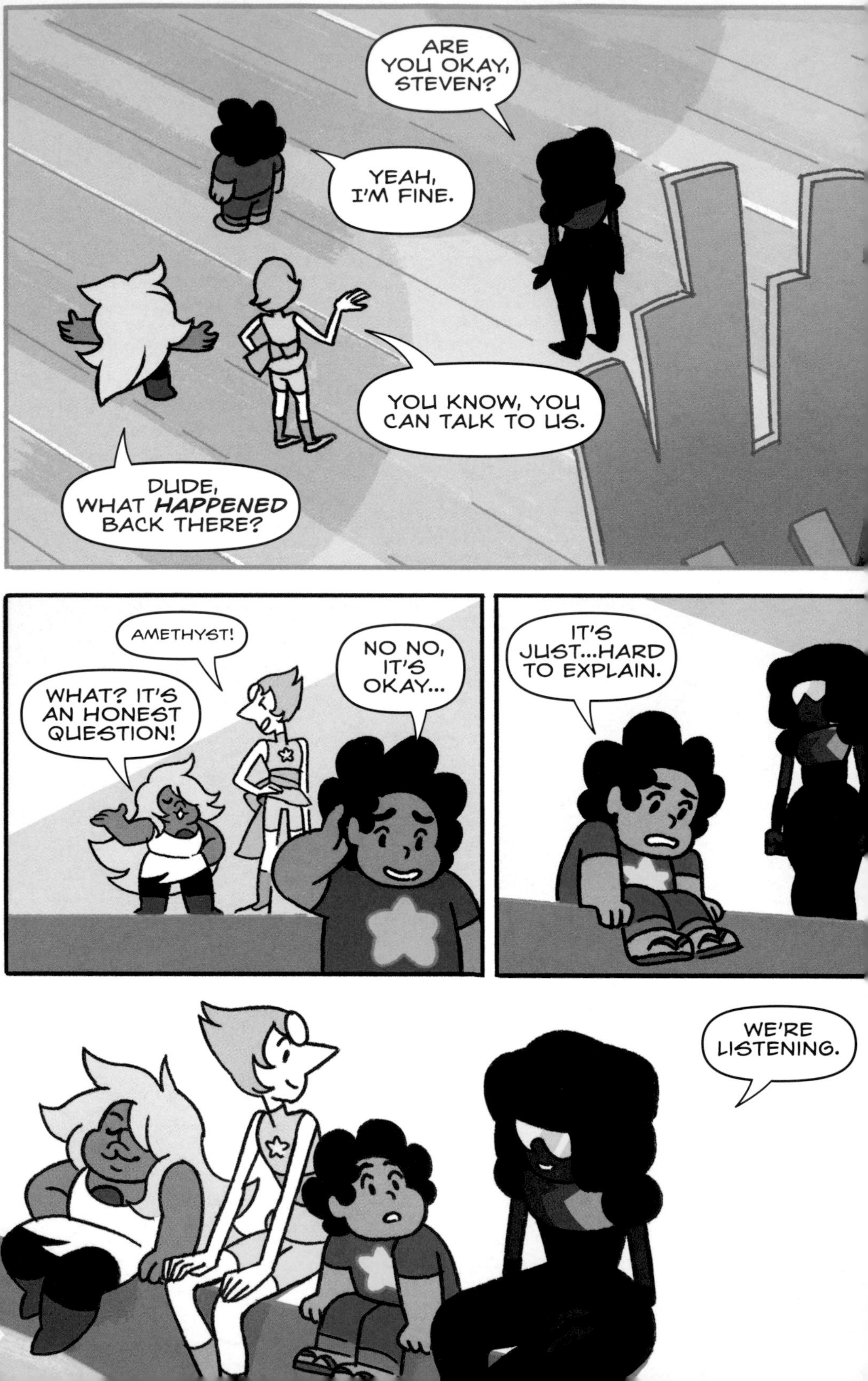
ARE YOU OKAY, STEVEN?
YEAH, I'M FINE.
YOU KNOW, YOU CAN TALK TO US.
DUDE, WHAT *HAPPENED* BACK THERE?
AMETHYST!
WHAT? IT'S AN HONEST QUESTION!
NO NO, IT'S OKAY...
IT'S JUST...HARD TO EXPLAIN.
WE'RE LISTENING.

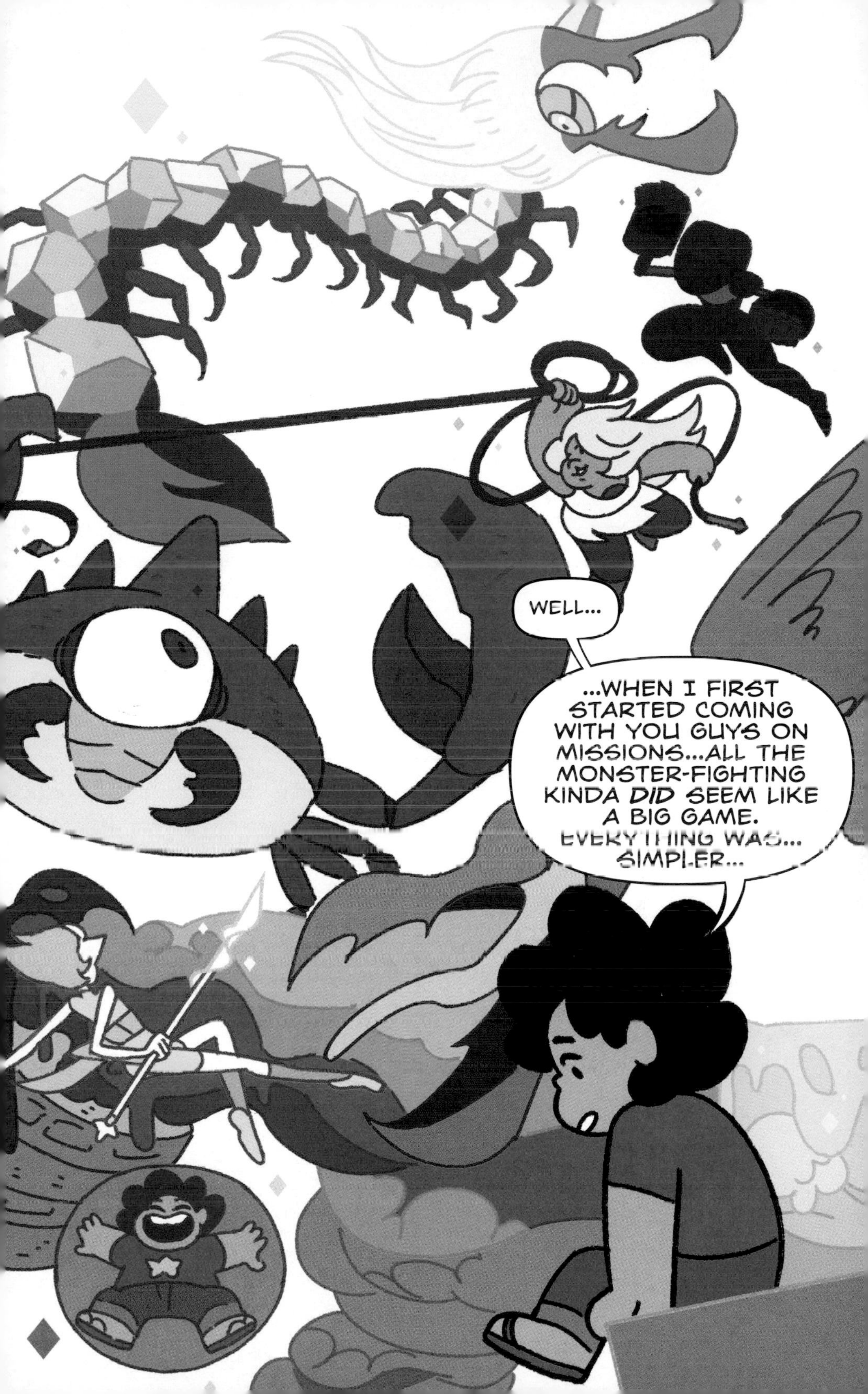
WELL...
...WHEN I FIRST STARTED COMING WITH YOU GUYS ON MISSIONS...ALL THE MONSTER-FIGHTING KINDA DID SEEM LIKE A BIG GAME. EVERYTHING WAS... SIMPLER...

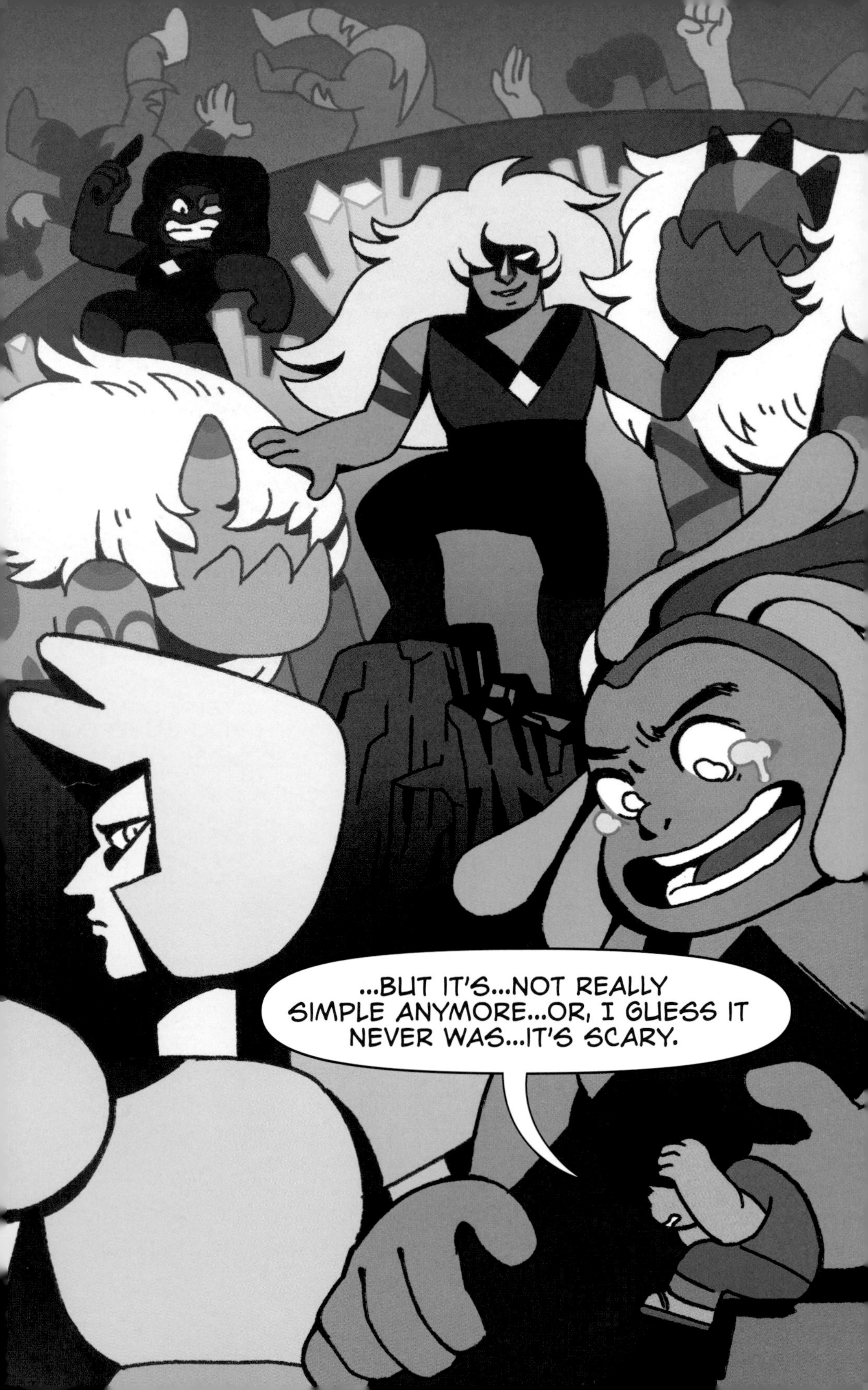
...BUT IT'S...NOT REALLY SIMPLE ANYMORE...OR, I GUESS IT NEVER WAS...IT'S SCARY.

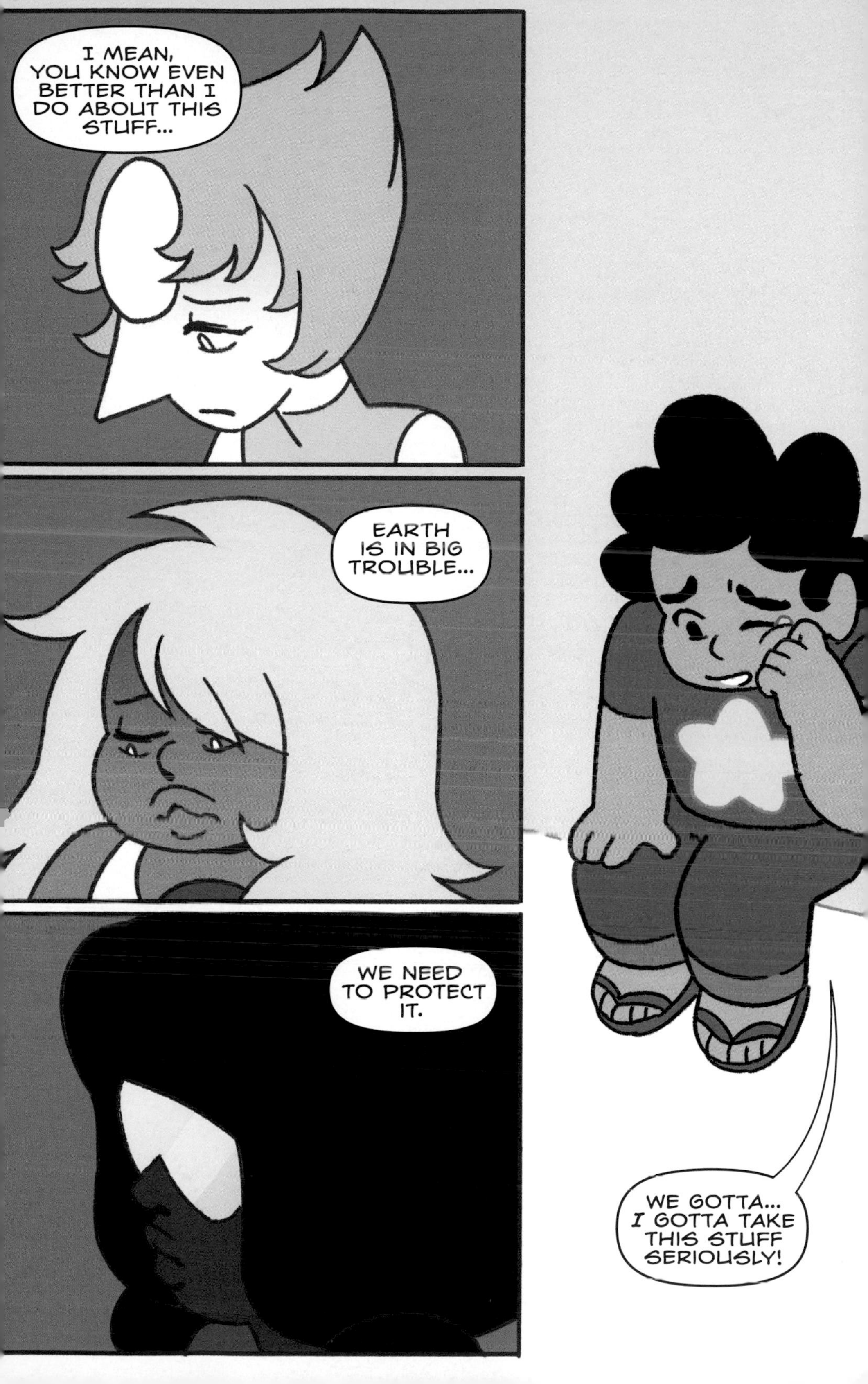
I MEAN, YOU KNOW EVEN BETTER THAN I DO ABOUT THIS STUFF...
EARTH IS IN BIG TROUBLE...
WE NEED TO PROTECT IT.
WE GOTTA... *I* GOTTA TAKE THIS STUFF SERIOUSLY!

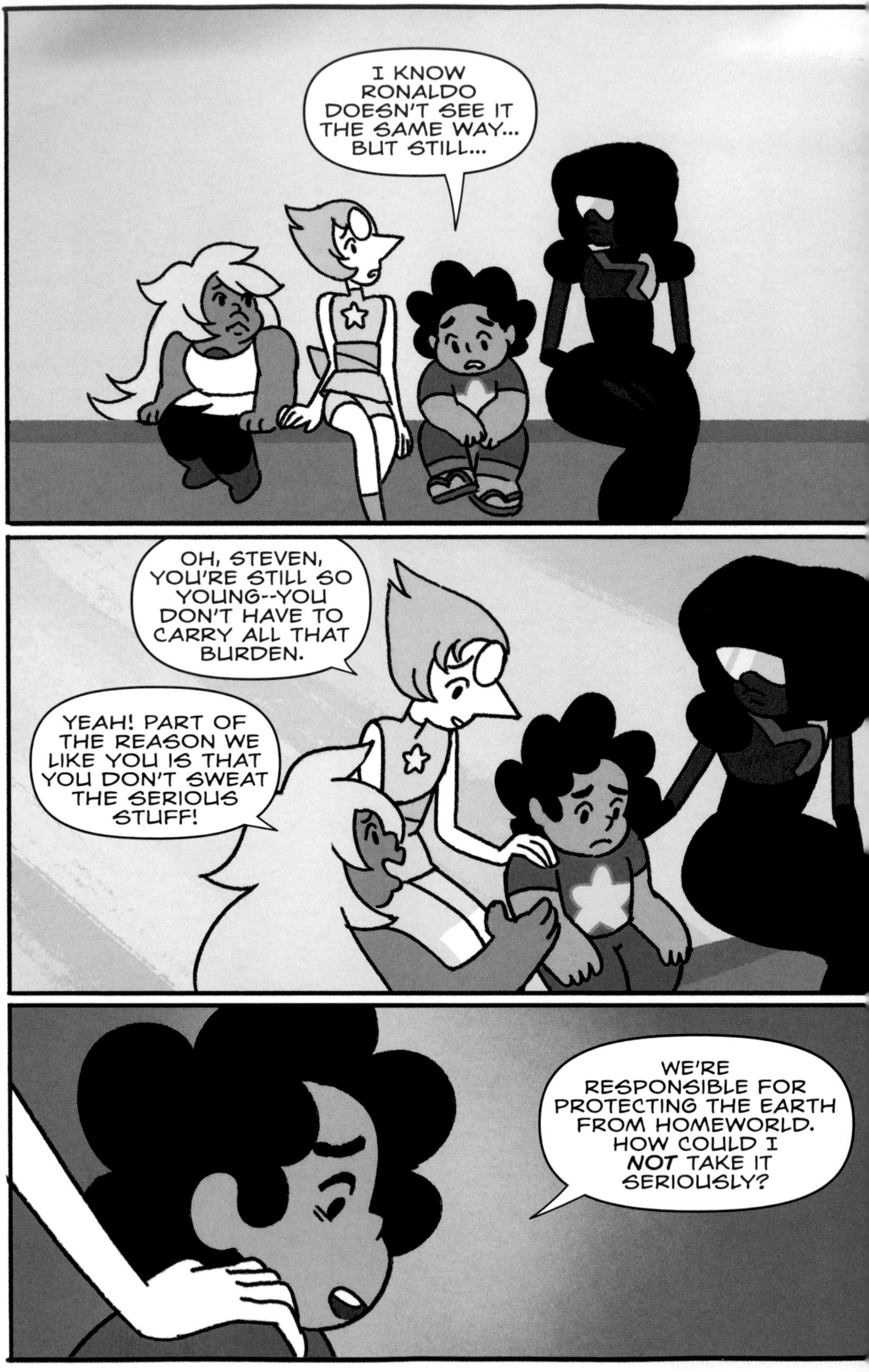
I KNOW RONALDO DOESN'T SEE IT THE SAME WAY... BUT STILL...
OH, STEVEN, YOU'RE STILL SO YOUNG--YOU DON'T HAVE TO CARRY ALL THAT BURDEN.
YEAH! PART OF THE REASON WE LIKE YOU IS THAT YOU DON'T SWEAT THE SERIOUS STUFF!
WE'RE RESPONSIBLE FOR PROTECTING THE EARTH FROM HOMEWORLD. HOW COULD I ***NOT*** TAKE IT SERIOUSLY?

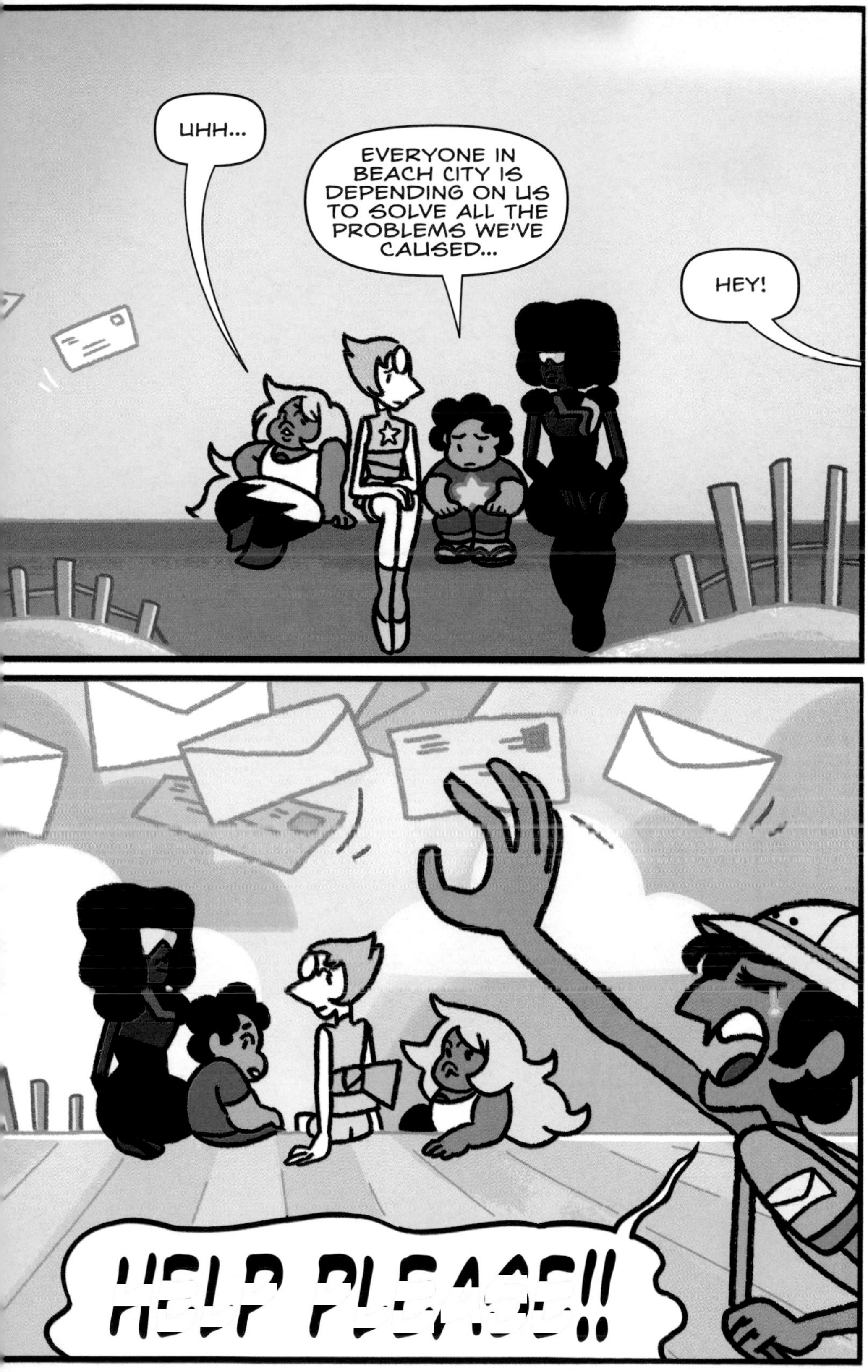
UHH...
EVERYONE IN BEACH CITY IS DEPENDING ON US TO SOLVE ALL THE PROBLEMS WE'VE CAUSED...
HEY!
HELP PLEASE!!

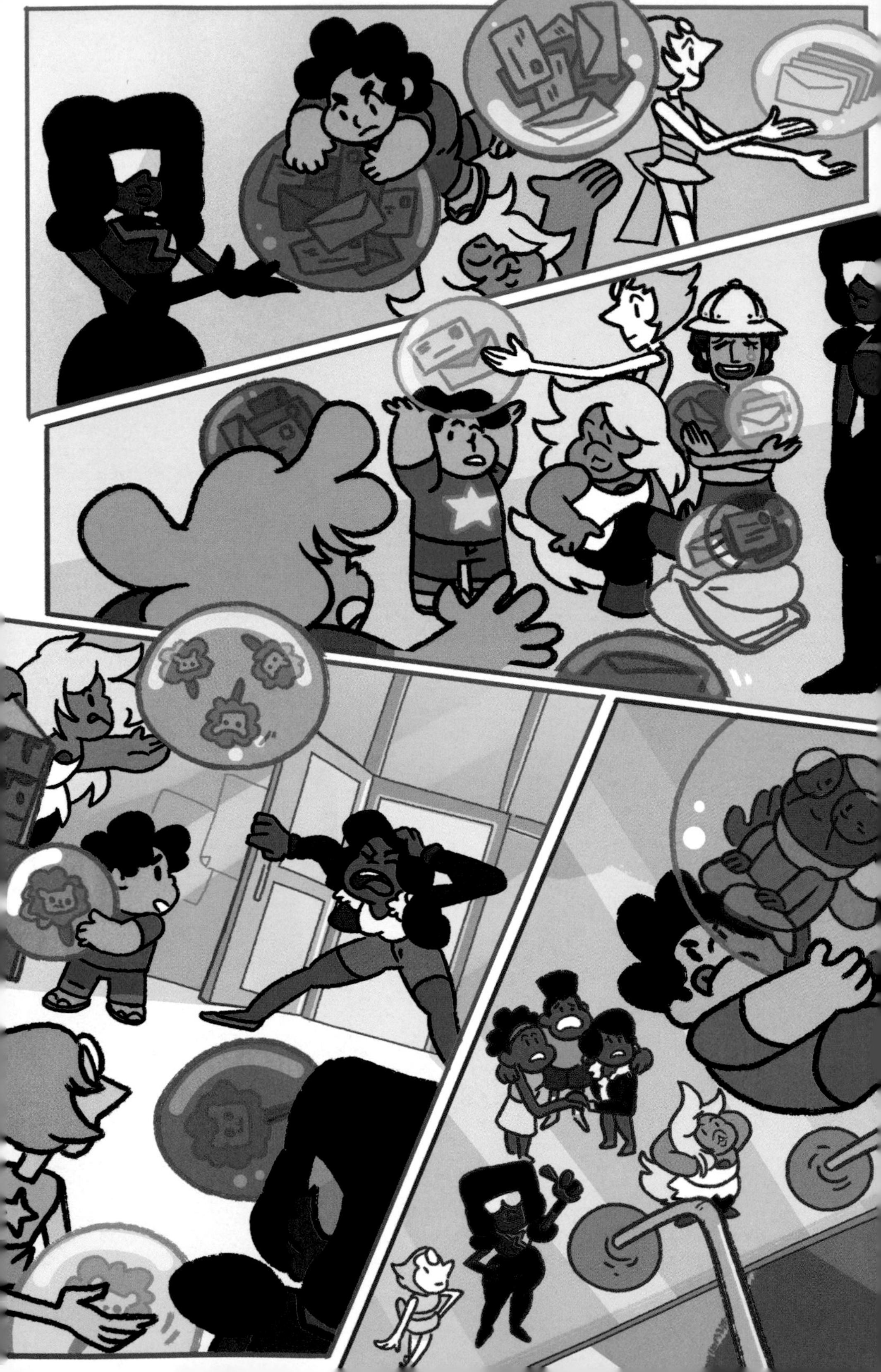

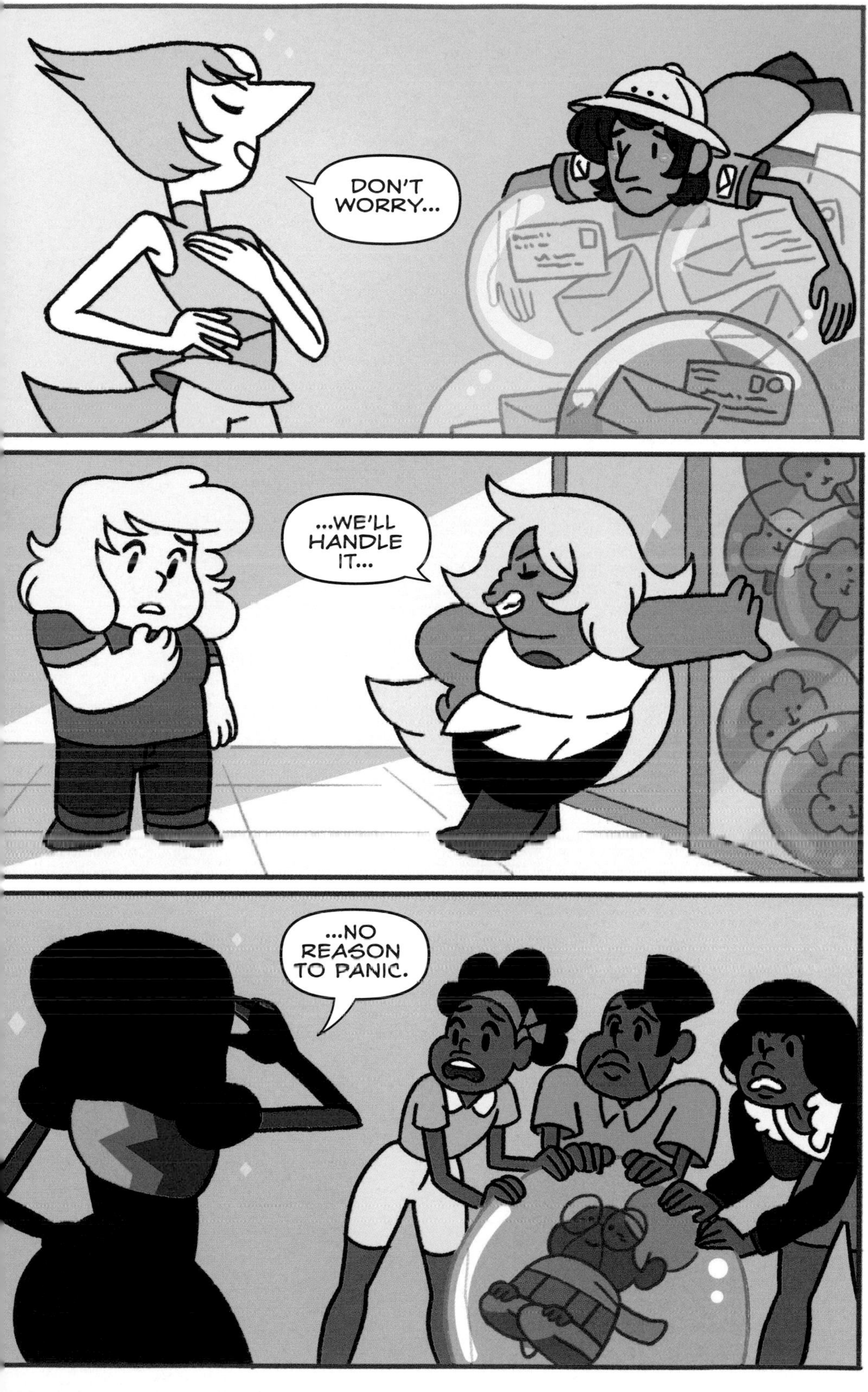
DON'T WORRY...
DO
...WE'LL HANDLE IT...
...NO REASON TO PANIC.

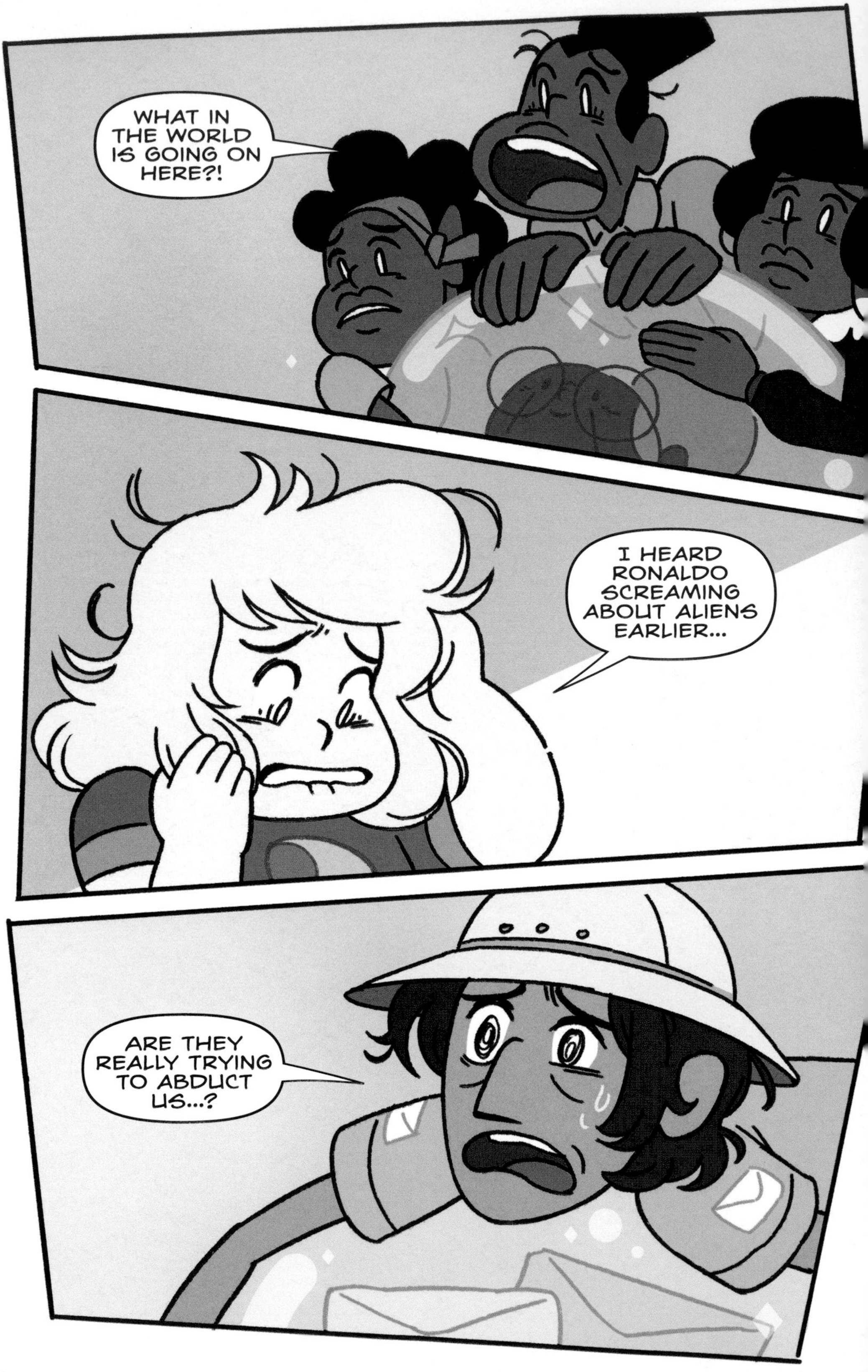
WHAT IN THE WORLD IS GOING ON HERE?!
I HEARD RONALDO SCREAMING ABOUT ALIENS EARLIER...
ARE THEY REALLY TRYING TO ABDUCT US...?

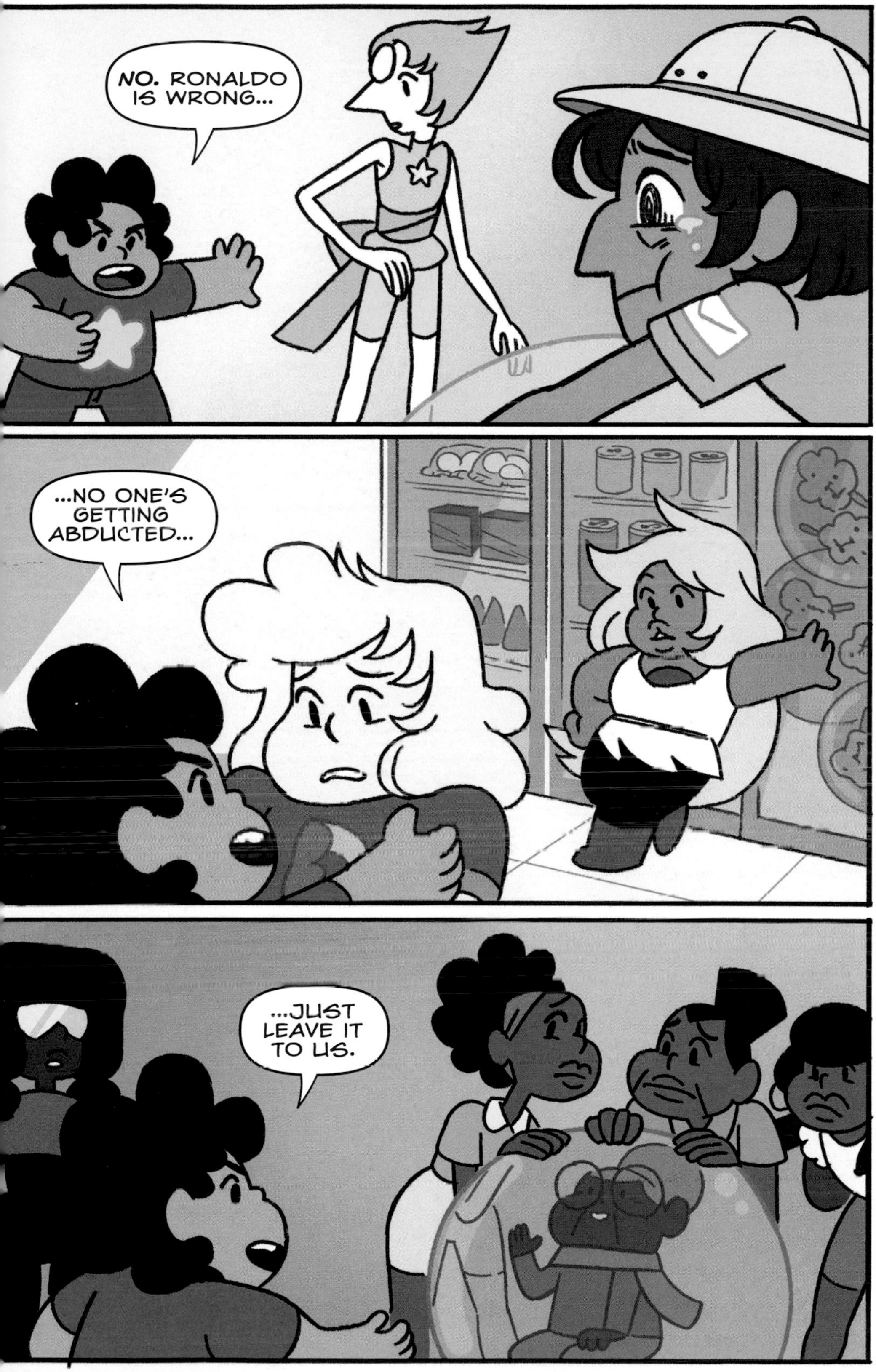
NO. RONALDO IS WRONG...
...NO ONE'S GETTING ABDUCTED...
...JUST LEAVE IT TO US.

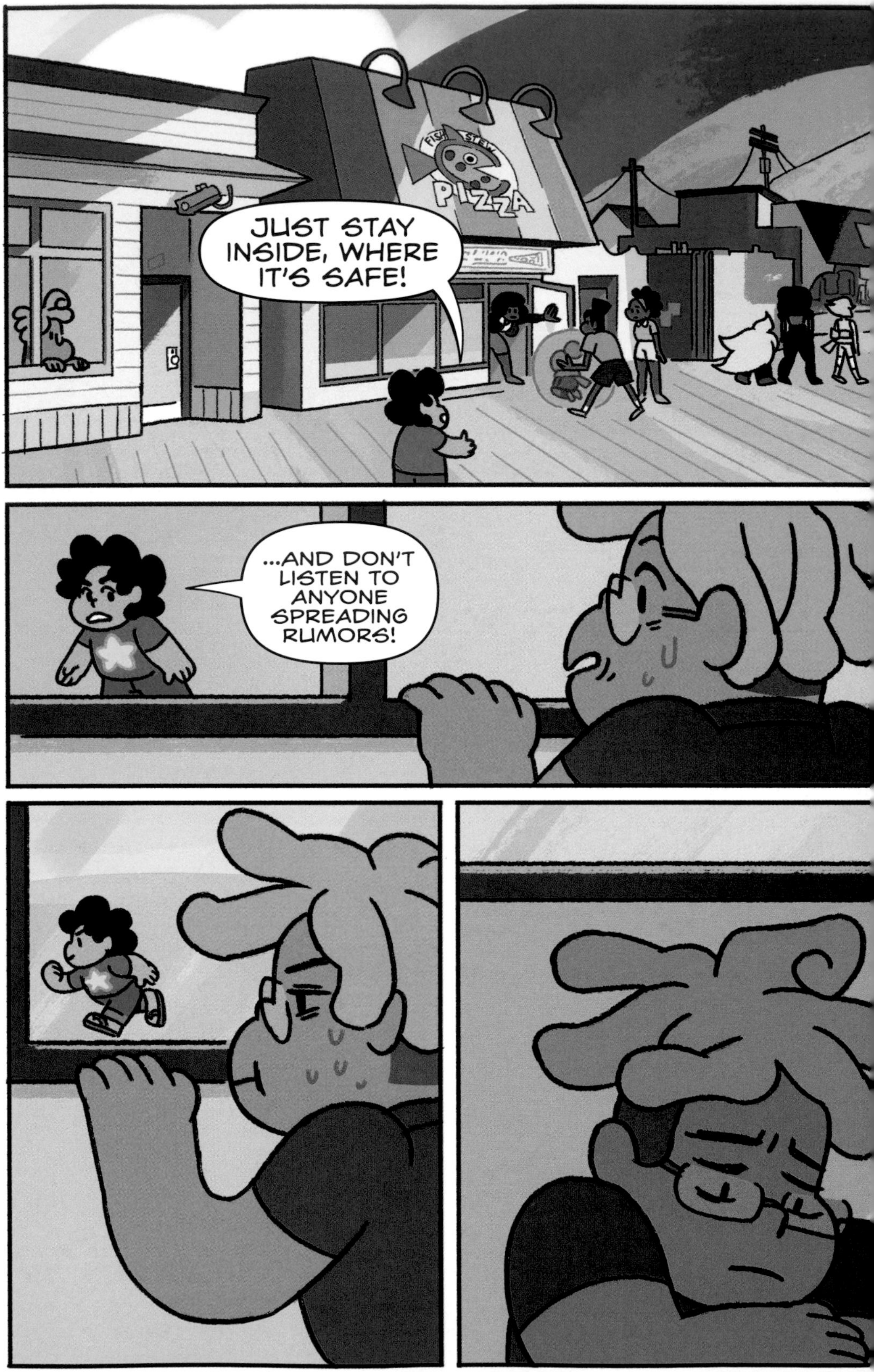
JUST STAY INSIDE, WHERE IT'S SAFE!
FISH STEW PIZZA
...AND DON'T LISTEN TO ANYONE SPREADING RUMORS!

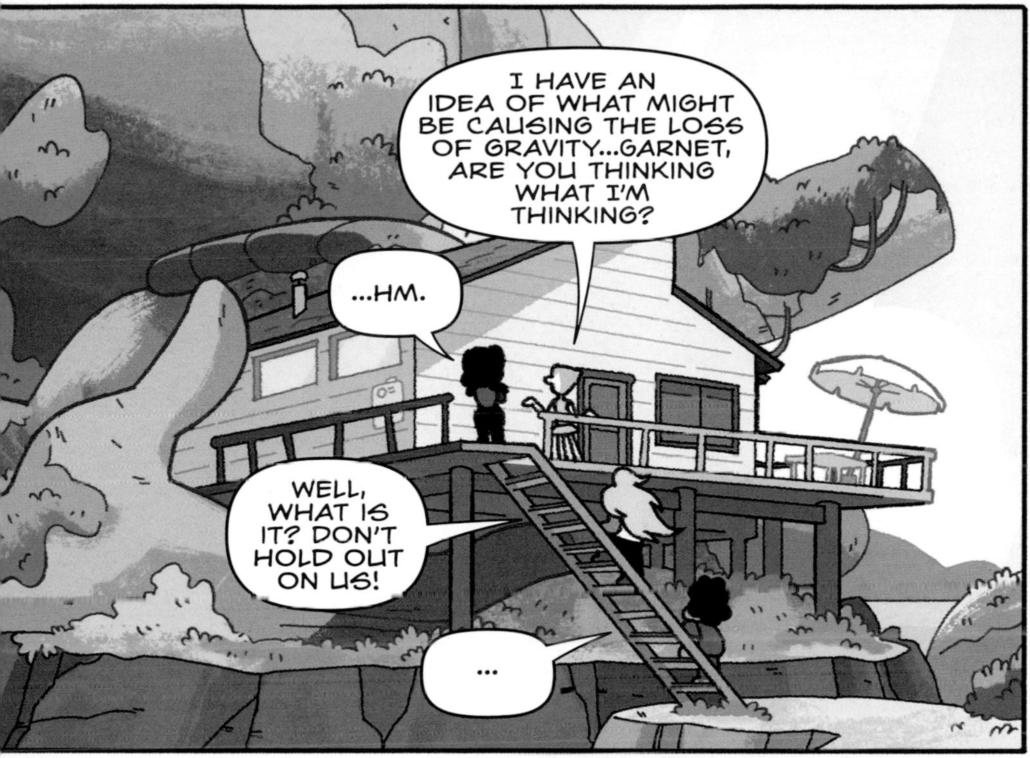
I HAVE AN IDEA OF WHAT MIGHT BE CAUSING THE LOSS OF GRAVITY...GARNET, ARE YOU THINKING WHAT I'M THINKING?
...HM.
WELL, WHAT IS IT? DON'T HOLD OUT ON US!
...

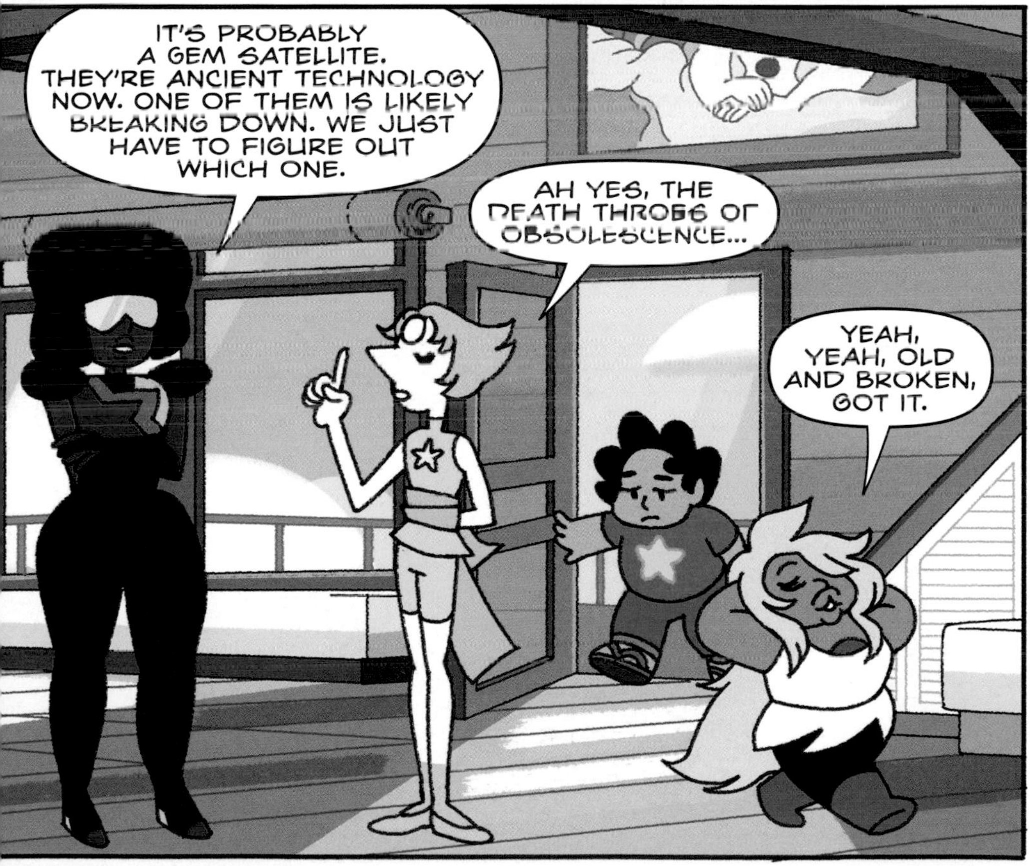
IT'S PROBABLY A GEM SATELLITE. THEY'RE ANCIENT TECHNOLOGY NOW. ONE OF THEM IS LIKELY BREAKING DOWN. WE JUST HAVE TO FIGURE OUT WHICH ONE.
AH YES, THE DEATH THROES OF OBSOLESCENCE...
YEAH, YEAH, OLD AND BROKEN, GOT IT.

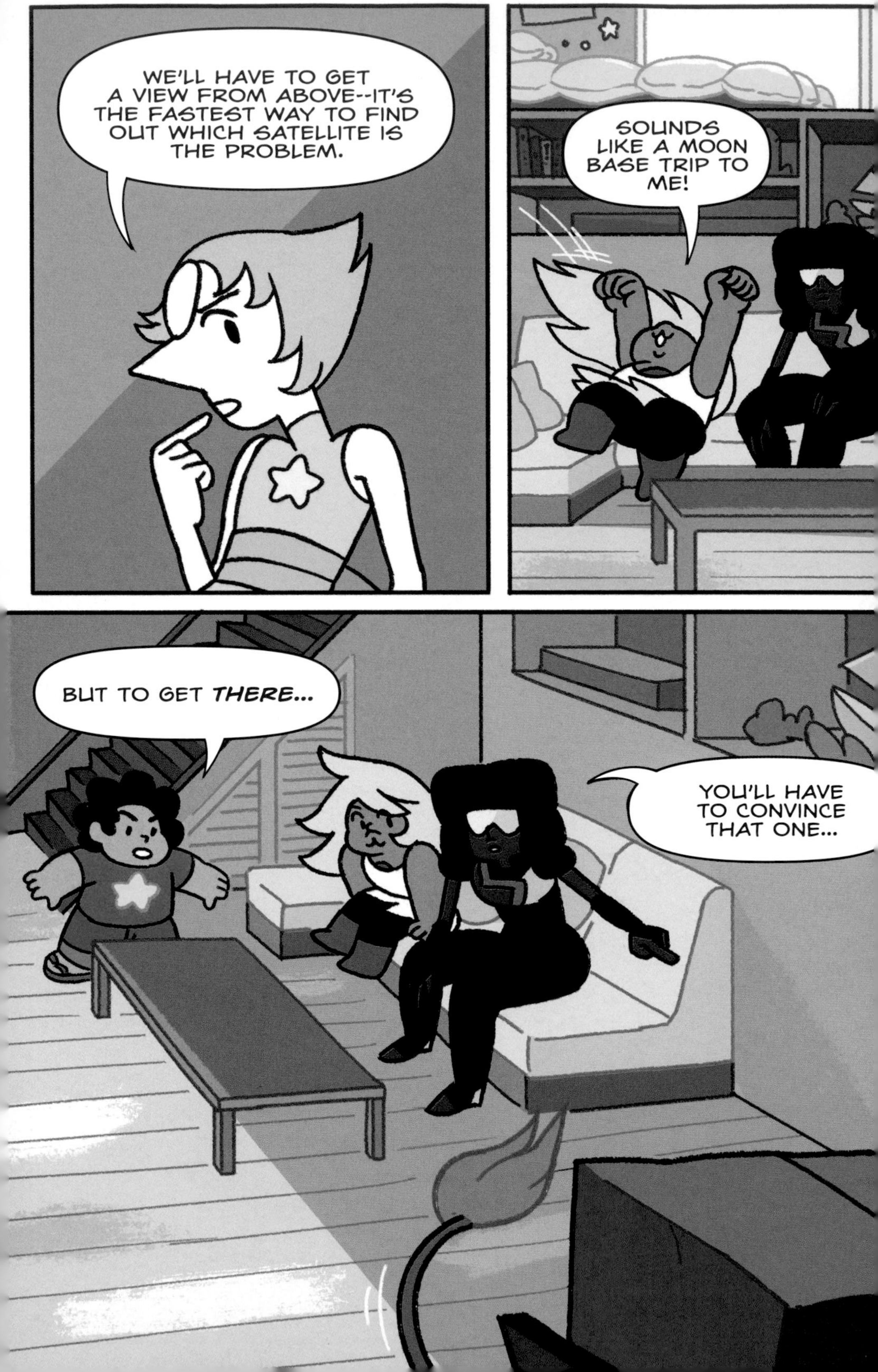
WE'LL HAVE TO GET A VIEW FROM ABOVE--IT'S THE FASTEST WAY TO FIND OUT WHICH SATELLITE IS THE PROBLEM.
SOUNDS LIKE A MOON BASE TRIP TO ME!
BUT TO GET *THERE*...
YOU'LL HAVE TO CONVINCE THAT ONE...

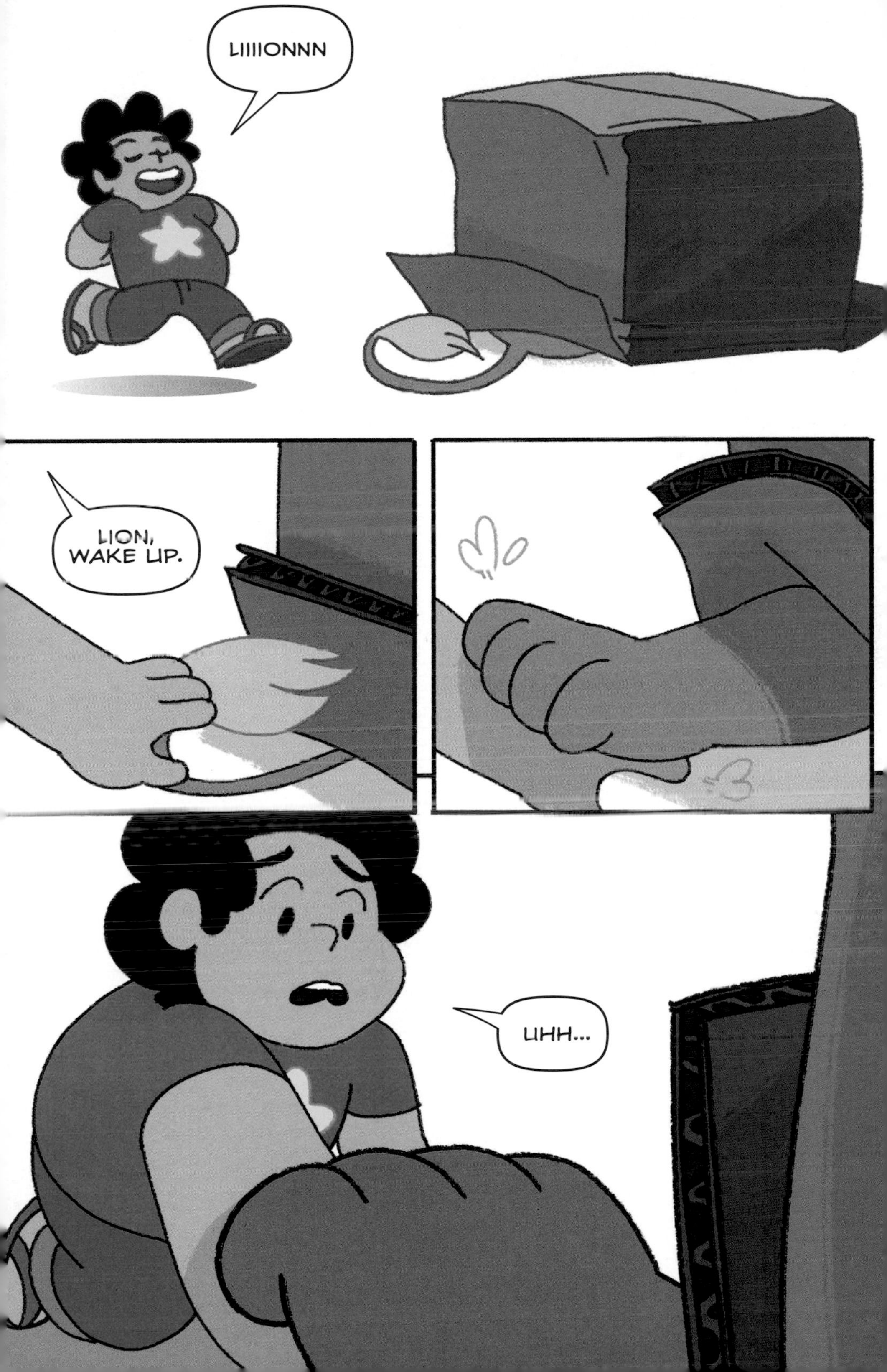
LIIIIONNN
LION, WAKE UP.
UHH...

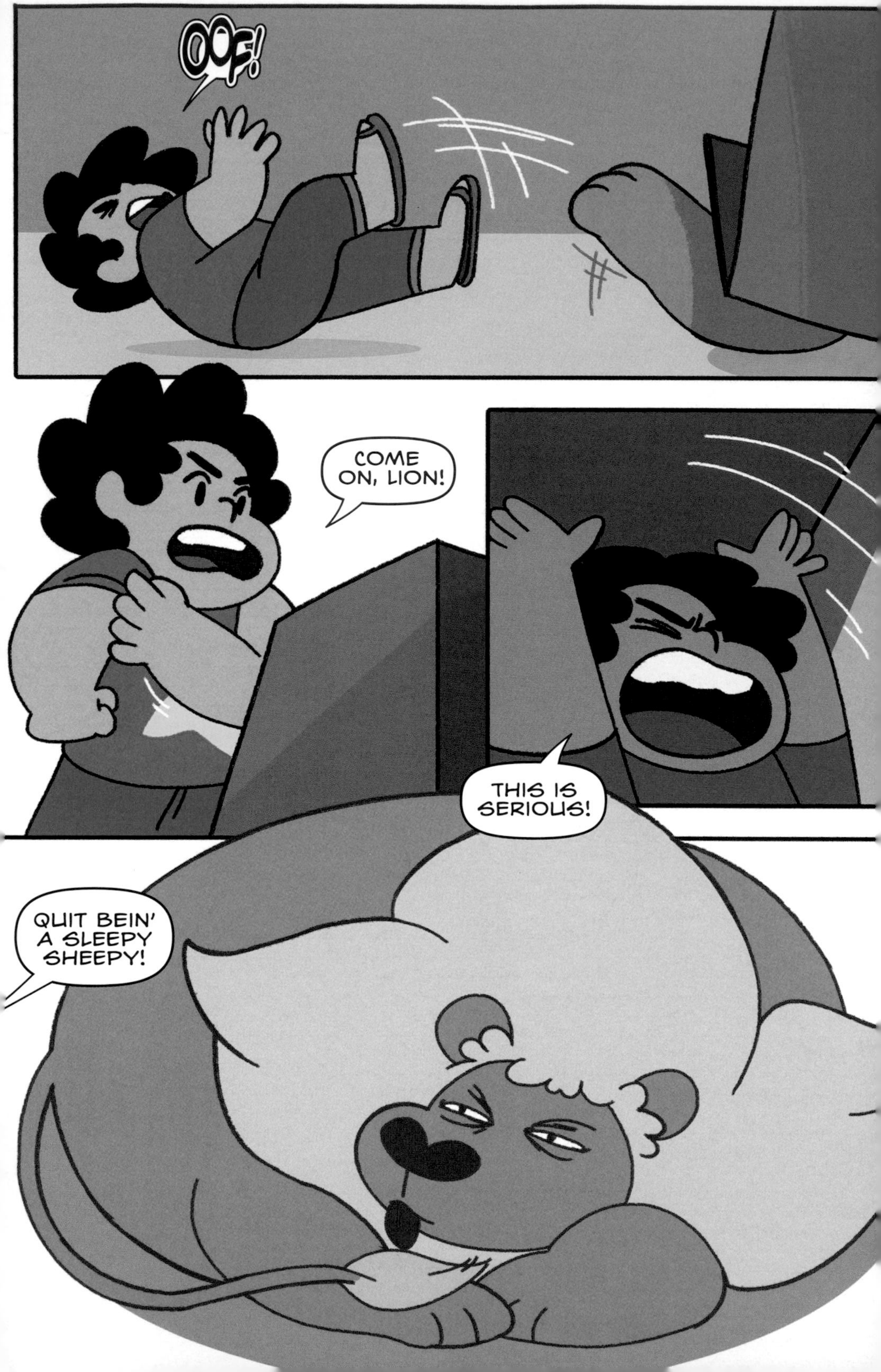
OOF!
COME ON, LION!
THIS IS SERIOUS!
QUIT BEIN' A SLEEPY SHEEPY!

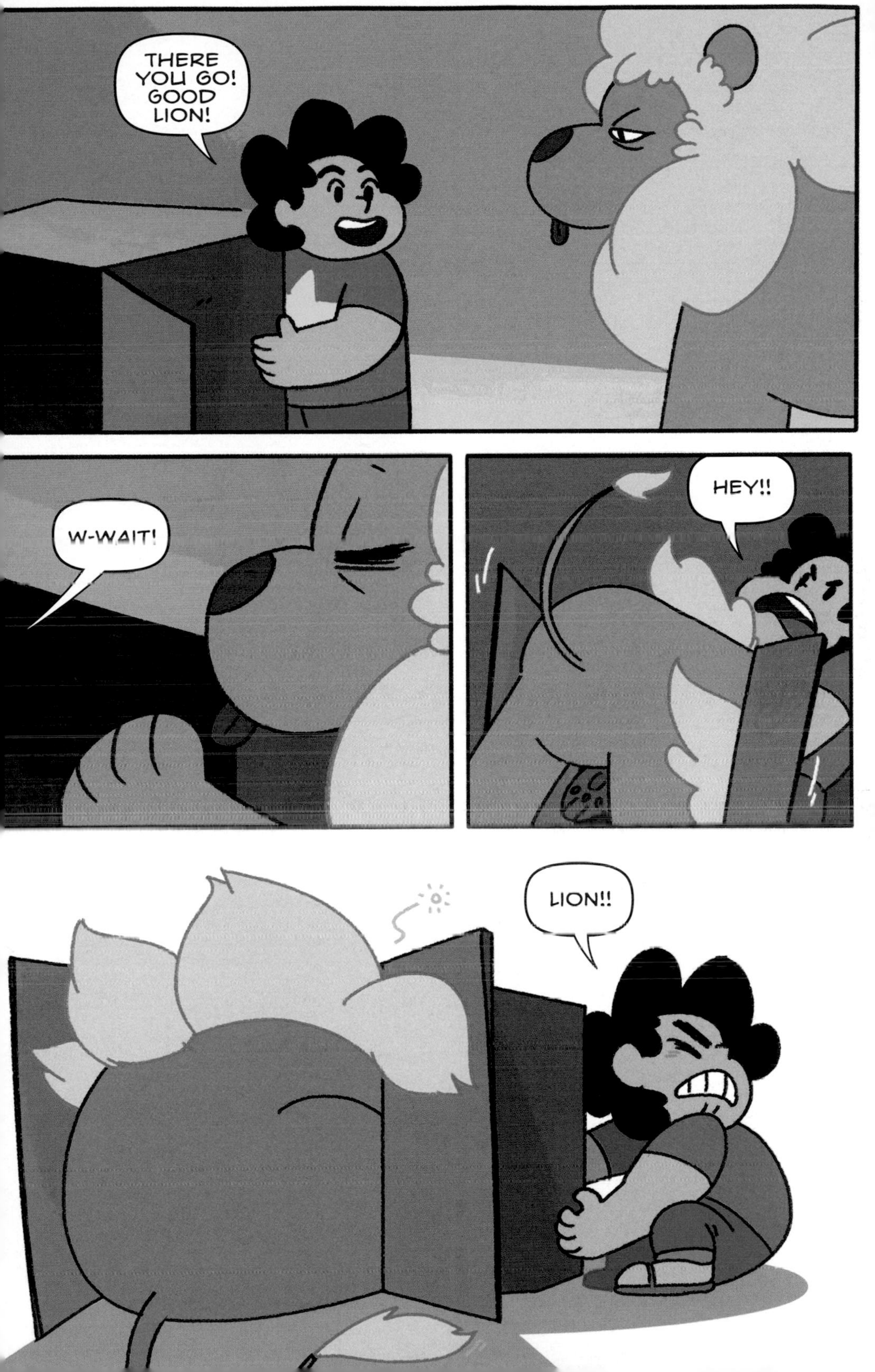
THERE YOU GO! GOOD LION!
W-WAIT!
HEY!!
LION!!

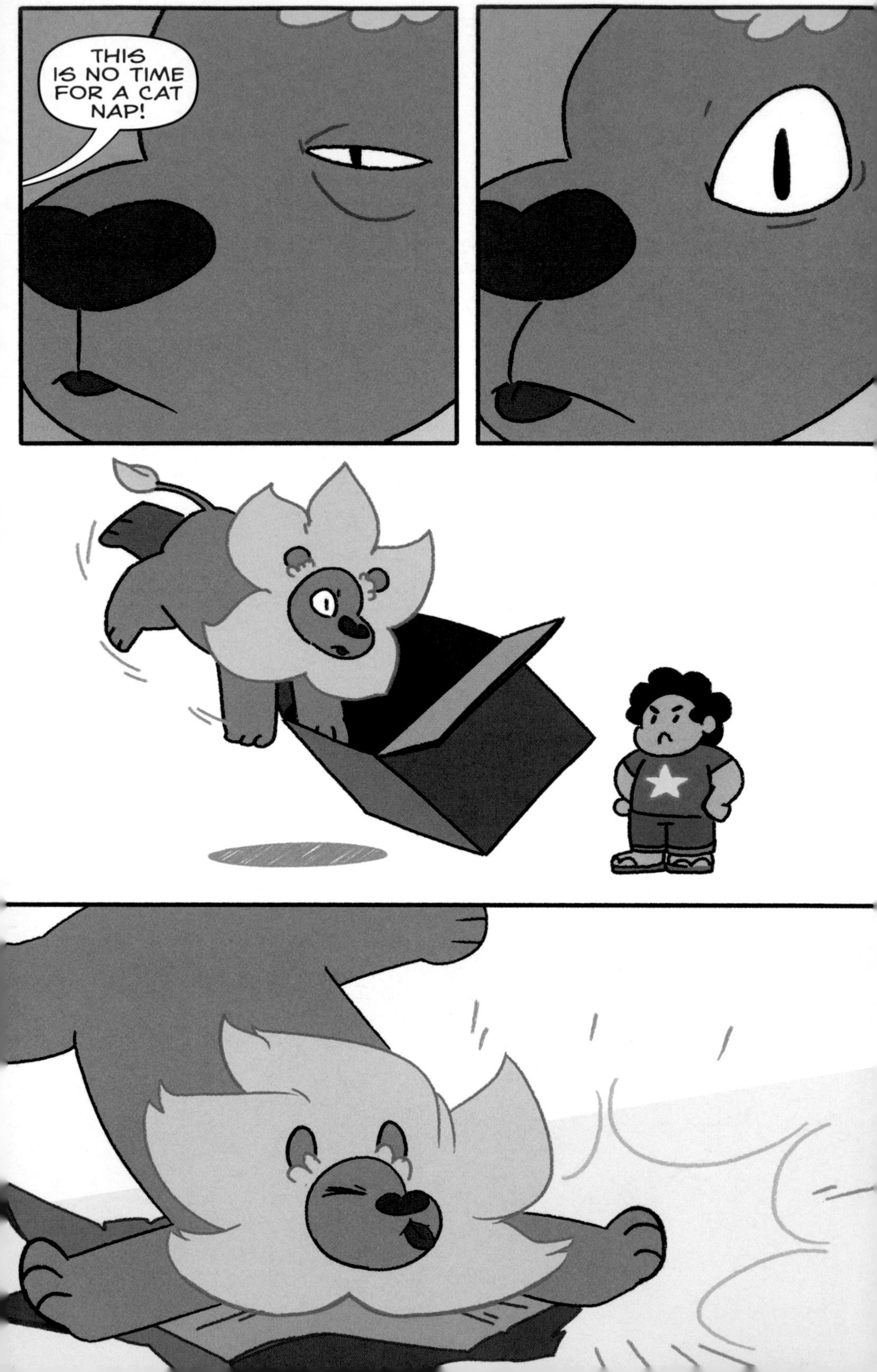
THIS IS NO TIME FOR A CAT NAP!

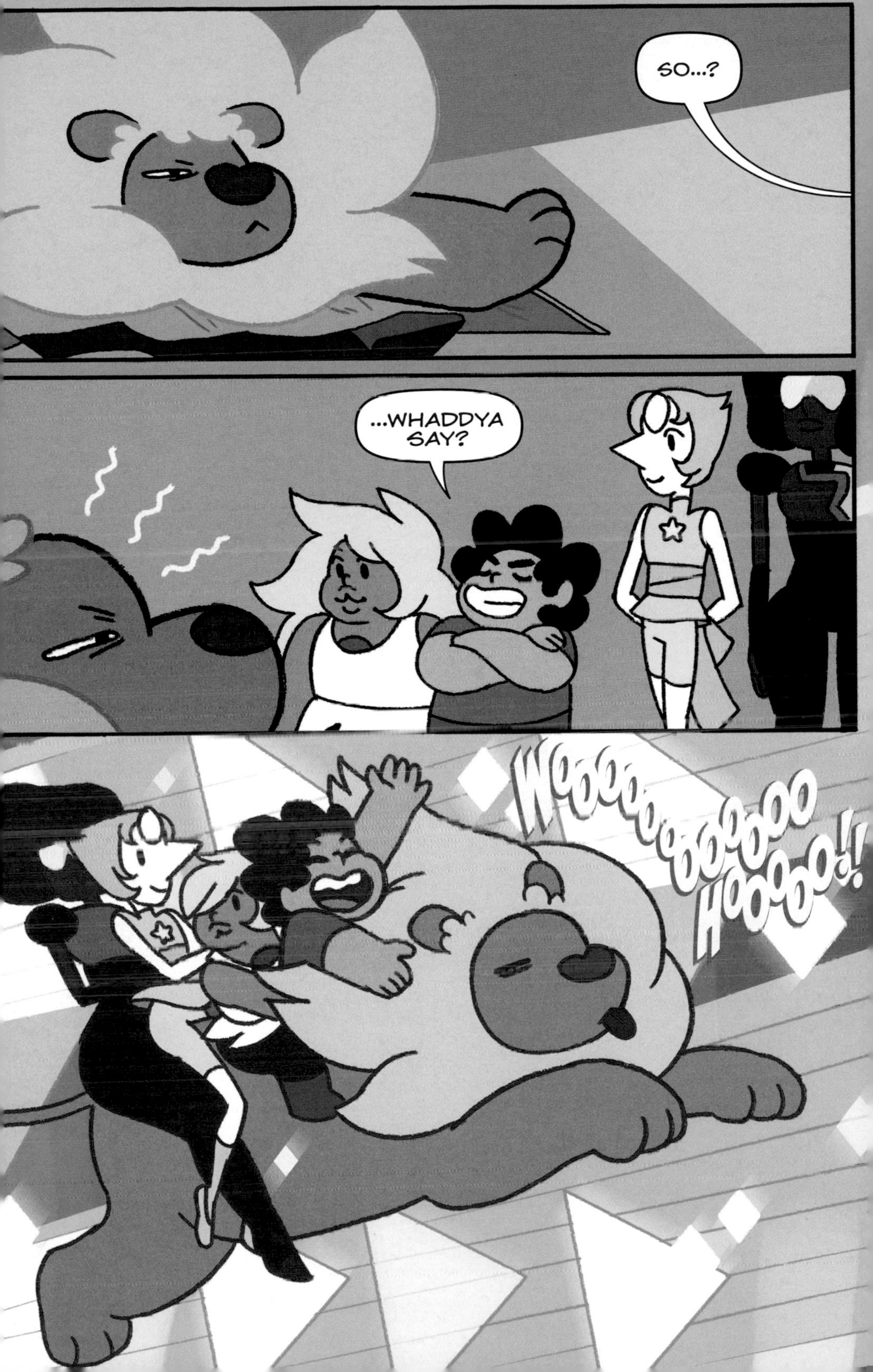
SO...?
...WHADDYA SAY?
WOOOOOOOOOOOOO HOOOOO!!

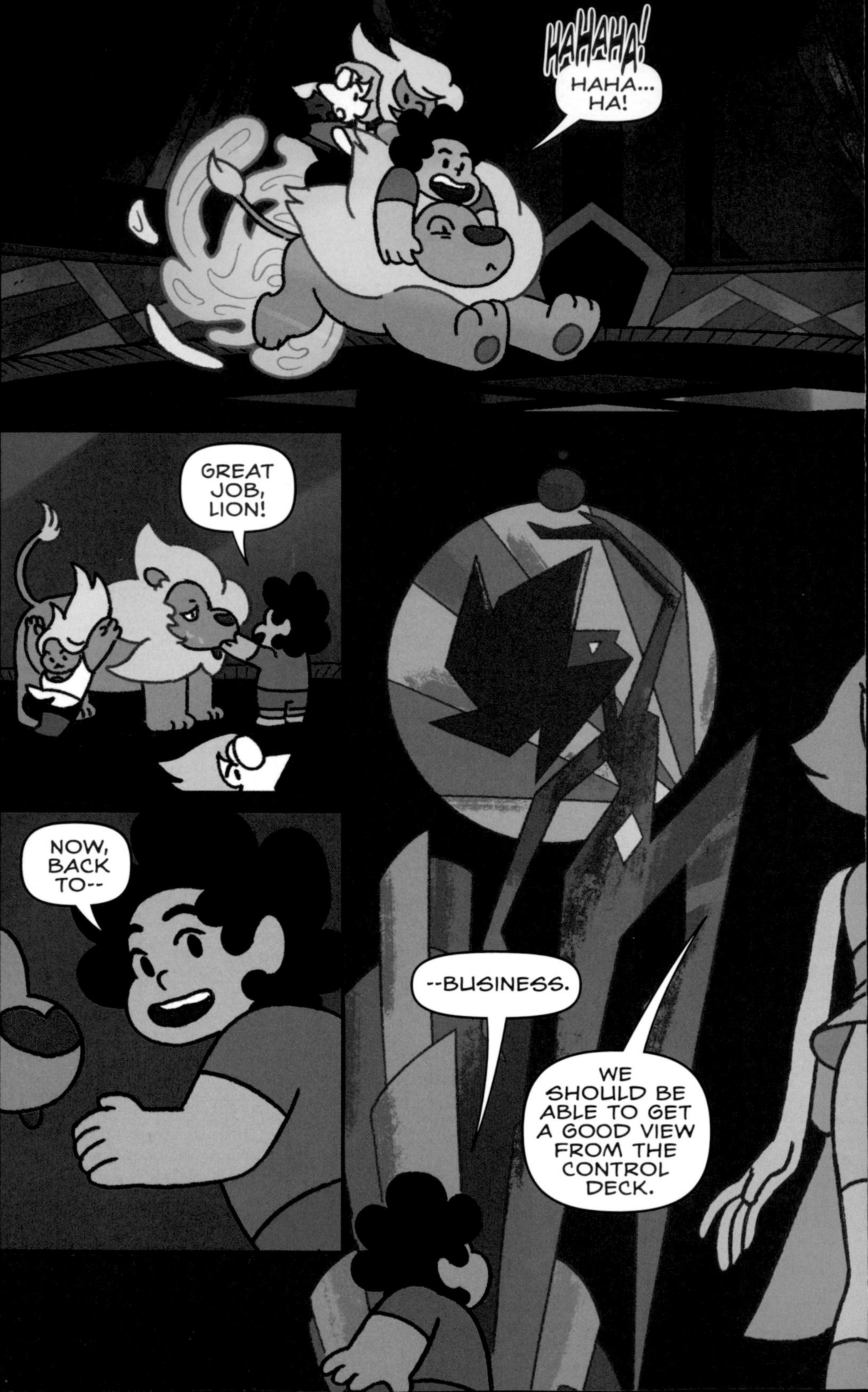
HAHAHA!
HAHA... HA!
GREAT JOB, LION!
NOW, BACK TO--
--BUSINESS.
WE SHOULD BE ABLE TO GET A GOOD VIEW FROM THE CONTROL DECK.

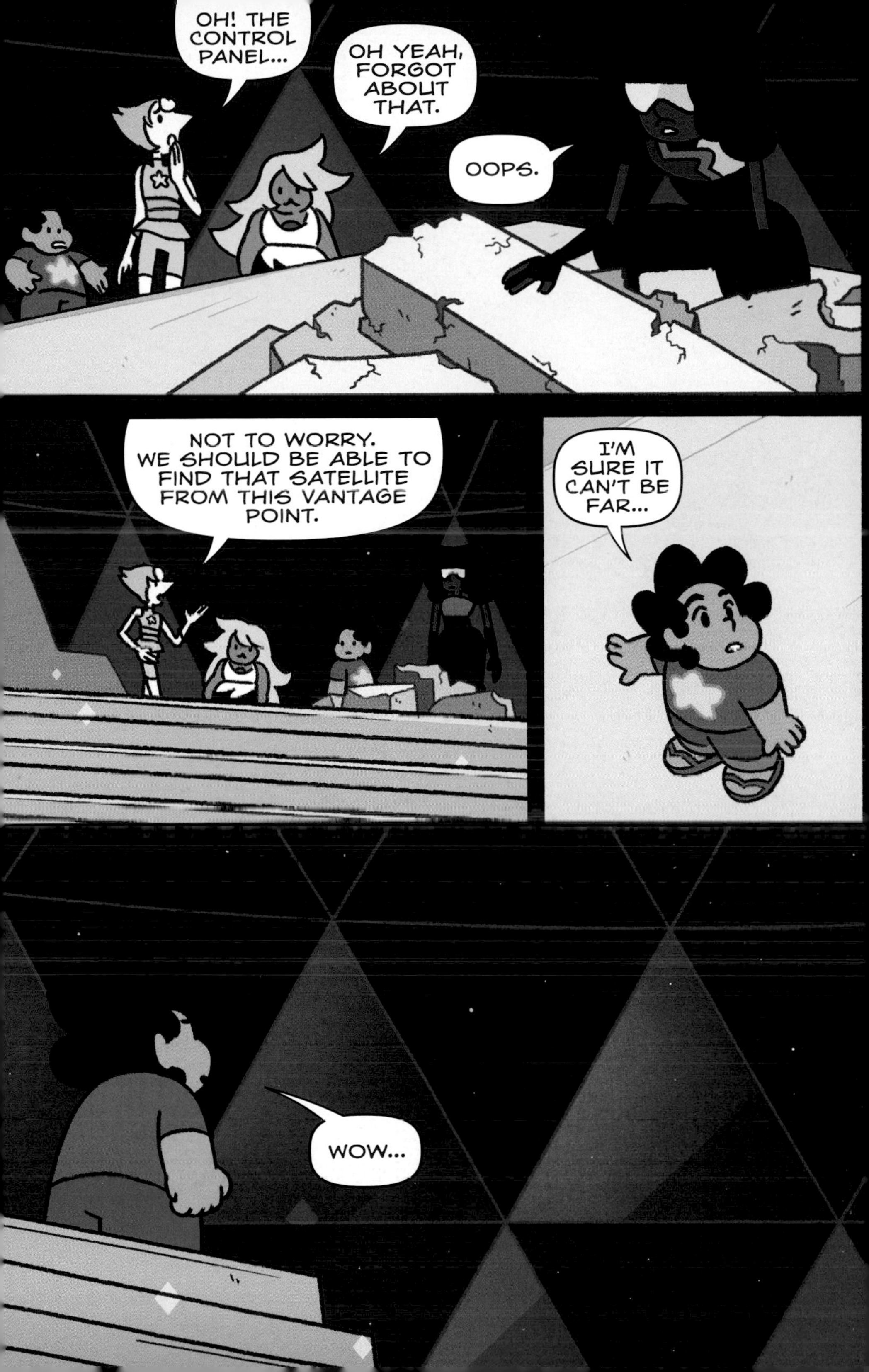
OH! THE CONTROL PANEL...
OH YEAH, FORGOT ABOUT THAT.
OOPS.
NOT TO WORRY. WE SHOULD BE ABLE TO FIND THAT SATELLITE FROM THIS VANTAGE POINT.
I'M SURE IT CAN'T BE FAR...
WOW...

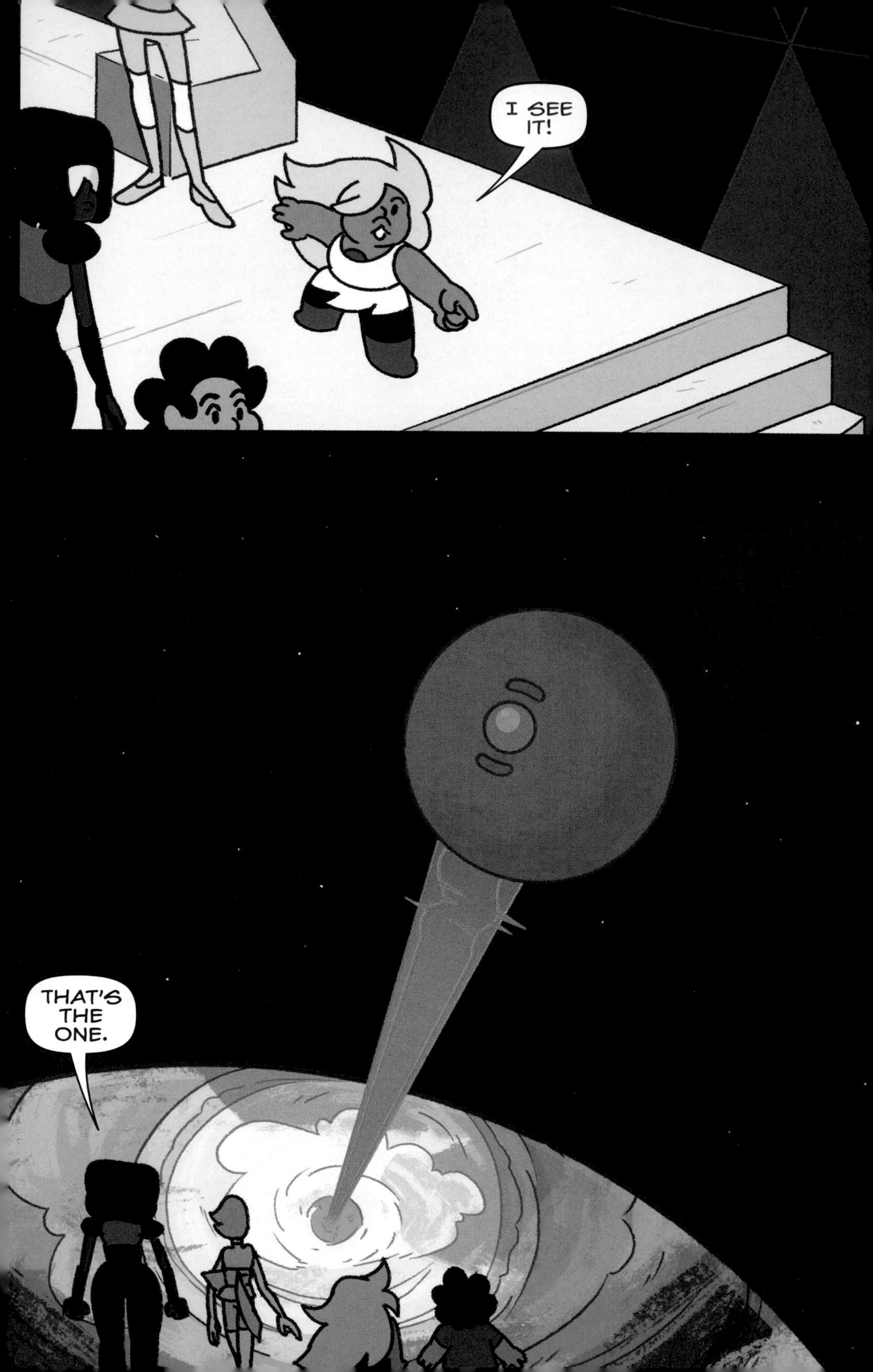
I SEE IT!
THAT'S THE ONE.

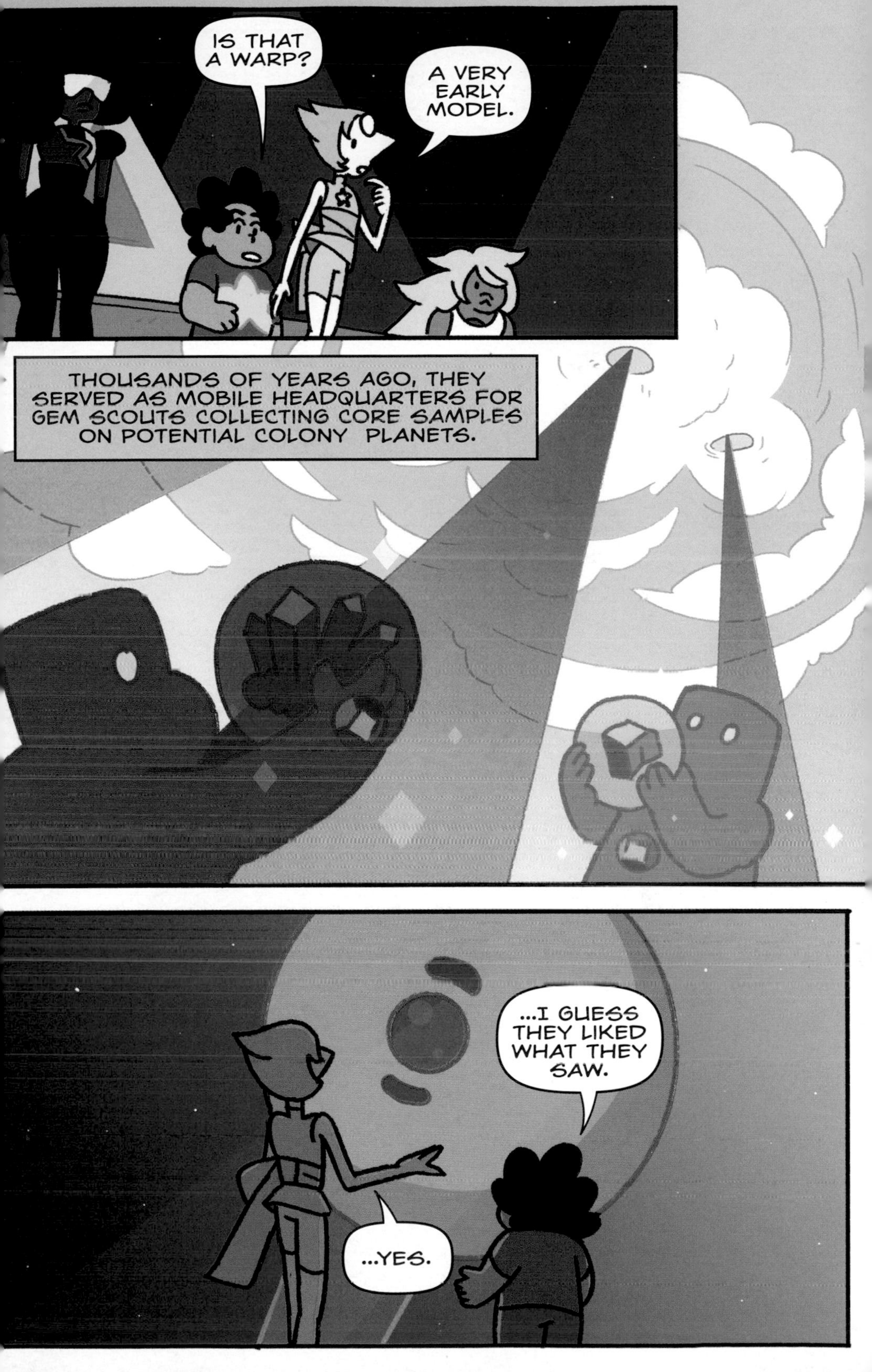
IS THAT A WARP?
A VERY EARLY MODEL.
THOUSANDS OF YEARS AGO, THEY SERVED AS MOBILE HEADQUARTERS FOR GEM SCOUTS COLLECTING CORE SAMPLES ON POTENTIAL COLONY PLANETS.
...I GUESS THEY LIKED WHAT THEY SAW.
...YES.

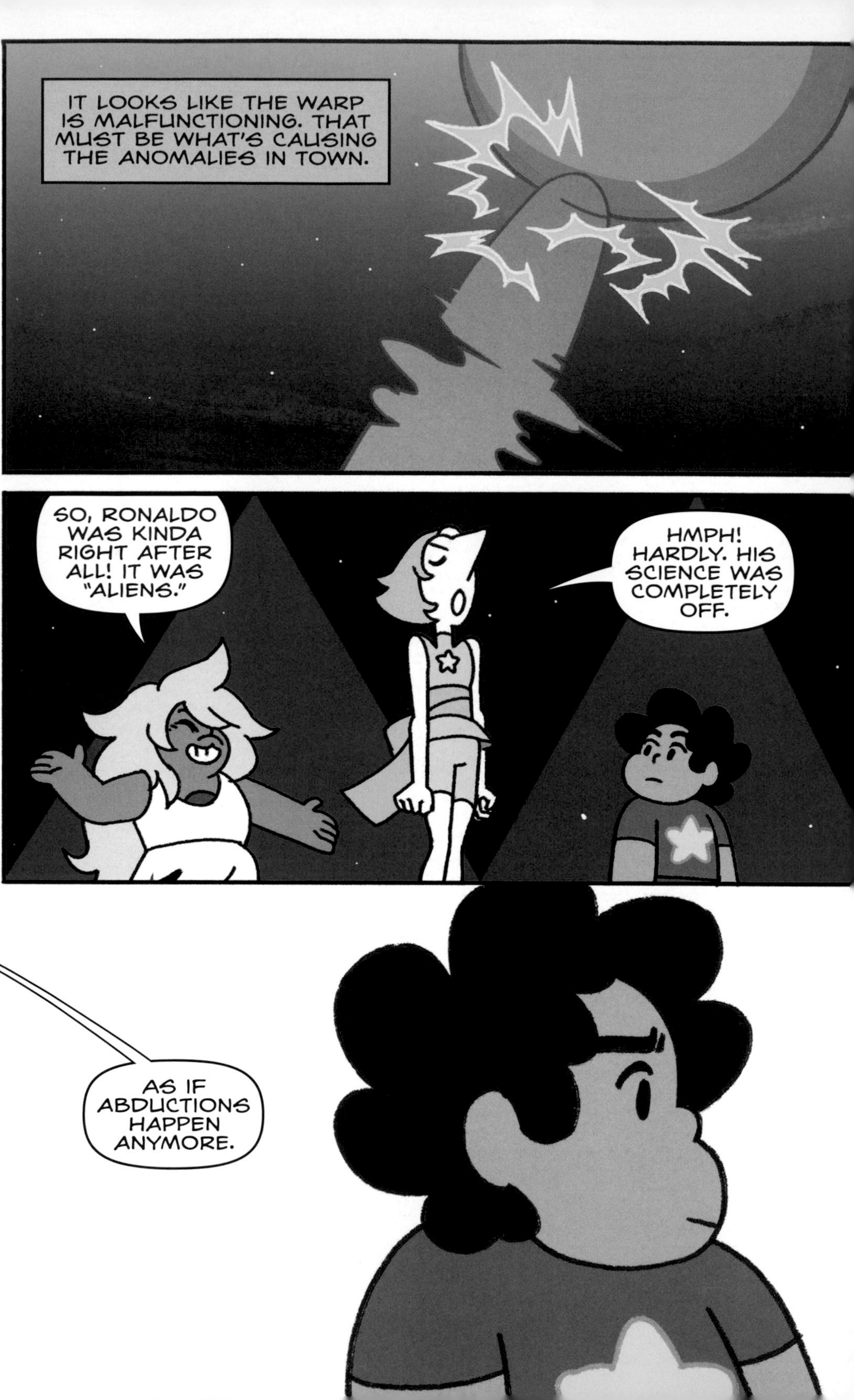
IT LOOKS LIKE THE WARP IS MALFUNCTIONING. THAT MUST BE WHAT'S CAUSING THE ANOMALIES IN TOWN.
SO, RONALDO WAS KINDA RIGHT AFTER ALL! IT WAS "ALIENS."
HMPH! HARDLY. HIS SCIENCE WAS COMPLETELY OFF.
AS IF ABDUCTIONS HAPPEN ANYMORE.

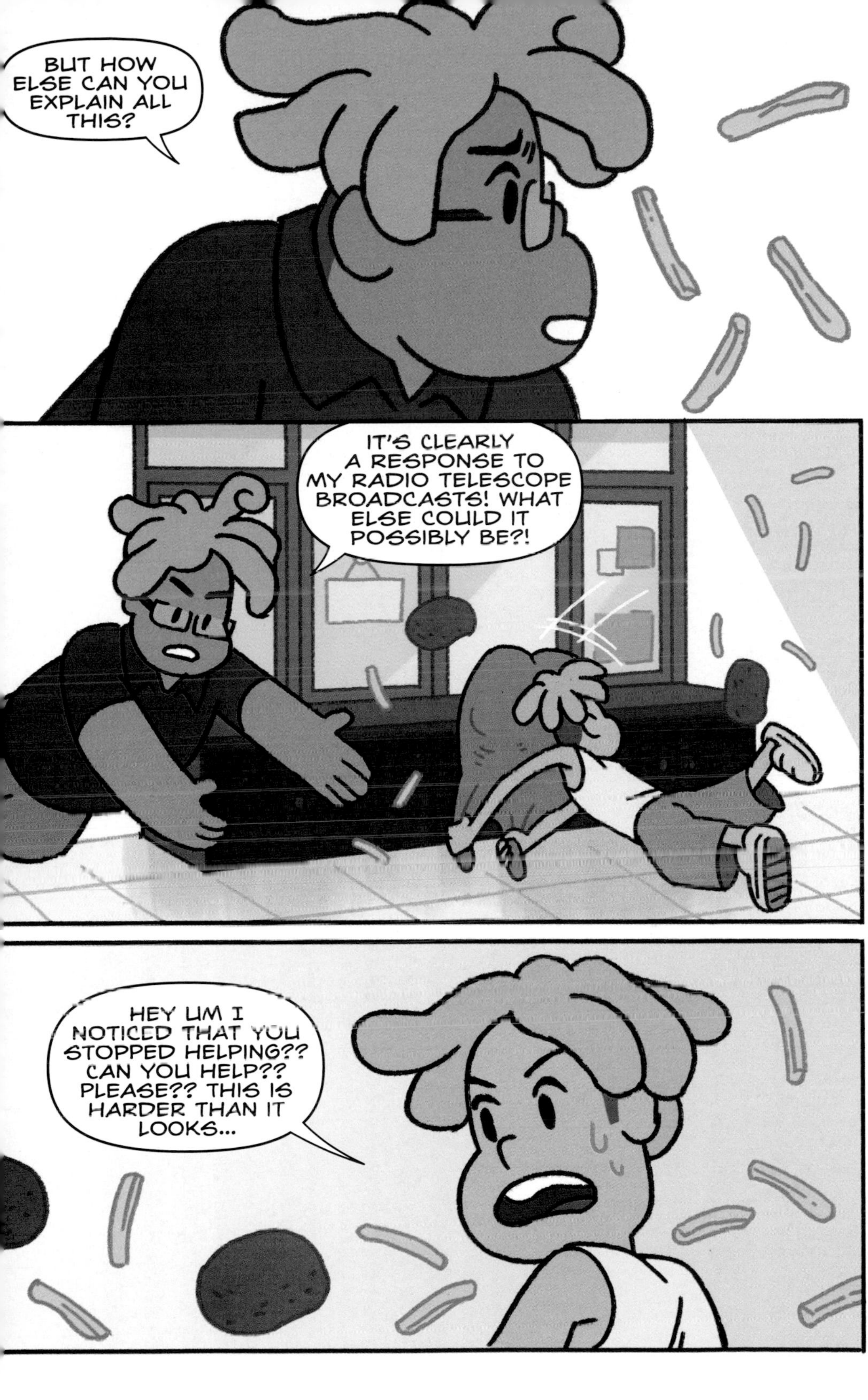

BUT HOW ELSE CAN YOU EXPLAIN ALL THIS?
IT'S CLEARLY A RESPONSE TO MY RADIO TELESCOPE BROADCASTS! WHAT ELSE COULD IT POSSIBLY BE?!
HEY UM I NOTICED THAT YOU STOPPED HELPING?? CAN YOU HELP?? PLEASE?? THIS IS HARDER THAN IT LOOKS...

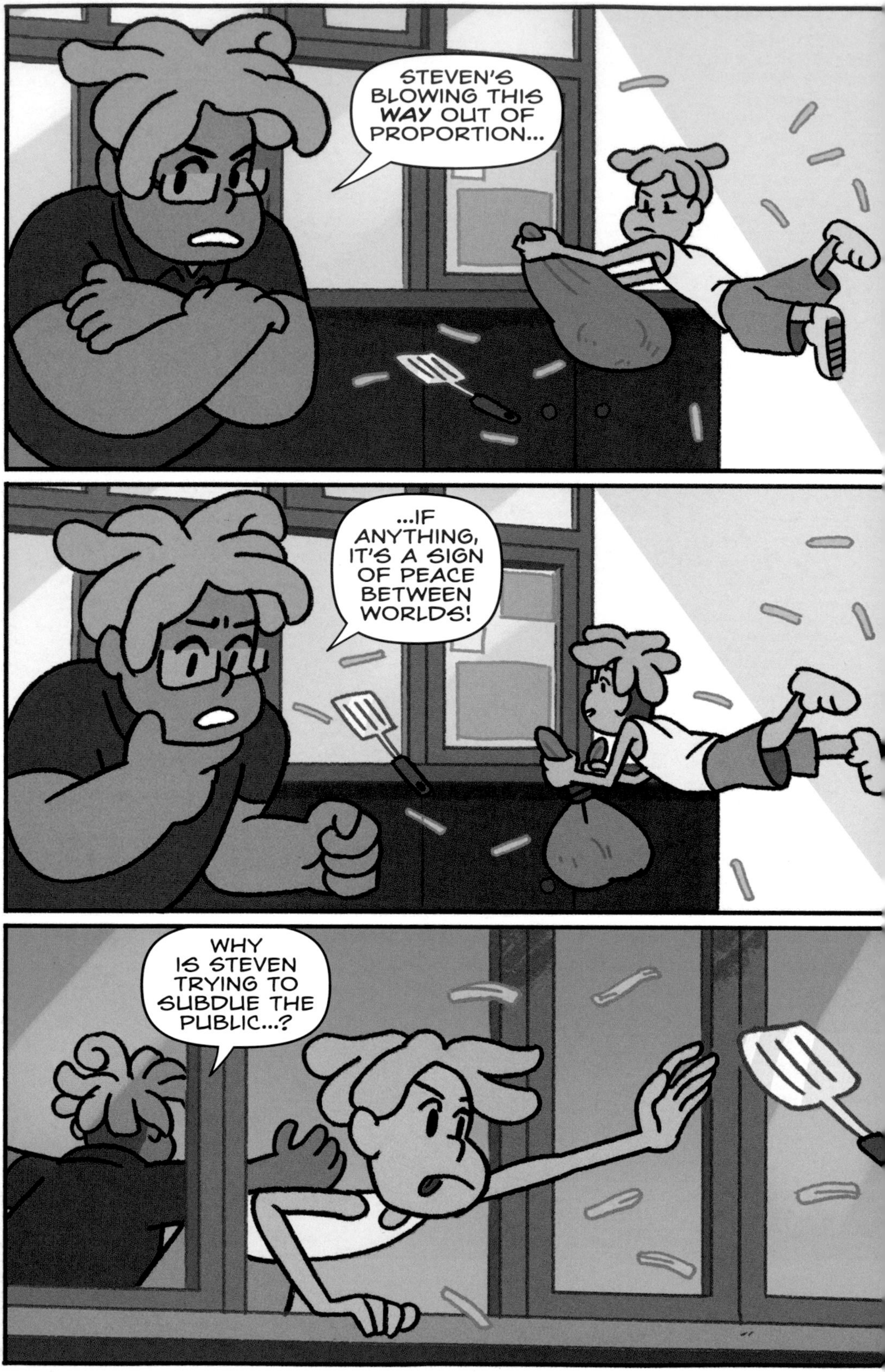
STEVEN'S BLOWING THIS WAY OUT OF PROPORTION...
...IF ANYTHING, IT'S A SIGN OF PEACE BETWEEN WORLDS!
WHY IS STEVEN TRYING TO SUBDUE THE PUBLIC...?

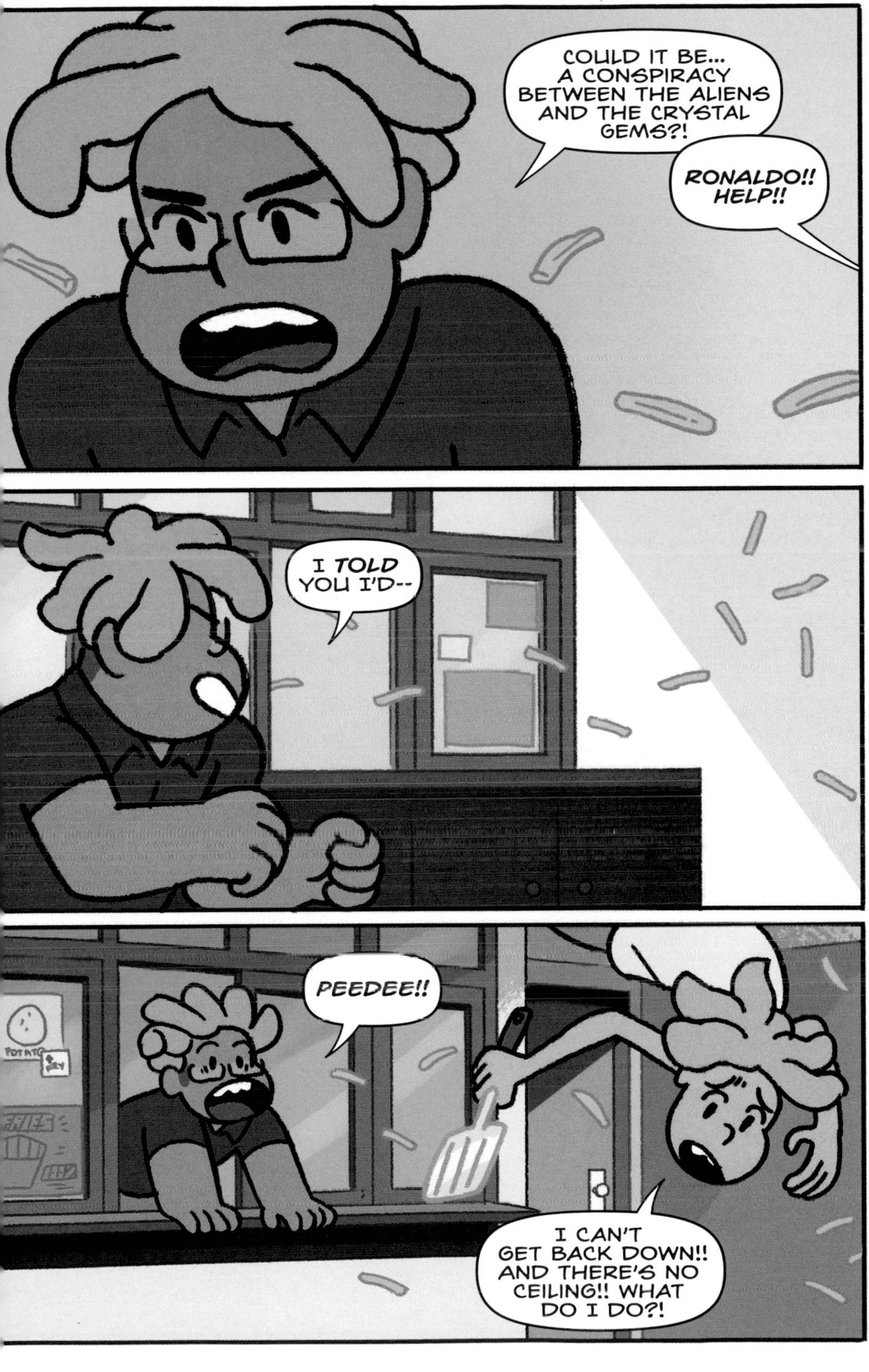
COULD IT BE... A CONSPIRACY BETWEEN THE ALIENS AND THE CRYSTAL GEMS?!
RONALDO!! HELP!!
I TOLD YOU I'D--
PEEDEE!!
I CAN'T GET BACK DOWN!! AND THERE'S NO CEILING!! WHAT DO I DO?!

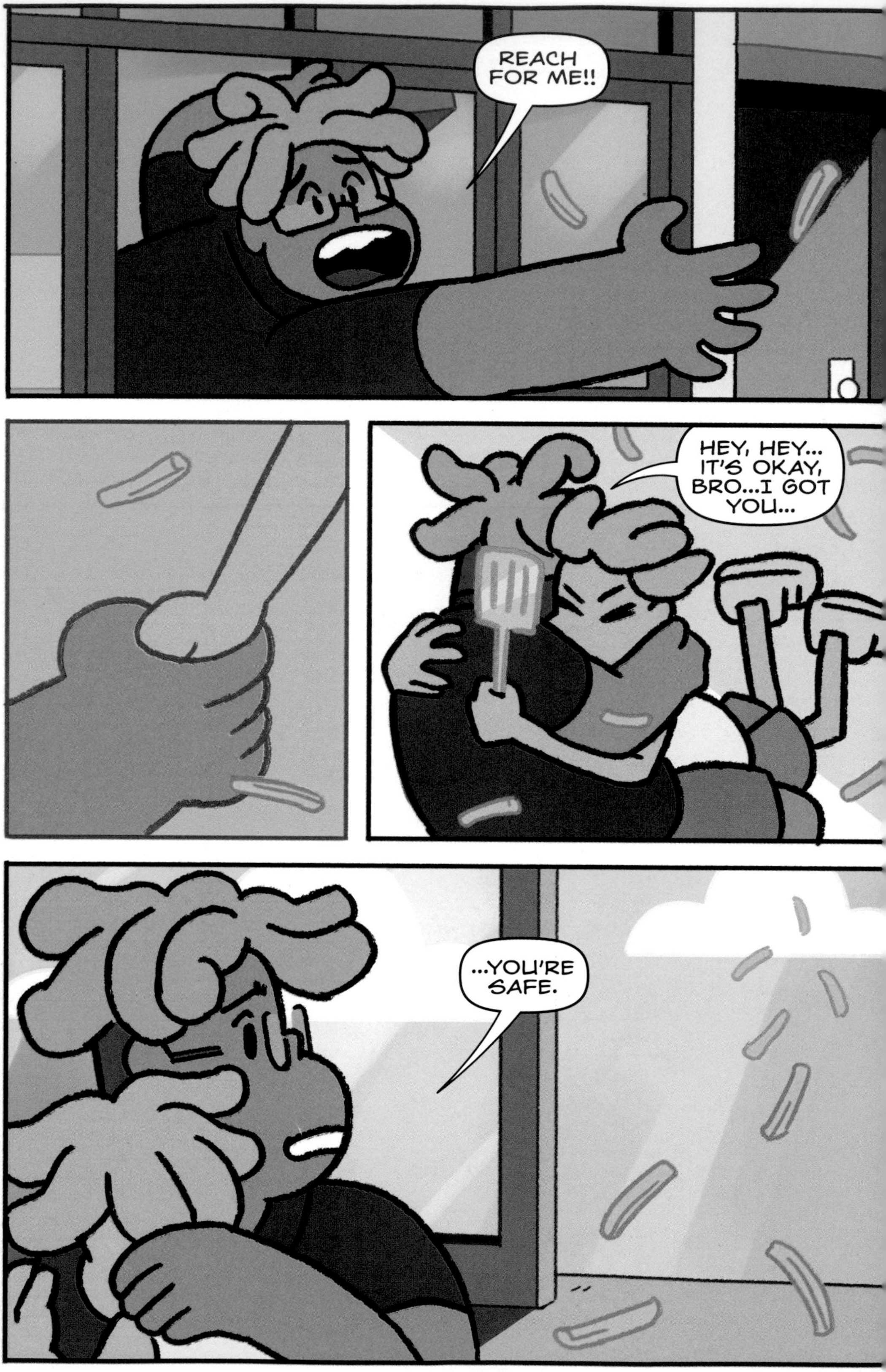
REACH FOR ME!!
HEY, HEY... IT'S OKAY, BRO...I GOT YOU...
...YOU'RE SAFE.

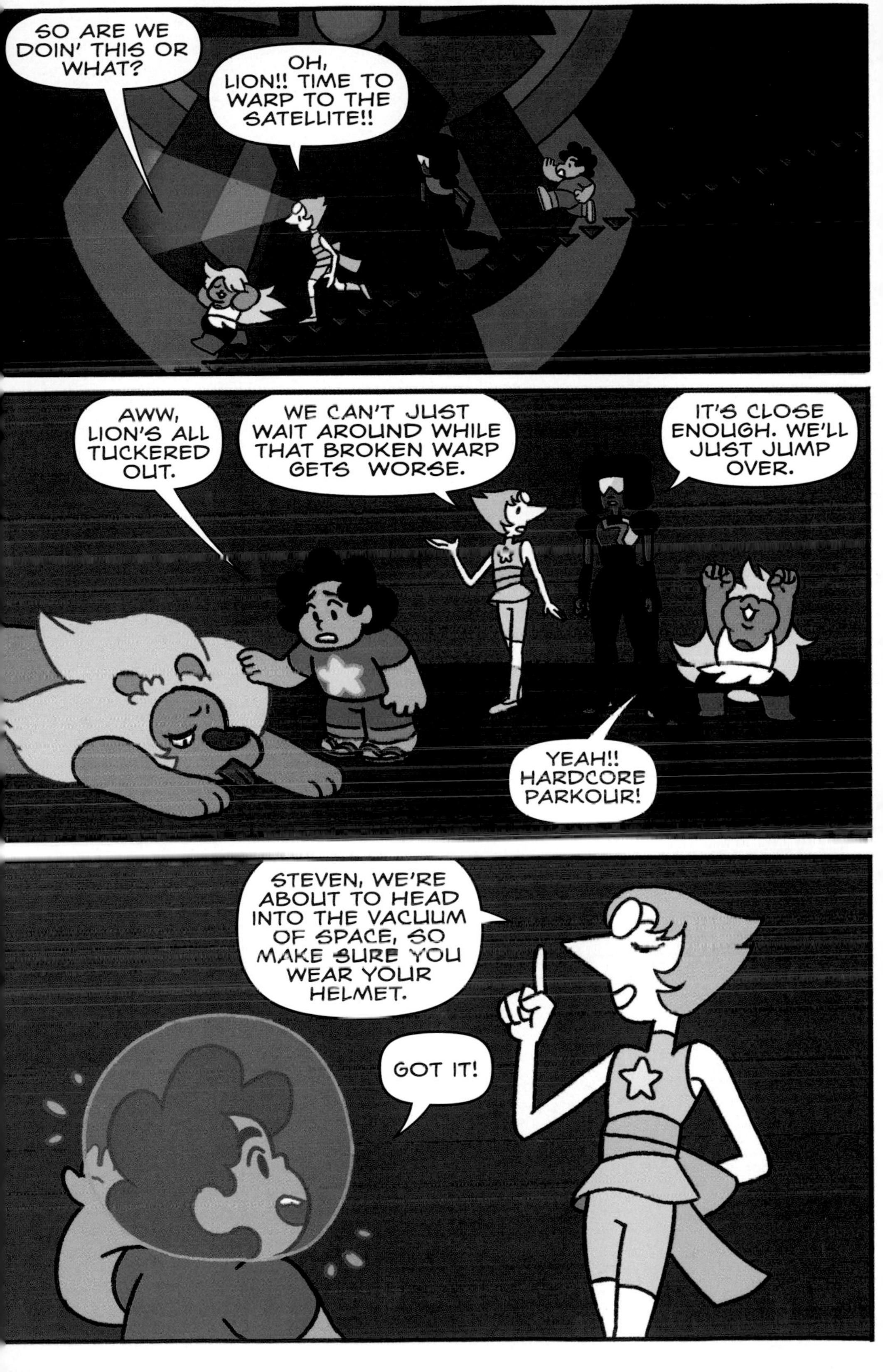
SO ARE WE DOIN' THIS OR WHAT?
OH, LION!! TIME TO WARP TO THE SATELLITE!!
AWW, LION'S ALL TUCKERED OUT.
WE CAN'T JUST WAIT AROUND WHILE THAT BROKEN WARP GETS WORSE.
IT'S CLOSE ENOUGH. WE'LL JUST JUMP OVER.
YEAH!! HARDCORE PARKOUR!
STEVEN, WE'RE ABOUT TO HEAD INTO THE VACUUM OF SPACE, SO MAKE SURE YOU WEAR YOUR HELMET.
GOT IT!

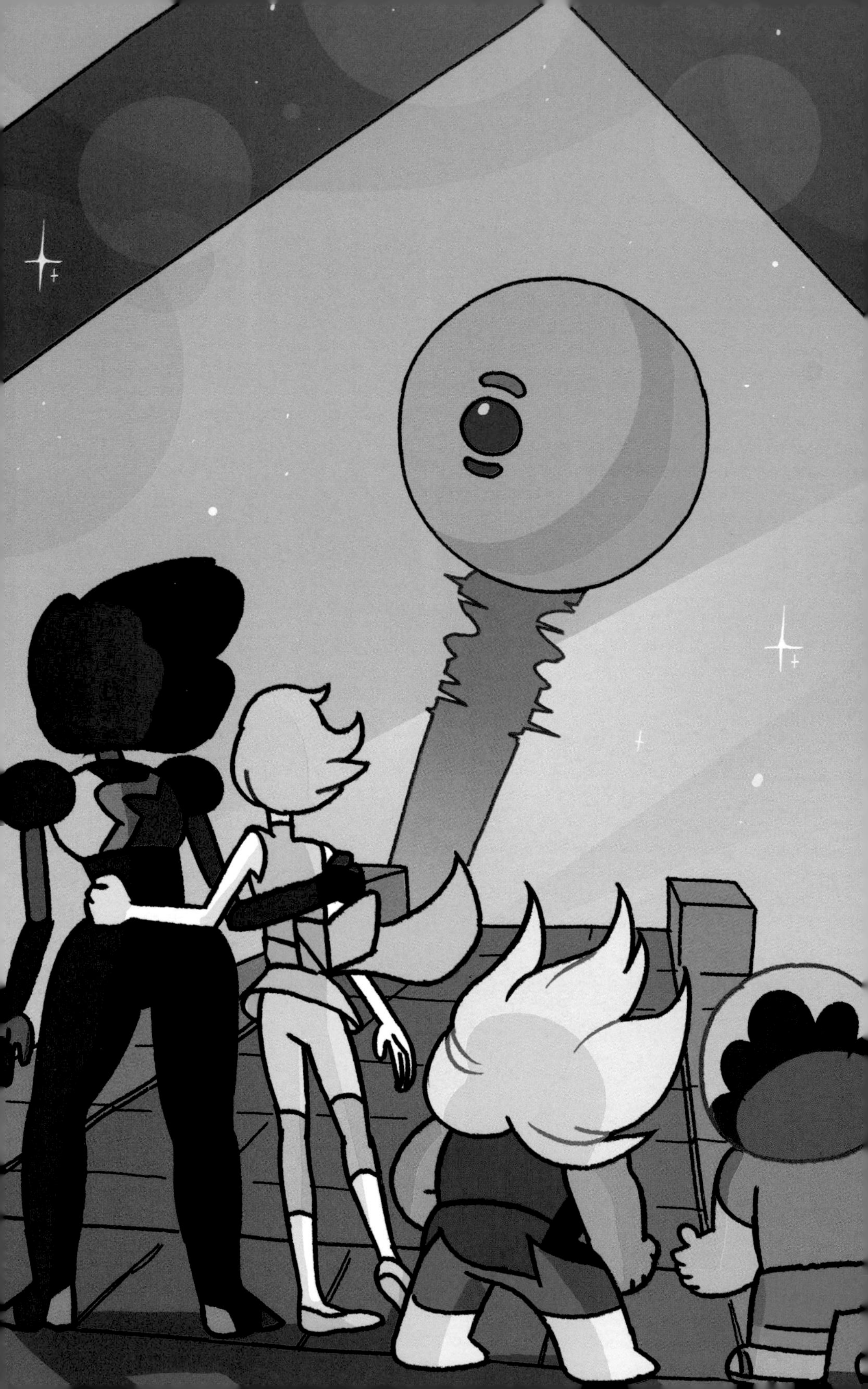

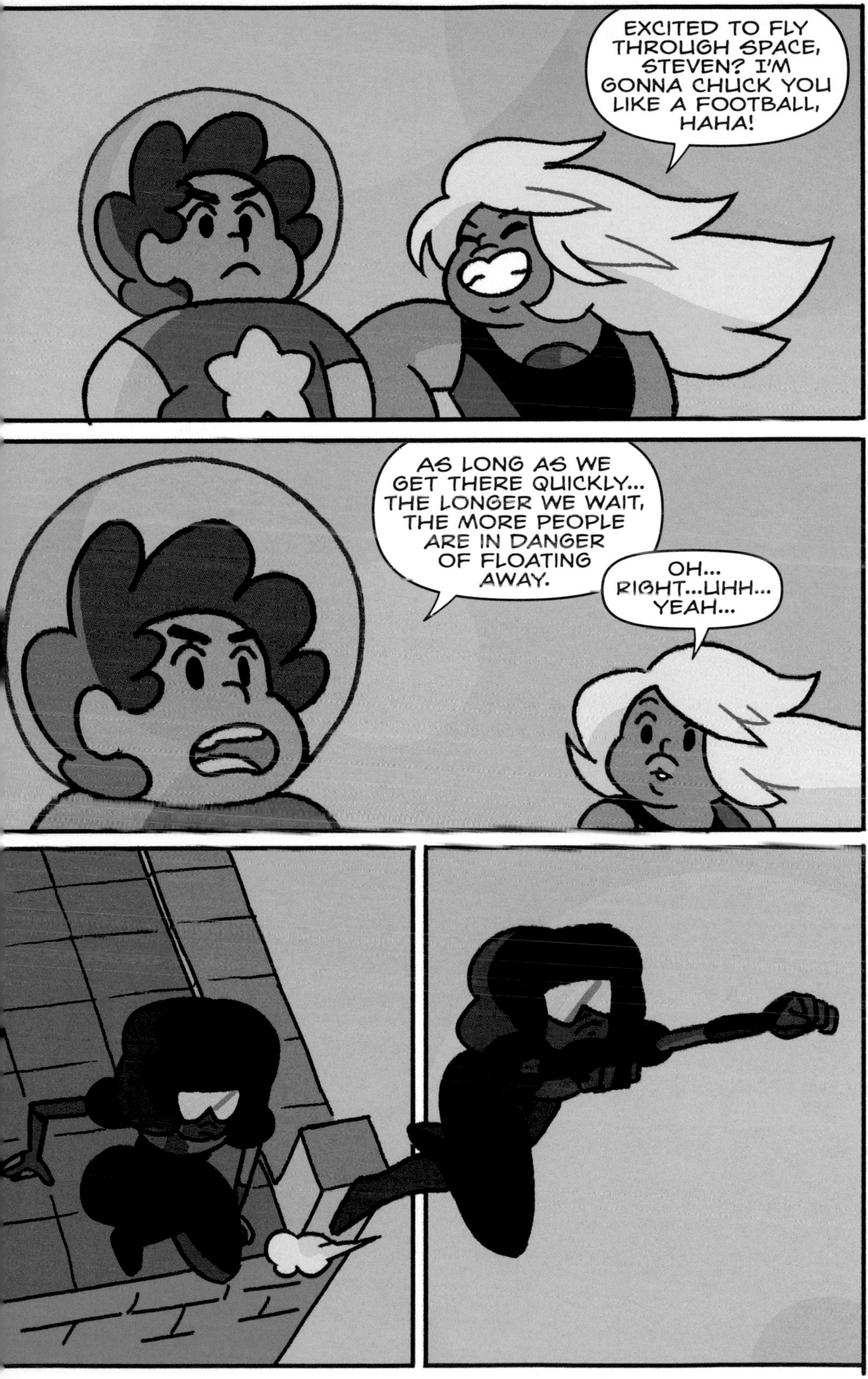
EXCITED TO FLY THROUGH SPACE, STEVEN? I'M GONNA CHUCK YOU LIKE A FOOTBALL, HAHA!
AS LONG AS WE GET THERE QUICKLY... THE LONGER WE WAIT, THE MORE PEOPLE ARE IN DANGER OF FLOATING AWAY.
OH... RIGHT...UHH... YEAH...

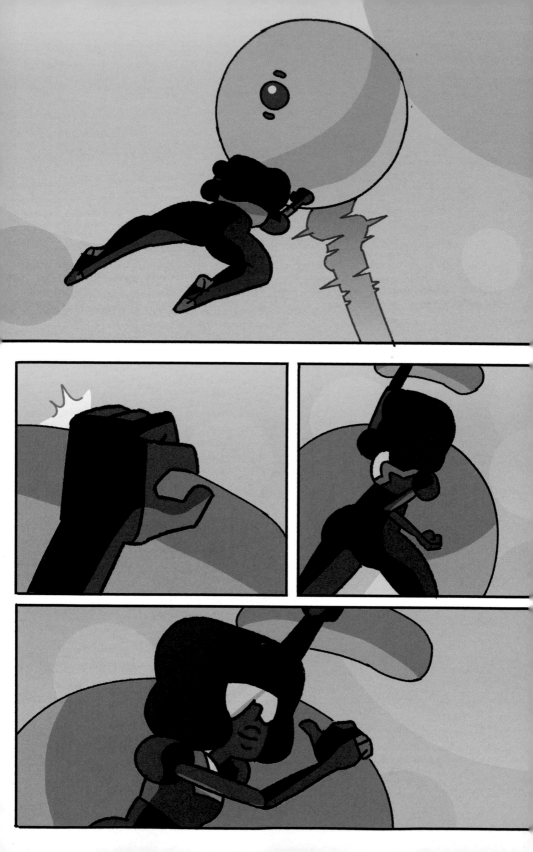

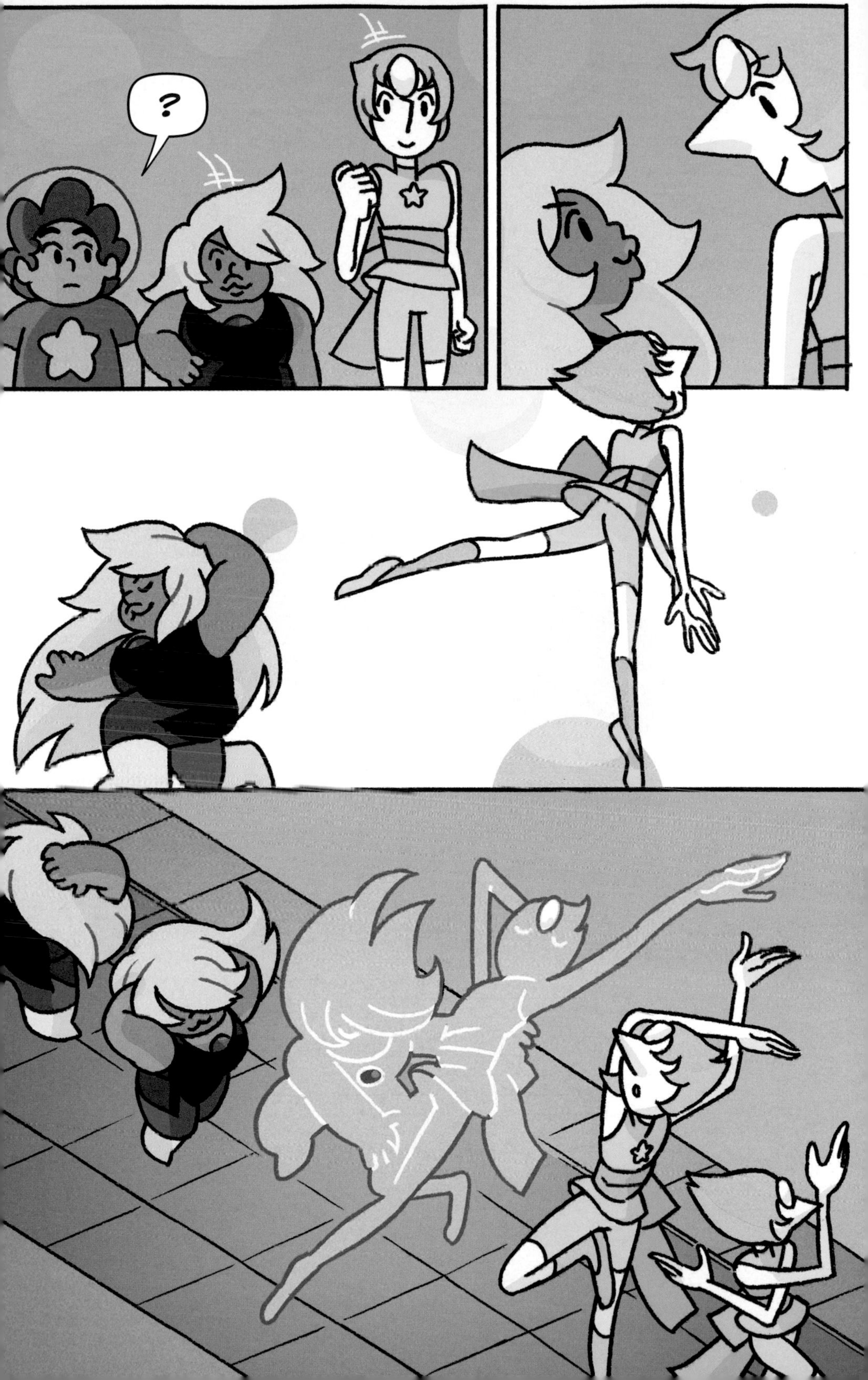
?

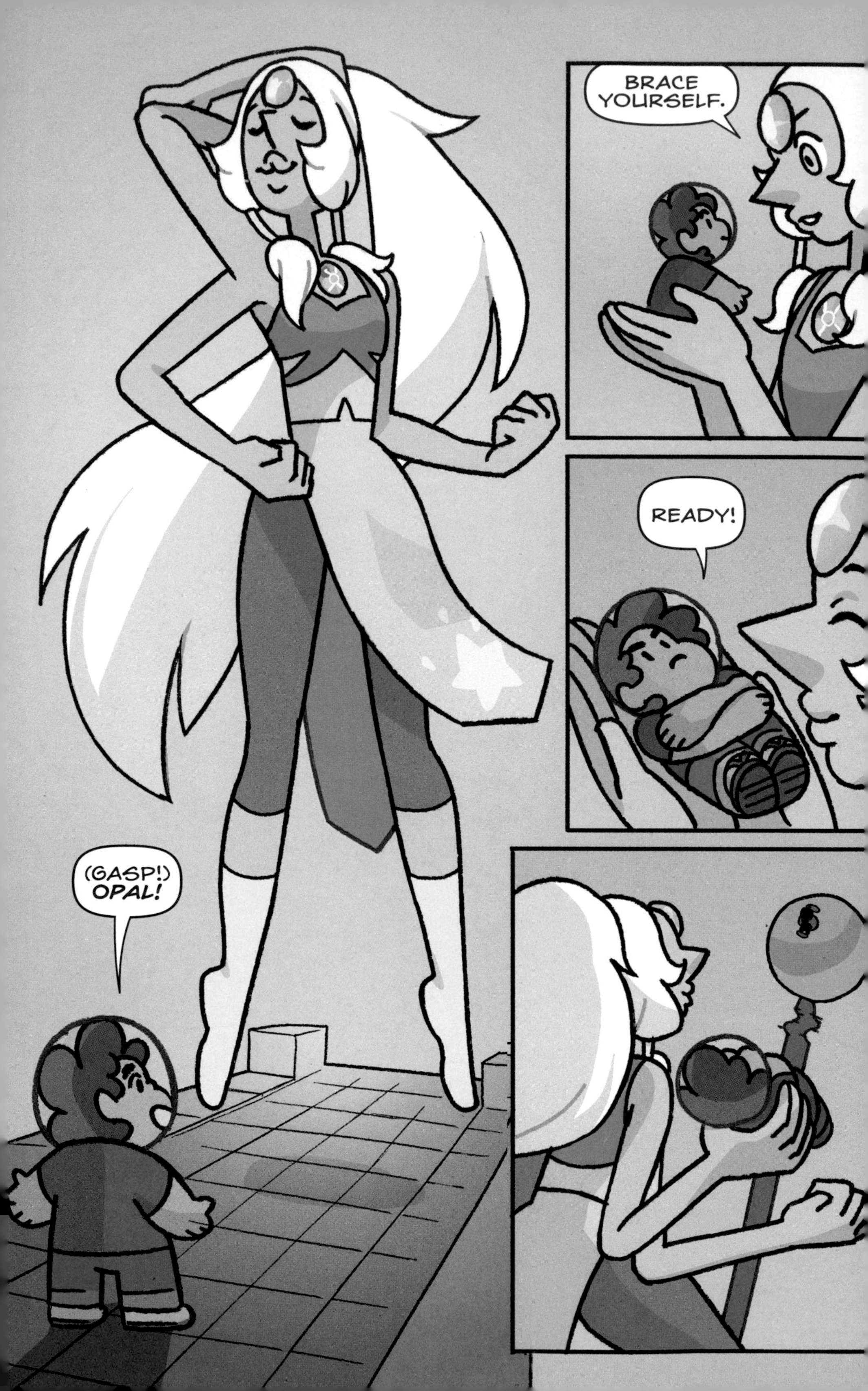
(GASP!) OPAL!
BRACE YOURSELF.
READY!

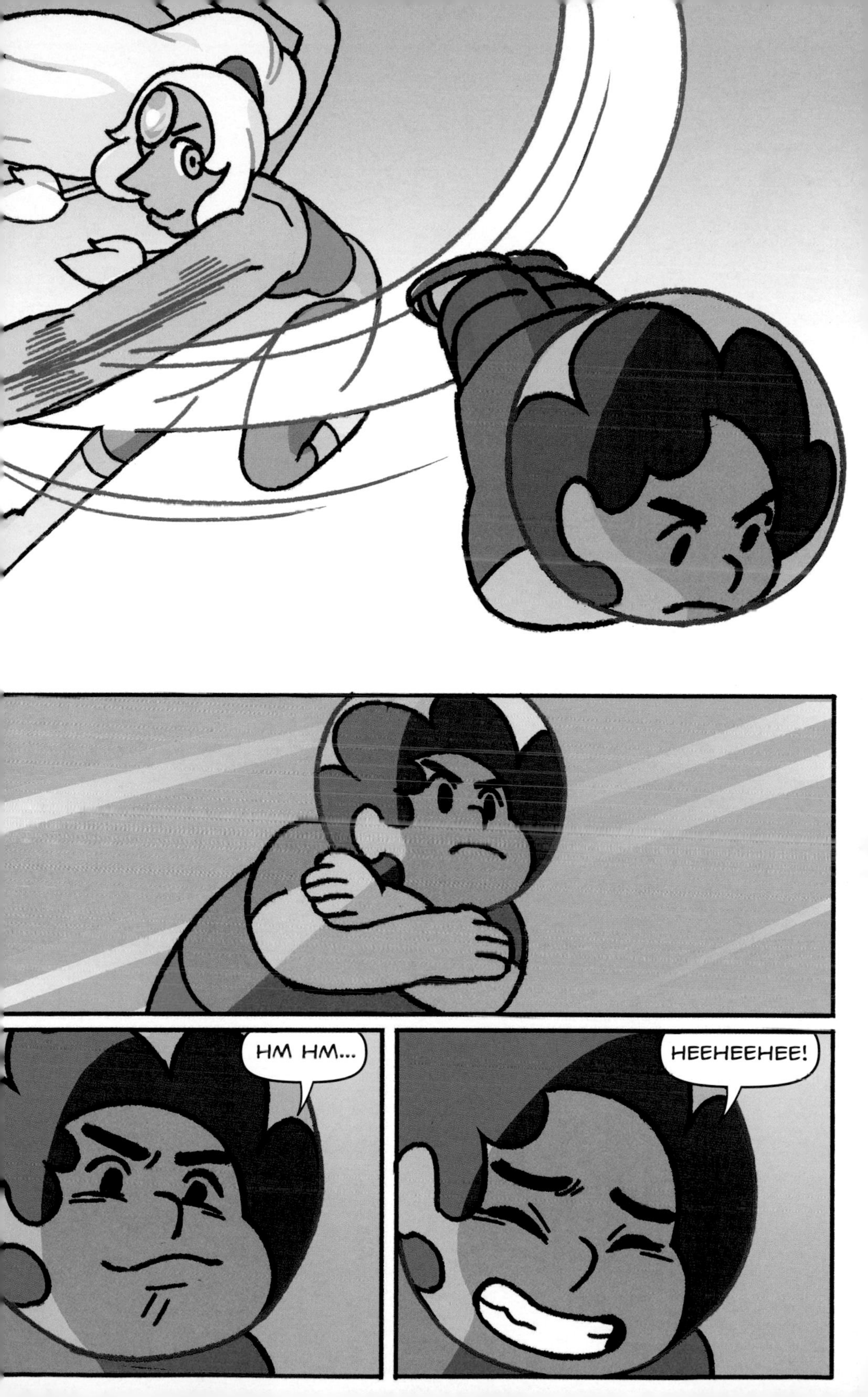
HM HM...
HEEHEEHEE!

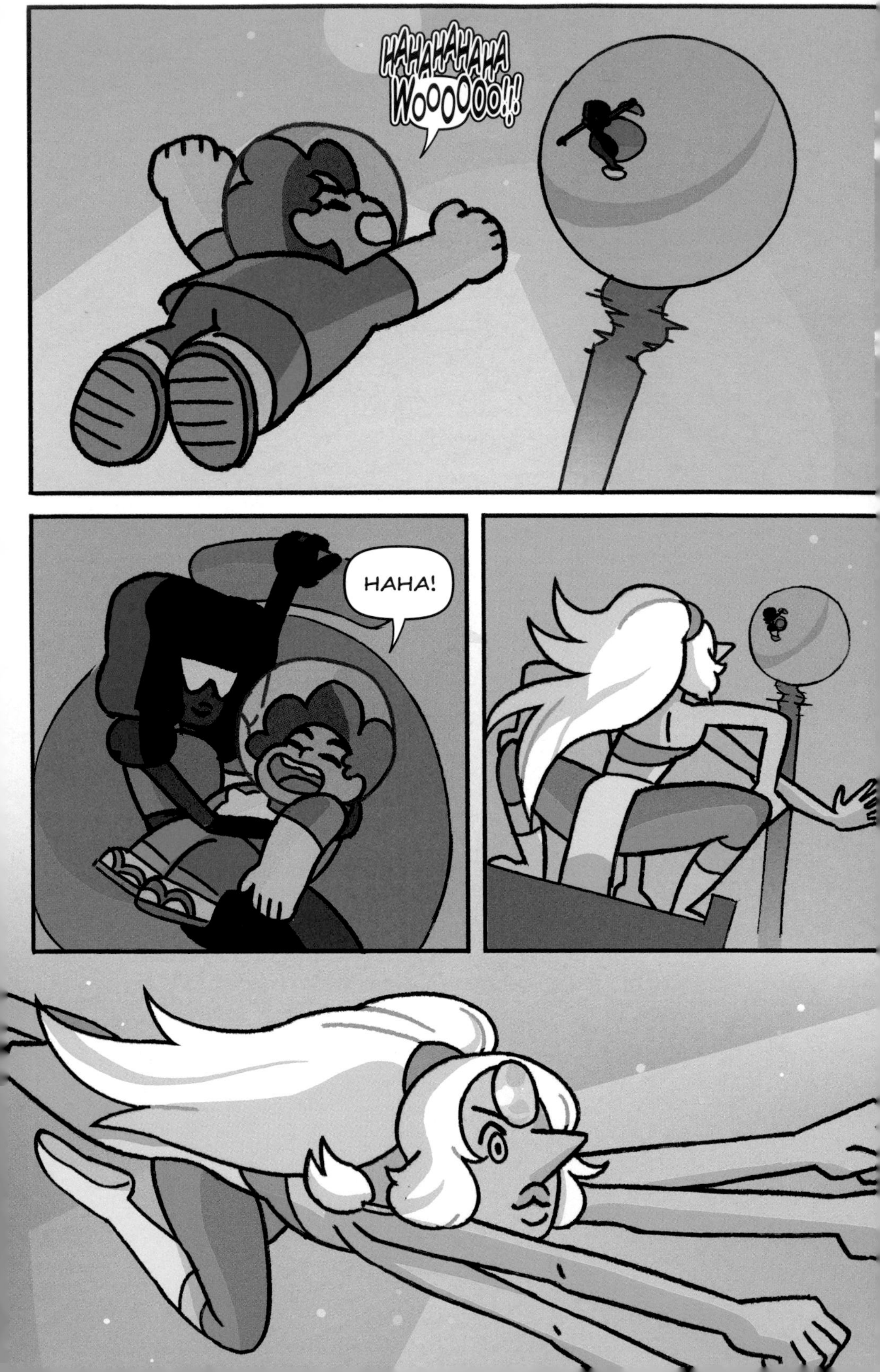
HAHAHAHAHA WOOOOOO!!!
HAHA!

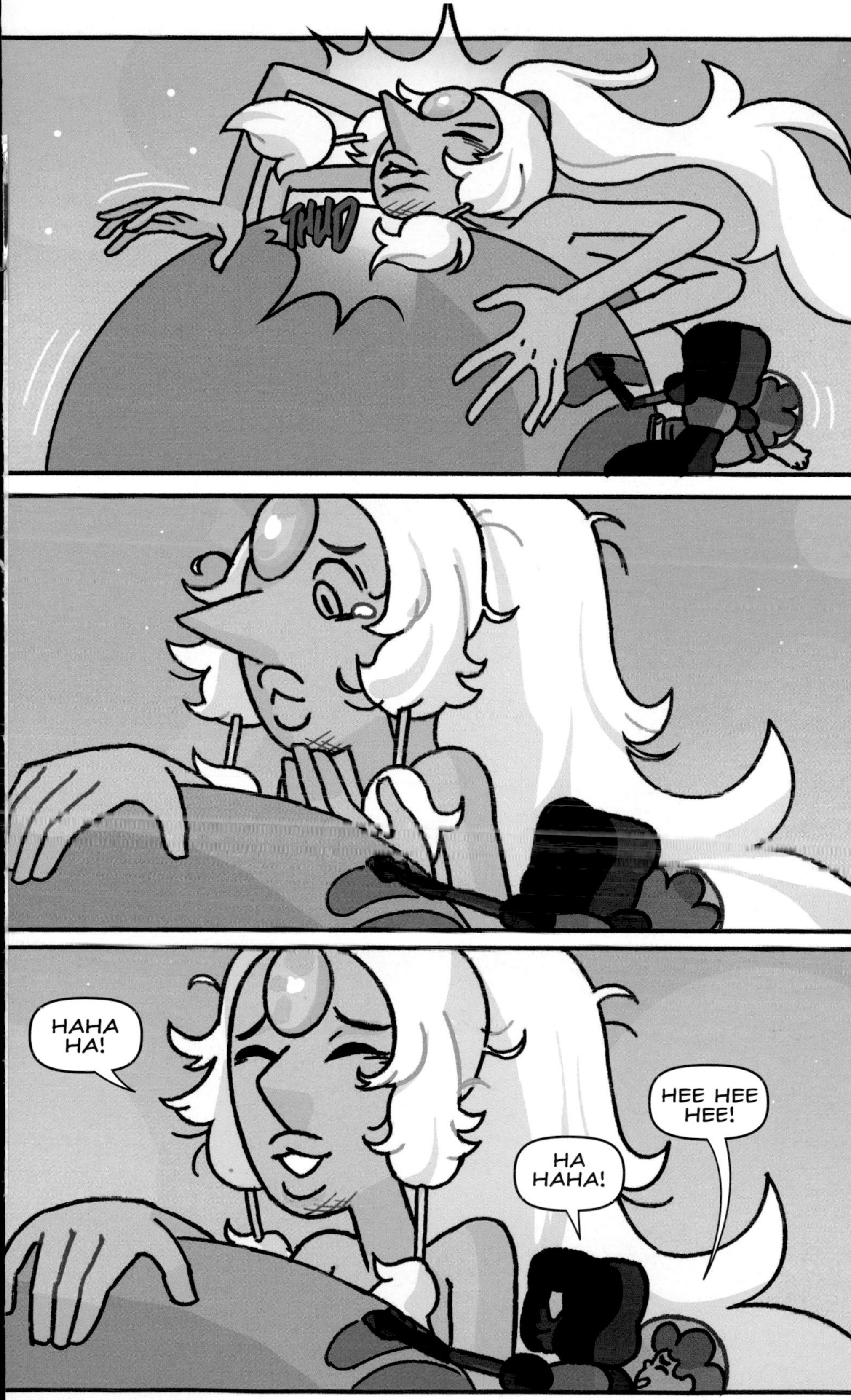
THUD
HAHA HA!
HA HAHA!
HEE HEE HEE!

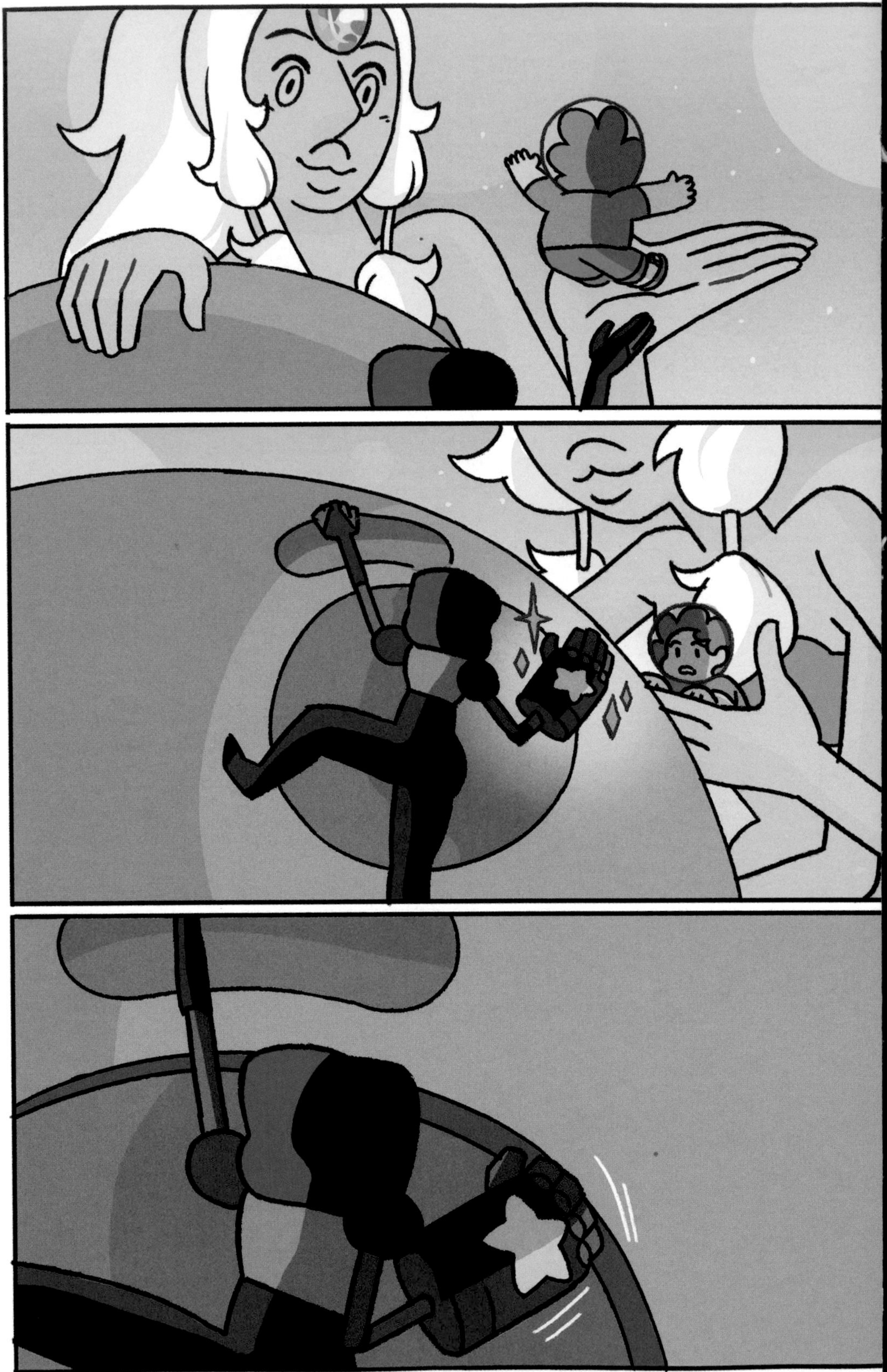

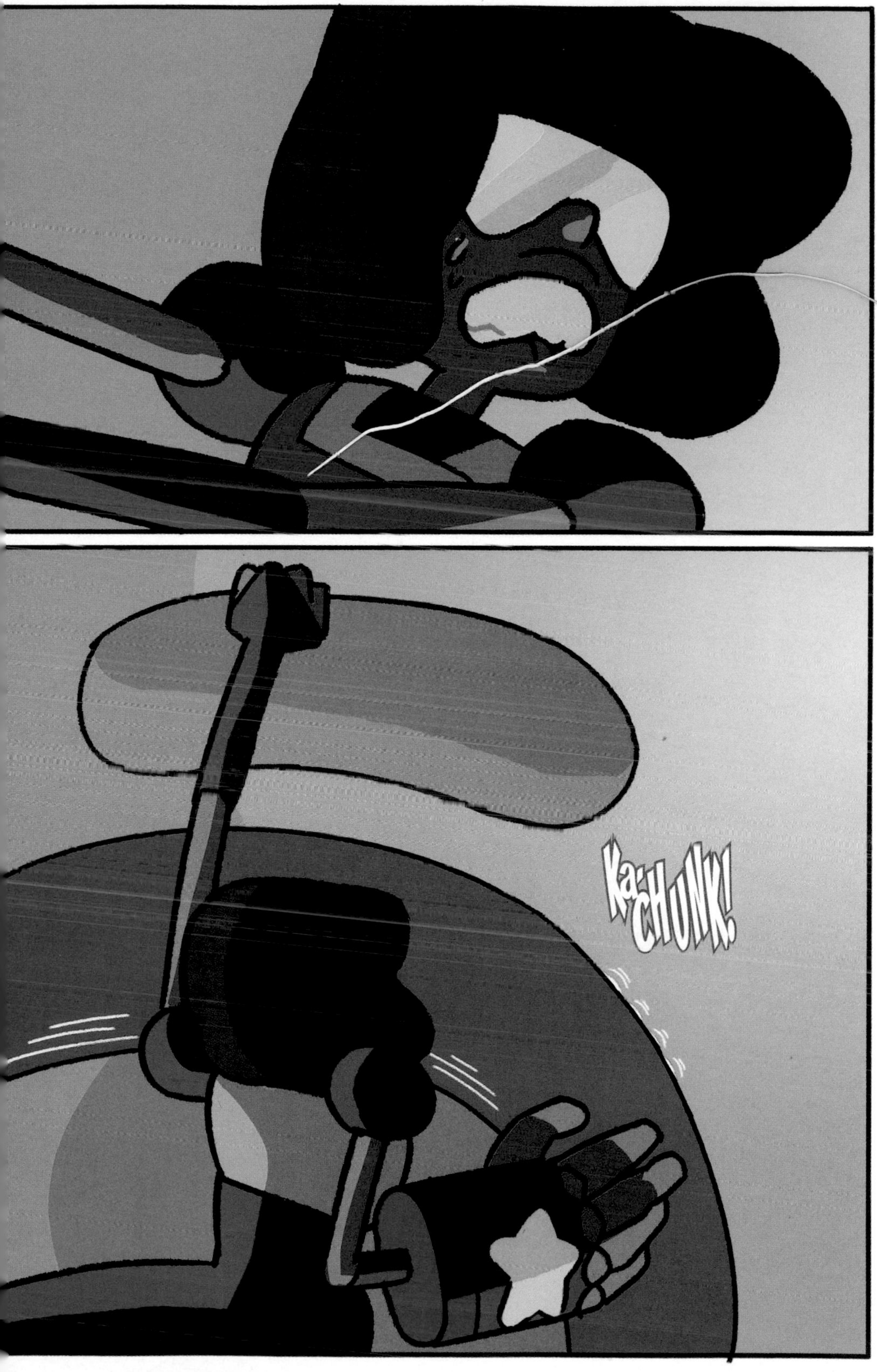
KA-CHUNK!

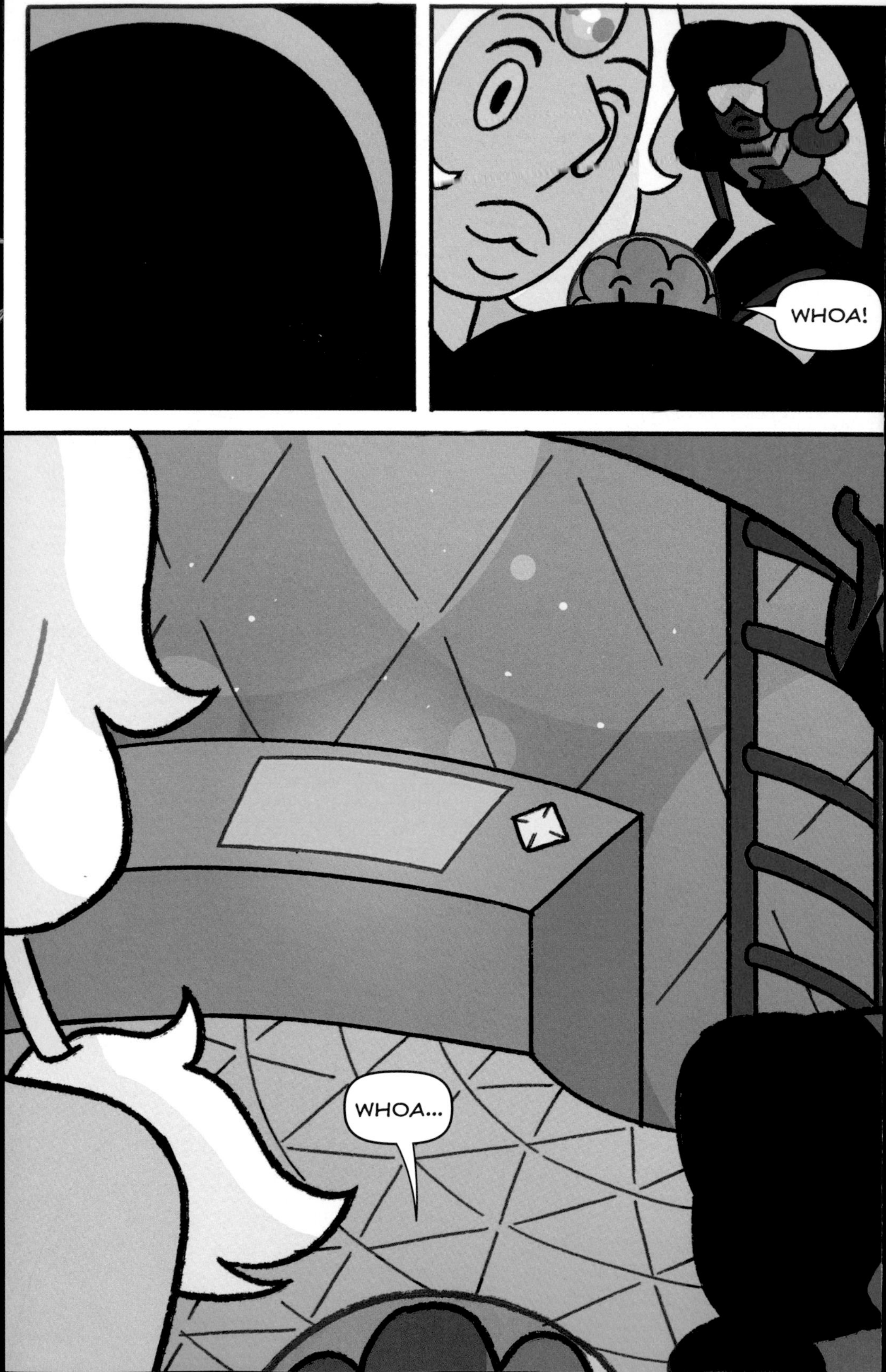
WHOA!
WHOA...

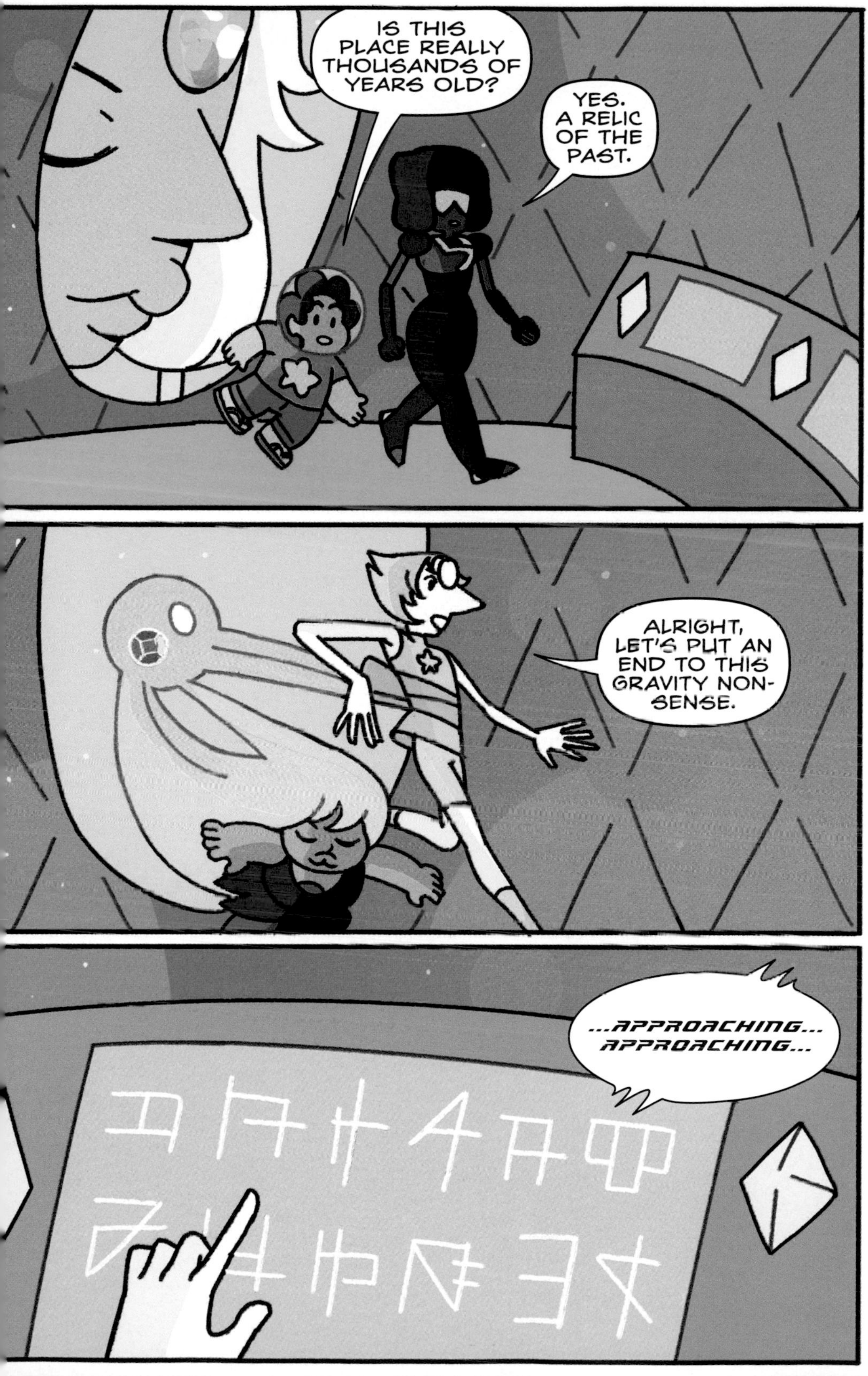

IS THIS PLACE REALLY THOUSANDS OF YEARS OLD?
YES. A RELIC OF THE PAST.
ALRIGHT, LET'S PUT AN END TO THIS GRAVITY NON-SENSE.
...APPROACHING... APPROACHING...

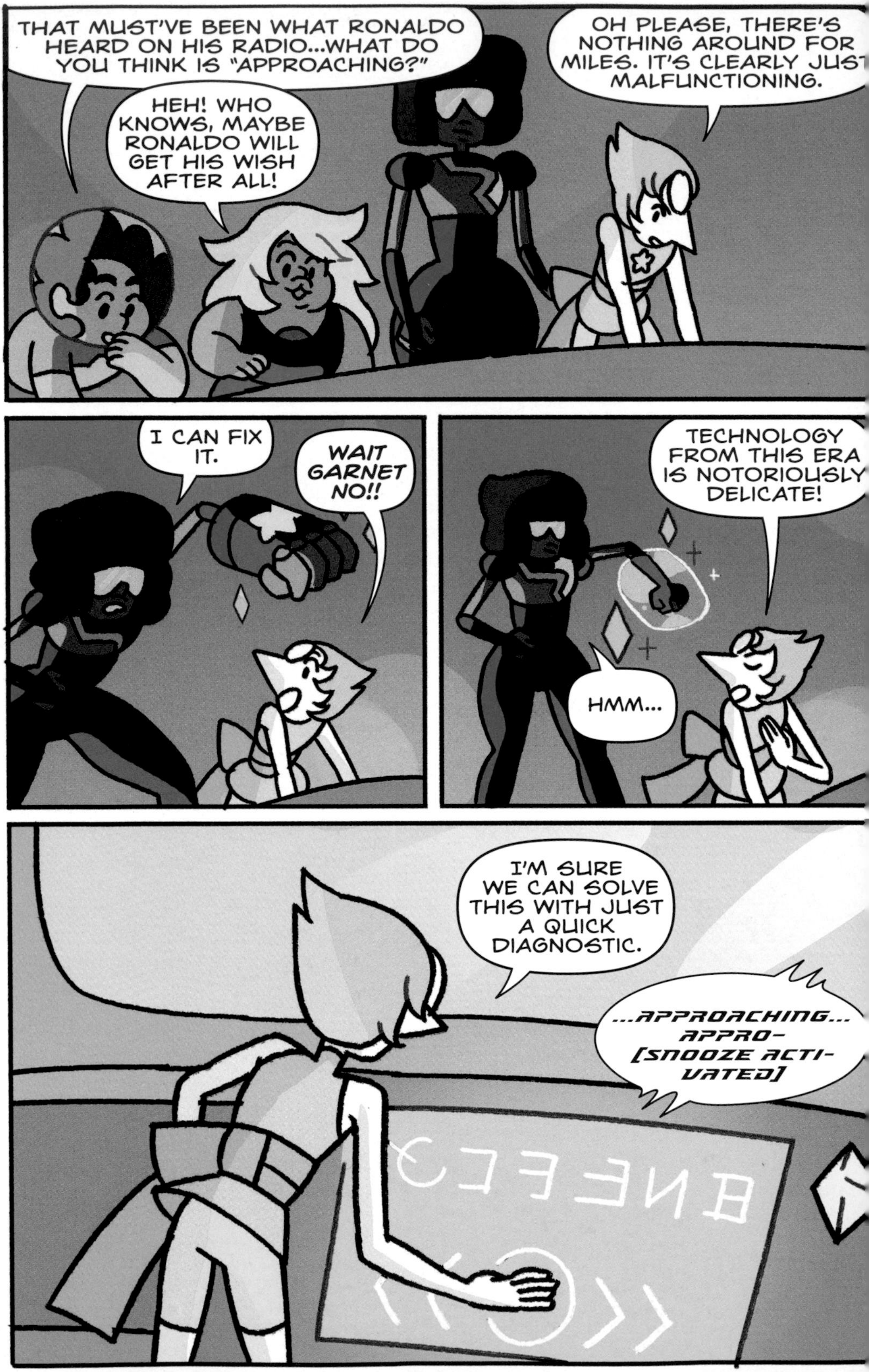
THAT MUST'VE BEEN WHAT RONALDO HEARD ON HIS RADIO...WHAT DO YOU THINK IS "APPROACHING?"
HEH! WHO KNOWS, MAYBE RONALDO WILL GET HIS WISH AFTER ALL!
OH PLEASE, THERE'S NOTHING AROUND FOR MILES. IT'S CLEARLY JUST MALFUNCTIONING.
I CAN FIX IT.
WAIT GARNET NO!!
TECHNOLOGY FROM THIS ERA IS NOTORIOUSLY DELICATE!
HMM...
I'M SURE WE CAN SOLVE THIS WITH JUST A QUICK DIAGNOSTIC.
...APPROACHING... APPRO- [SNOOZE ACTI-VATED]

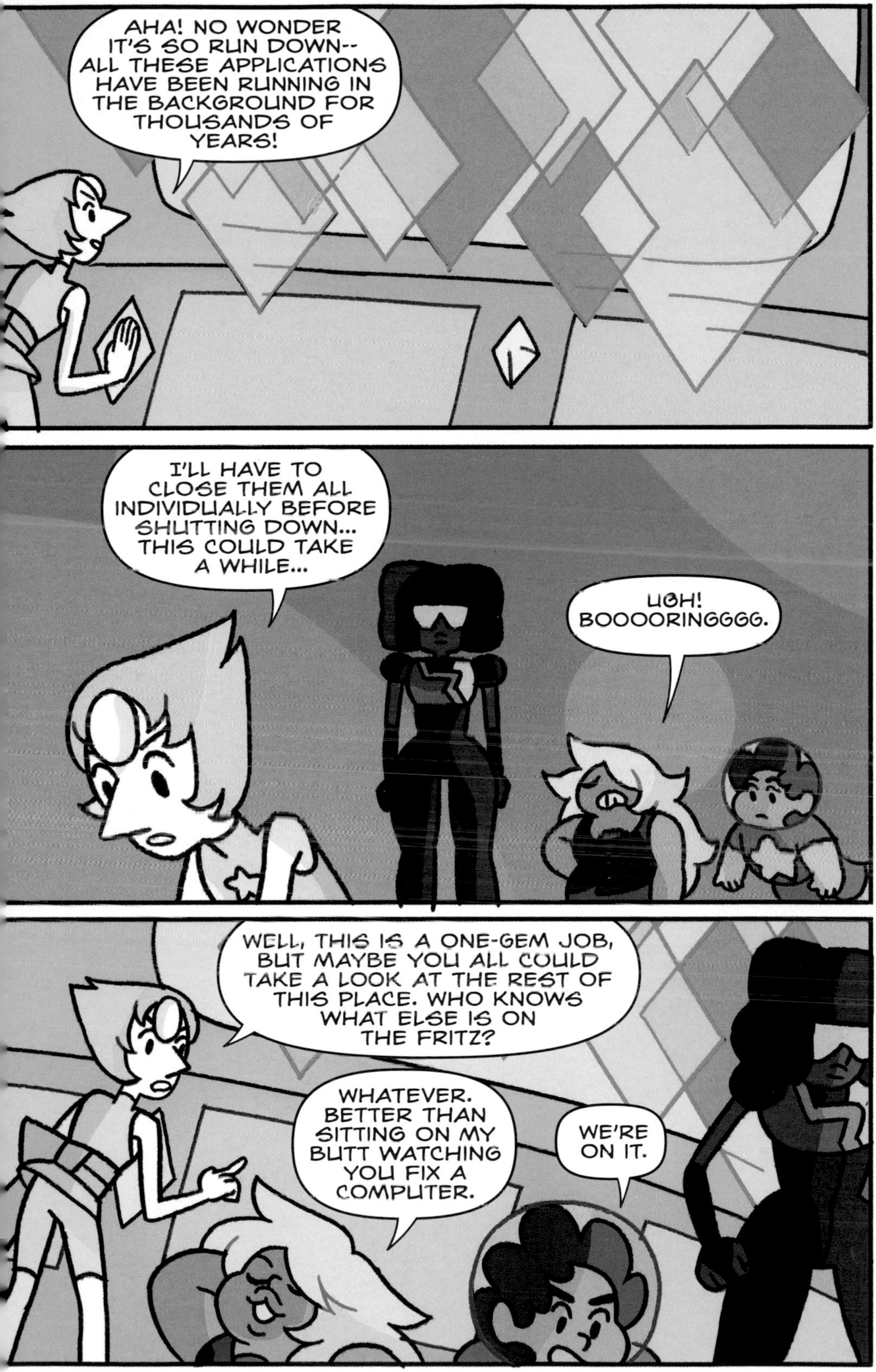
AHA! NO WONDER IT'S SO RUN DOWN--ALL THESE APPLICATIONS HAVE BEEN RUNNING IN THE BACKGROUND FOR THOUSANDS OF YEARS!
I'LL HAVE TO CLOSE THEM ALL INDIVIDUALLY BEFORE SHUTTING DOWN... THIS COULD TAKE A WHILE...
UGH! BOOOORINGGGG.
WELL, THIS IS A ONE-GEM JOB, BUT MAYBE YOU ALL COULD TAKE A LOOK AT THE REST OF THIS PLACE. WHO KNOWS WHAT ELSE IS ON THE FRITZ?
WHATEVER. BETTER THAN SITTING ON MY BUTT WATCHING YOU FIX A COMPUTER.
WE'RE ON IT.

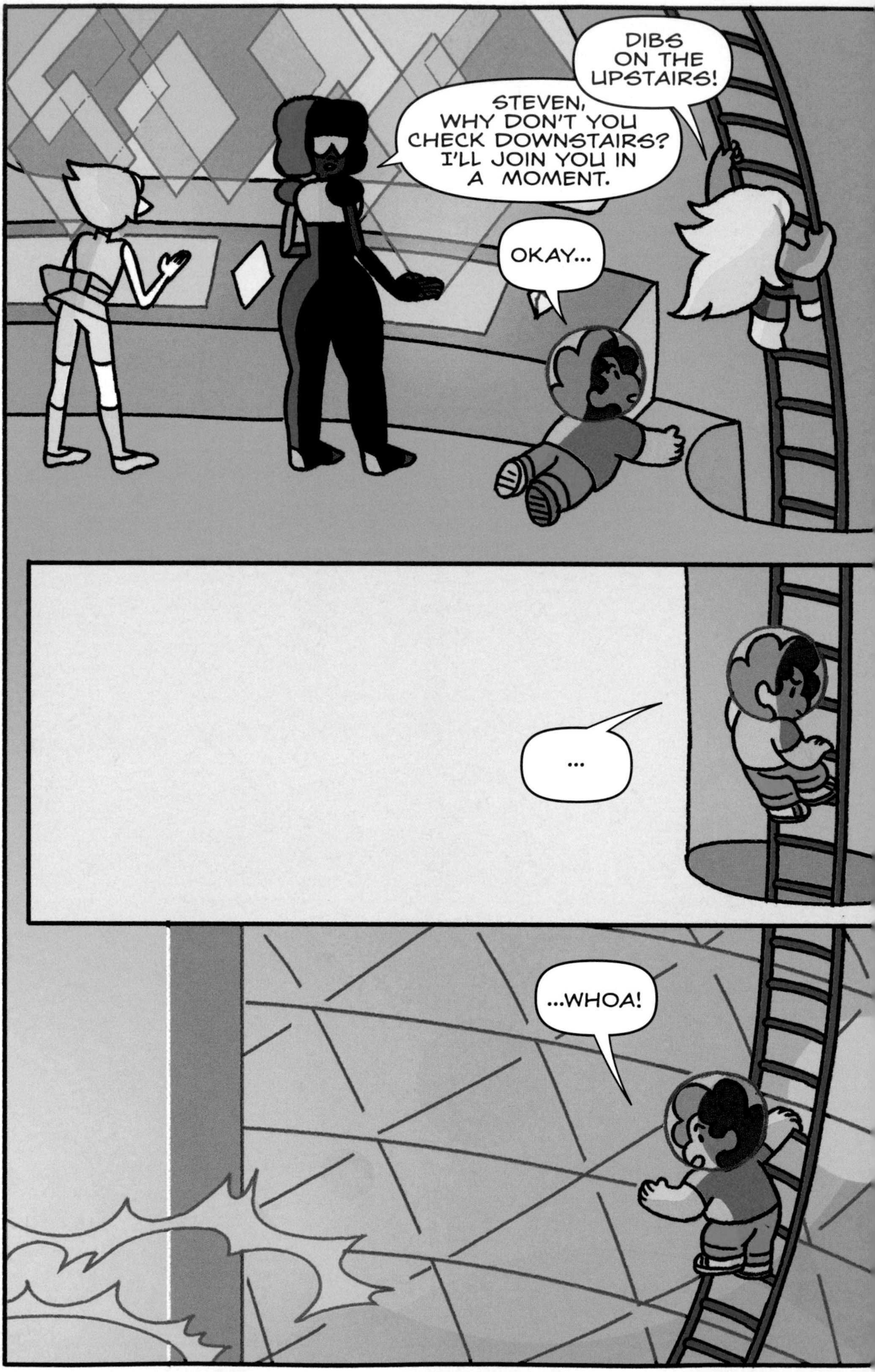
STEVEN, WHY DON'T YOU CHECK DOWNSTAIRS? I'LL JOIN YOU IN A MOMENT.
DIBS ON THE UPSTAIRS!
OKAY...
...
...WHOA!

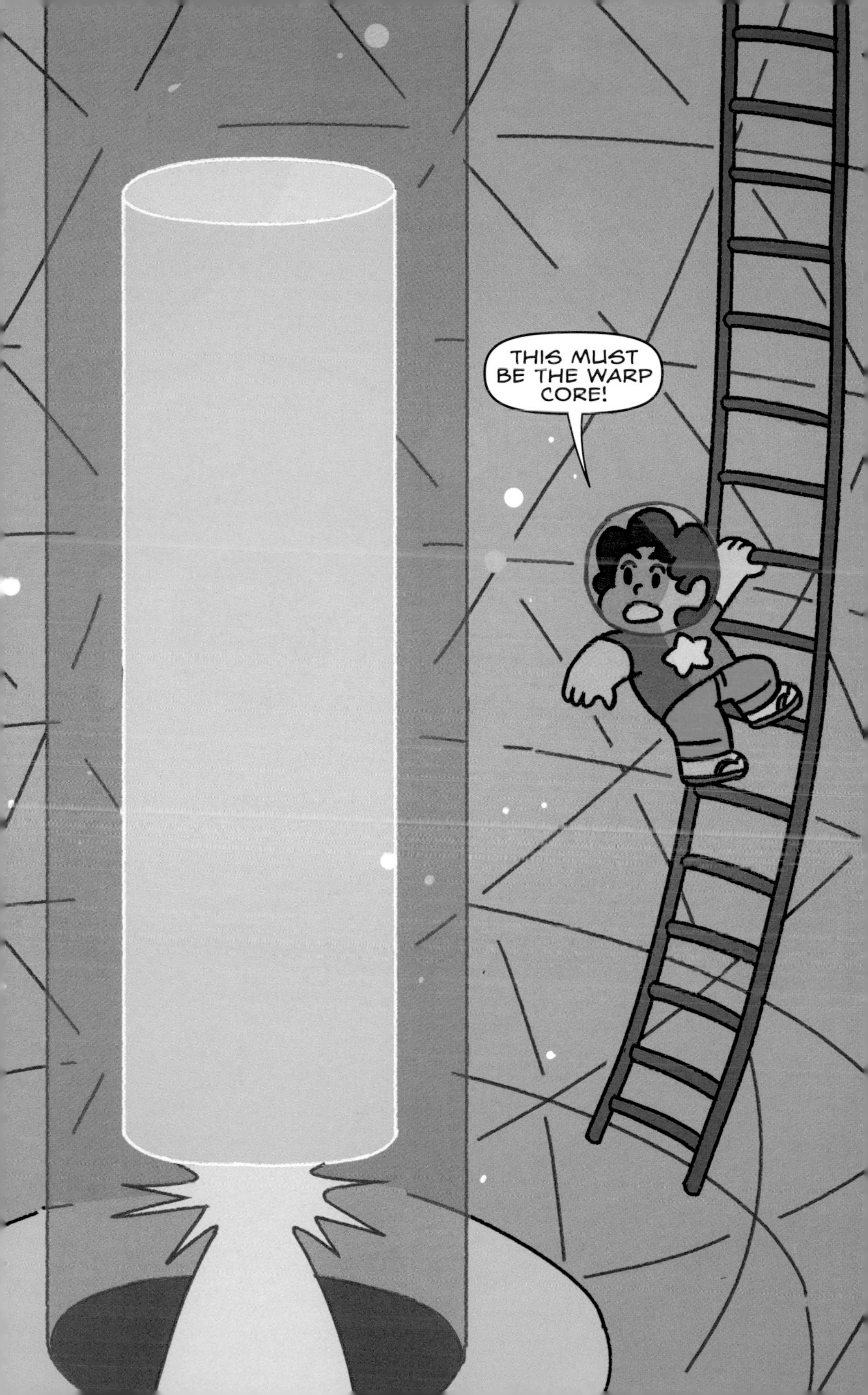
THIS MUST BE THE WARP CORE!

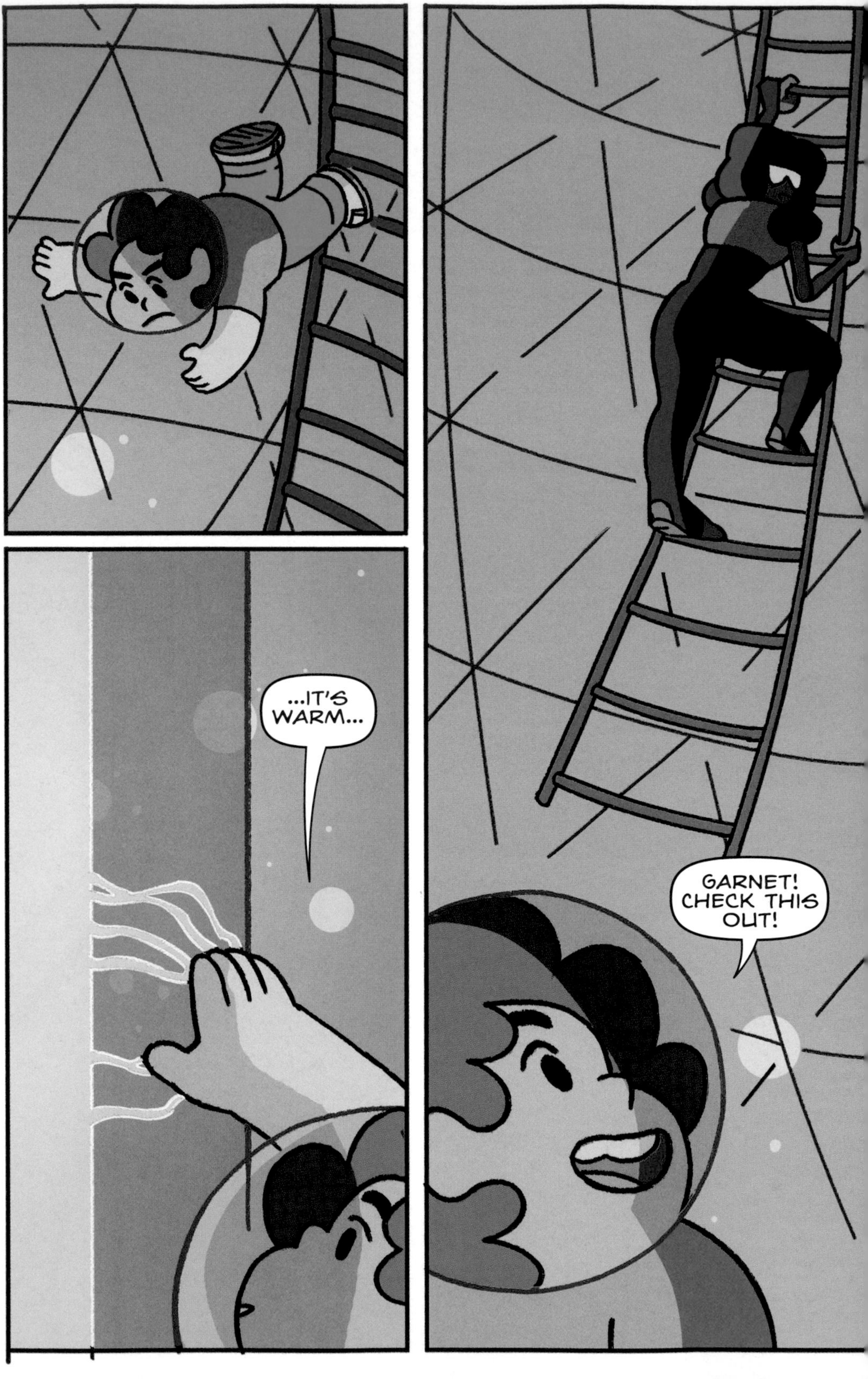
...IT'S WARM...
GARNET! CHECK THIS OUT!

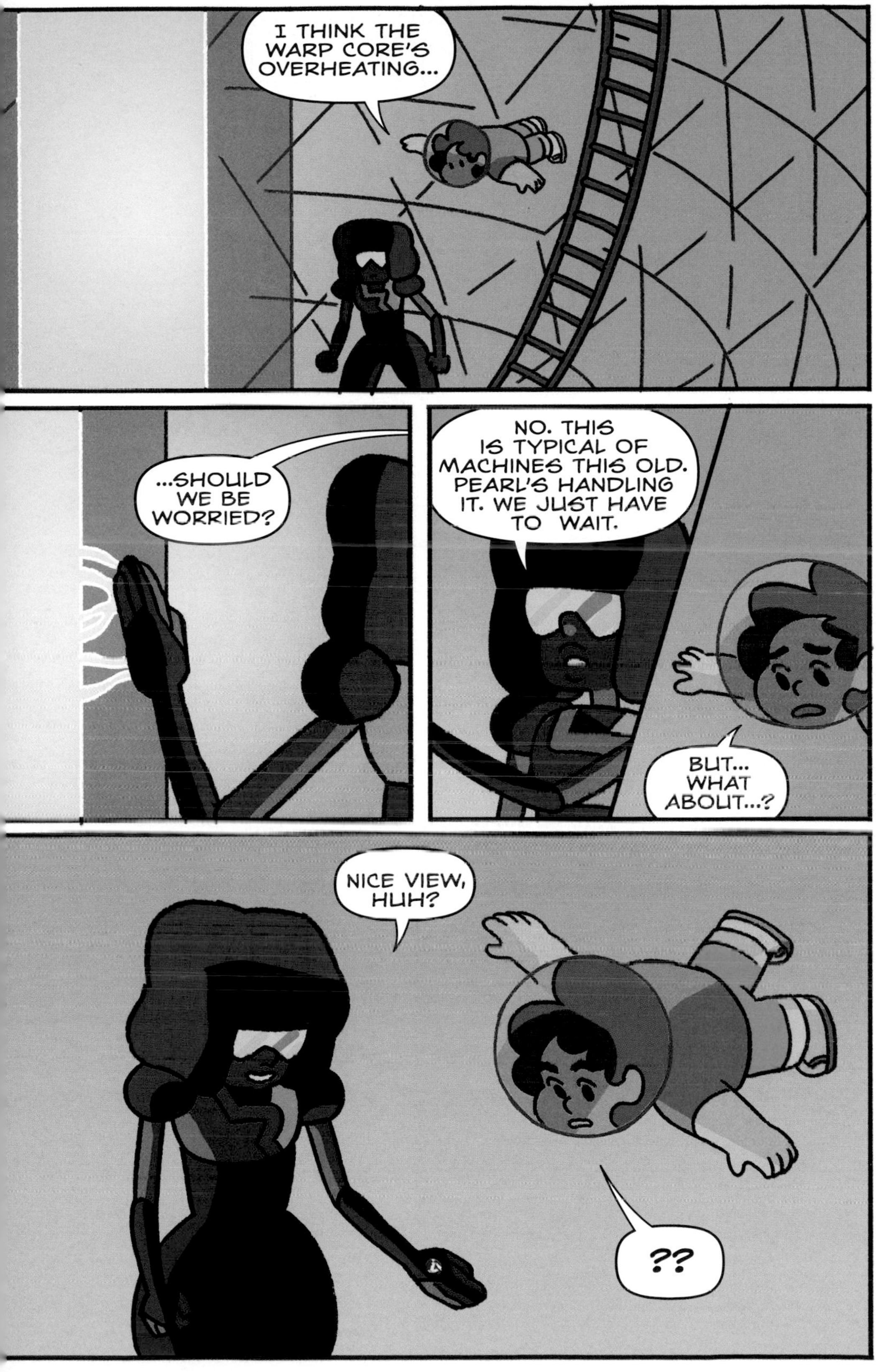
I THINK THE WARP CORE'S OVERHEATING...
...SHOULD WE BE WORRIED?
NO. THIS IS TYPICAL OF MACHINES THIS OLD. PEARL'S HANDLING IT. WE JUST HAVE TO WAIT.
BUT... WHAT ABOUT...?
NICE VIEW, HUH?
??

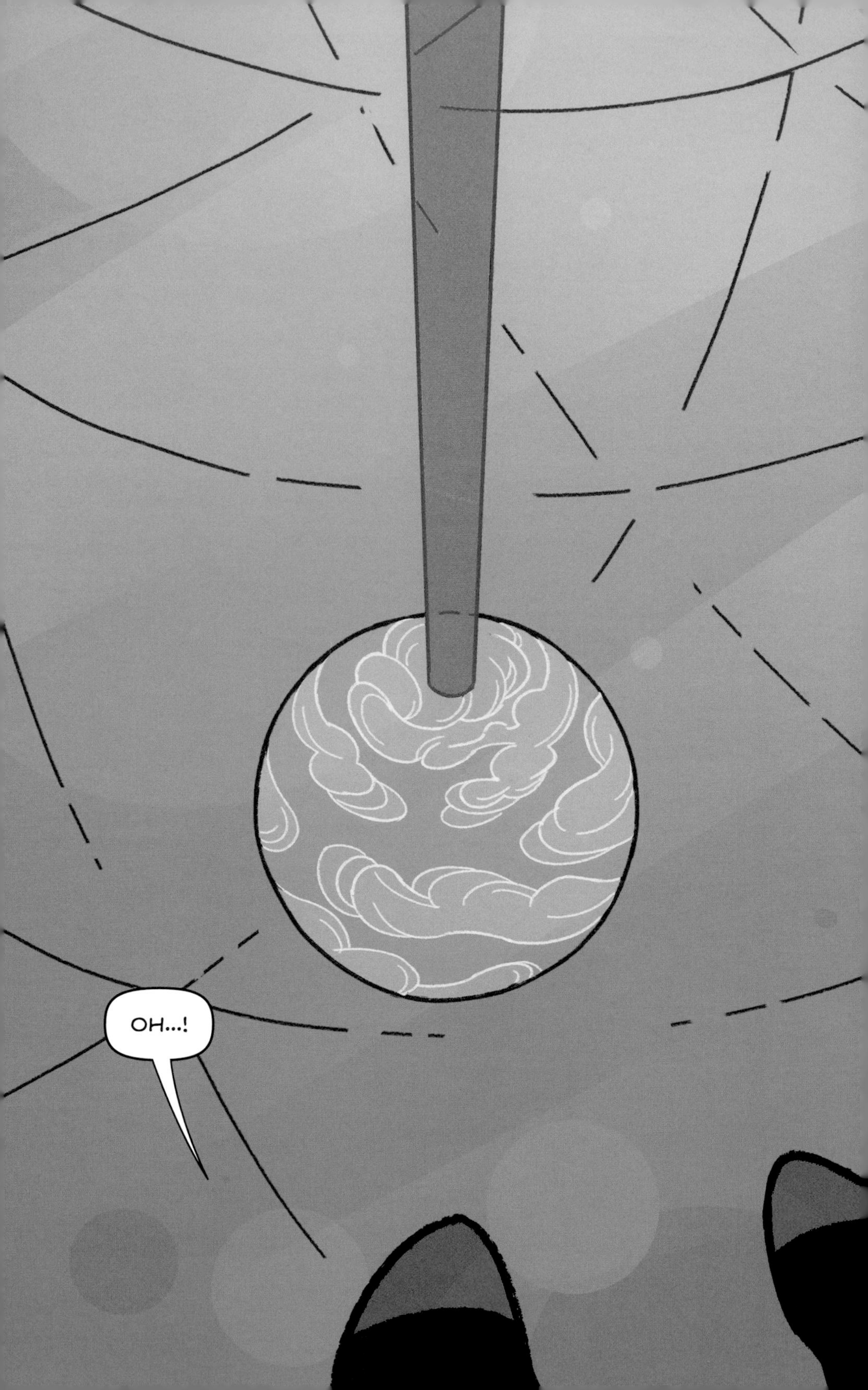
OH...!

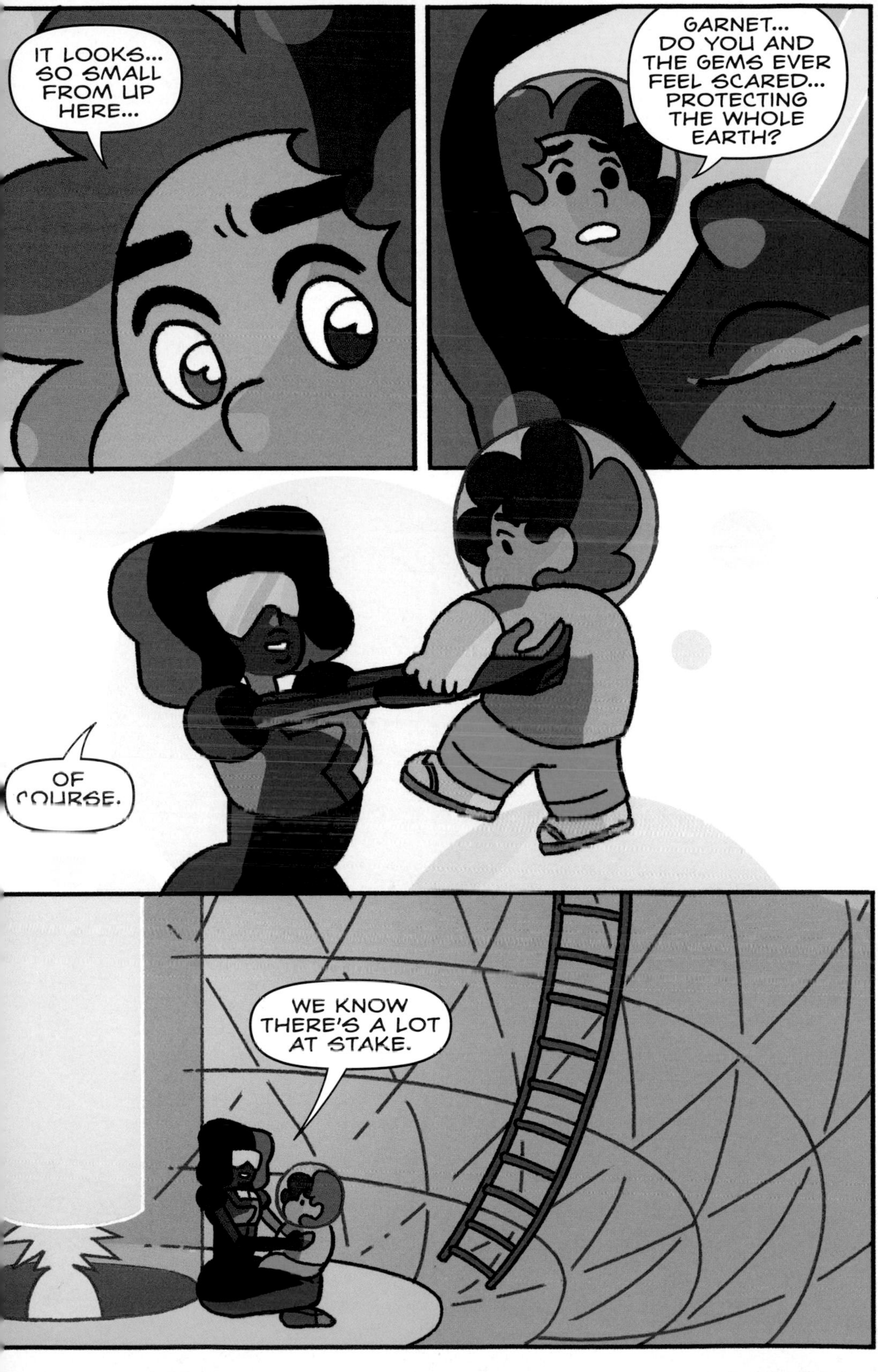
IT LOOKS... SO SMALL FROM UP HERE...
GARNET... DO YOU AND THE GEMS EVER FEEL SCARED... PROTECTING THE WHOLE EARTH?
OF COURSE.
WE KNOW THERE'S A LOT AT STAKE.

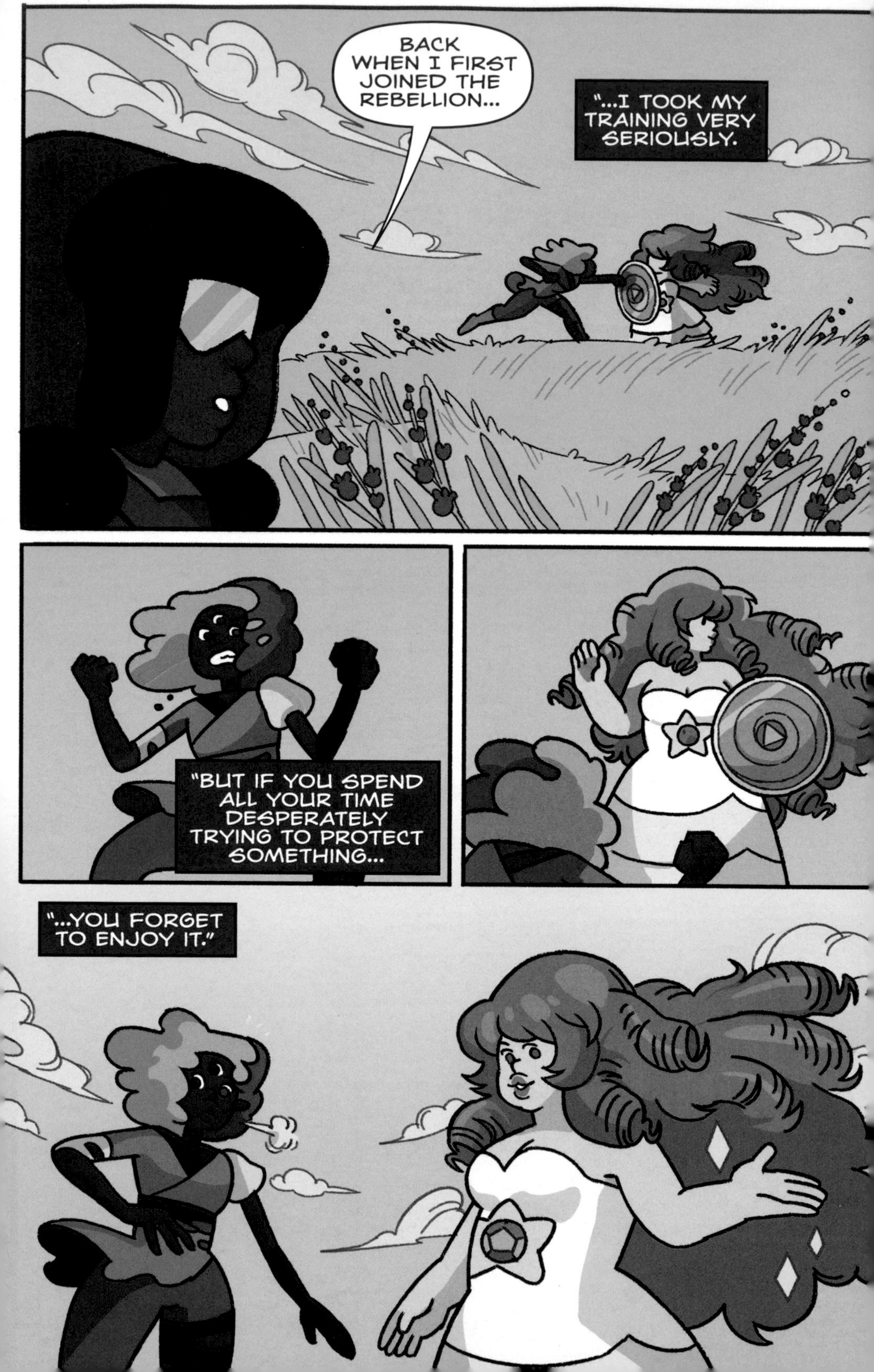

BACK WHEN I FIRST JOINED THE REBELLION...
"...I TOOK MY TRAINING VERY SERIOUSLY.
"BUT IF YOU SPEND ALL YOUR TIME DESPERATELY TRYING TO PROTECT SOMETHING...
"...YOU FORGET TO ENJOY IT."

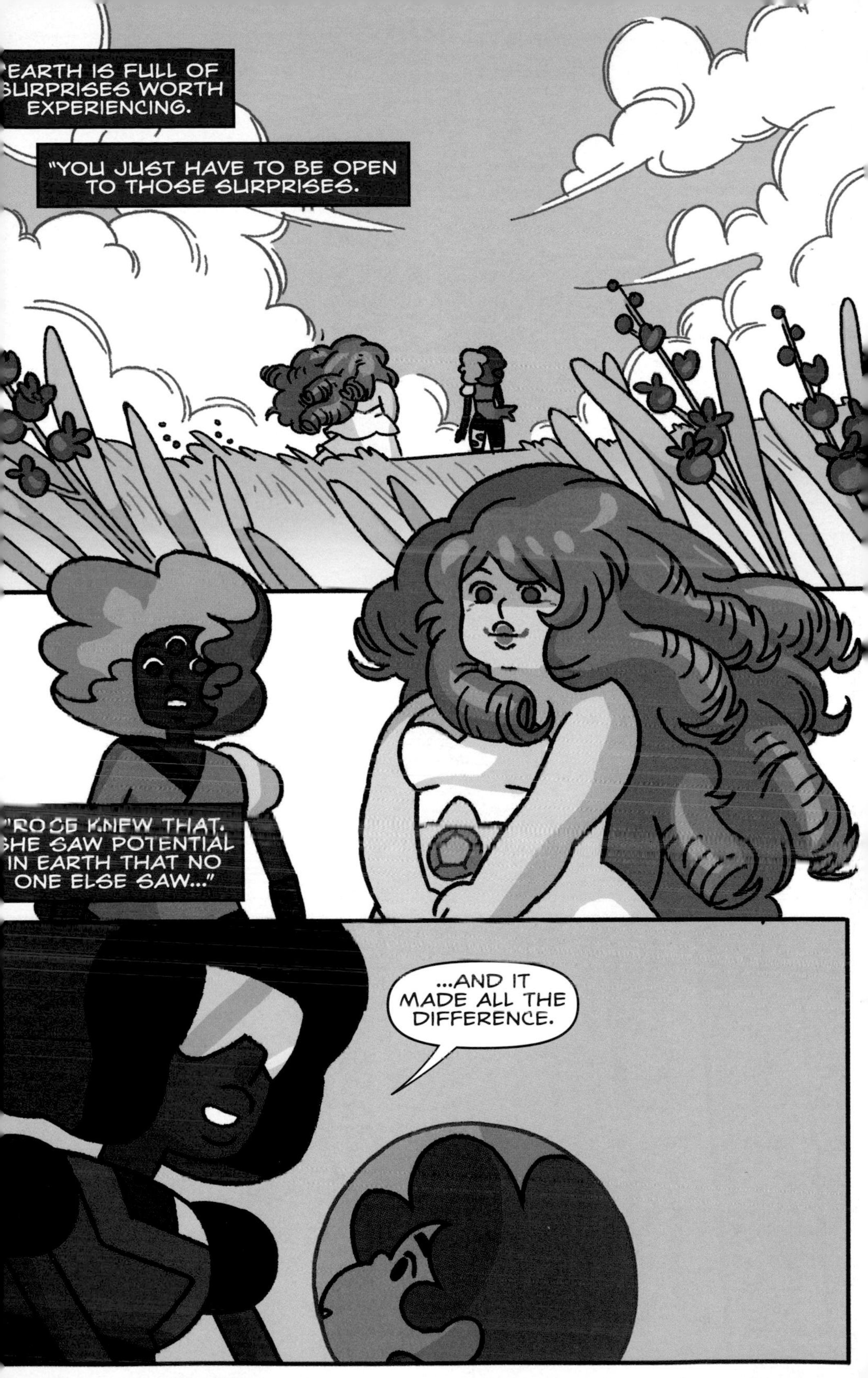
EARTH IS FULL OF SURPRISES WORTH EXPERIENCING.
"YOU JUST HAVE TO BE OPEN TO THOSE SURPRISES.
"ROSE KNEW THAT. SHE SAW POTENTIAL IN EARTH THAT NO ONE ELSE SAW..."
...AND IT MADE ALL THE DIFFERENCE.

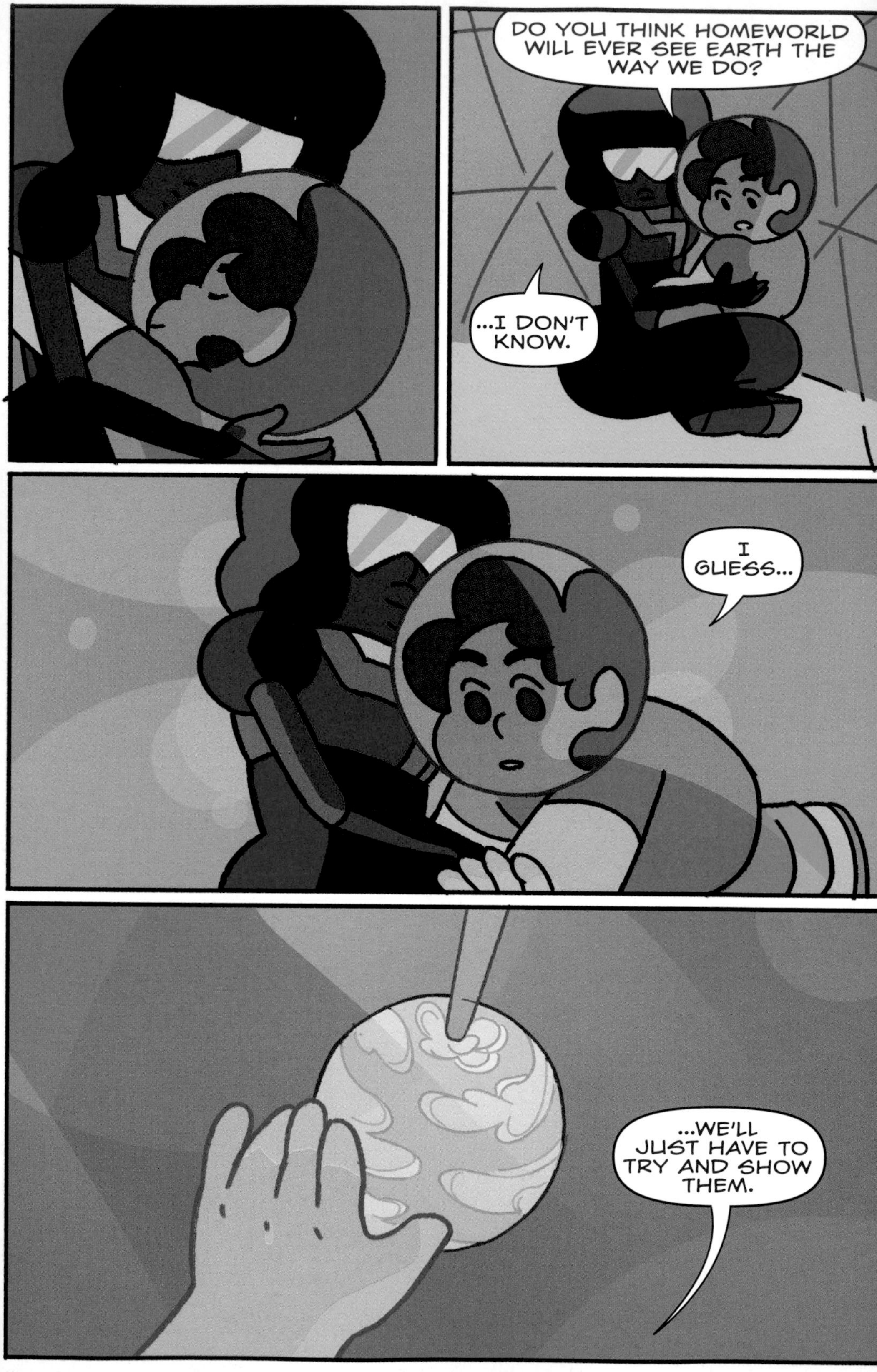
DO YOU THINK HOMEWORLD WILL EVER SEE EARTH THE WAY WE DO?
...I DON'T KNOW.
I GUESS...
...WE'LL JUST HAVE TO TRY AND SHOW THEM.

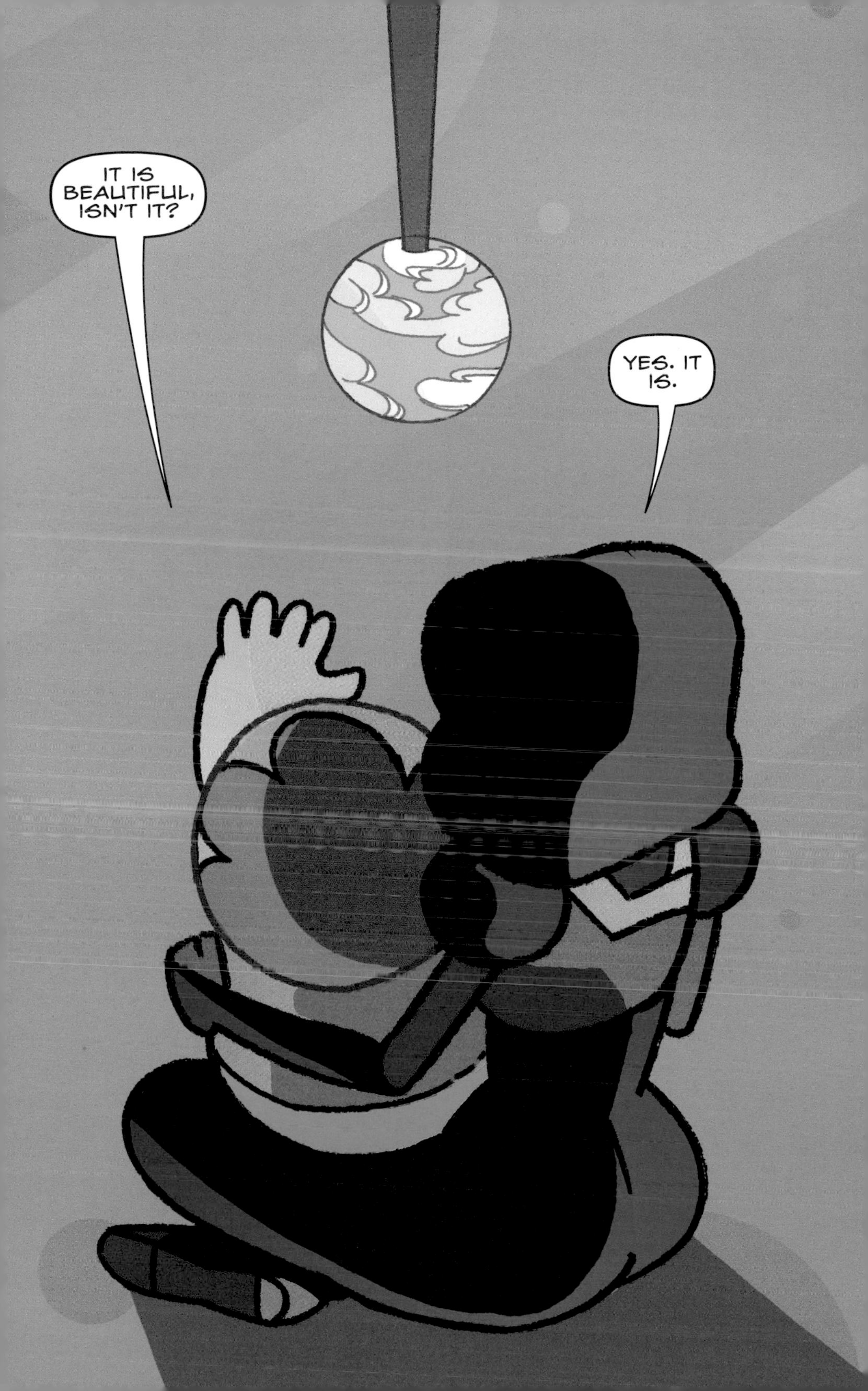
IT IS BEAUTIFUL, ISN'T IT?
YES. IT IS.

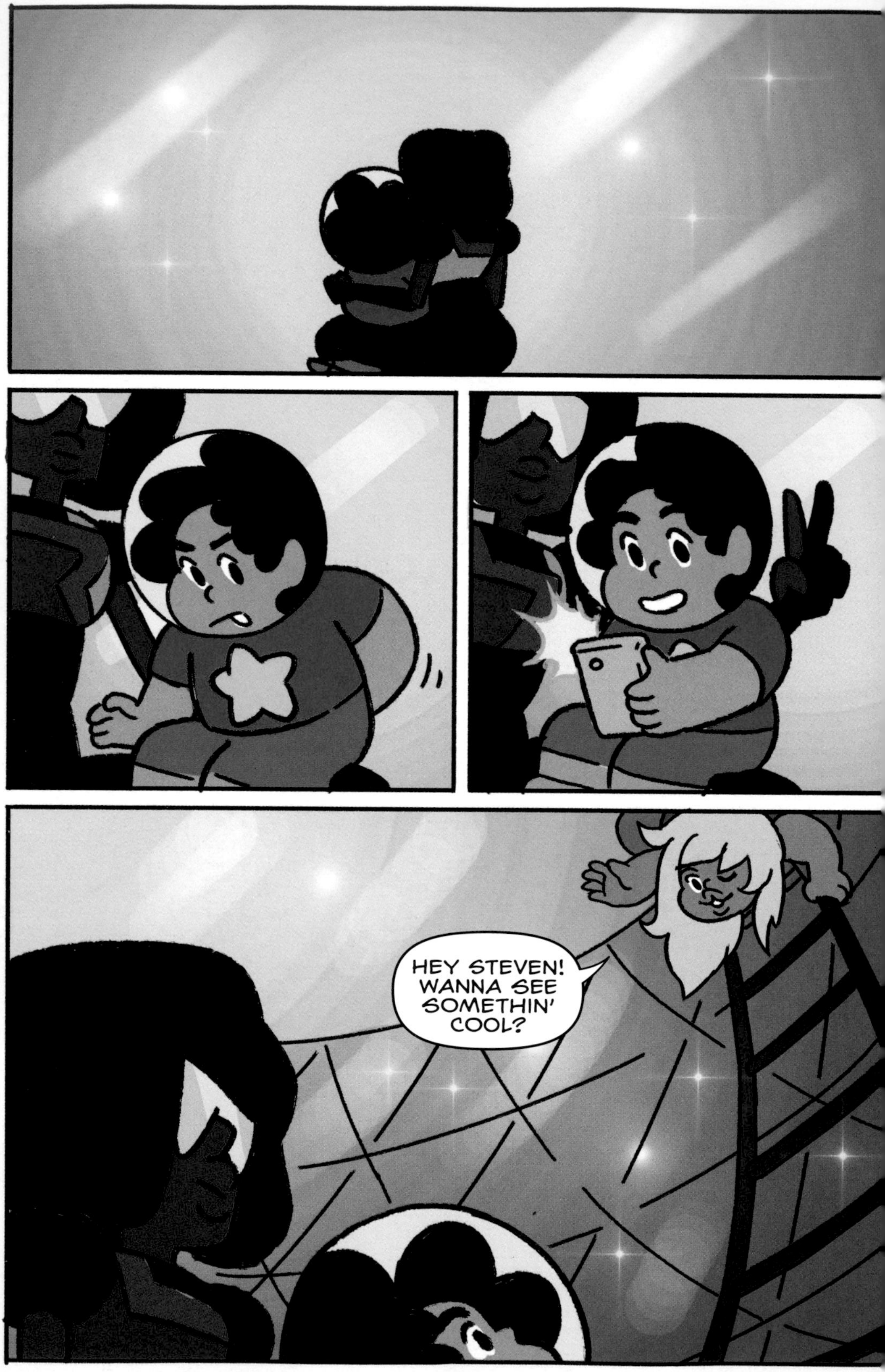
HEY STEVEN! WANNA SEE SOMETHIN' COOL?

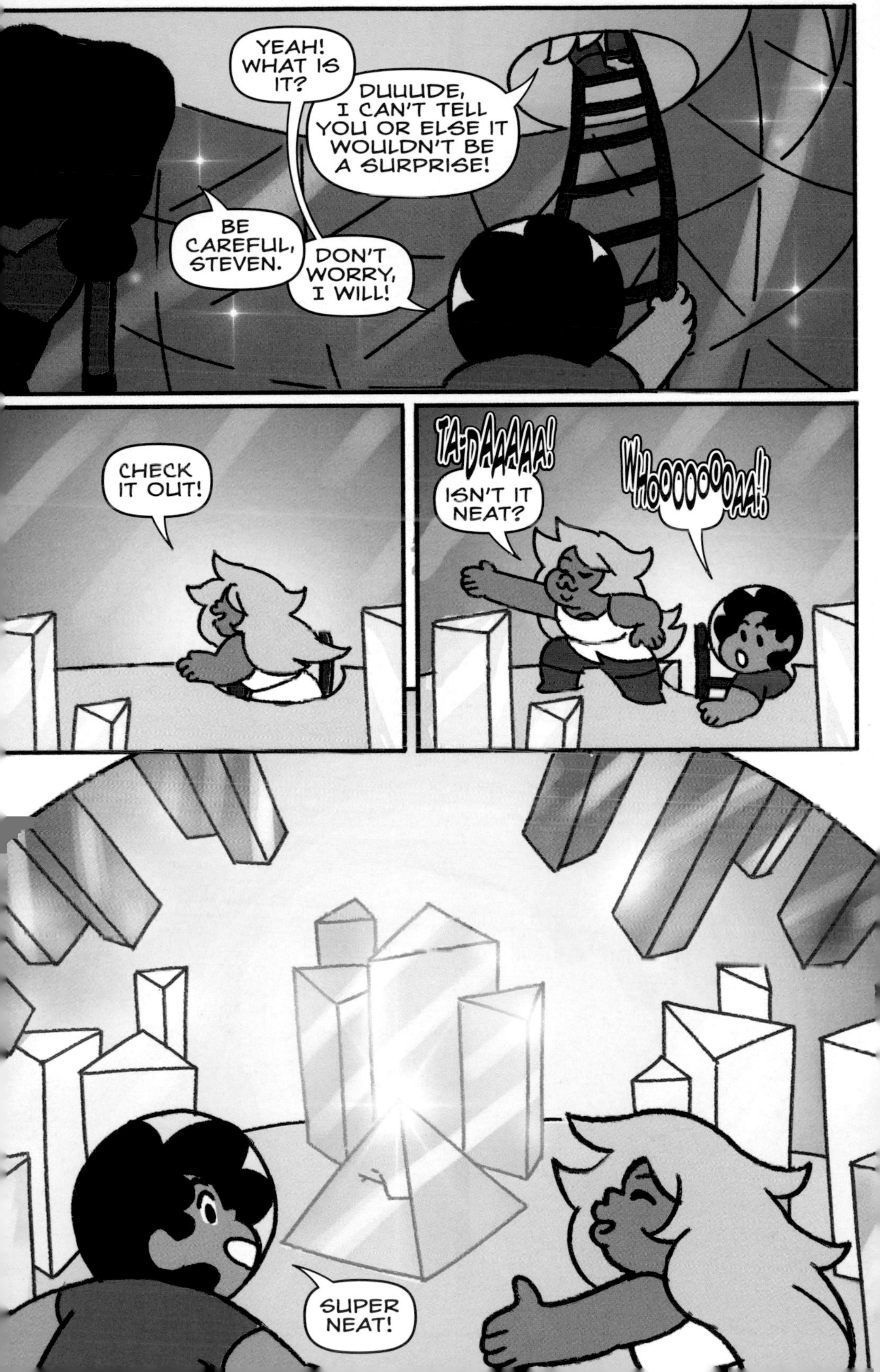
YEAH! WHAT IS IT?
DUUUDE, I CAN'T TELL YOU OR ELSE IT WOULDN'T BE A SURPRISE!
BE CAREFUL, STEVEN.
DON'T WORRY, I WILL!
CHECK IT OUT!
TA-DAAAAA!
ISN'T IT NEAT?
WHOOOOOOOAA!!
SUPER NEAT!

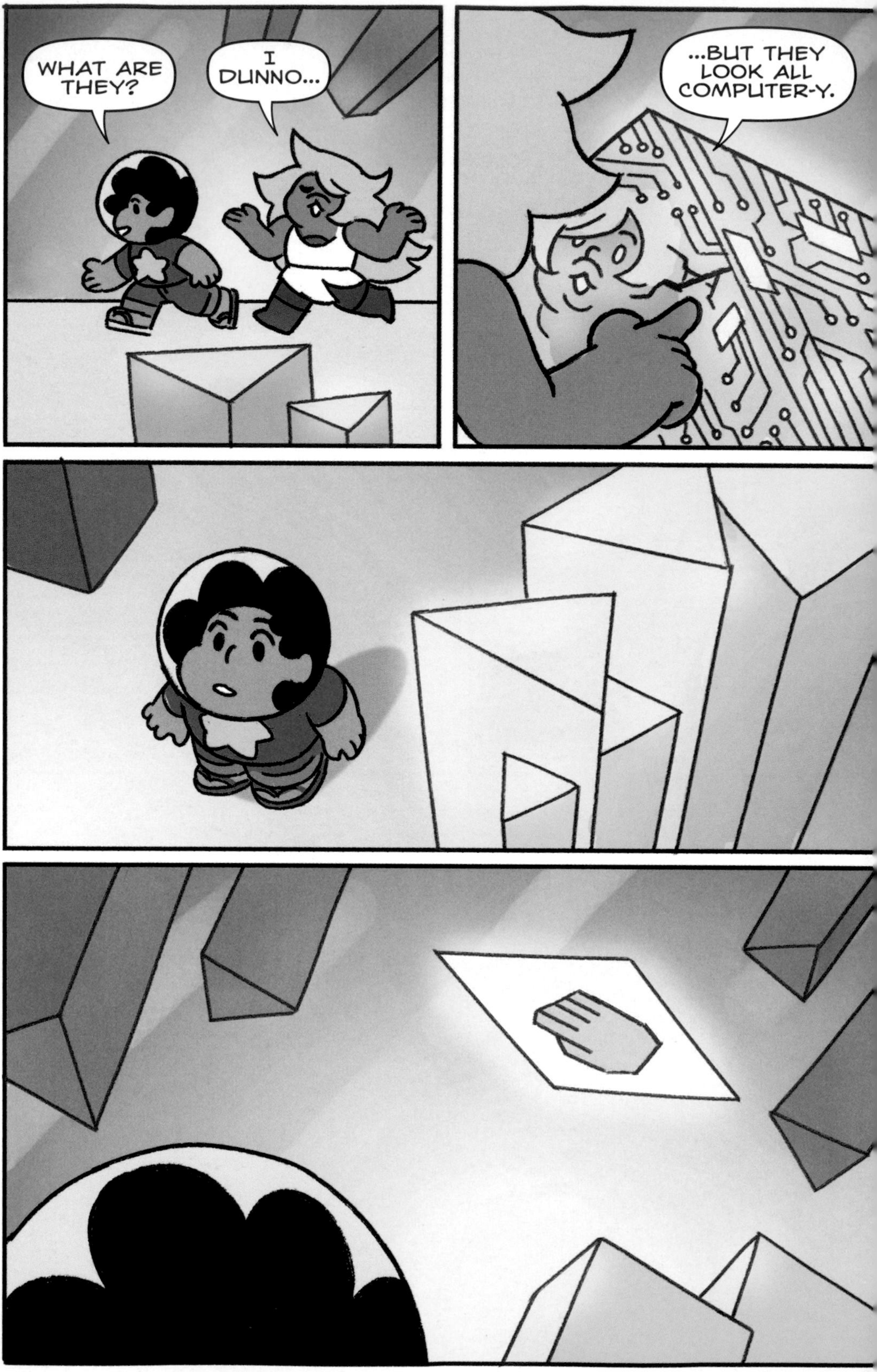
WHAT ARE THEY?
I DUNNO...
...BUT THEY LOOK ALL COMPUTER-Y.

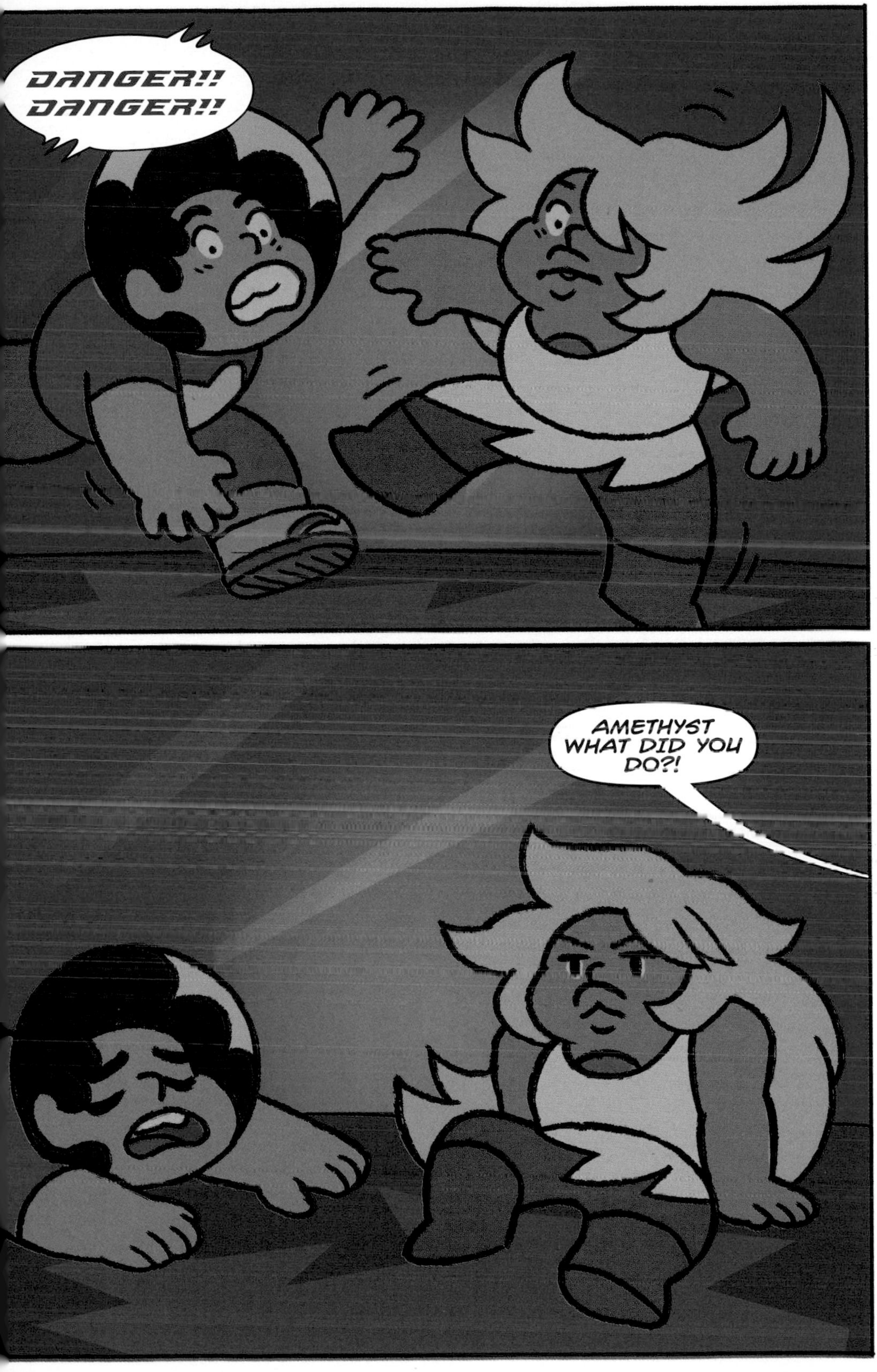
DANGER!! DANGER!!
AMETHYST WHAT DID YOU DO?!

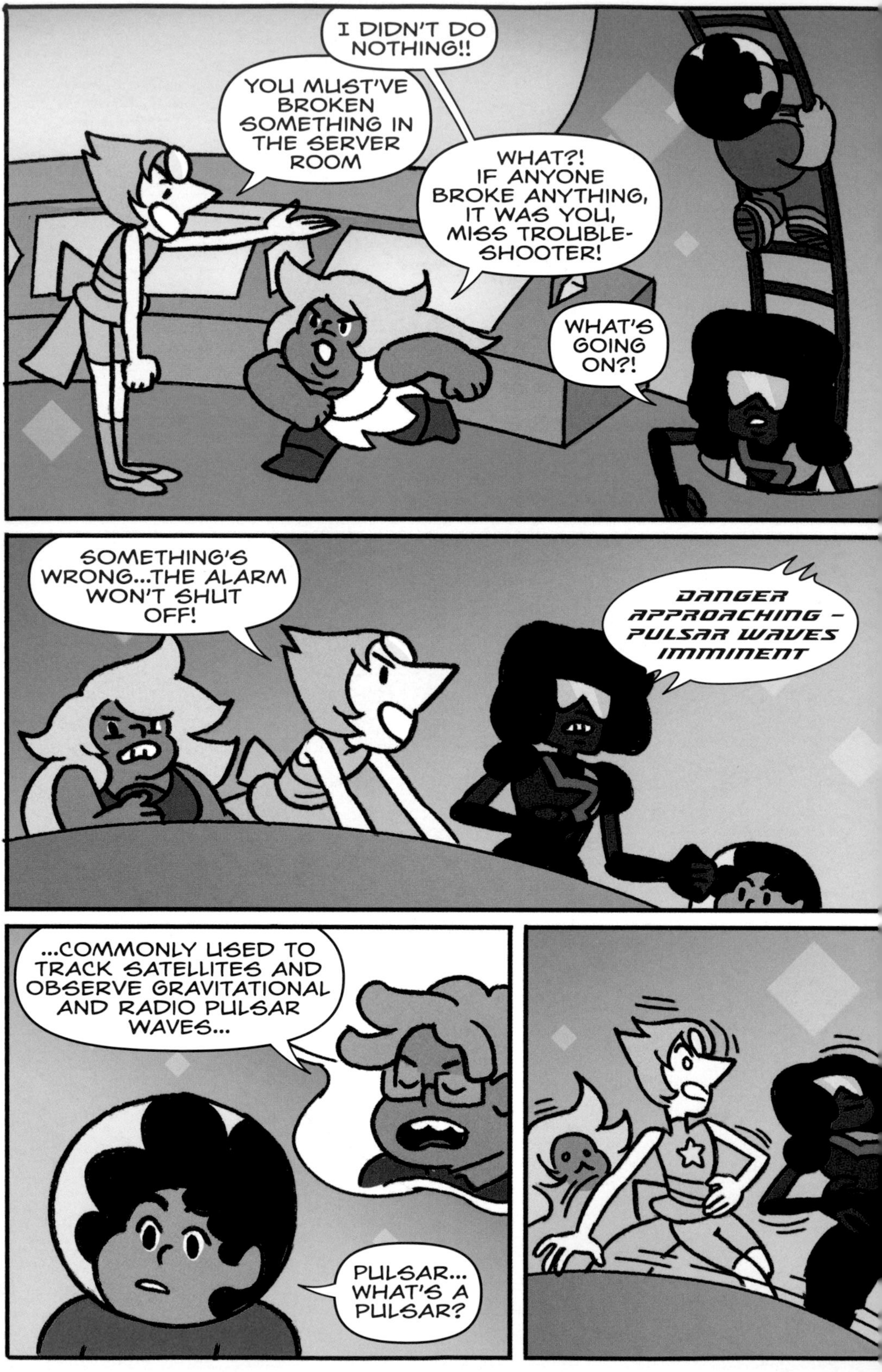
YOU MUST'VE BROKEN SOMETHING IN THE SERVER ROOM
I DIDN'T DO NOTHING!!
WHAT?! IF ANYONE BROKE ANYTHING, IT WAS YOU, MISS TROUBLE-SHOOTER!
WHAT'S GOING ON?!
SOMETHING'S WRONG...THE ALARM WON'T SHUT OFF!
DANGER APPROACHING – PULSAR WAVES IMMINENT
...COMMONLY USED TO TRACK SATELLITES AND OBSERVE GRAVITATIONAL AND RADIO PULSAR WAVES...
PULSAR... WHAT'S A PULSAR?

AAAAH! WHAT'S HAPPENING?!

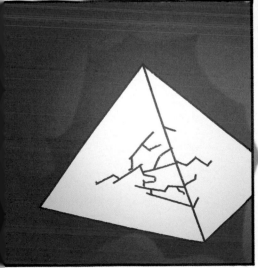

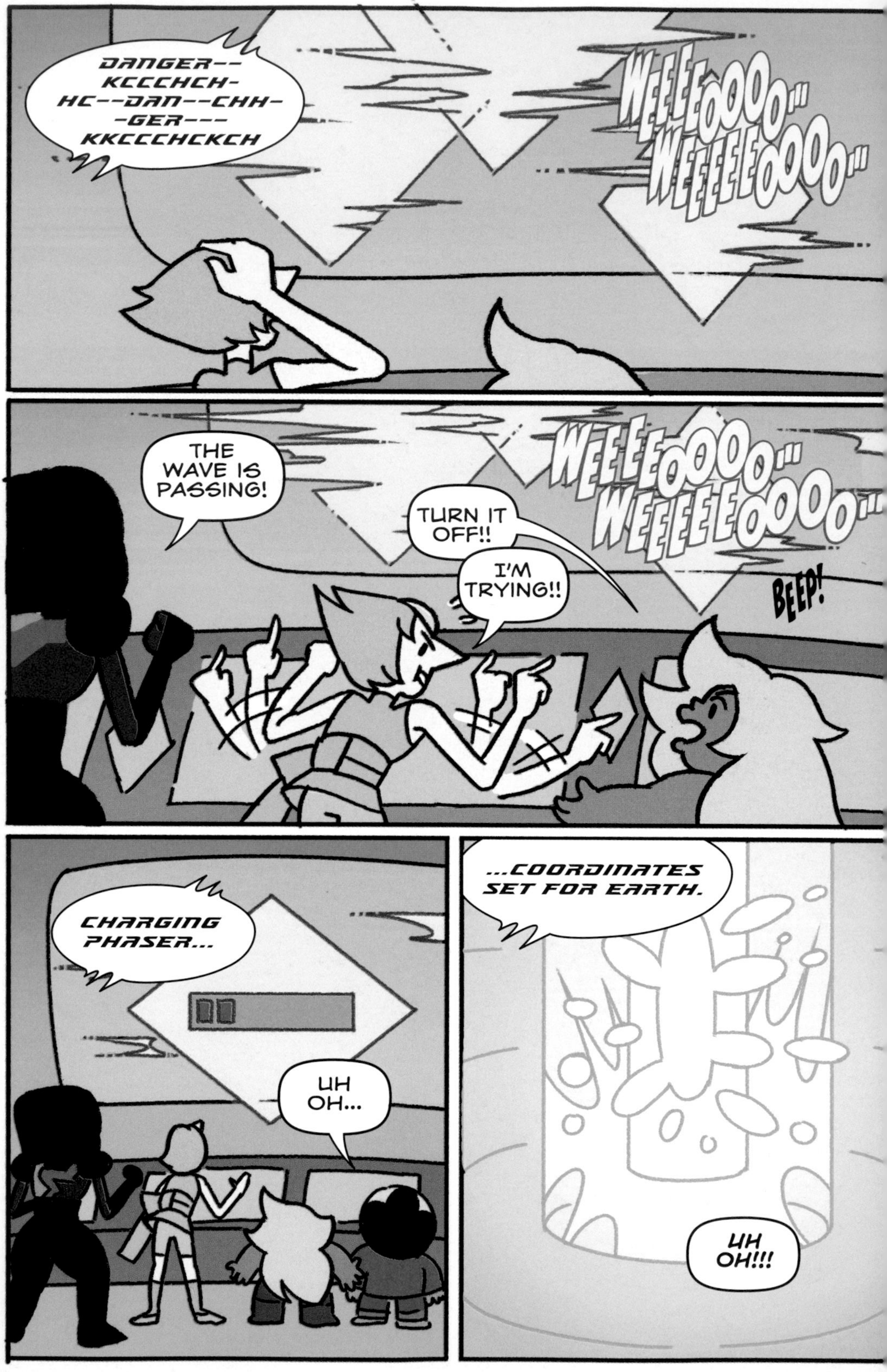
DANGER-- KCCCHCH- HC--DAN--CHH- -GER--- KKCCCHCKCH
WEEEEOOOO-"
WEEEEEOOOO-"
THE WAVE IS PASSING!
WEEEEOOOO-"
WEEEEEOOOO-"
TURN IT OFF!!
I'M TRYING!!
BEEP!
CHARGING PHASER...
UH OH...
...COORDINATES SET FOR EARTH.
UH OH!!!

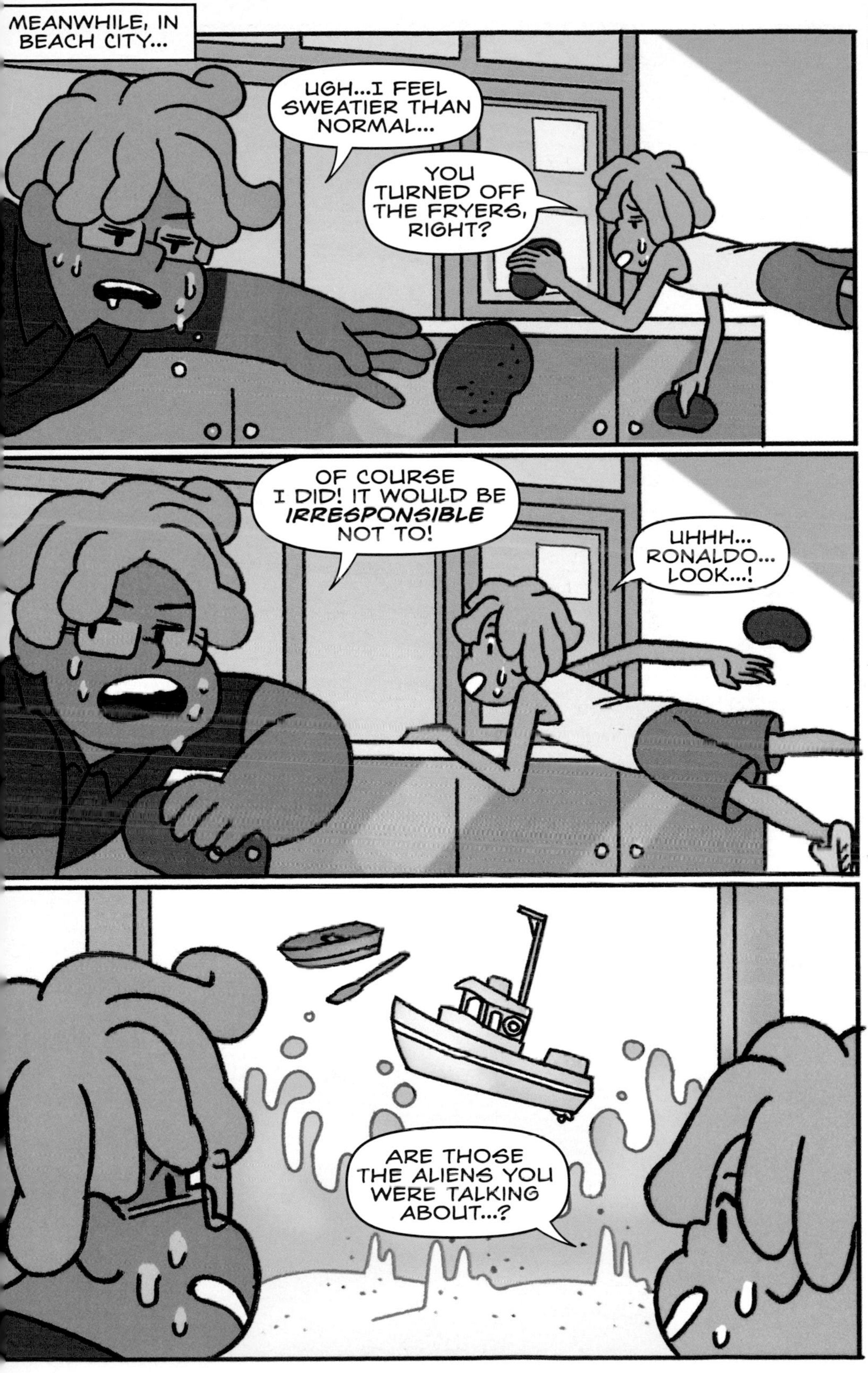
MEANWHILE, IN BEACH CITY...
UGH...I FEEL SWEATIER THAN NORMAL...
YOU TURNED OFF THE FRYERS, RIGHT?
OF COURSE I DID! IT WOULD BE *IRRESPONSIBLE* NOT TO!
UHHH... RONALDO... LOOK...!
ARE THOSE THE ALIENS YOU WERE TALKING ABOUT...?

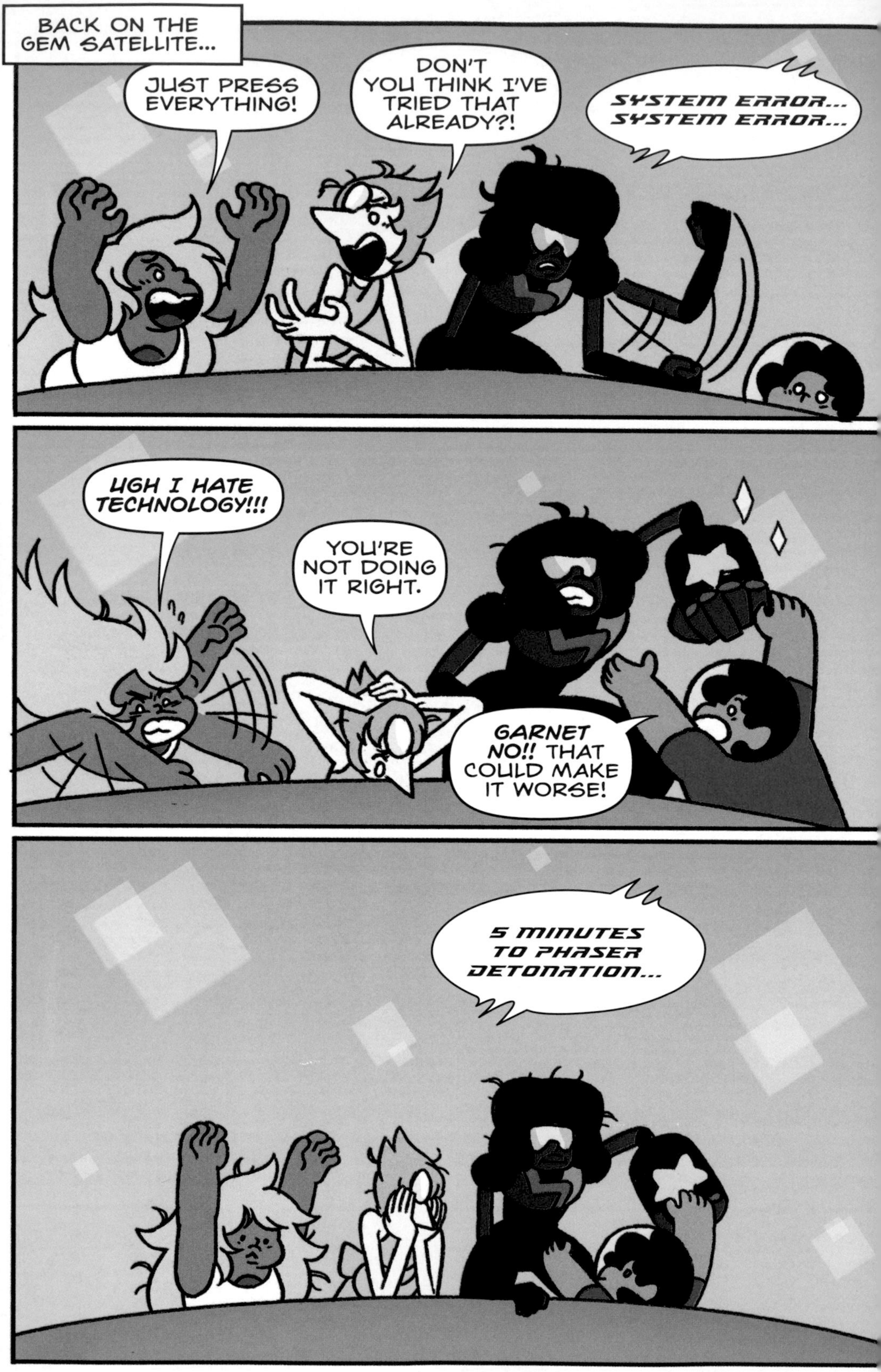
BACK ON THE GEM SATELLITE...
JUST PRESS EVERYTHING!
DON'T YOU THINK I'VE TRIED THAT ALREADY?!
SYSTEM ERROR... SYSTEM ERROR...
UGH I HATE TECHNOLOGY!!!
YOU'RE NOT DOING IT RIGHT.
GARNET NO!! THAT COULD MAKE IT WORSE!
5 MINUTES TO PHASER DETONATION...

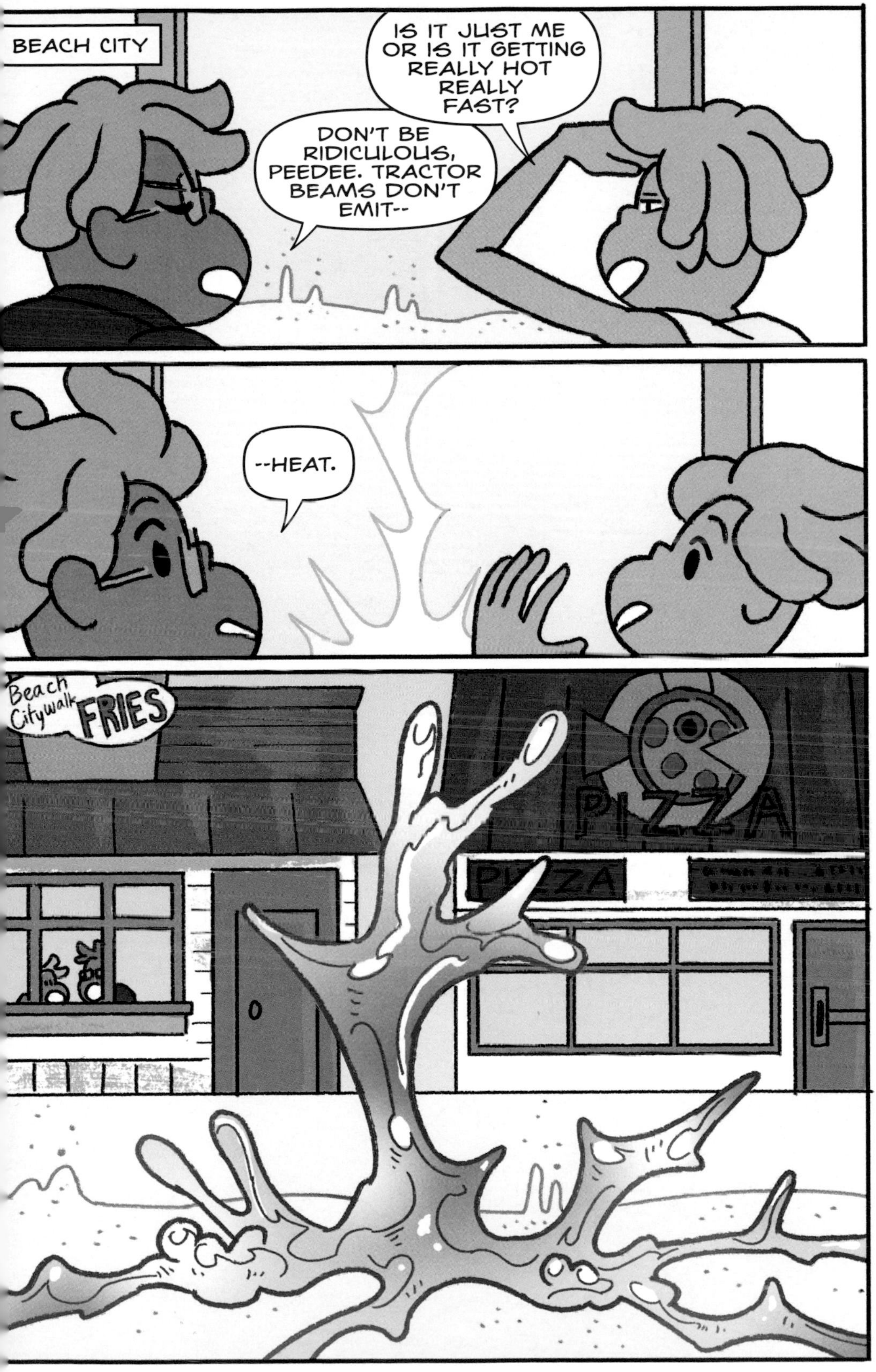
BEACH CITY
IS IT JUST ME OR IS IT GETTING REALLY HOT REALLY FAST?
DON'T BE RIDICULOUS, PEEDEE. TRACTOR BEAMS DON'T EMIT--
--HEAT.
Beach Citywalk FRIES
PIZZA
PIZZA

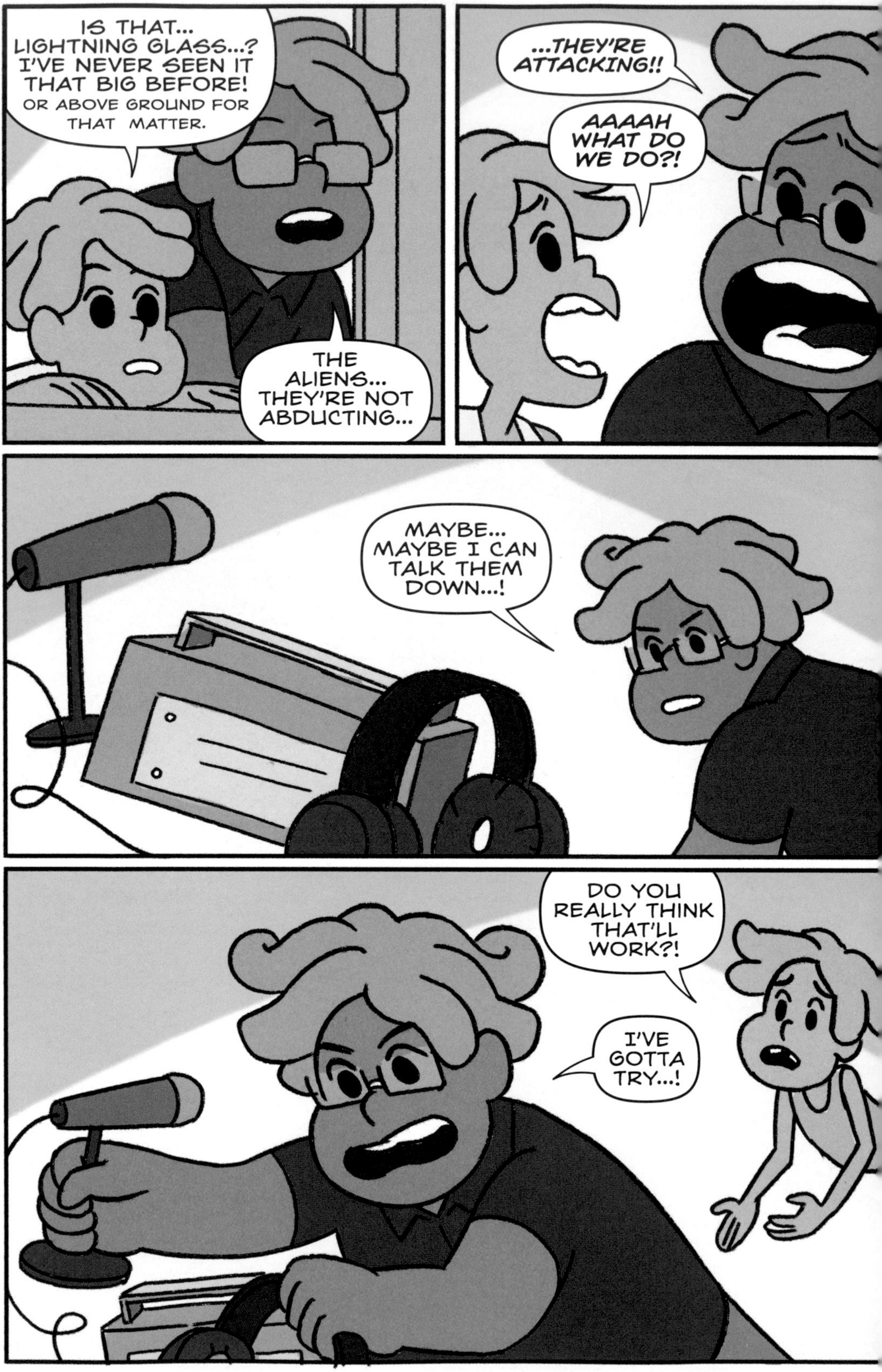
IS THAT... LIGHTNING GLASS...? I'VE NEVER SEEN IT THAT BIG BEFORE! OR ABOVE GROUND FOR THAT MATTER.
THE ALIENS... THEY'RE NOT ABDUCTING...
...THEY'RE ATTACKING!!
AAAAH WHAT DO WE DO?!
MAYBE... MAYBE I CAN TALK THEM DOWN...!
DO YOU REALLY THINK THAT'LL WORK?!
I'VE GOTTA TRY...!

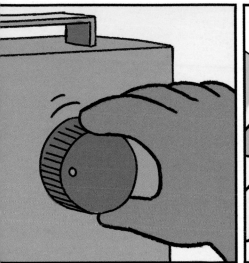

TESTING TESTING!! HELLO! THIS IS RONALDO FRYMAN OF EARTH CONTACTING ALL ALIEN INVADERS!

PLEASE DON'T KILL US!

I KNOW YOU HAVE NO REASON TO BELIEVE US, BUT THIS IS A PEACEFUL PLANET...

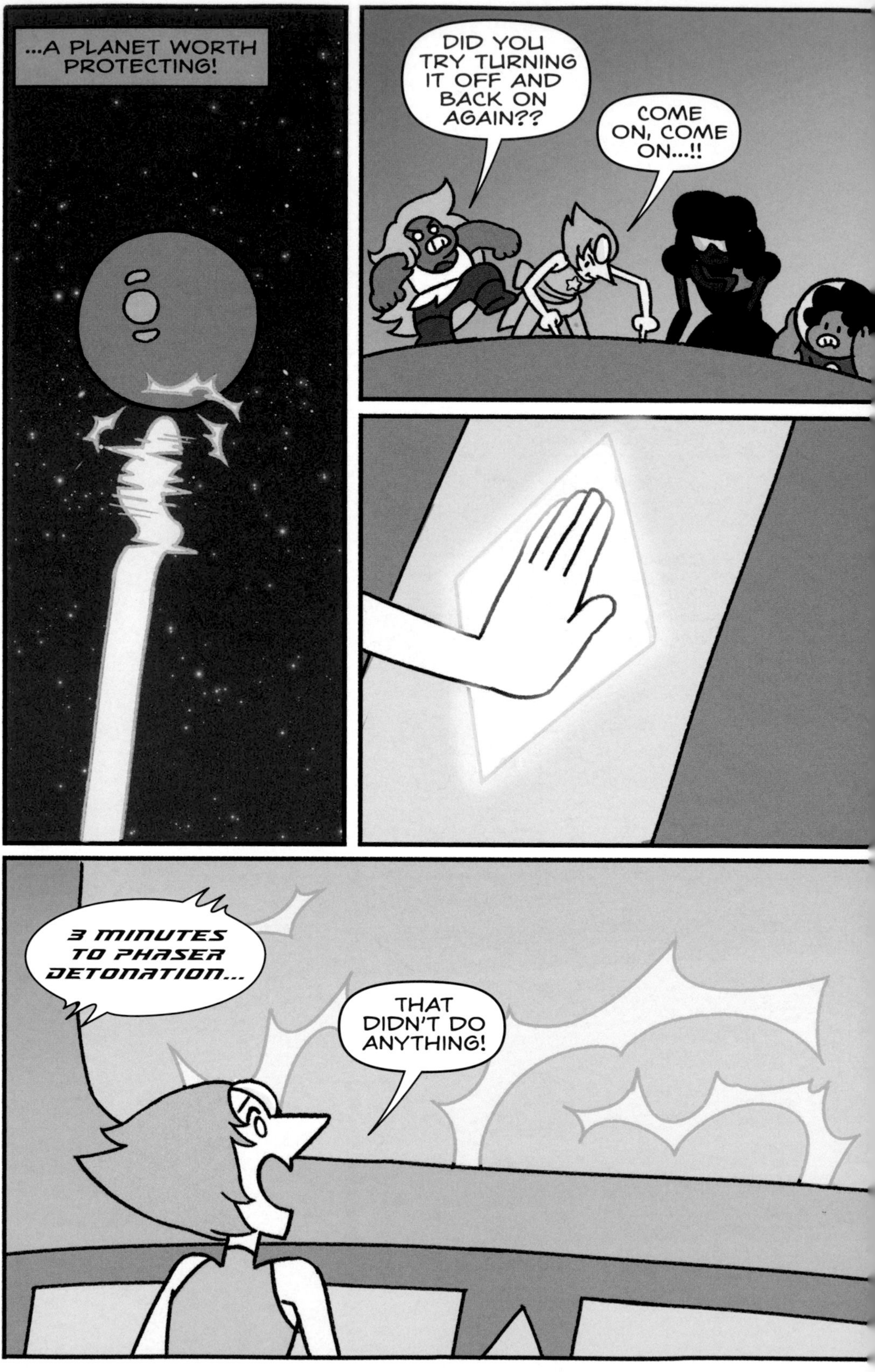
...A PLANET WORTH PROTECTING!
DID YOU TRY TURNING IT OFF AND BACK ON AGAIN??
COME ON, COME ON...!!
3 MINUTES TO PHASER DETONATION...
THAT DIDN'T DO ANYTHING!

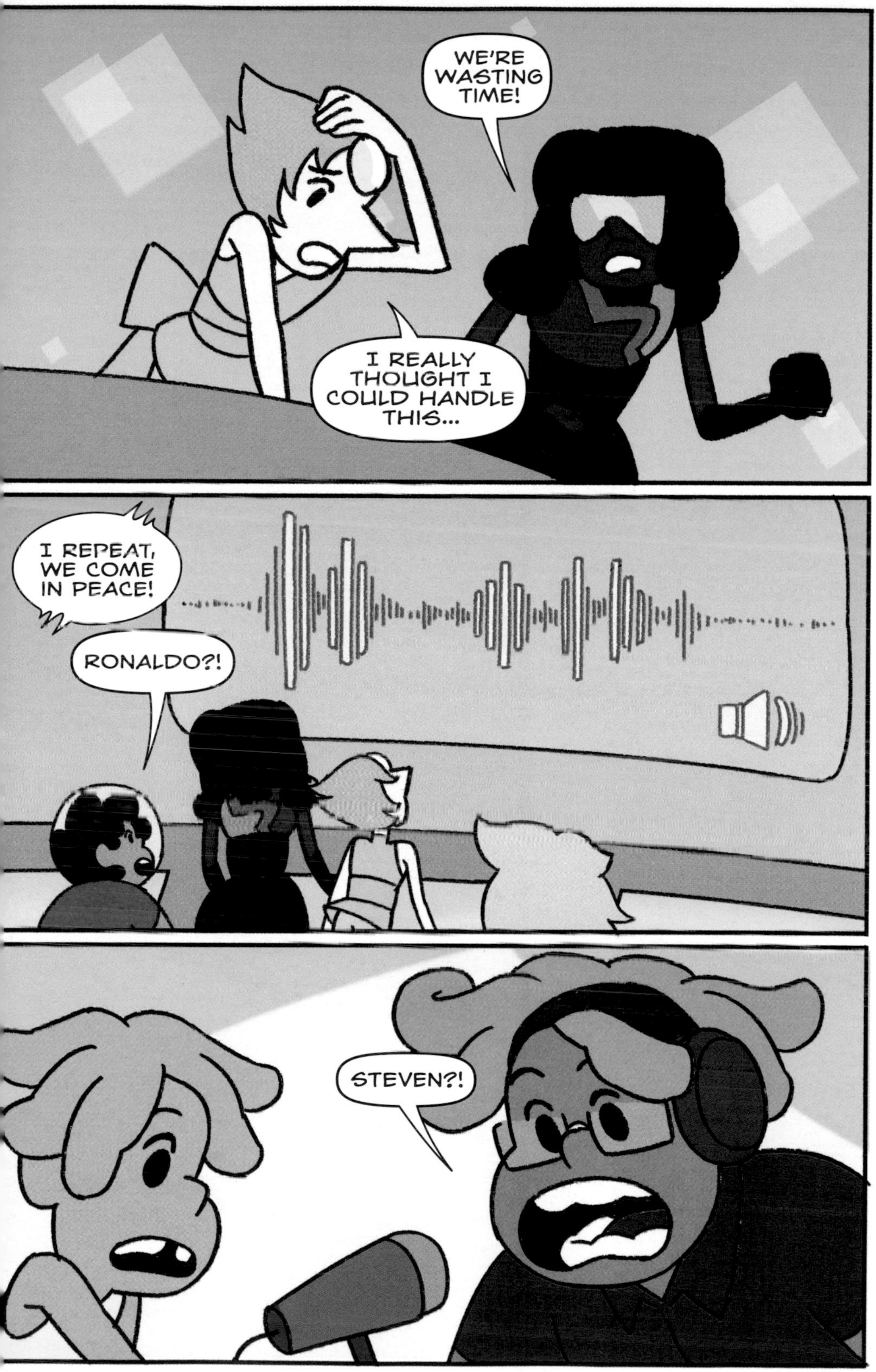
WE'RE WASTING TIME!
I REALLY THOUGHT I COULD HANDLE THIS...
I REPEAT, WE COME IN PEACE!
RONALDO?!
STEVEN?!

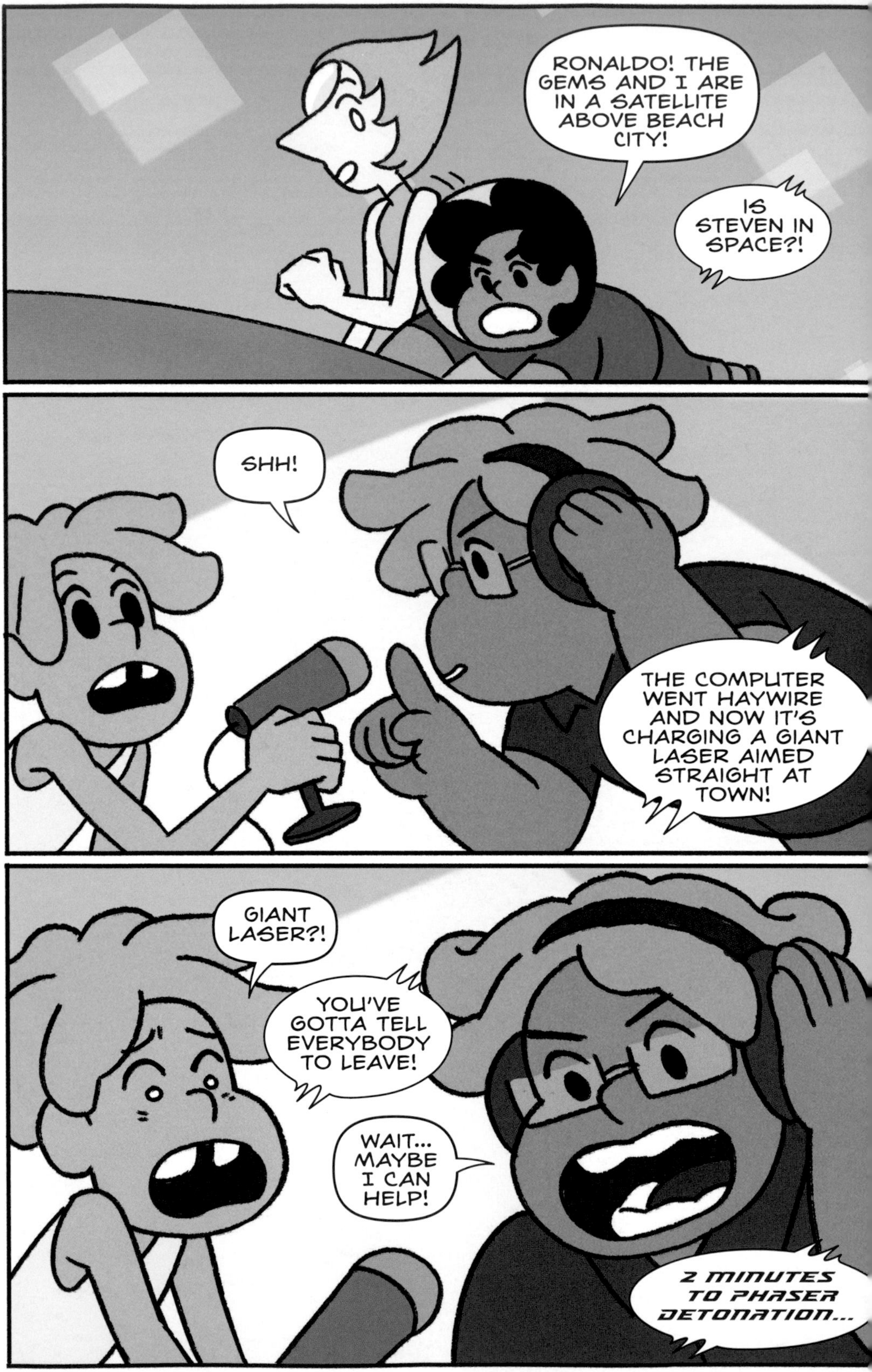
RONALDO! THE GEMS AND I ARE IN A SATELLITE ABOVE BEACH CITY!
IS STEVEN IN SPACE?!
SHH!
THE COMPUTER WENT HAYWIRE AND NOW IT'S CHARGING A GIANT LASER AIMED STRAIGHT AT TOWN!
GIANT LASER?!
YOU'VE GOTTA TELL EVERYBODY TO LEAVE!
WAIT... MAYBE I CAN HELP!
2 MINUTES TO PHASER DETONATION...

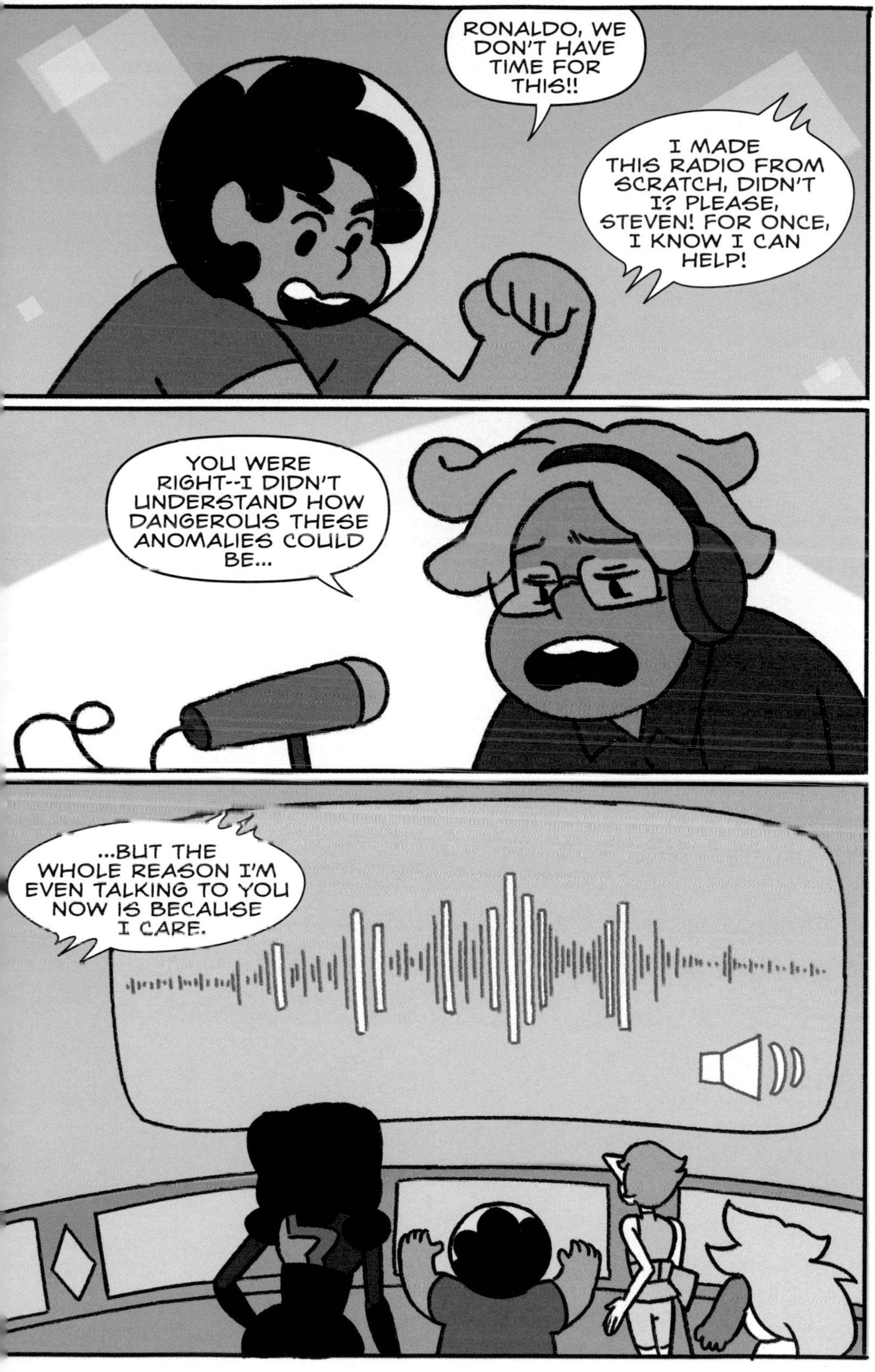
RONALDO, WE DON'T HAVE TIME FOR THIS!!
I MADE THIS RADIO FROM SCRATCH, DIDN'T I? PLEASE, STEVEN! FOR ONCE, I KNOW I CAN HELP!
YOU WERE RIGHT--I DIDN'T UNDERSTAND HOW DANGEROUS THESE ANOMALIES COULD BE...
...BUT THE WHOLE REASON I'M EVEN TALKING TO YOU NOW IS BECAUSE I CARE.

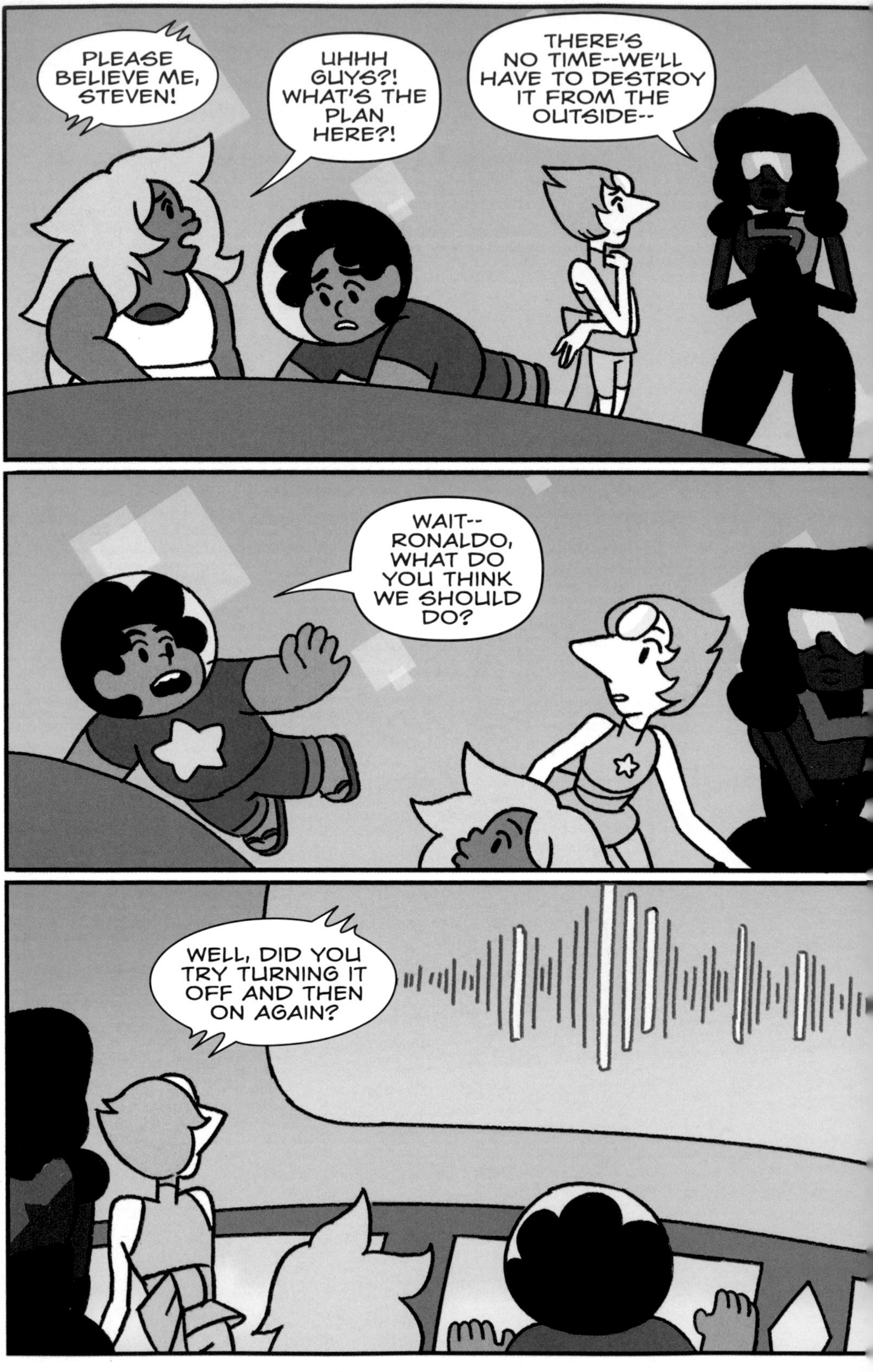
PLEASE BELIEVE ME, STEVEN!
UHHH GUYS?! WHAT'S THE PLAN HERE?!
THERE'S NO TIME--WE'LL HAVE TO DESTROY IT FROM THE OUTSIDE--
WAIT-- RONALDO, WHAT DO YOU THINK WE SHOULD DO?
WELL, DID YOU TRY TURNING IT OFF AND THEN ON AGAIN?

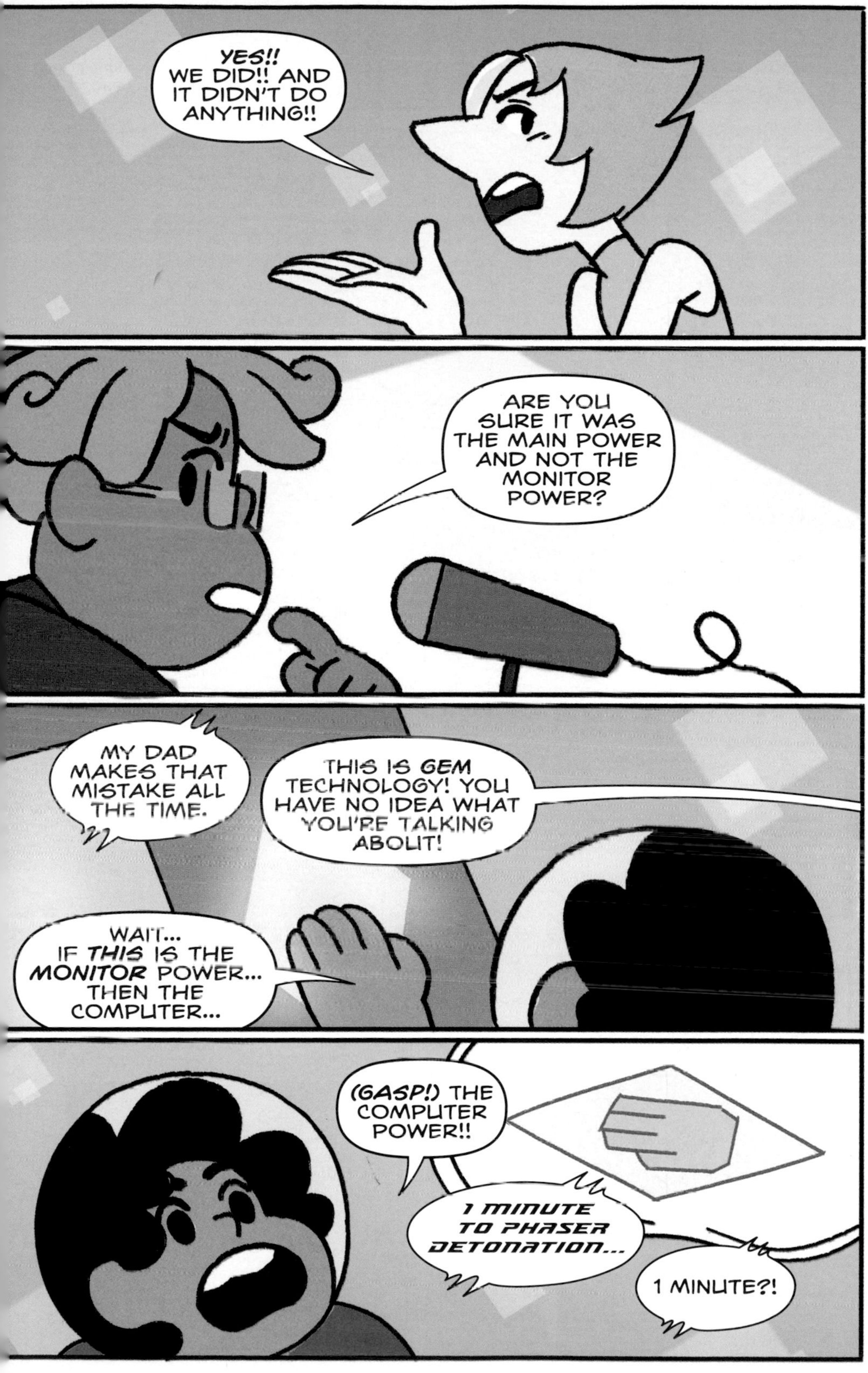
YES!! WE DID!! AND IT DIDN'T DO ANYTHING!!
ARE YOU SURE IT WAS THE MAIN POWER AND NOT THE MONITOR POWER?
MY DAD MAKES THAT MISTAKE ALL THE TIME.
THIS IS GEM TECHNOLOGY! YOU HAVE NO IDEA WHAT YOU'RE TALKING ABOUT!
WAIT... IF THIS IS THE MONITOR POWER... THEN THE COMPUTER...
(GASP!) THE COMPUTER POWER!!
1 MINUTE TO PHASER DETONATION...
1 MINUTE?!

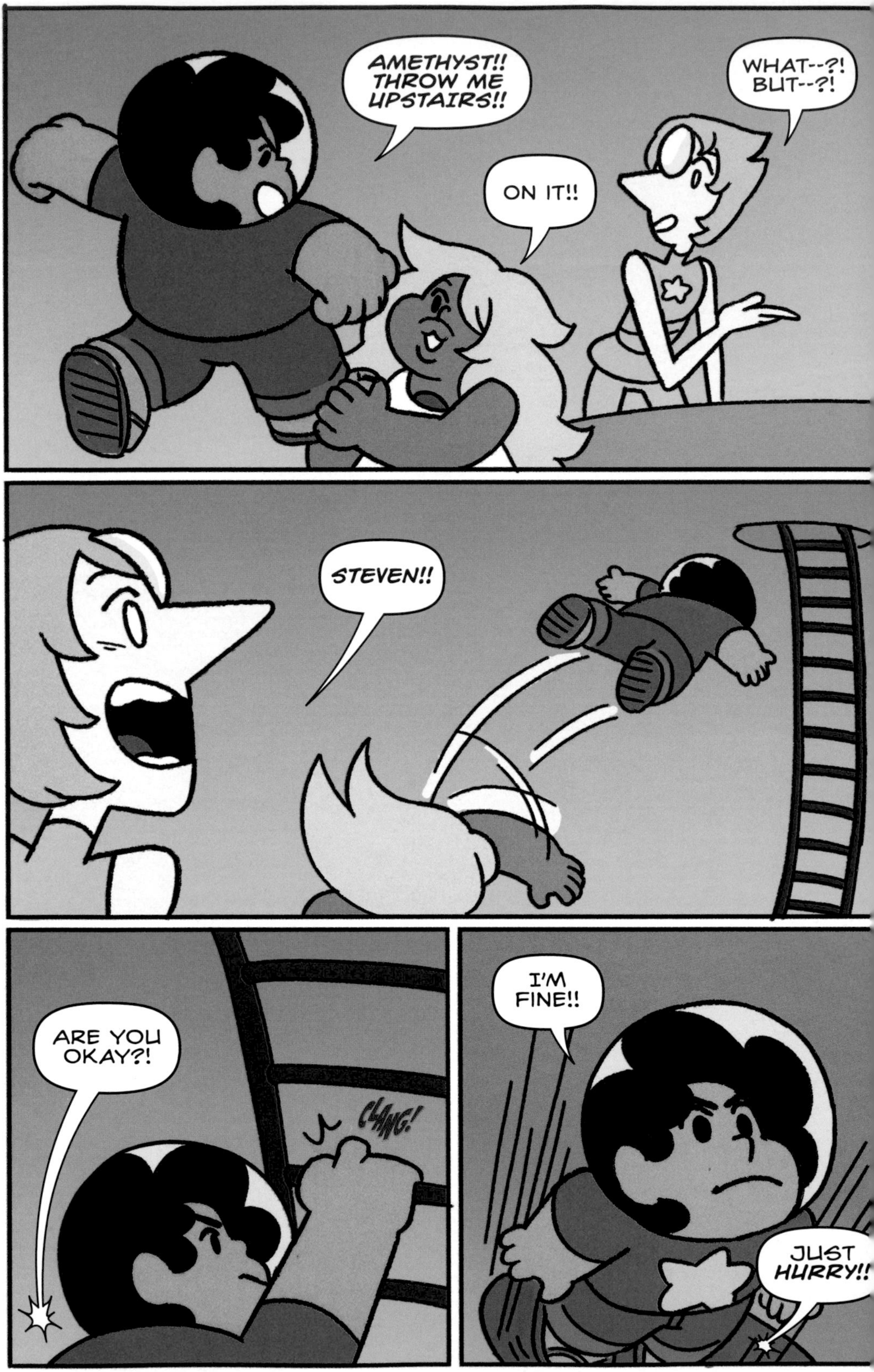
AMETHYST!! THROW ME UPSTAIRS!!
ON IT!!
WHAT--?! BUT--?!
STEVEN!!
ARE YOU OKAY?!
CLANG!
I'M FINE!!
JUST HURRY!!

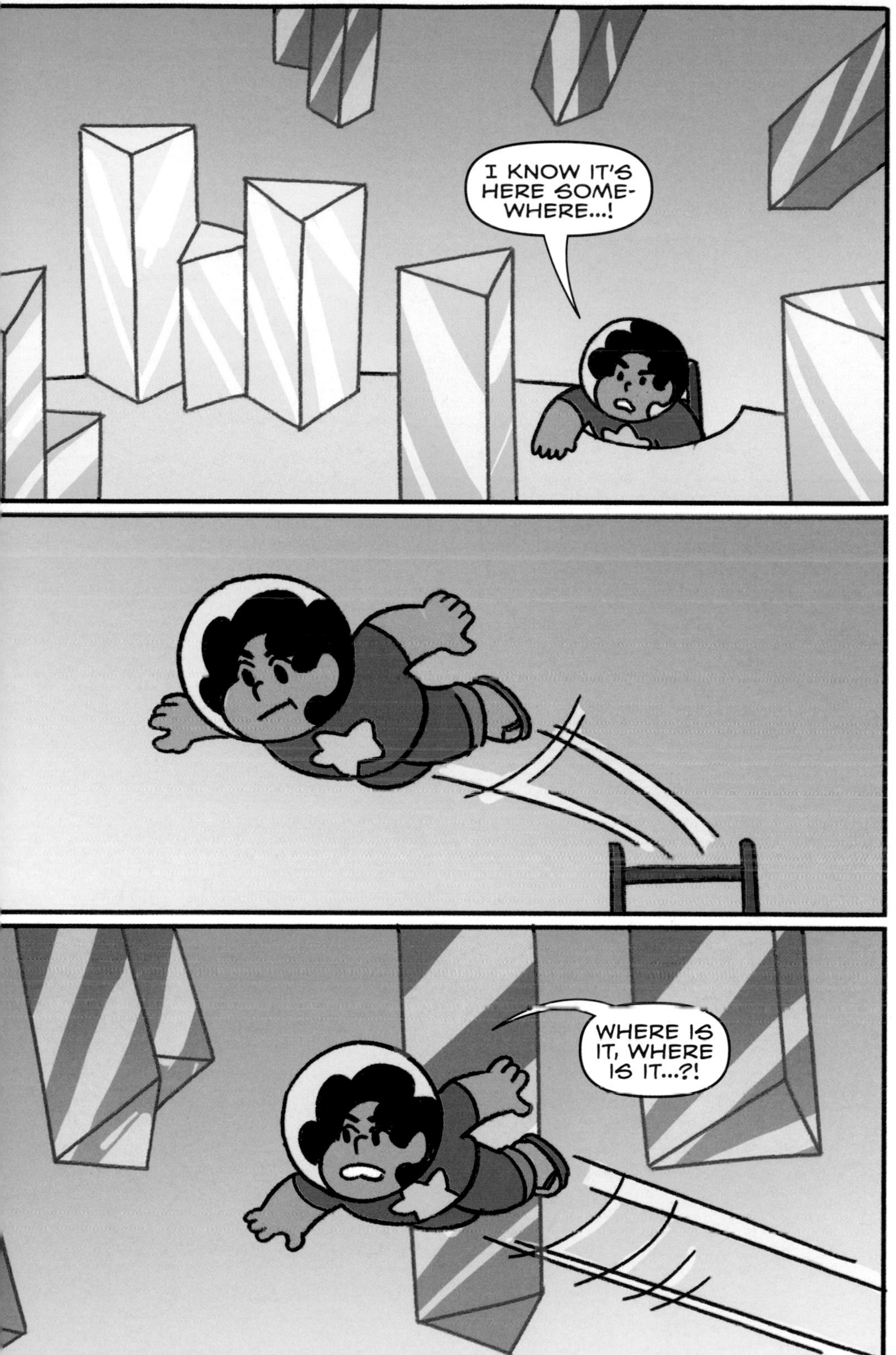
I KNOW IT'S HERE SOME-WHERE...!
WHERE IS IT, WHERE IS IT...?!

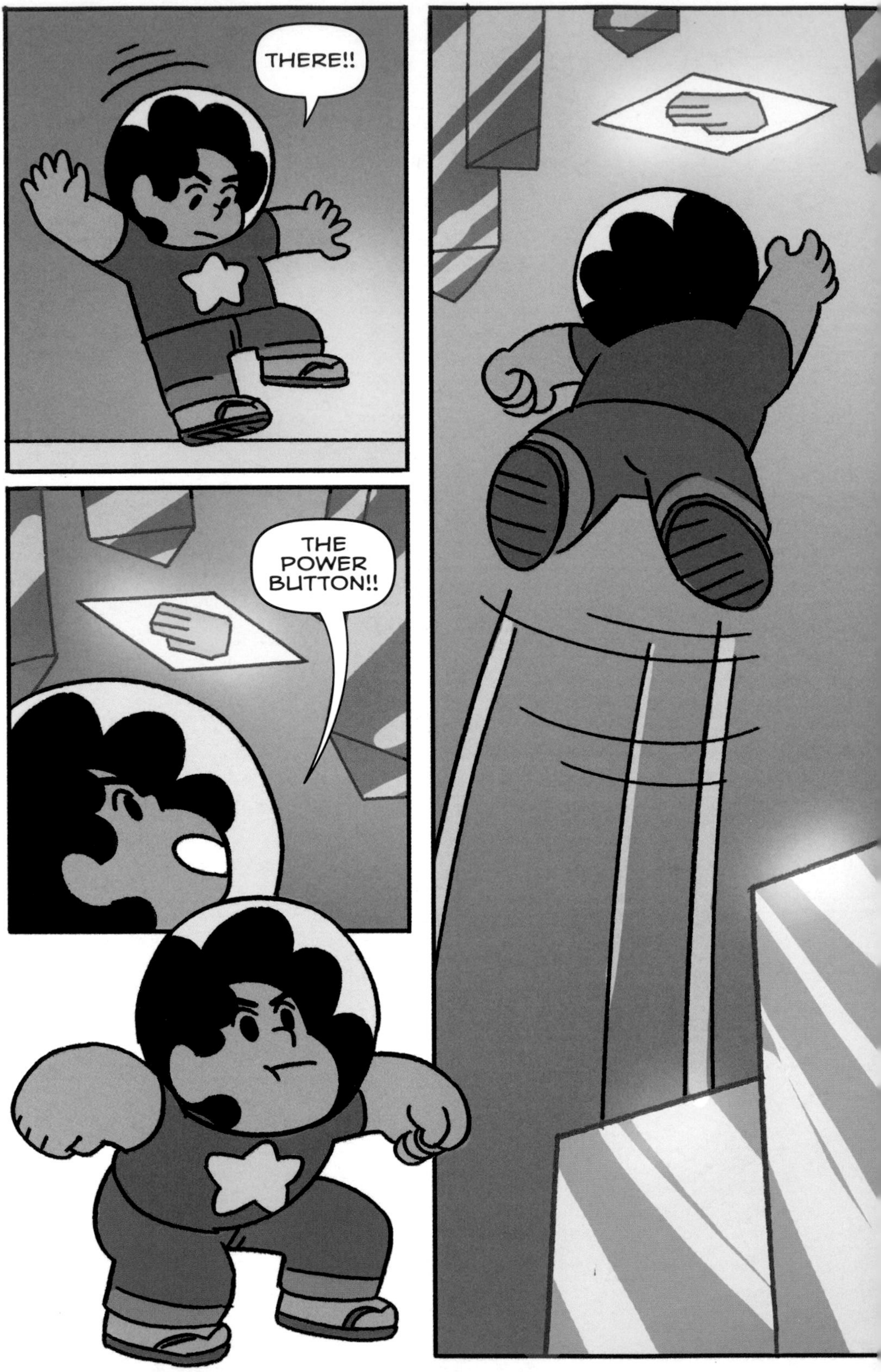
THERE!!
THE POWER BUTTON!!

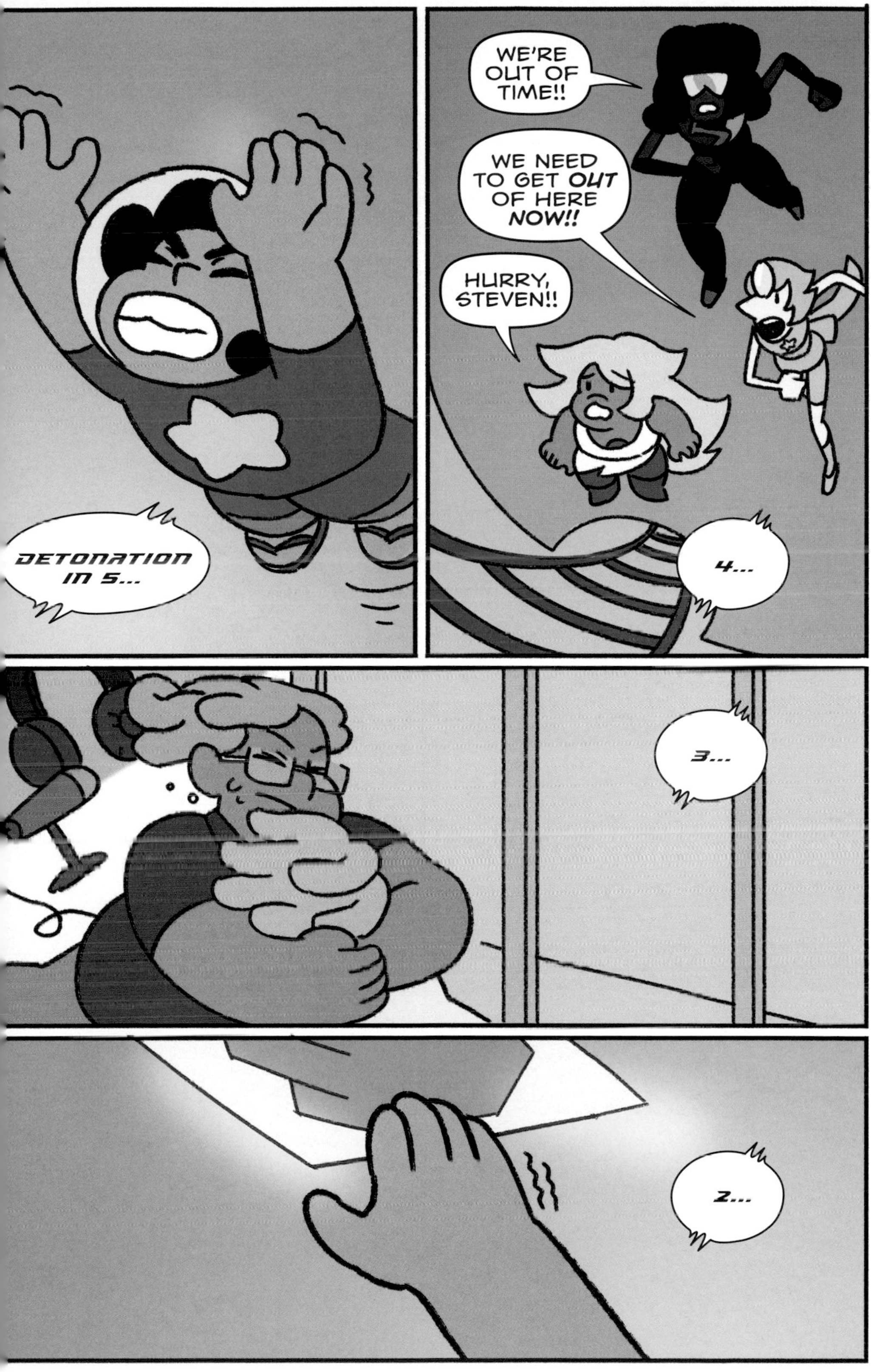
DETONATION IN 5...
WE'RE OUT OF TIME!!
WE NEED TO GET OUT OF HERE NOW!!
HURRY, STEVEN!!
4...
3...
2...

1...

BYOOOOOOOOOOOMMM

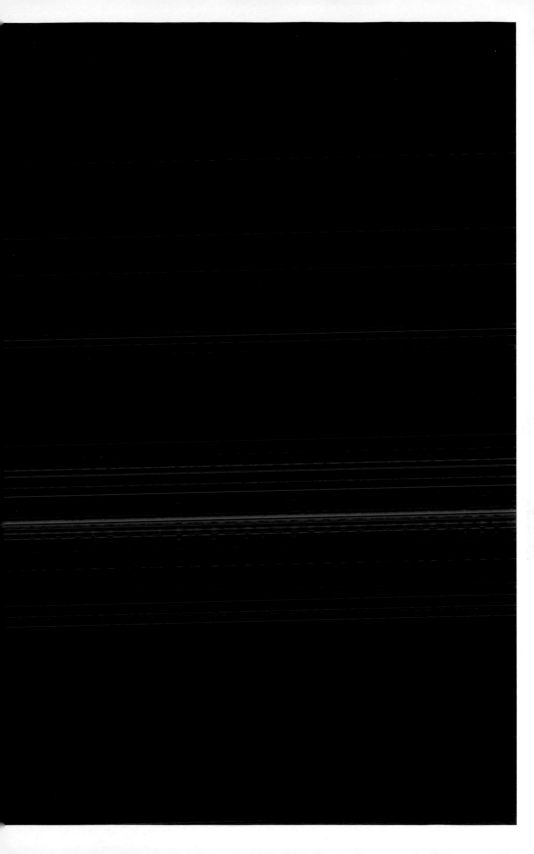

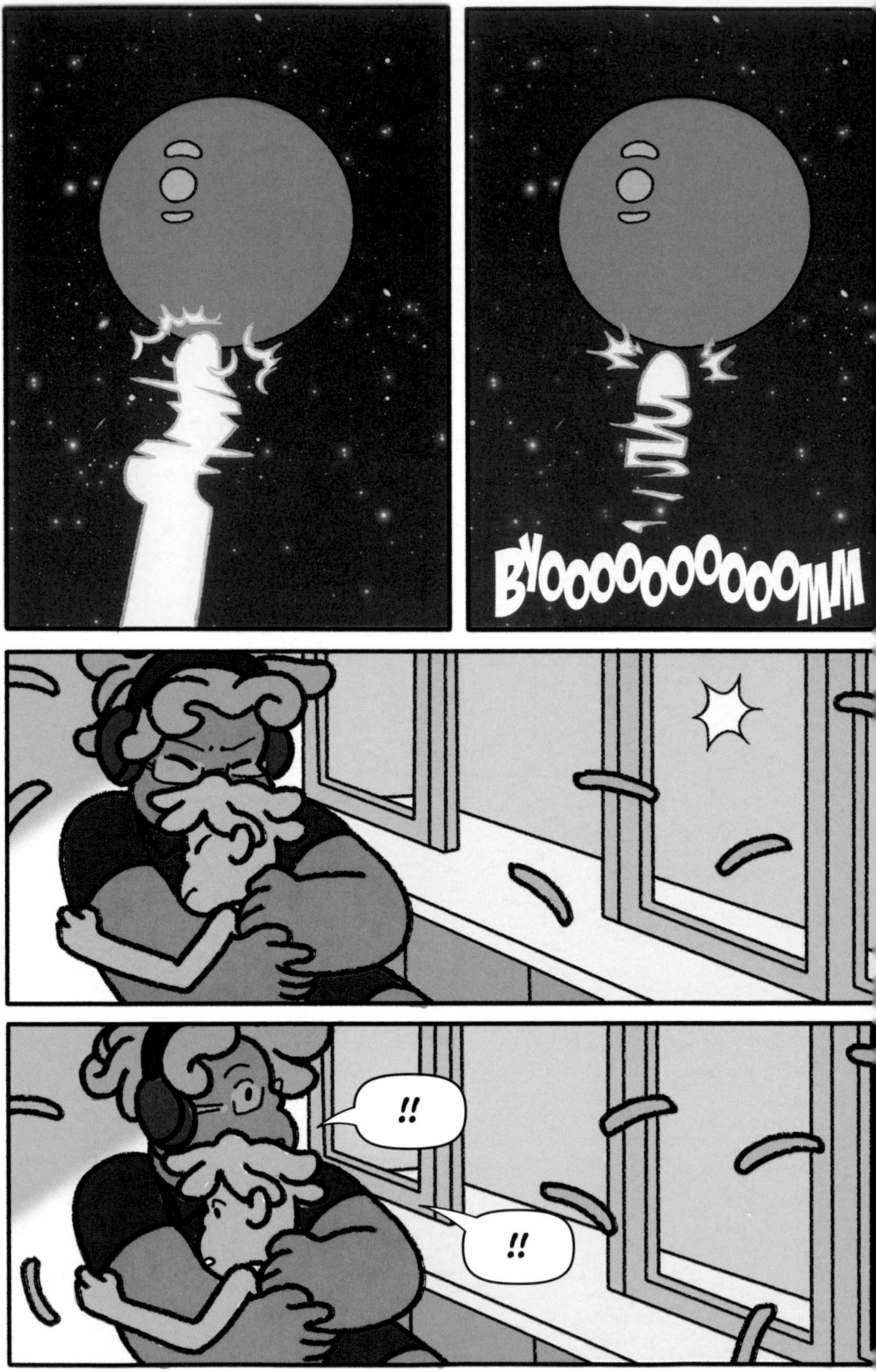
BYOOOOOOOOOOMM
!!
!!

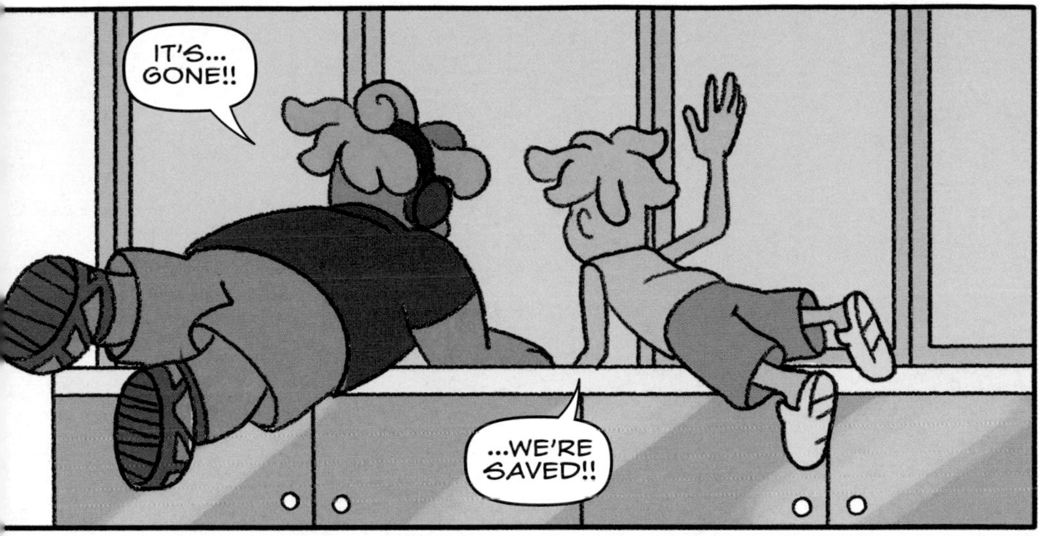
IT'S... GONE!!
...WE'RE SAVED!!
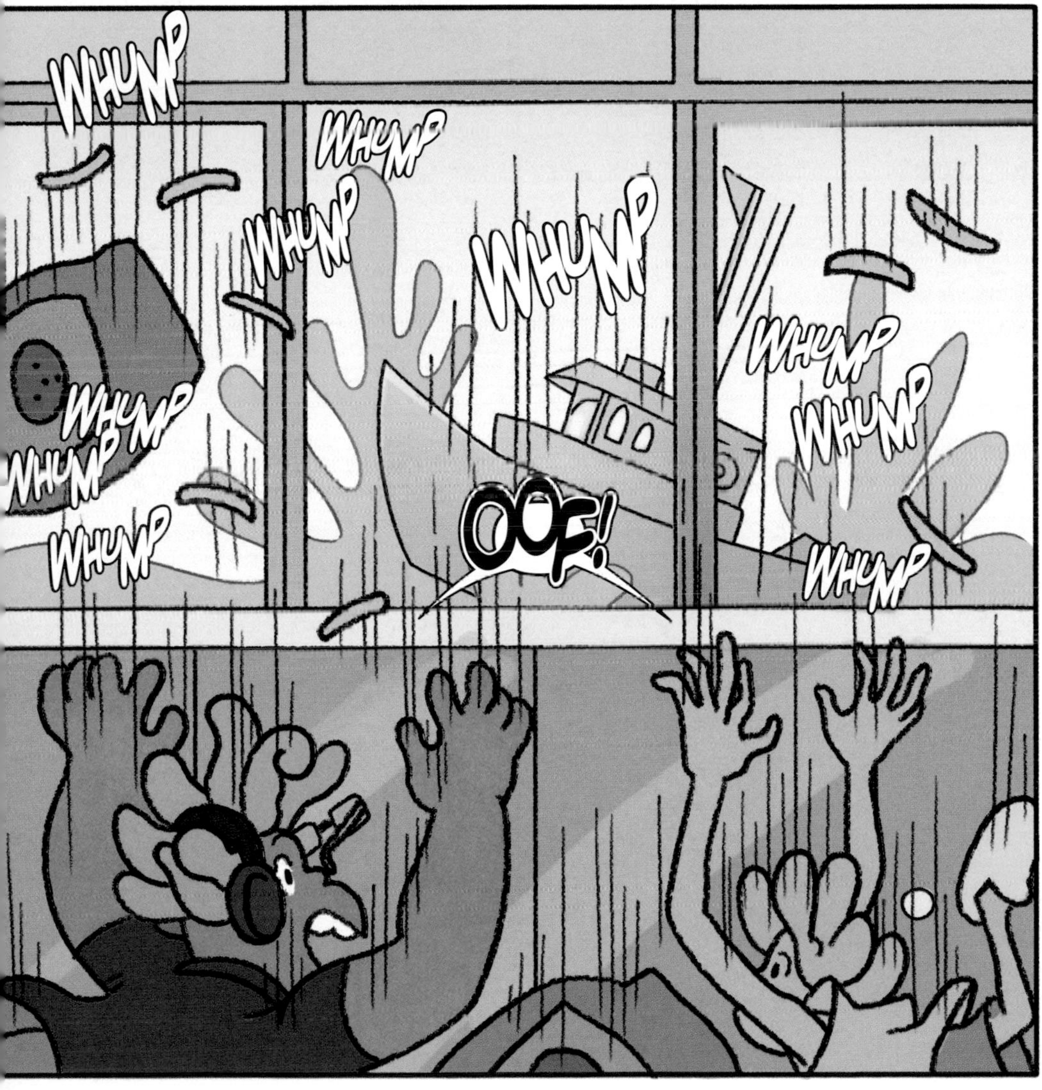
WHUMP
WHUMP
WHUMP
WHUMP
WHUMP
WHUMP
WHUMP
WHUMP
WHUMP
WHUMP
OOF!

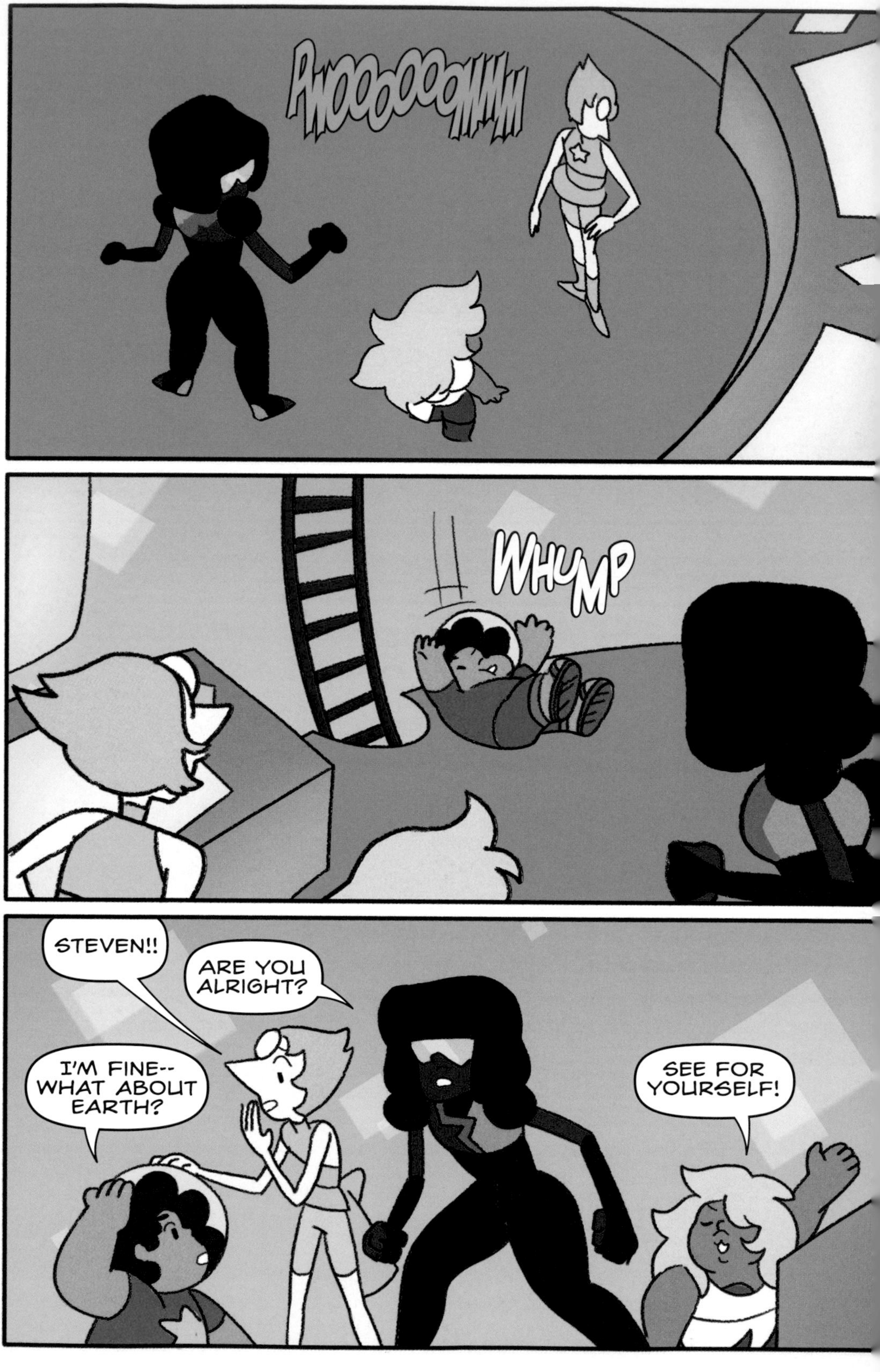
PWOOOOOOMMMM
WHUMP
STEVEN!!
ARE YOU ALRIGHT?
I'M FINE-- WHAT ABOUT EARTH?
SEE FOR YOURSELF!

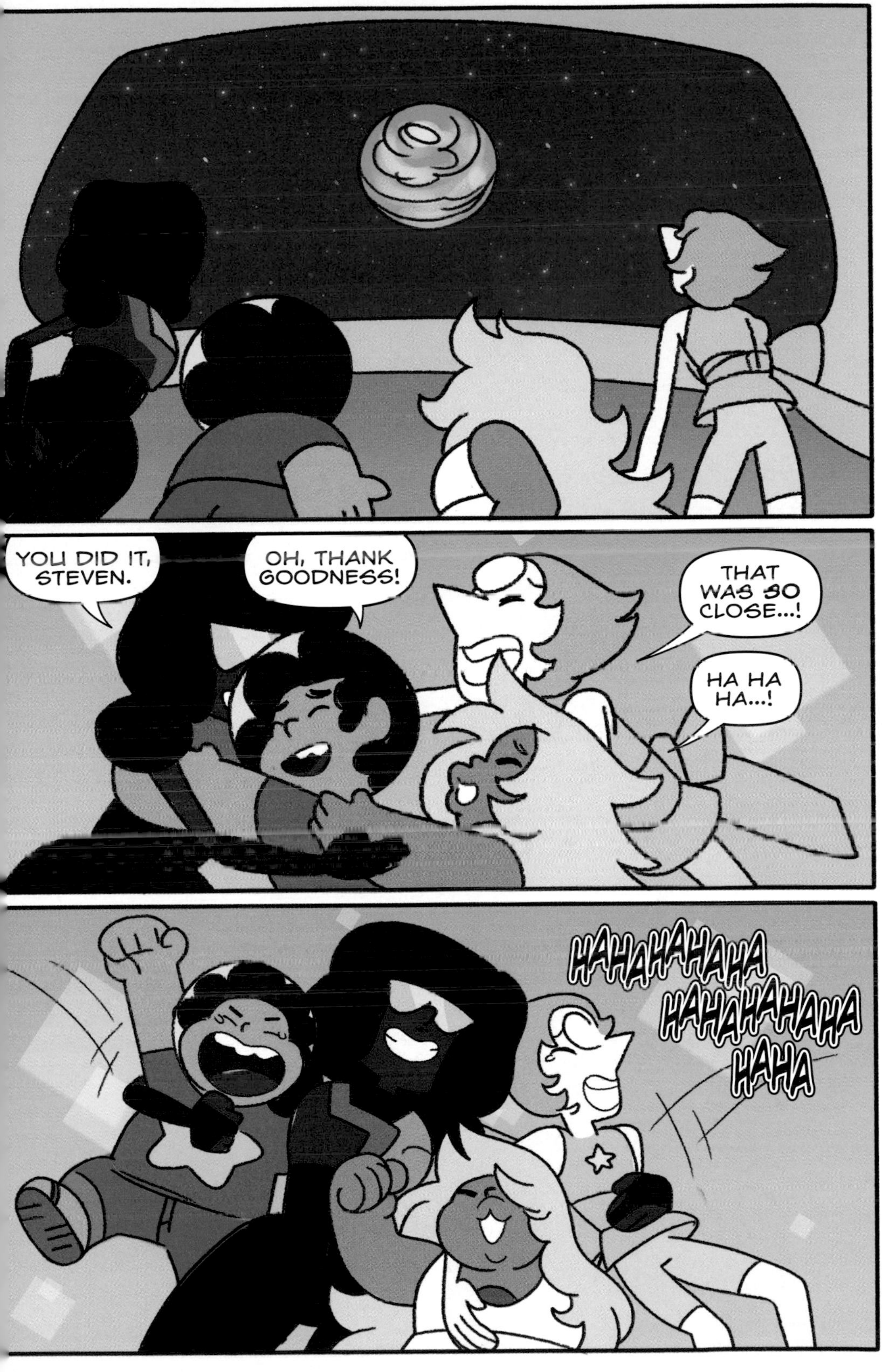
YOU DID IT, STEVEN.
OH, THANK GOODNESS!
THAT WAS SO CLOSE...!
HA HA HA...!
HAHAHAHAHA HAHAHAHAHA HAHA

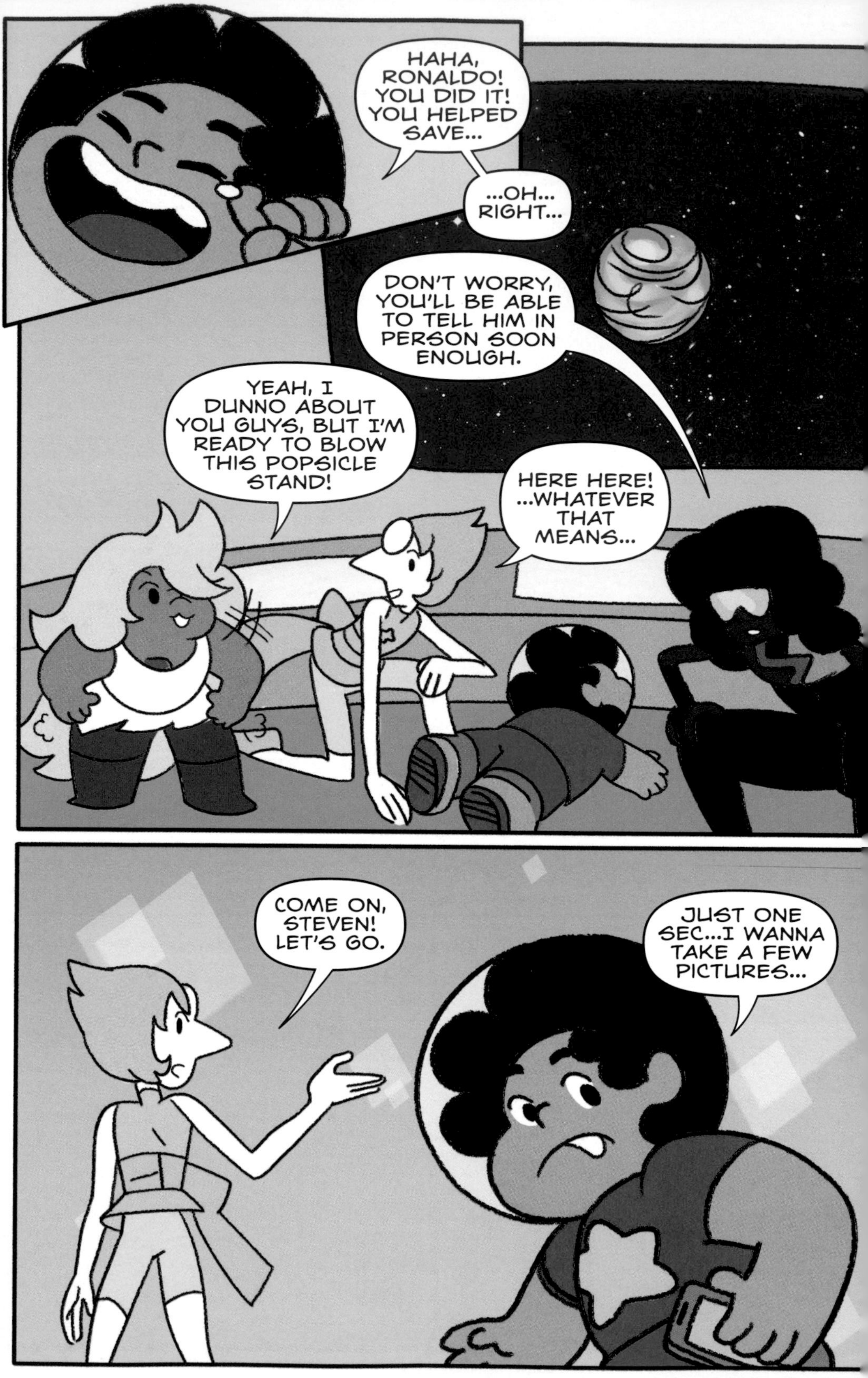
HAHA, RONALDO! YOU DID IT! YOU HELPED SAVE...
...OH... RIGHT...
DON'T WORRY, YOU'LL BE ABLE TO TELL HIM IN PERSON SOON ENOUGH.
YEAH, I DUNNO ABOUT YOU GUYS, BUT I'M READY TO BLOW THIS POPSICLE STAND!
HERE HERE! ...WHATEVER THAT MEANS...
COME ON, STEVEN! LET'S GO.
JUST ONE SEC...I WANNA TAKE A FEW PICTURES...

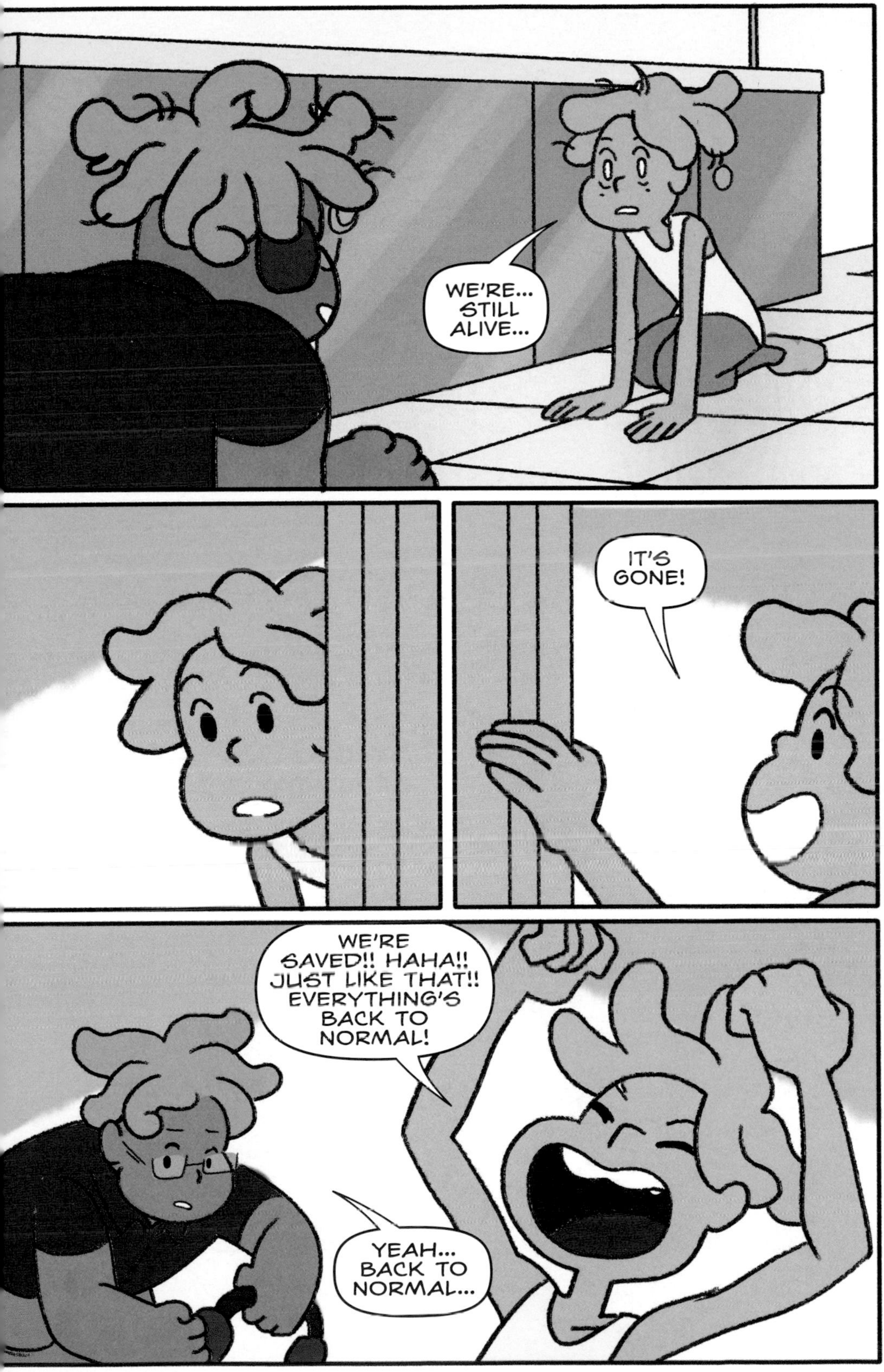
WE'RE... STILL ALIVE...
IT'S GONE!
WE'RE SAVED!! HAHA!! JUST LIKE THAT!! EVERYTHING'S BACK TO NORMAL!
YEAH... BACK TO NORMAL...

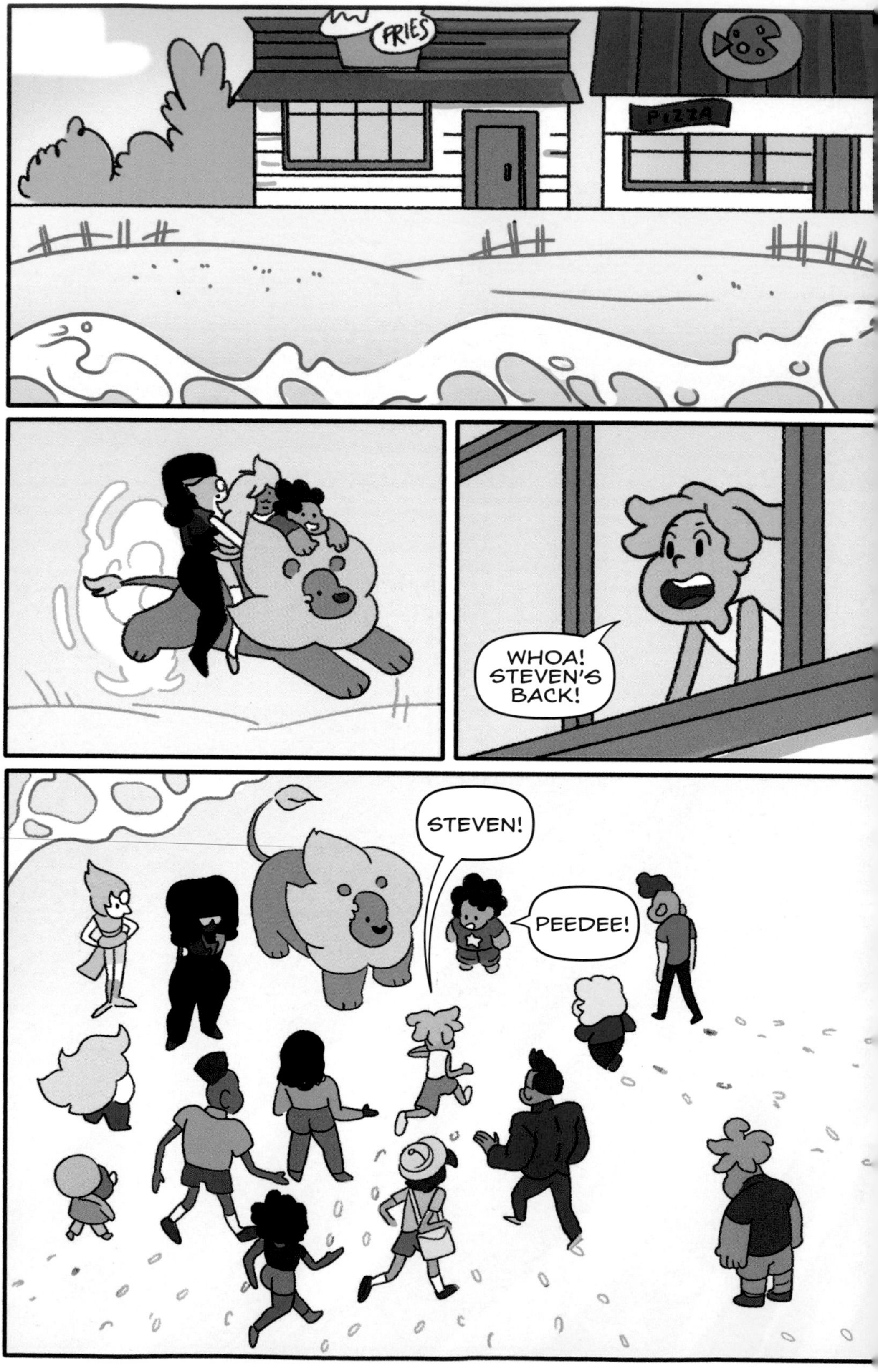
FRIES
PIZZA
WHOA! STEVEN'S BACK!
STEVEN!
PEEDEE!

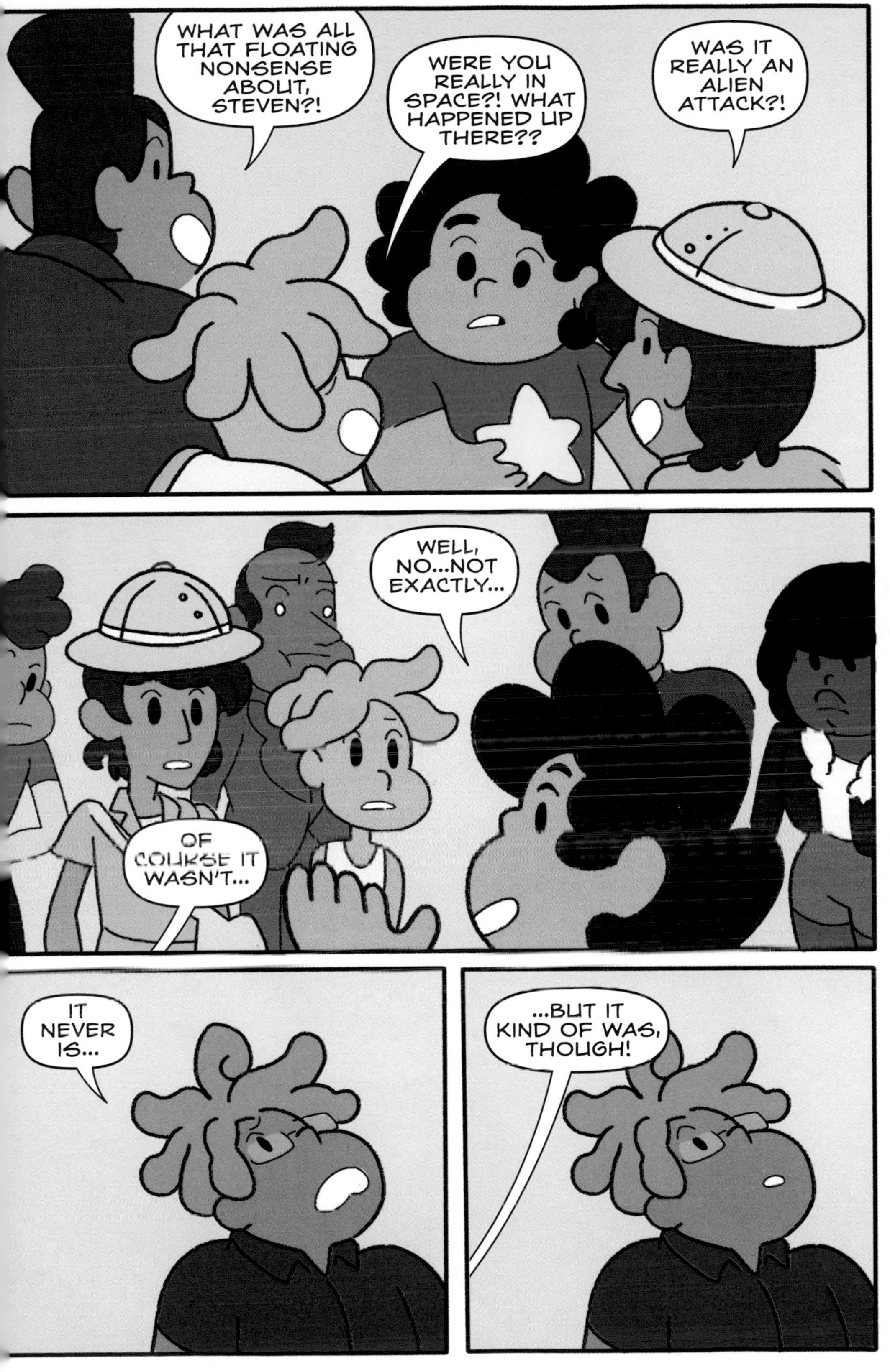
WHAT WAS ALL THAT FLOATING NONSENSE ABOUT, STEVEN?!
WERE YOU REALLY IN SPACE?! WHAT HAPPENED UP THERE??
WAS IT REALLY AN ALIEN ATTACK?!
WELL, NO...NOT EXACTLY...
OF COURSE IT WASN'T...
IT NEVER IS...
...BUT IT KIND OF WAS, THOUGH!

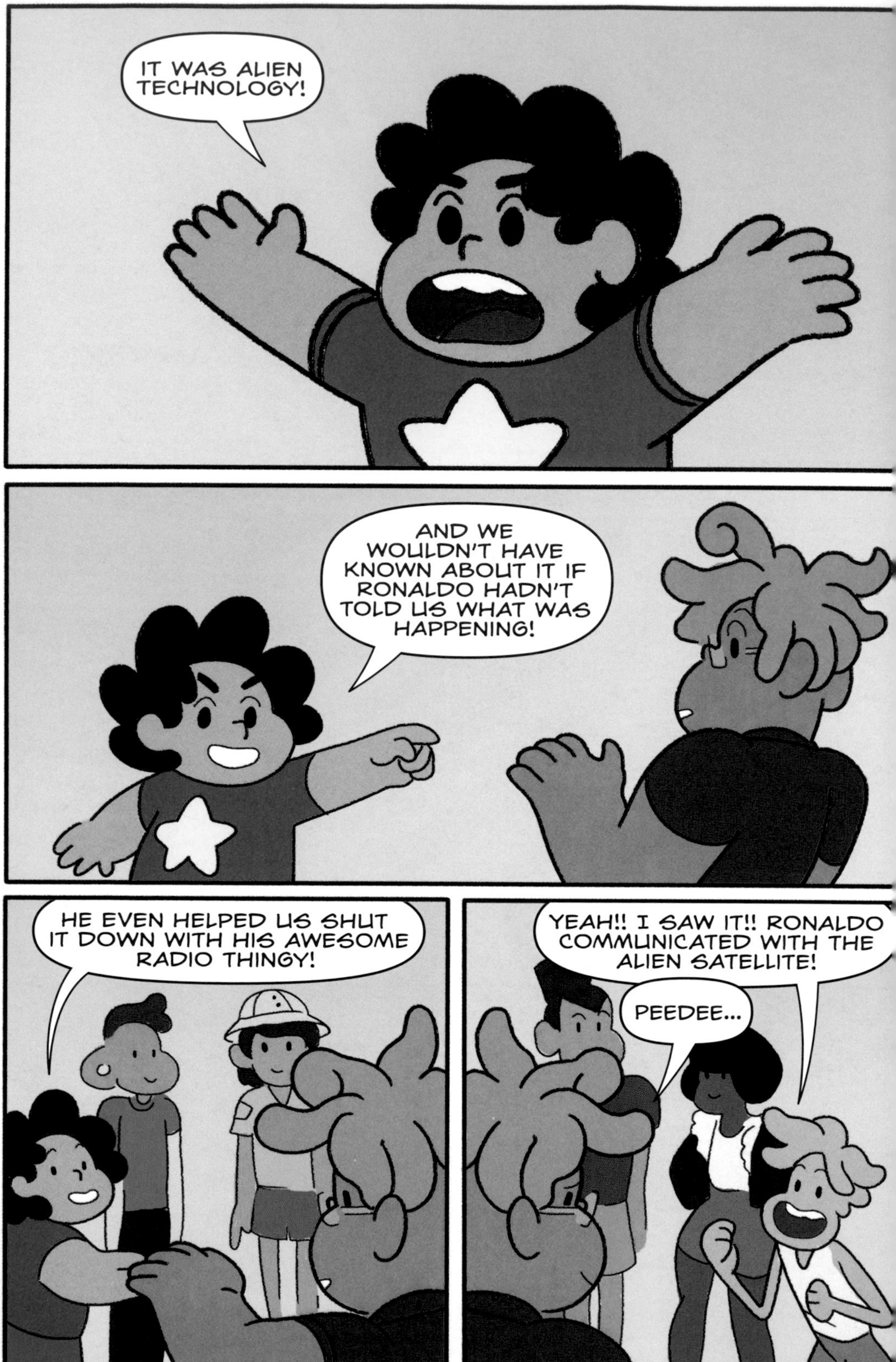
IT WAS ALIEN TECHNOLOGY!
AND WE WOULDN'T HAVE KNOWN ABOUT IT IF RONALDO HADN'T TOLD US WHAT WAS HAPPENING!
HE EVEN HELPED US SHUT IT DOWN WITH HIS AWESOME RADIO THINGY!
YEAH!! I SAW IT!! RONALDO COMMUNICATED WITH THE ALIEN SATELLITE!
PEEDEE...

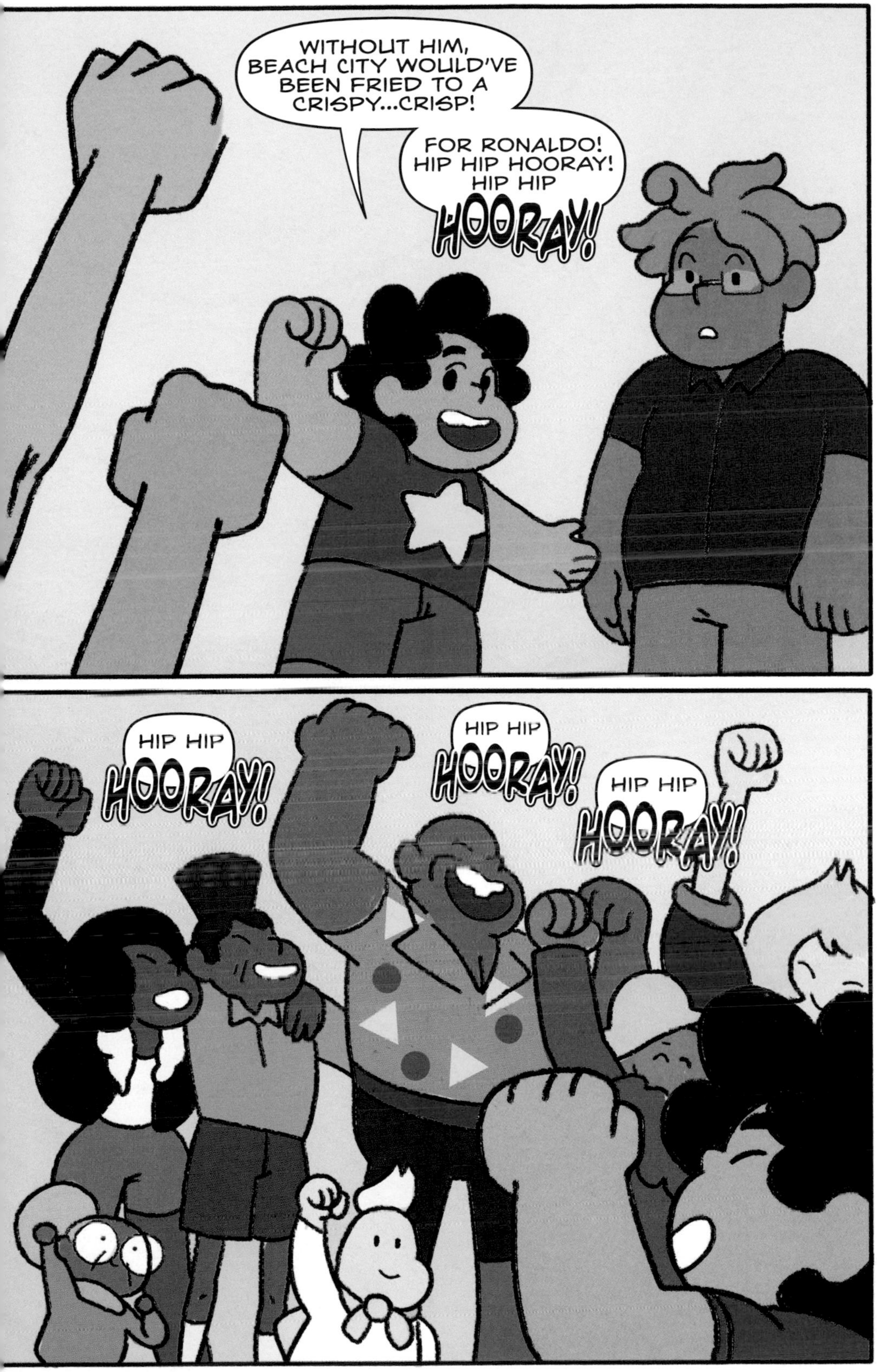
WITHOUT HIM, BEACH CITY WOULD'VE BEEN FRIED TO A CRISPY...CRISP!
FOR RONALDO! HIP HIP HOORAY! HIP HIP
HOORAY!
HIP HIP
HOORAY!
HIP HIP
HOORAY!
HIP HIP
HOORAY!

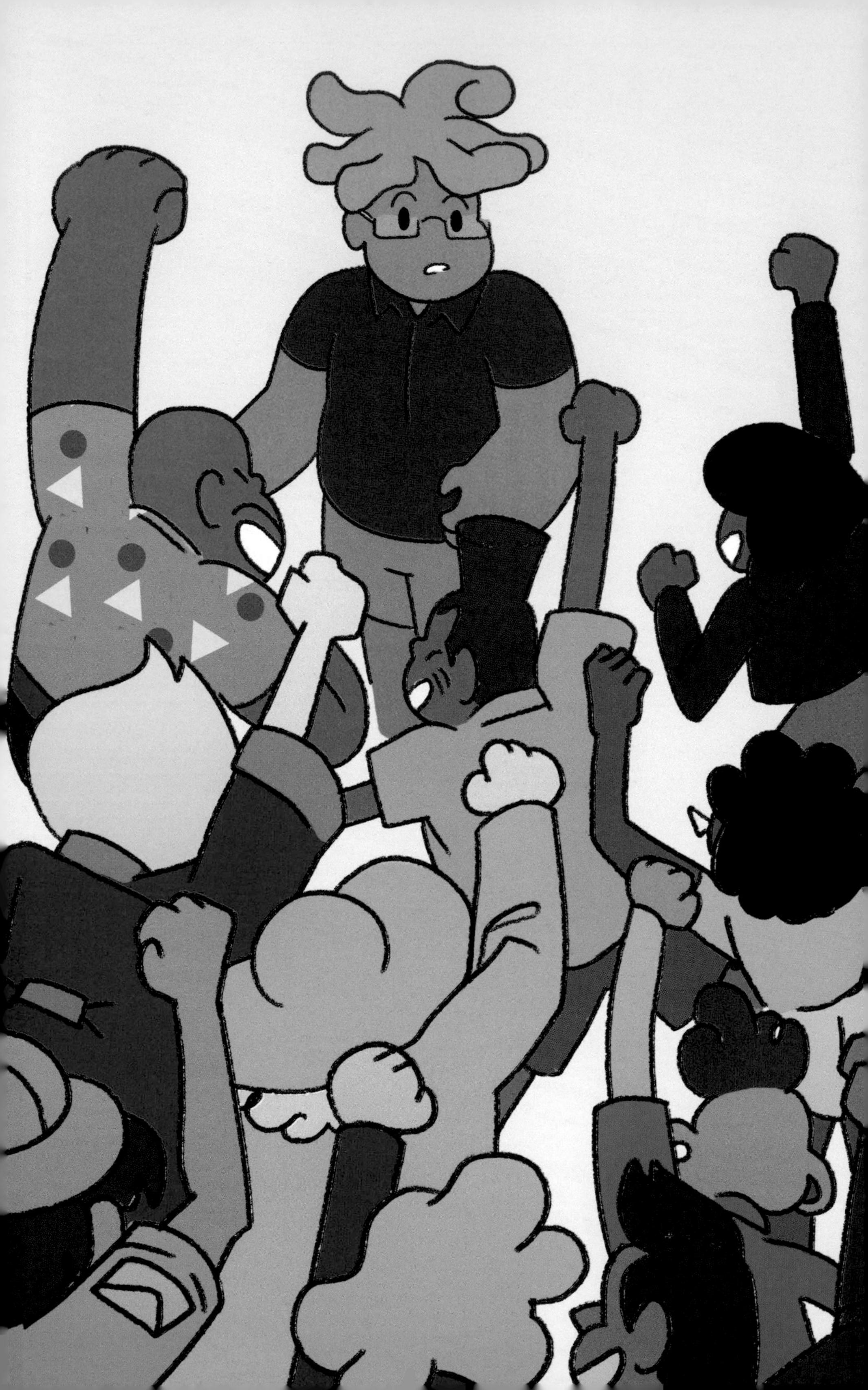

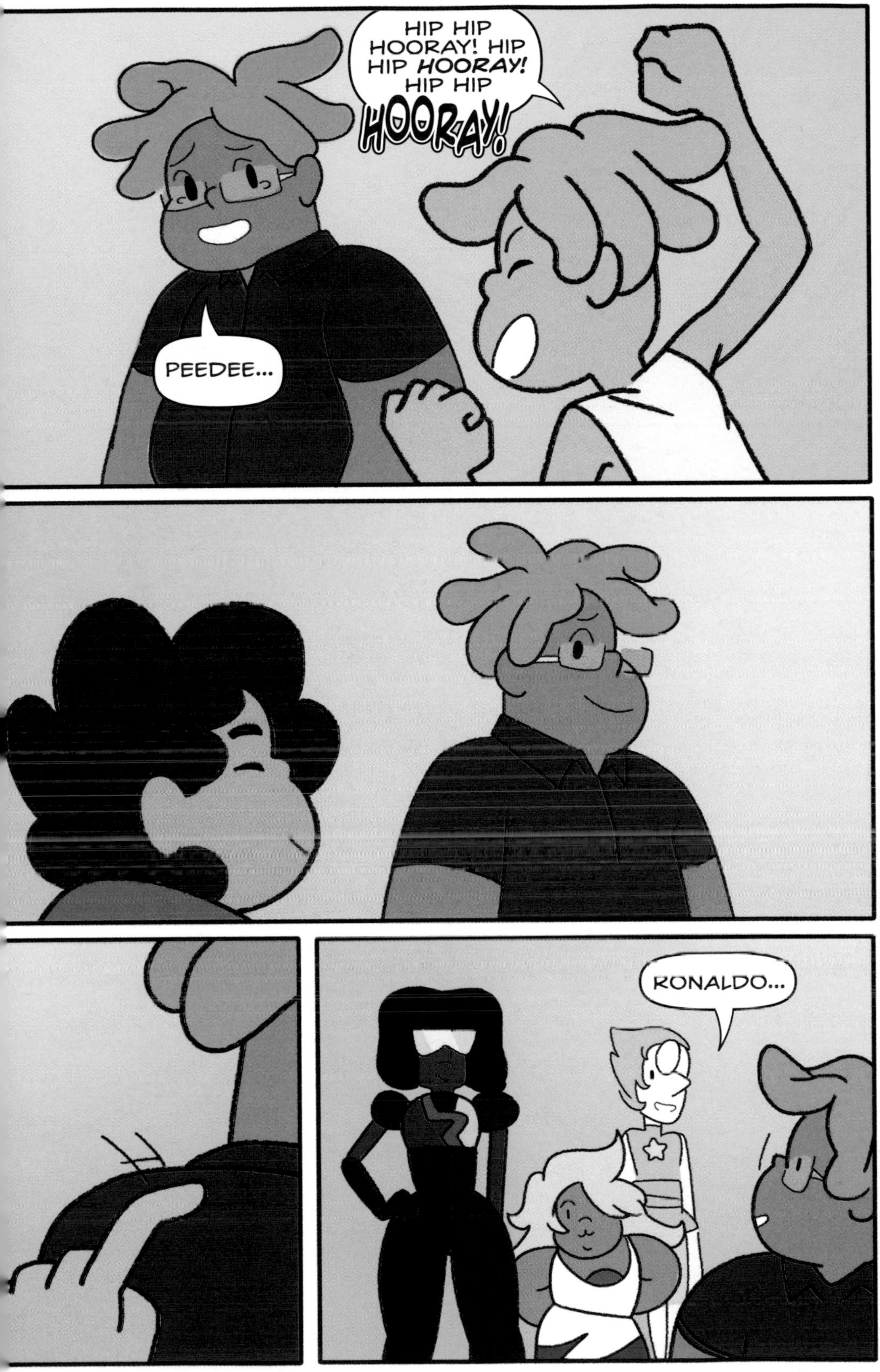
HIP HIP HOORAY! HIP HIP *HOORAY!* HIP HIP
HOORAY!
PEEDEE...
RONALDO...

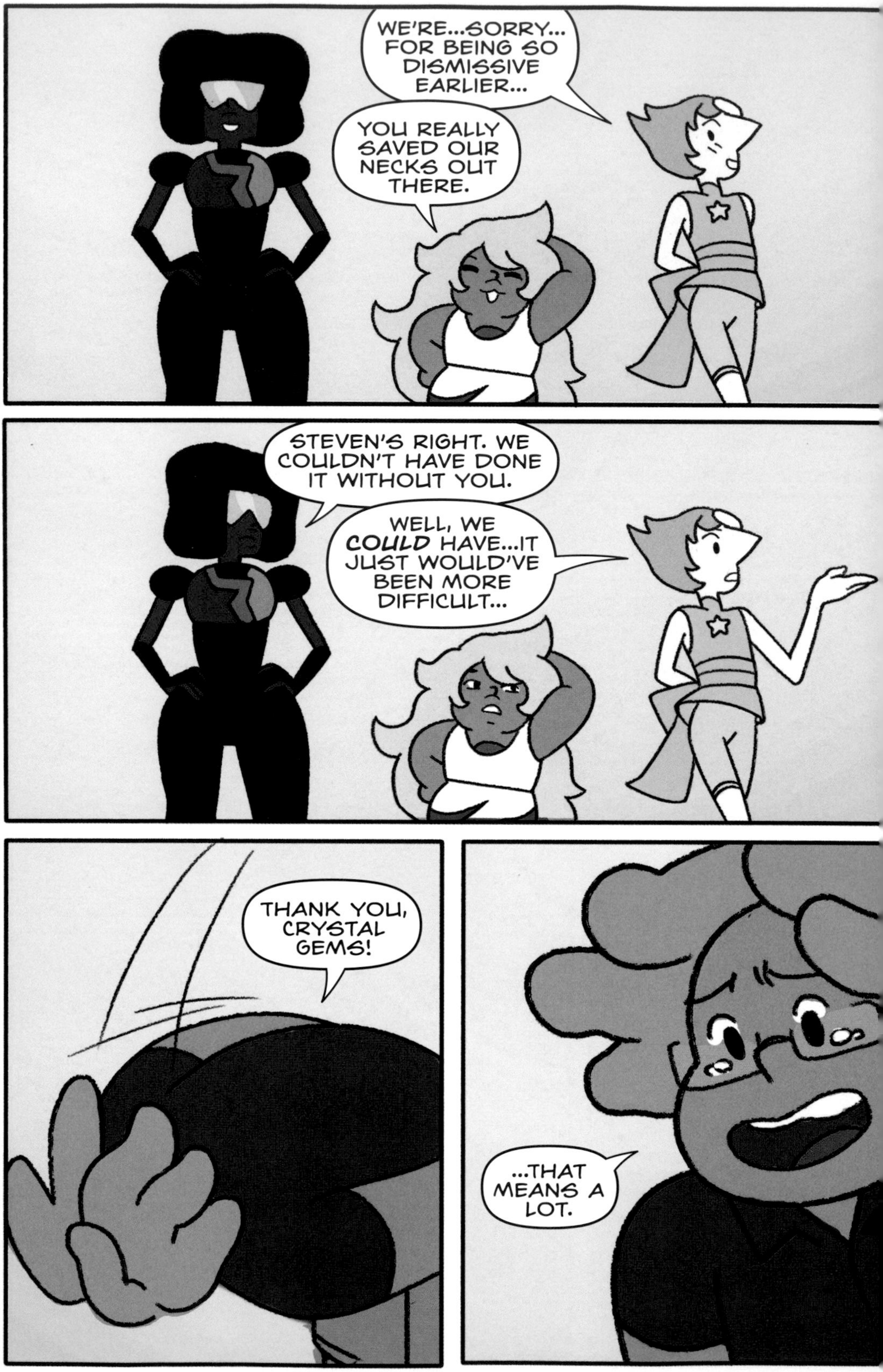
WE'RE...SORRY... FOR BEING SO DISMISSIVE EARLIER...
YOU REALLY SAVED OUR NECKS OUT THERE.
STEVEN'S RIGHT. WE COULDN'T HAVE DONE IT WITHOUT YOU.
WELL, WE *COULD* HAVE...IT JUST WOULD'VE BEEN MORE DIFFICULT...
THANK YOU, CRYSTAL GEMS!
...THAT MEANS A LOT.

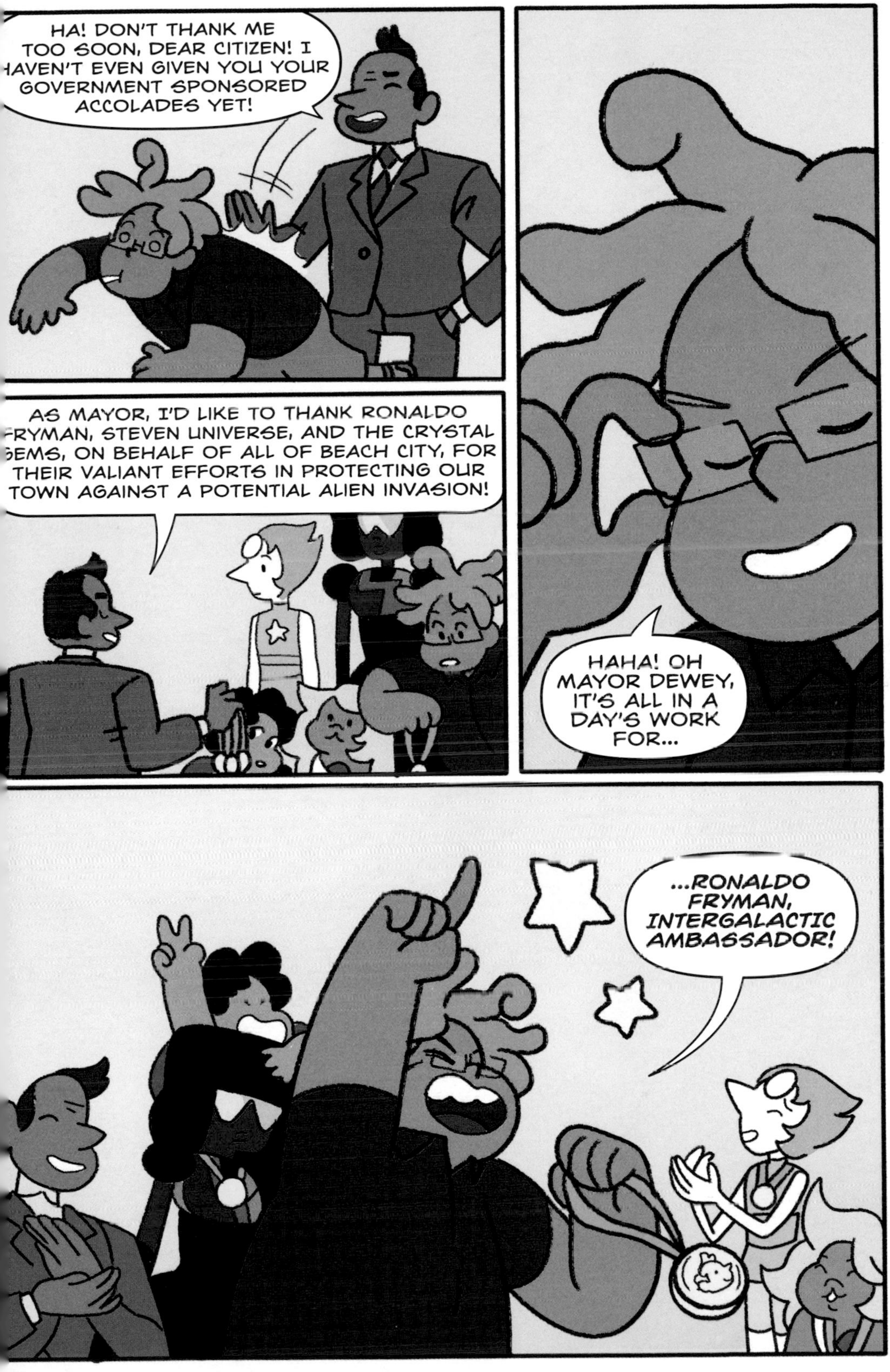
HA! DON'T THANK ME TOO SOON, DEAR CITIZEN! I HAVEN'T EVEN GIVEN YOU YOUR GOVERNMENT SPONSORED ACCOLADES YET!
AS MAYOR, I'D LIKE TO THANK RONALDO FRYMAN, STEVEN UNIVERSE, AND THE CRYSTAL GEMS, ON BEHALF OF ALL OF BEACH CITY, FOR THEIR VALIANT EFFORTS IN PROTECTING OUR TOWN AGAINST A POTENTIAL ALIEN INVASION!
HAHA! OH MAYOR DEWEY, IT'S ALL IN A DAY'S WORK FOR...
...RONALDO FRYMAN, INTERGALACTIC AMBASSADOR!

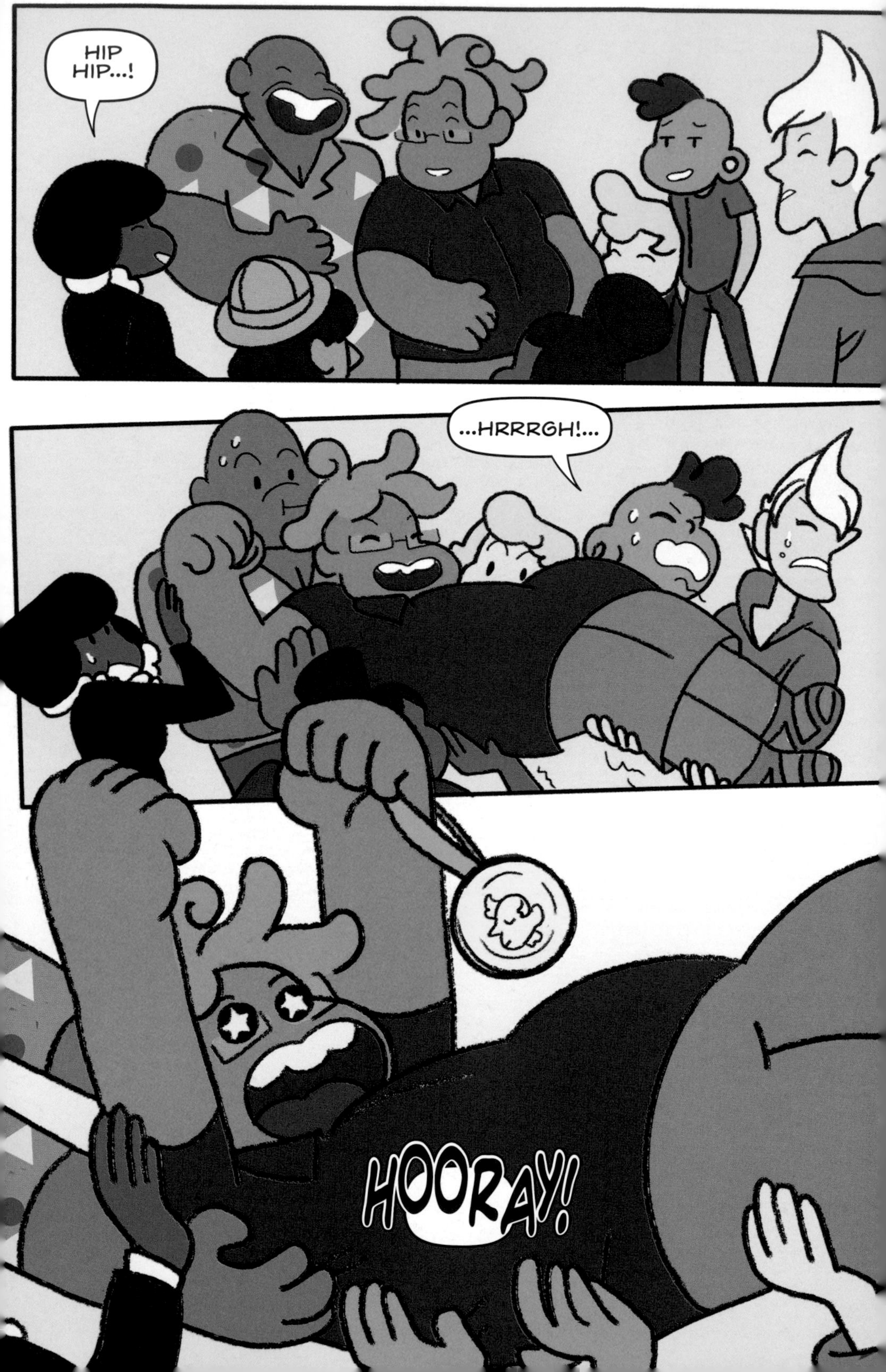
HIP HIP...!
...HRRRGH!...
HOORAY!

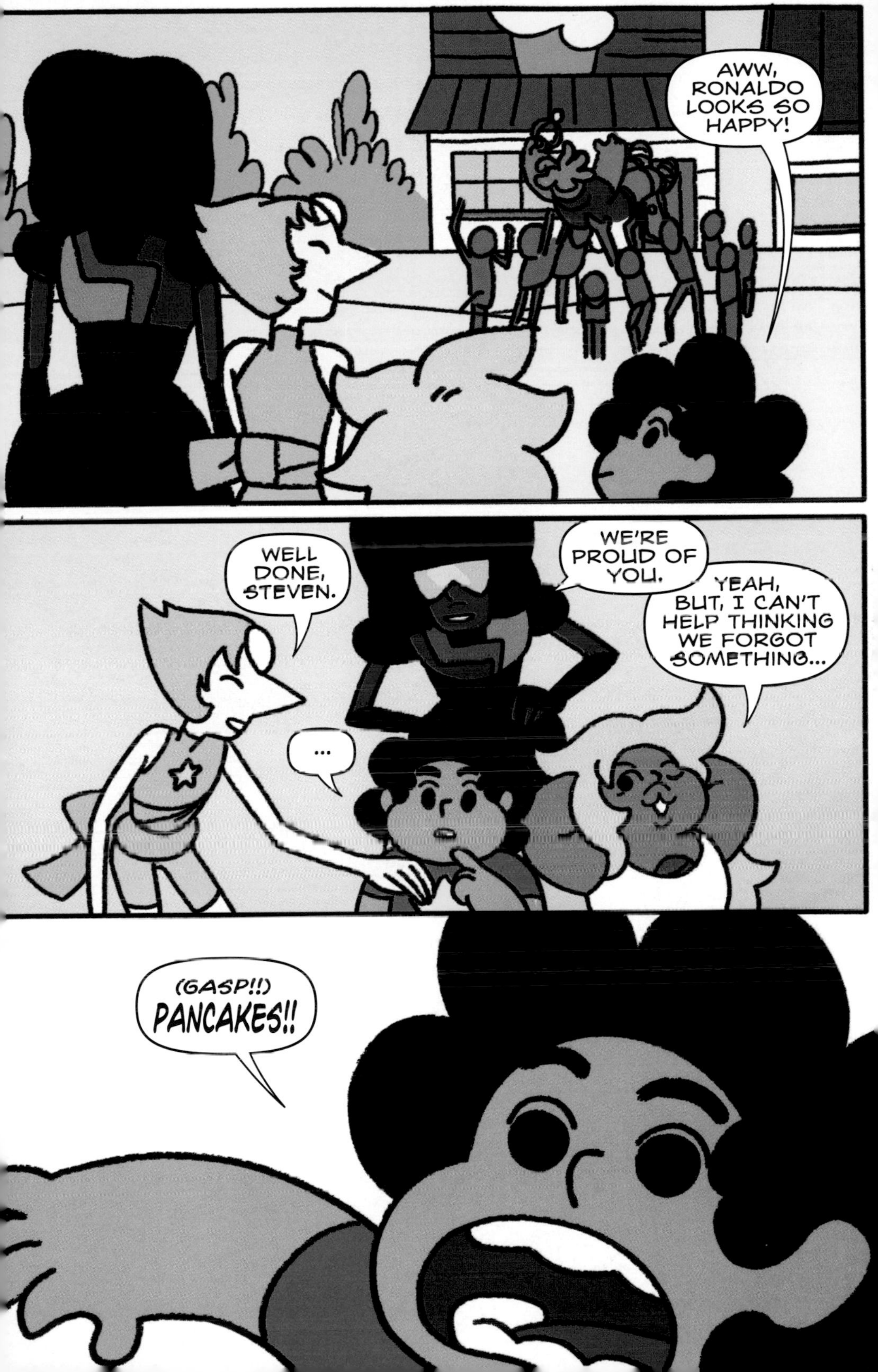
AWW, RONALDO LOOKS SO HAPPY!
WELL DONE, STEVEN.
WE'RE PROUD OF YOU.
YEAH, BUT, I CAN'T HELP THINKING WE FORGOT SOMETHING...
...
(GASP!!) PANCAKES!!

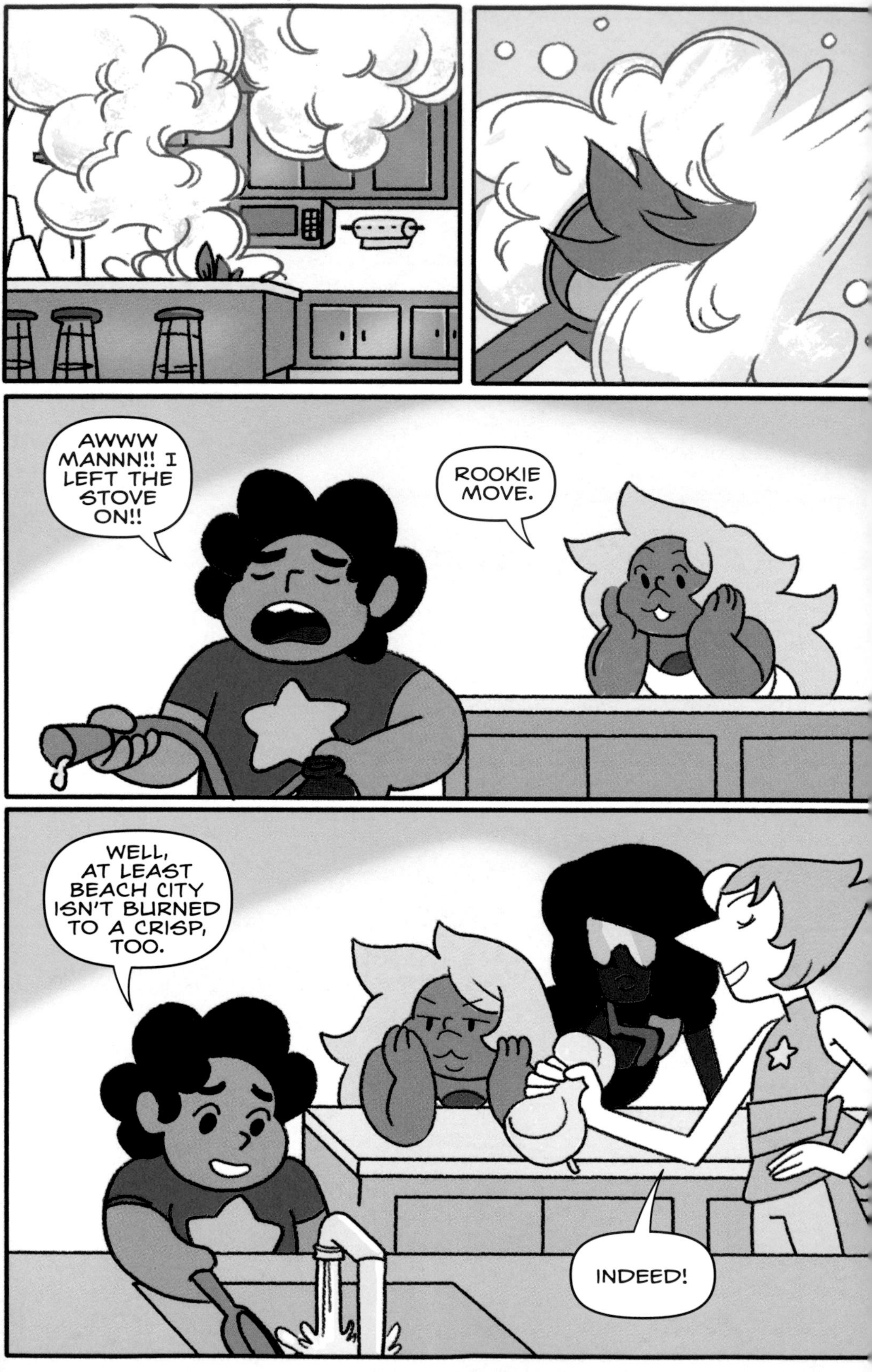
AWWW MANNN!! I LEFT THE STOVE ON!!
ROOKIE MOVE.
WELL, AT LEAST BEACH CITY ISN'T BURNED TO A CRISP, TOO.
INDEED!

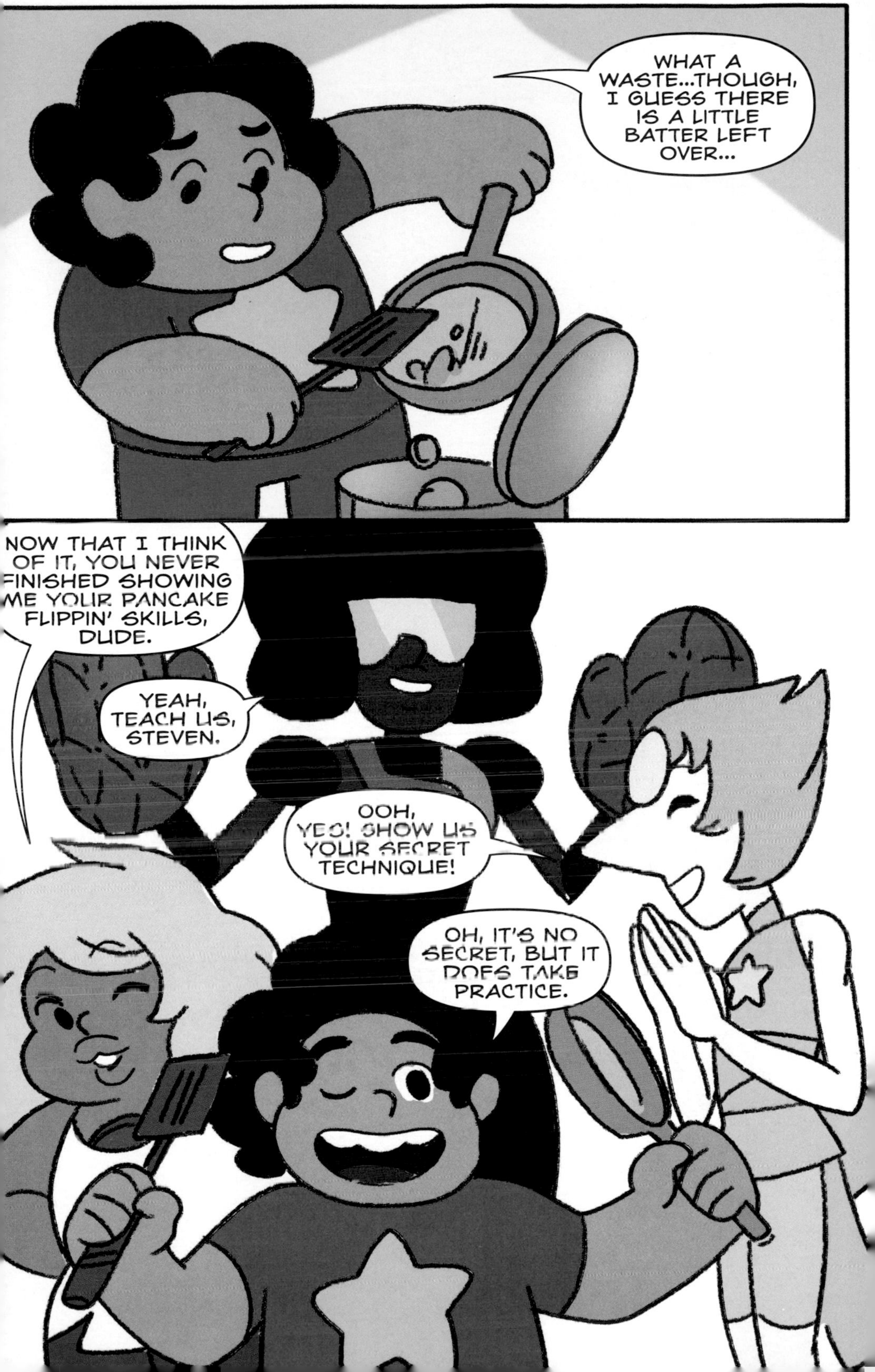
WHAT A WASTE...THOUGH, I GUESS THERE IS A LITTLE BATTER LEFT OVER...
NOW THAT I THINK OF IT, YOU NEVER FINISHED SHOWING ME YOUR PANCAKE FLIPPIN' SKILLS, DUDE.
YEAH, TEACH US, STEVEN.
OOH, YES! SHOW US YOUR SECRET TECHNIQUE!
OH, IT'S NO SECRET, BUT IT DOES TAKE PRACTICE.

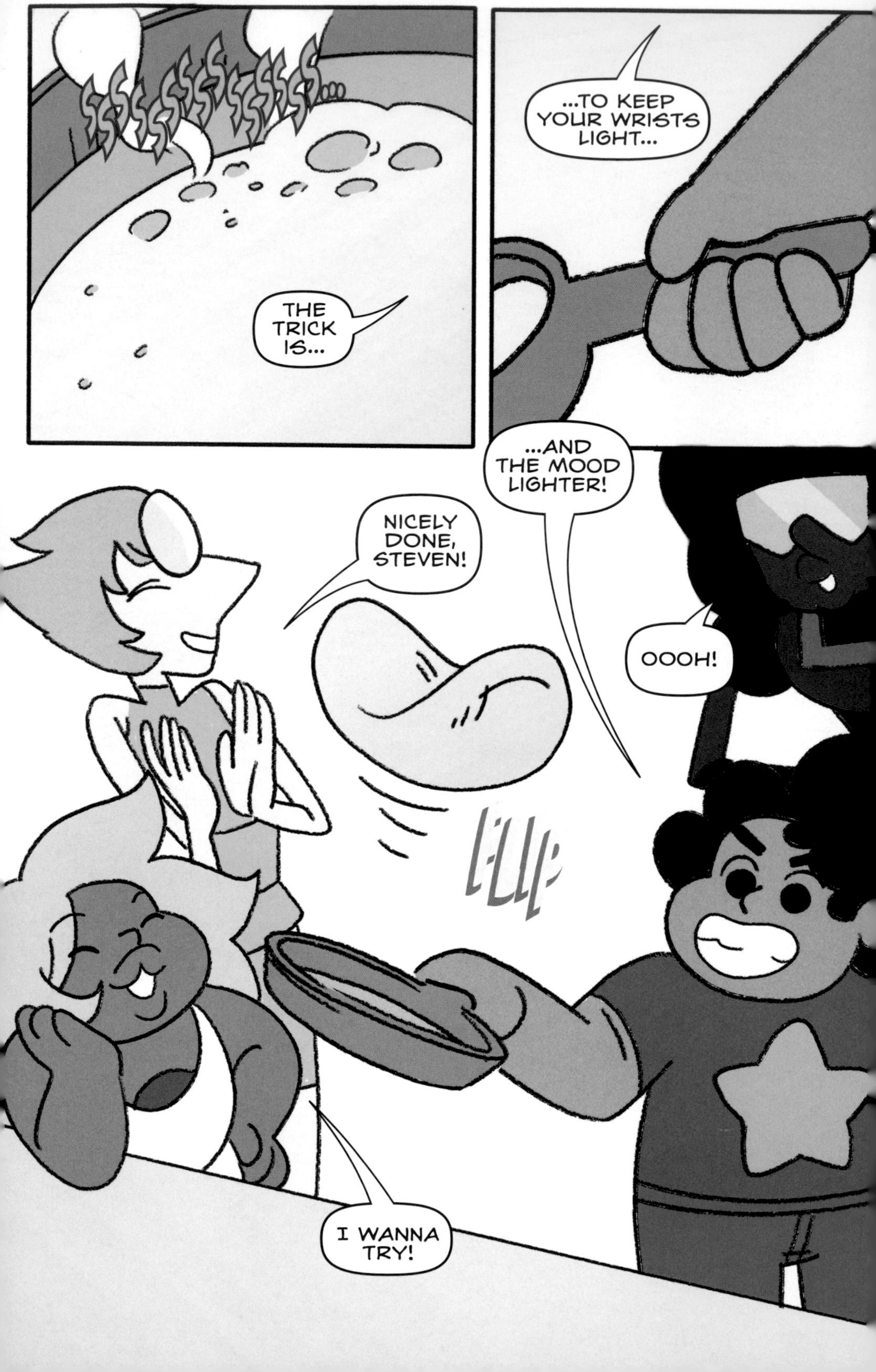
THE TRICK IS...
...TO KEEP YOUR WRISTS LIGHT...
...AND THE MOOD LIGHTER!
NICELY DONE, STEVEN!
OOOH!
I WANNA TRY!

 by Roswell Roigan

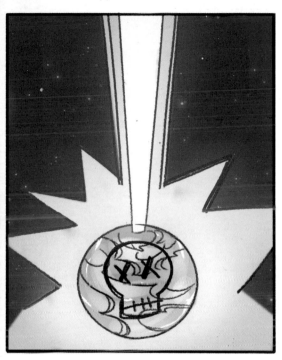

THE END...OR IS IT?!

BEACH CITY CAME IN CLOSE PROXIMITY TO NEAR *DISASTER* TODAY, YOU GUYS! IT WAS JUST EARLIER TODAY THAT I PICKED UP AN *ALIEN MESSAGE* ON MY RADIO TELESCOPE (SHOUT-OUT TO ROZWELLER47 FOR THE KIT--CHECK OUT HER E.T.BAY PAGE!) ANNOUNCING AN *IMMINENT APPROACH.* THIS APPROACH QUICKLY PROVED LESS FRIENDLY AND MORE...*FOE-LY!*

ACCORDING TO THE CRYSTAL GEMS' INVESTIGATION, THE MESSAGE CAME FROM AN *ALIEN CRAFT* ORBITING EARTH, CHARGING ITS PHASER FOR *ATTACK!!* THANKFULLY, I WAS ABLE TO DISABLE THEIR WEAPONS SYSTEMS REMOTELY WITH SOME SIMPLE I.T. TROUBLESHOOTING, BUT FOR A HOT, HOT SECOND THERE, OUR FAIR PLANET COULD'VE BEEN *TOAST,* LITERALLY! CHECK OUT THESE *EXCLUSIVE* PHOTOS OF THE ALIEN CRAFT, TAKEN BY BEACH CITY'S VERY OWN STEVEN UNIVERSE... BELOW THE FOLD IS A PHOTO OF THE CONTROL PANEL, A SLEEK, FUTURISTIC DEVICE.

HERE'S THE CONTROL PANEL OF THE ALIEN CRAFT. AS YOU CAN SEE, THEIR TECHNOLOGY HAS FAR SURPASSED OUR OWN. I WAS ABLE TO FIND THE SATELLITE'S SPECIFIC FREQUENCY AND COMMUNICATE WITH IT VIA RADIO. THE CONNECTION WAS SURPRISINGLY GOOD CONSIDERING THE CIRCUMSTANCES.

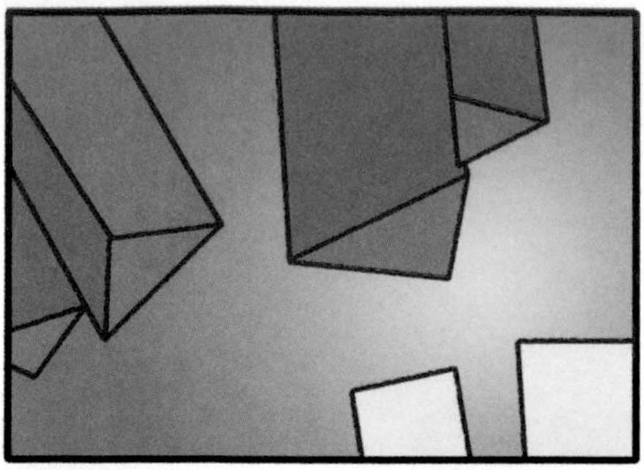

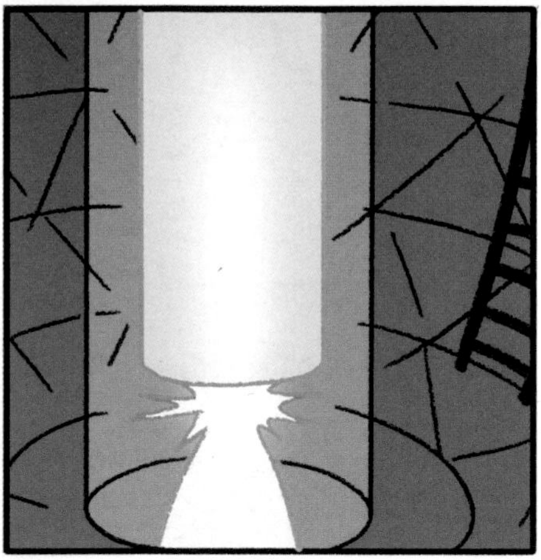

IF YOU ASK ME, IT'S NO COINCIDENCE THAT THESE COMPUTER CHIPS ARE DESIGNED LIKE STALAGMITE AND STALACTITE ROCK FORMATIONS. ALL THE MORE EVIDENCE FOR MY POLYMORPHIC SENTIENT ROCK PEOPLE THEORY!

LAST IS A PHOTO OF THE WARP CORE TAKEN FROM INSIDE THE LOWER LEVEL OBSERVATORY.

THIS ENERGY CORE IS PART TRACTOR BEAM, PART ELECTROMAGNETIC CANNON (OR SOMETHING LIKE THAT). BEFORE I REALIZED IT WAS A WEAPON, I WAS ALMOST ABDUCTED BY IT, LIFTED OFF THE GROUND HIGH INTO THE AIR! I'LL ADMIT, I WAS KINDA HOPING TO BE ABDUCTED SO I COULD FINALLY SPEARHEAD INTERGALACTI DIPLOMACY, BUT CLEARLY THE UNIVERSE JUST ISN'T READY TO MOVE PAST VIOLENT COLONIZATION OF FOREIGN PLANETS. STILL I HOLD OUT HOPE THAT PEACEFUL COHABITATION WITH ALIEN LIFE-FORMS IS COMING SOONER THAN LATER. UNTIL THEN STAY WEIRD, BEACH CITY!

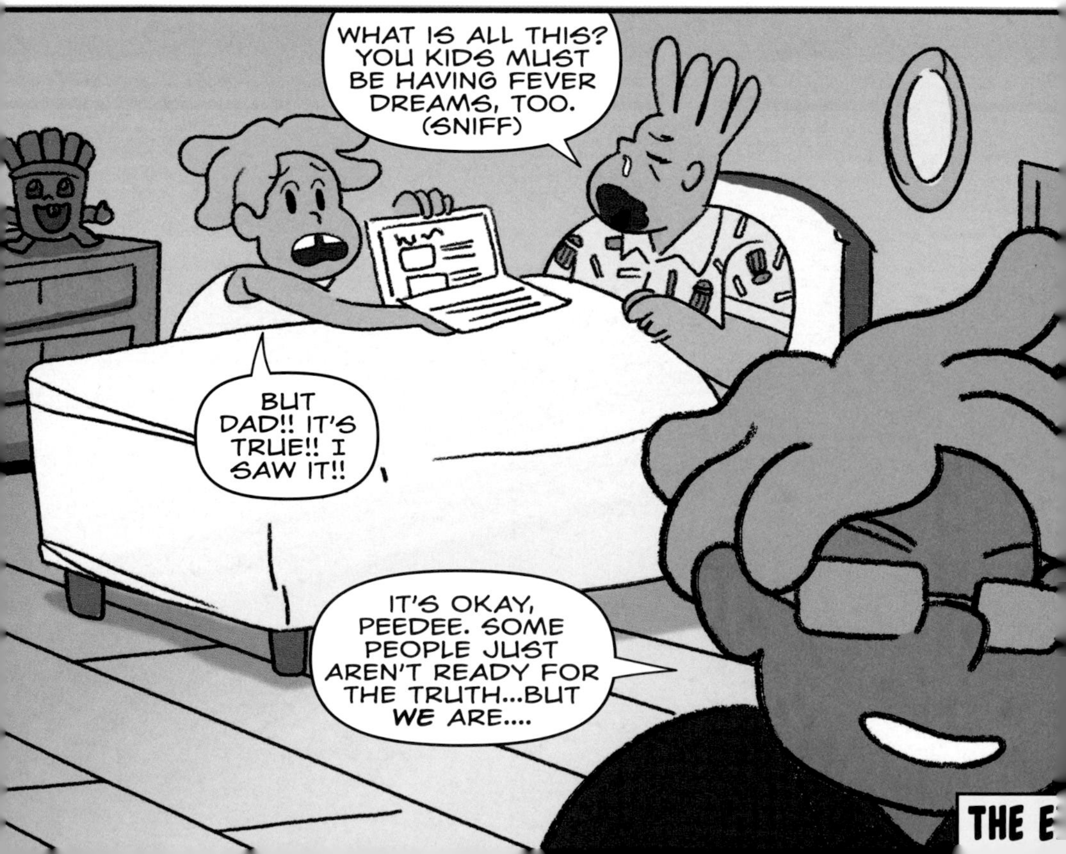
WHAT IS ALL THIS? YOU KIDS MUST BE HAVING FEVER DREAMS, TOO. (SNIFF)
BUT DAD!! IT'S TRUE!! I SAW IT!!
IT'S OKAY, PEEDEE. SOME PEOPLE JUST AREN'T READY FOR THE TRUTH...BUT *WE* ARE....
THE E

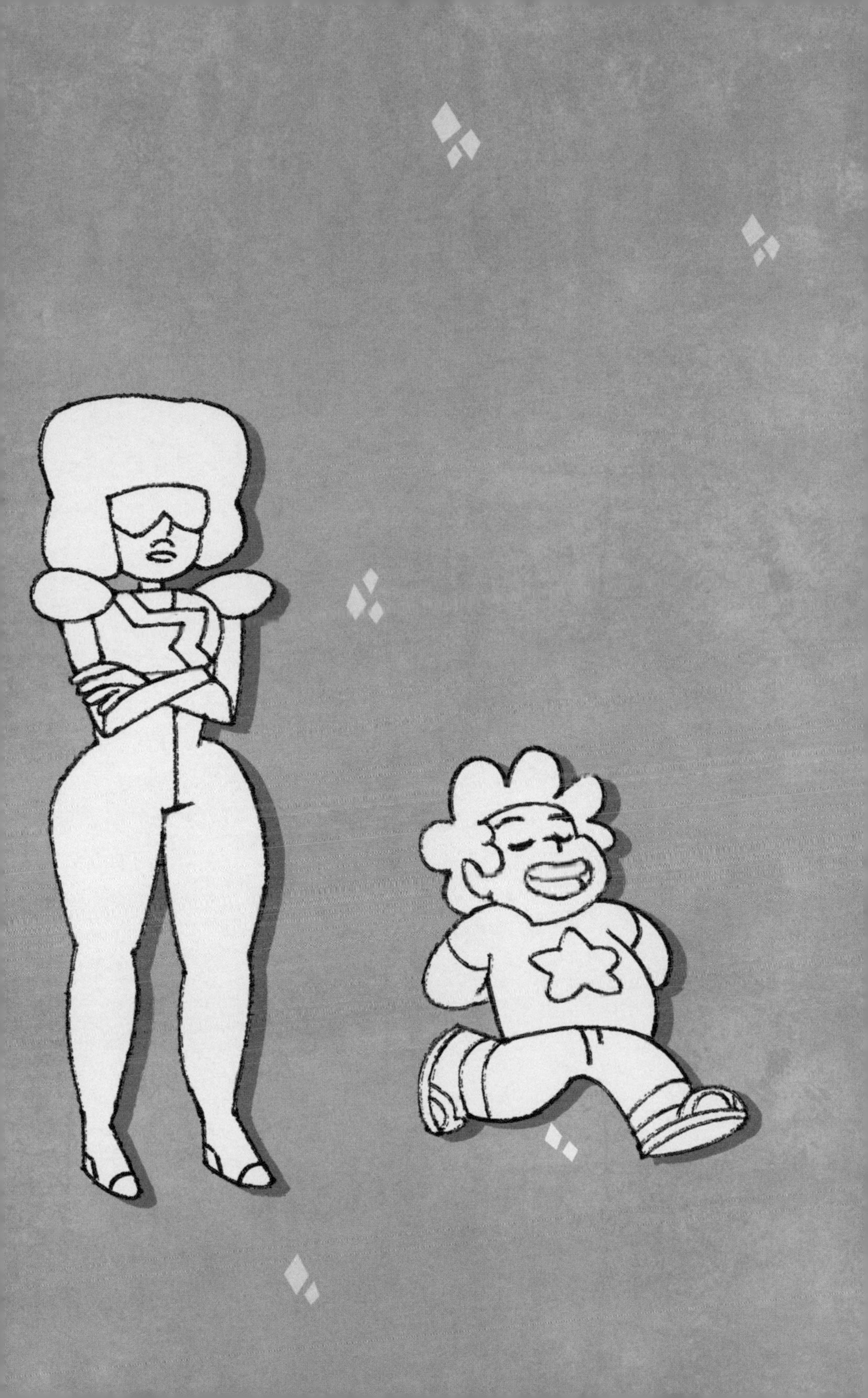

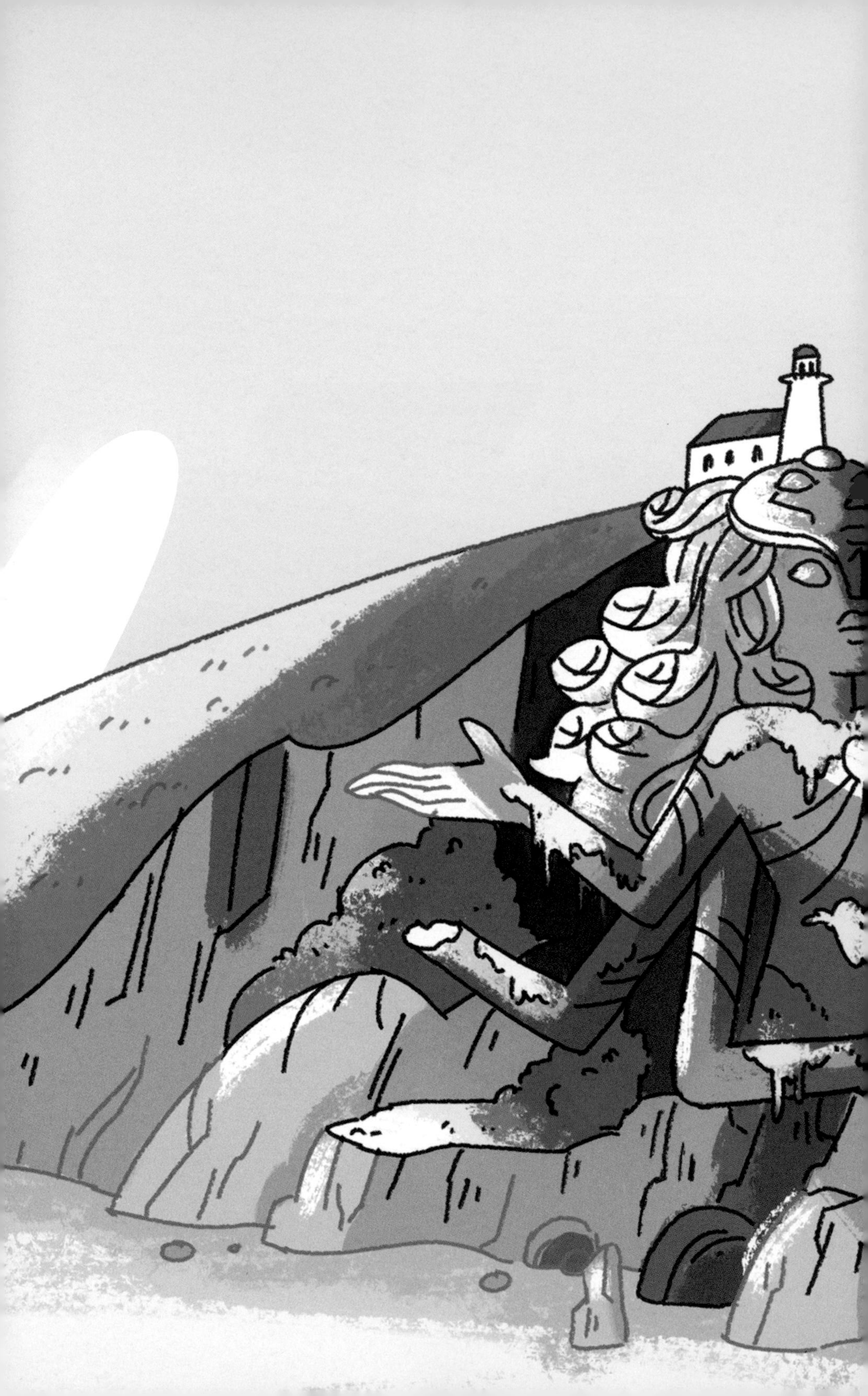

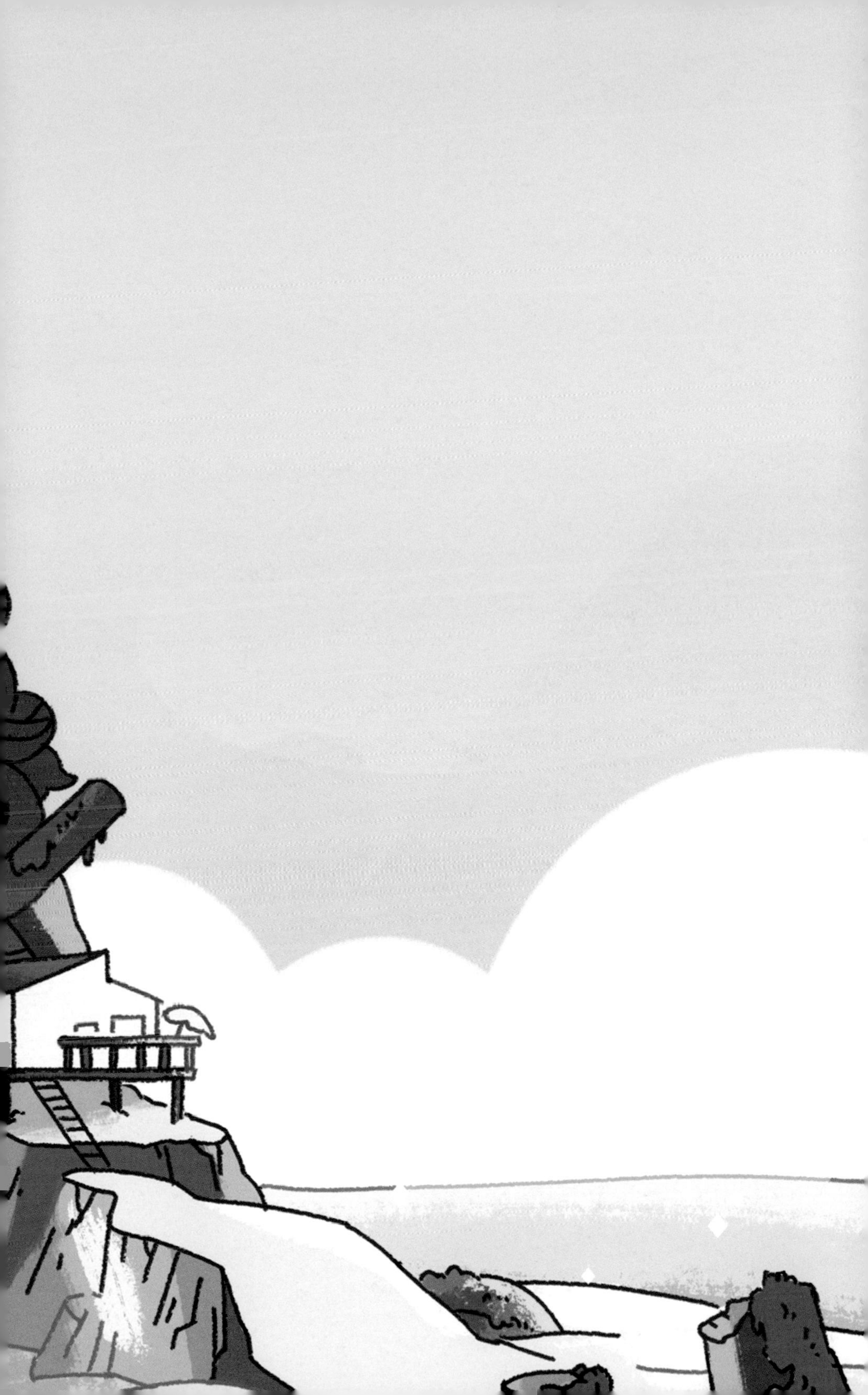

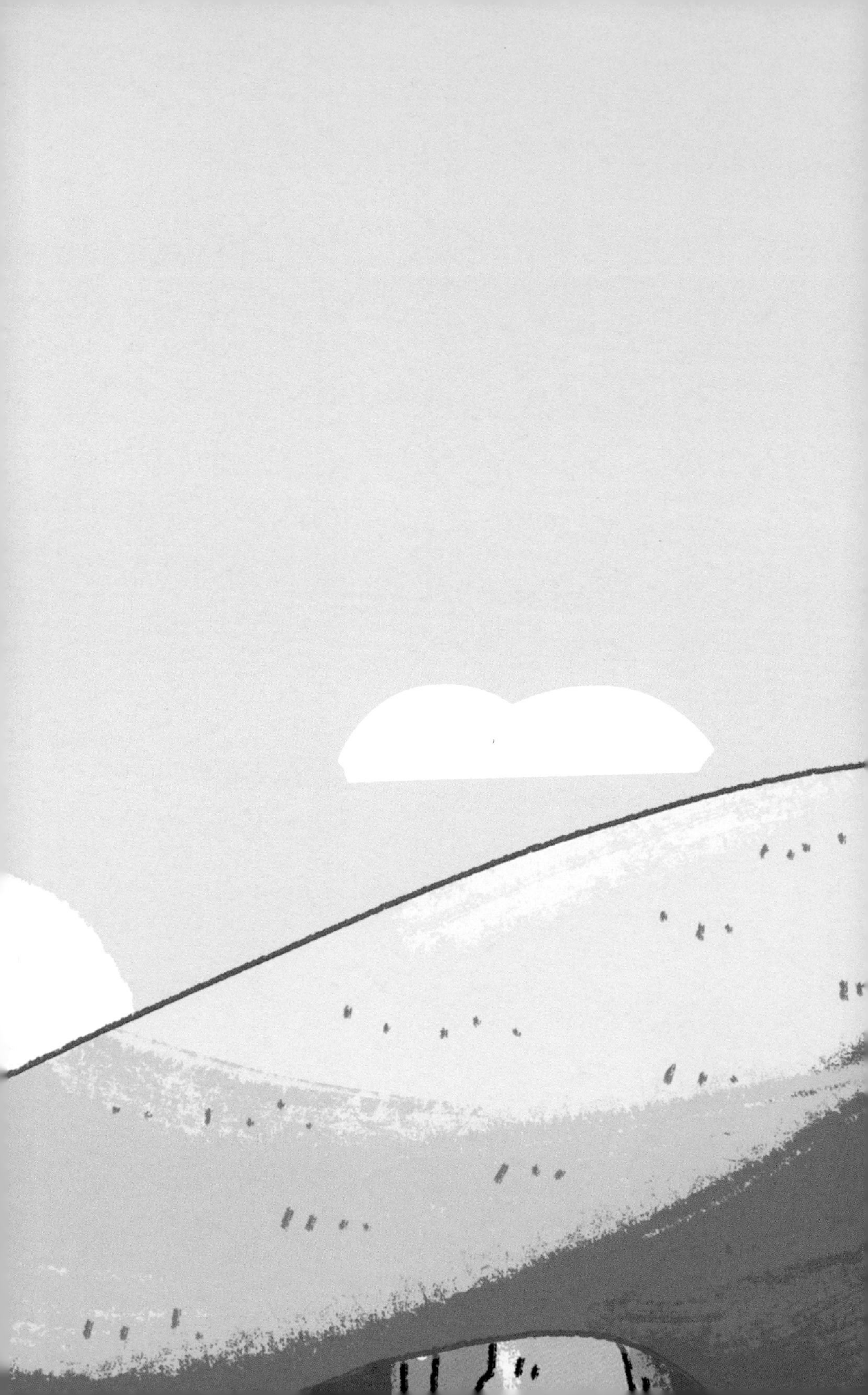

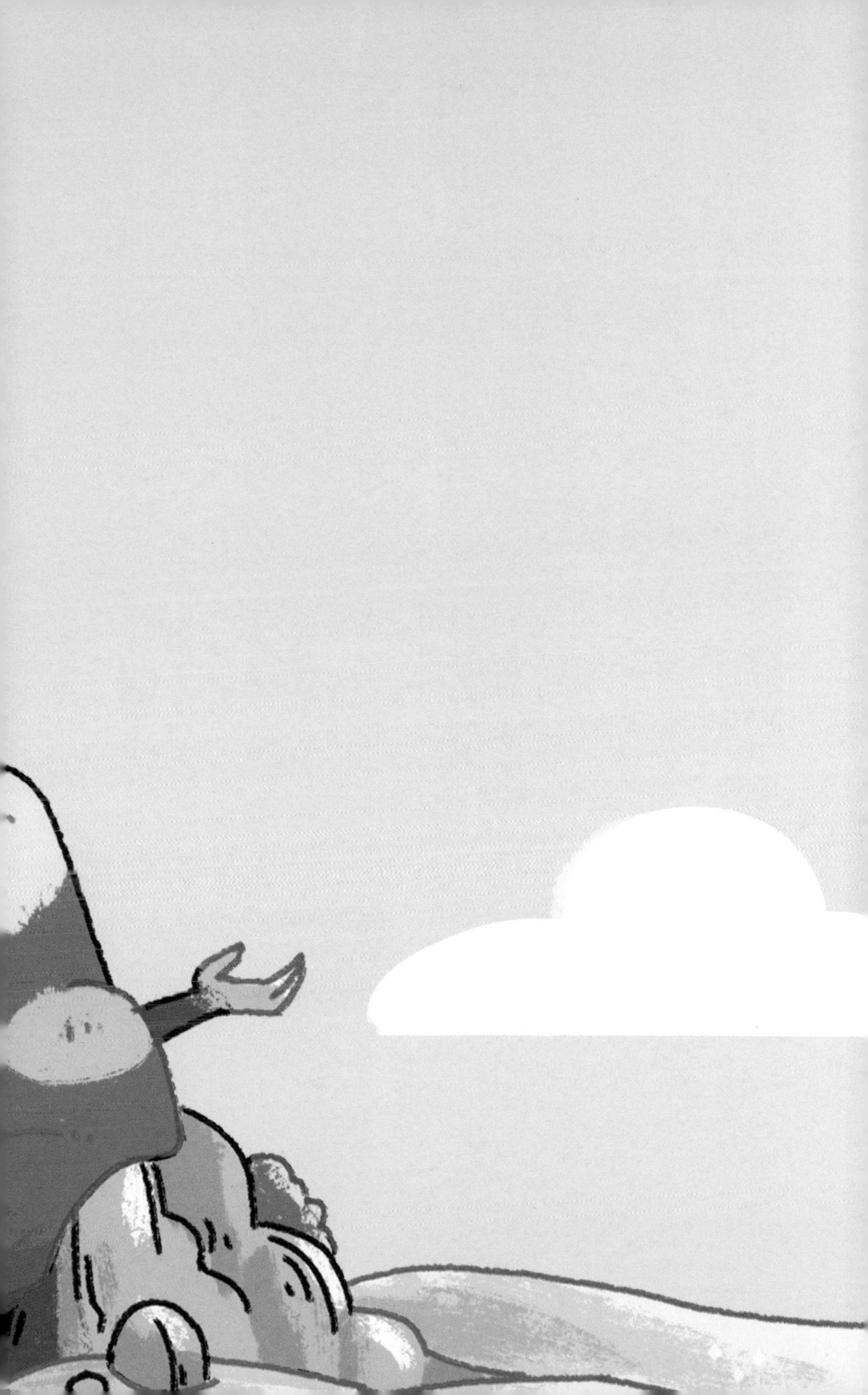

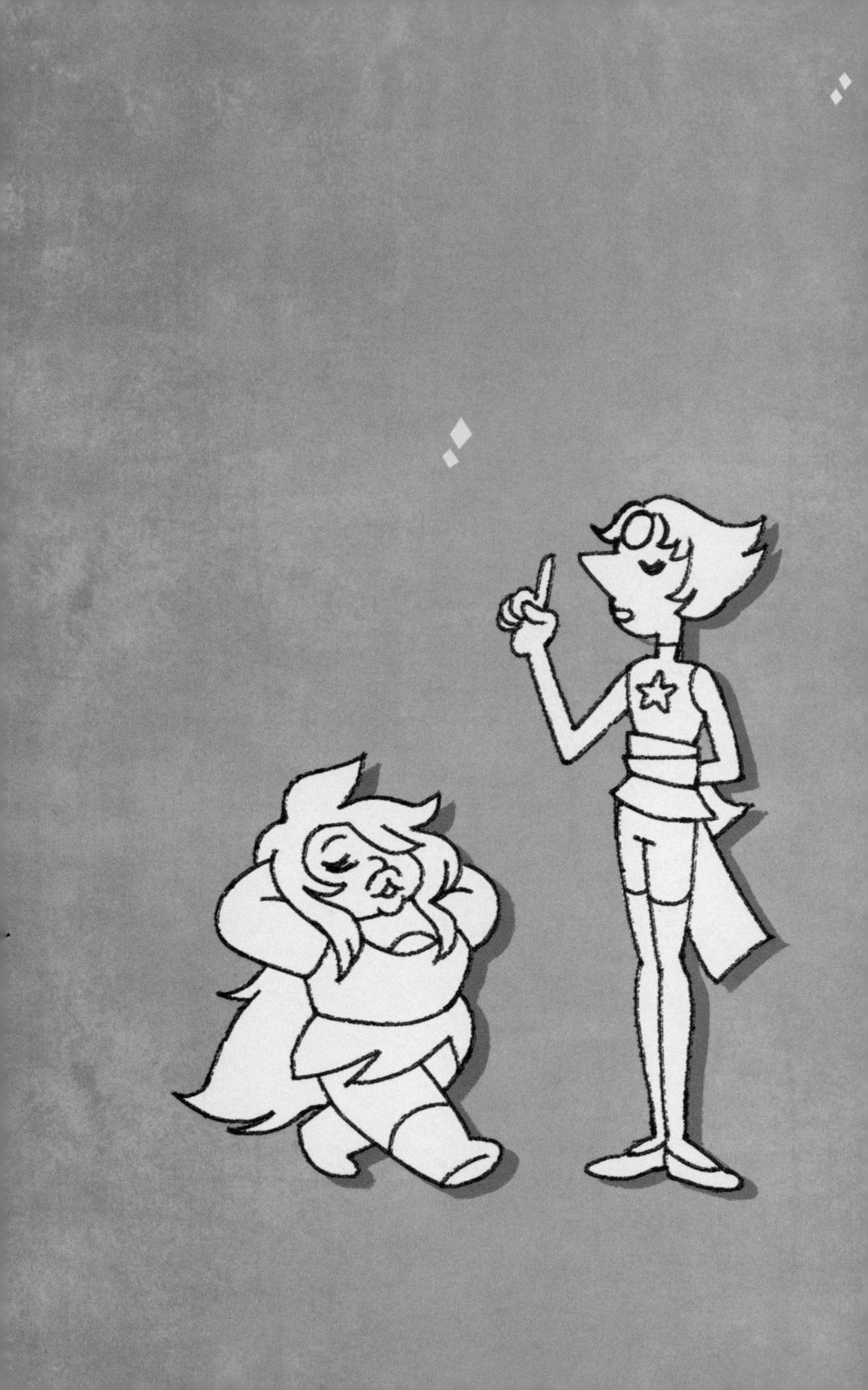

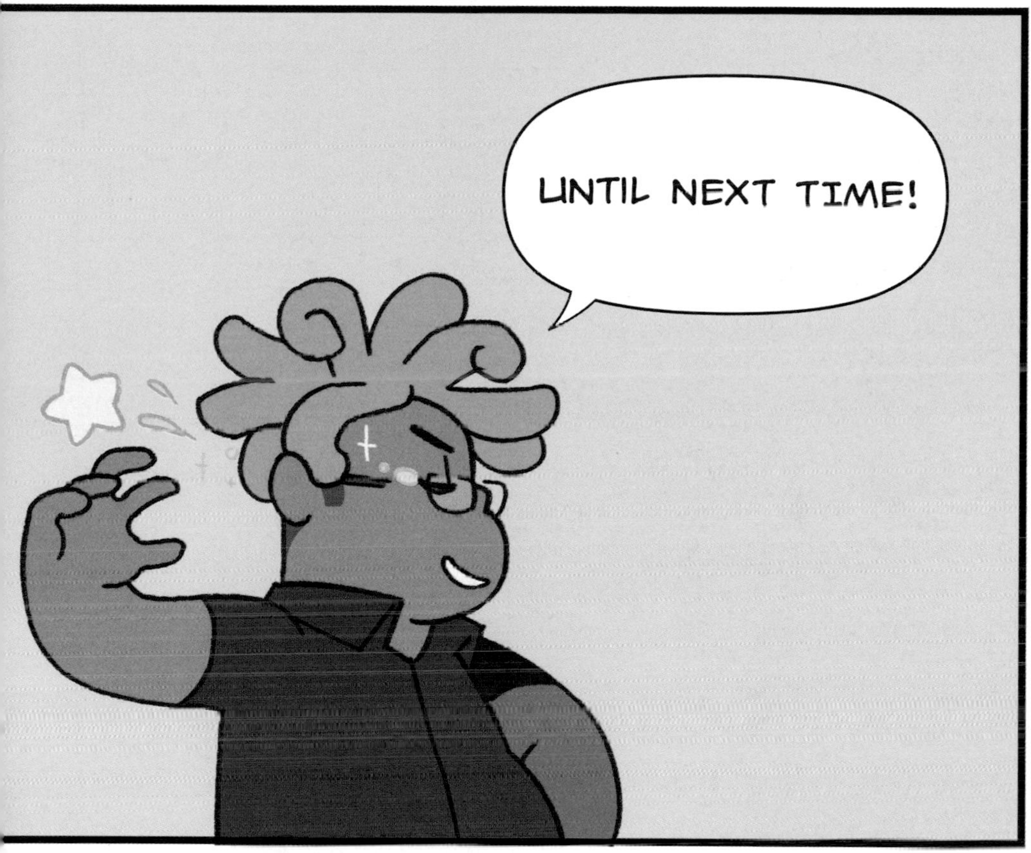
UNTIL NEXT TIME!

DISCOVER
EXPLOSIVE NEW WORLDS

ADVENTURE TIME

Sam Sykes · Selina Espiritu · Sarah Stern
Brave Chef Brianna

KELLY THOMPSON BRIANNE DROUHARD M. VICTORIA ROBADO
MEGA PRINCESS

THE NOT-SO SECRET SOCIETY
DALEY · CRAFTS · CLARK · BRUNI
KEEP OUT
CAUTION

OVER THE GARDEN WALL

STEVEN UNIVERSE
VOLUME ONE

Adventure Time
Pendleton Ward and Others
Volume 1
ISBN: 978-1-60886-280-1 | $14.99 US
Volume 2
ISBN: 978-1-60886-323-5 | $14.99 US
Adventure Time: Islands
ISBN: 978-1-60886-972-5 | $9.99 US

The Amazing World of Gumball
Ben Bocquelet and Others
Volume 1
ISBN: 978-1-60886-488-1 | $14.99 US
Volume 2
ISBN: 978-1-60886-793-6 | $14.99 US

Brave Chef Brianna
Sam Sykes, Selina Espiritu
ISBN: 978-1-68415-050-2 | $14.99 US

Mega Princess
Kelly Thompson, Brianne Drouhard
ISBN: 978-1-68415-007-6 | $14.99 US

The Not-So Secret Society
Matthew Daley, Arlene Daley, Wook Jin Clark
ISBN: 978-1-60886-997-8 | $9.99 US

Over the Garden Wall
Patrick McHale, Jim Campbell and Others
Volume 1
ISBN: 978-1-60886-940-4 | $14.99 US
Volume 2
ISBN: 978-1-68415-006-9 | $14.99 US

Steven Universe
Rebecca Sugar and Others
Volume 1
ISBN: 978-1-60886-706-6 | $14.99 US
Volume 2
ISBN: 978-1-60886-796-7 | $14.99 US

Steven Universe & The Crystal Gems
ISBN: 978-1-60886-921-3 | $14.99 US

Steven Universe: Too Cool for School
ISBN: 978-1-60886-771-4 | $14.99 US

kaboom!™

AVAILABLE AT YOUR LOCAL COMICS SHOP AND BOOKSTORE
To find a comics shop in your area, call 1-888-266-4226
WWW.**BOOM-STUDIOS**.COM

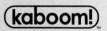